Noel

Noel

Gage Irving

ISBN:	Hardcover	978-1-5245-8053-7
	Softcover	978-1-4931-2043-7
	eBook	978-1-4931-2044-4

Cover art and design—Antoinette Beck
Graphics—Kinga.me

Print information available on the last page.

Rev. date: 07/10/2018

To order additional copies of this book, contact:
Xlibris
1-888-795-4274
www.Xlibris.com
Orders@Xlibris.com
552399

CONTENTS

The Prologue

Five gargantuan whirlpools called gyres swirl through the earth's oceans unrestrained. Debris floating into one of these global currents will finally end up in its stagnant center. In the past, this flotsam was biodegradable, quickly disappearing without a trace. That is no longer the case. The industrial revolution erupted like a demented volcano in the 1900's, ushering in manufacture on a massive scale. The resulting waste coming out of the factories was tossed into landfills and rivers, ponds and oceans without a second thought; an endless flow of poisonous lava. The centers of all five of the gyres were overwhelmed by manmade debris, and that terrible flood became a deluge.

The gyre in the northern Pacific Ocean was deemed the worst of the group with the highest amount of rubbish. Those in power remained indifferent to the possible repercussions coming out of their carelessness, and they barreled into the millennium at breakneck speed. The environmentally aware nicknamed the fouled center of the gyre in the pacific, the Trash Vortex. It's estimated to be twice the size of Texas. No one really knows exactly where the actually border of this listless eye really ends, but thousands of miles of open water has been overcome with crap within that circling current. Whether it's a ripped drop cloth, or a vinyl console wrenched from the inside of an automobile, most of it cannot degrade. After twenty years or so, the console would disintegrate down to the smallest particle industrialized plastic polymer can go, and no farther. In this neustonic state, it is biologically inactive, yet tiny enough to invade and sicken the bodies of the living and interfere with the oxygenation of sea water. This degradation of the water and the biological intrusion is widening out across the oceans. Seals basking on the glacier ice at the North Pole hundreds of miles away from the vortex, now have tiny pieces of plastic imbedded in their blubber.

In the middle of the gyres, the flotsam slowly sinks down in a column beneath the surface, and birds, fish, mammals and algae ingest it to their peril. The inorganic and biological dreck pounds through the watery heart of the world without end, and the Trash Vortex has become a colossal beaker jam-packed with stuff that should not be there. A contaminated soup of our own unbridled excess had been percolating out there for years. Has the impossible taken place? Life of a different sort could have awakened in an elemental and negative charge, and rooted itself in the badly wounded salt water to gestate and grow large enough to pull us to heel; a Frankenstein lurching out of the sea in a corporeal answer to an unsanctionable question none of us want to accept.

The Second Coming

Turning and turning in the widening gyre
The falcon cannot hear the falconer;
Things fall apart; the center cannot hold;
Mere anarchy is loosed upon the world,
The blood-dimmed tide is loosed, and everywhere
The ceremony of innocence is drowned;
The best lack all conviction, while the worst
Are full of passionate intensity.

Surely some revelation is at hand;
Surely the Second Coming is at hand.
The Second Coming! Hardly are those words out
When a vast image out of Spiritus Mundi
Troubles my sight: somewhere in sands of the desert
A shape with lion body and the head of a man,
A gaze blank and pitiless as the sun,
Is moving its slow thighs, while all about it
Reel shadows of the indignant desert birds.
The darkness drops again; but now I know
That twenty centuries of stony sleep
Were vexed to nightmare by a rocking cradle,
And what rough beast, its hour come round at last,
Slouches towards Bethlehem to be born?

William Butler Yeats (1920)

PART ONE

4:22AM Monday **February 11th, 2004** **The Ocean Swan; 6 degrees North of Kiritimati**

Six months ago, Walter Pratt had signed on as the ship's cook. Making breakfast for the seven men in the crew that morning was a juggling match for him as The Swan crossed the Pacific to unload their cargo at Mutsa Ogasana on the coast of Japan. The captain of the ship had turned the freighter south, out of the shipping lanes. He had been trying to avoid the storm, but the strategy hadn't worked. Walter held onto the top of the anchored work table in the middle of the galley as the floor slanted at an obscene angle and the salt container flew out of his hand and hit the ceiling. He wasn't going to be able to cook anything until it got calmer out there.

The diesel engines were pounding and growling under his feet, and the gale howled on the other side the porthole, but it didn't mask the sound of gunfire. Wally took off his apron, and swayed to the other side of the galley to hang it on a metal hook. Opening the door of the ship's pantry, he carefully stepped inside and sat down on the floor. The pantry was six by eight, and it was stocked with produce and grain, and Walter was busily arranging bags of potatoes and onions around his legs, torso and head. He was concealing himself, and he hoped that everyone on board had forgotten he was even there.

Running a day late from a paperwork snafu in France, it had been a disconcerting voyage from the get-go. The bureaucratic stall holding up the difficult job of lifting three nine ton casks off the dock and into the hold of the ship had finally straightened out, but the Swan should have left the dock hours ago. Captain Zack decided to go through the Panama Canal, as it would shave off quite a lot of time from the trip. That option hadn't worked out very well either. A low-grade disaster, in fact. During the ship's sedate ride through the canal itself, members of an environmental group called *Green Peace* illegally boarded The Ocean Swan to put up signs, and wave to the crowd, and it was a mad house on shore. News vans and trucks, and thousands of protesters lined the narrow waterway, and Zack dropped his head into his hands and groaned. They should have gone around the horn for a lot of reasons.

After the irritating and temporary invasion and scrutiny at the canal, the freighter docked at Puerto de Balboa for two days. She had to refuel and load in more supplies before the next ocean crossing. On the second night there, at one in the morning, the crew heard odd noises on the deck, and they all got up and looked around. Not finding anything, no one had an explanation for the strange sounds. Walter realigned a bag of onions right in front of his face, and the answer to that puzzle came to him. Every single one of the non-violent Green Peace group had left the ship before they'd left the canal, so what they'd heard in the middle of the night had been stowaways getting on board. *Armed and dangerous ones.*

When the Swan was roped to the commercial dock in Balboa two days ago, five eco-terrorists, dressed in black with duffle bags on their backs, crept on her at 12:55 AM. Like stygian mist, they were close to invisible on that moonless night. Their leader lifted a hatch on the front deck, and gestured to the rest to get through this opening and into the body of the ship. Following his direction, they gathered in an enclosure at the bow of the ship. It was called the chain locker, and hundreds of feet of anchor chain got stored there. Closing the heavy metal door behind them, they'd stay there for at least twenty-four hours while the ship was under power. With rations and plastic bottles to pee in during the interim, they'd hide there until the Swan was many miles off-shore before going into action. They'd wait until the only reinforcements the crew could rely on would be the frightening depth of the seawater rolling beneath them.

After the length of time they were relying on had passed, the well-armed group emerged from the locker. It'd been cramped in there, and they stretched out the kinks in their muscles for a couple of minutes before trotting down a narrow passage under the foredeck. They stopped in front of the bunk room, or the 'fo'c'sle'. Harris, the leader, silently pointed at two of the men in his team. They would surprise most of the crew while they were still asleep. The other two stumbled off on the tilting floor of the corridor to hunt down the man on watch, meanwhile Harris would silently sneak into the wheelhouse and subdue the captain on his own.

And the two madman left in front of the bunk room door began their assault by slamming it open and flicking the ceiling lights on at the same time. Startling and blinding the half-asleep with this simple boom and flash, their unpretentious foray worked without a hitch. The brigands herded the crew up the stairs to the mess hall pointing rifles straight at them. Rebellious ideas in their heads were snuffed out by the proximity of the guns. Pushing them inside the messhall, one of the masked men ordered them to sit along on the bench against the wall. The finger of his right hand trembled. It was only a hairsbreadth away from the trigger, and these muscular roustabouts remained powerless under the one-eyed stare of the barrel of his AK47. His companion tied their hands behind their backs without a problem, and when the situation was secure, they radioed out to the others.

Shawn was on watch, and seeing armed men race towards him on the transom didn't make him very happy. They were dressed like rejects from a grade B Zorro movie, and he would have laughed at them if they weren't holding machine guns. He instantly tried to get to the wheel house and radio the military base in Panama for help, but when he was halfway through the hatch a bullet plowed into his left leg and he was knocked off his feet. Whoever shot him must have been very good...with luck on his side. He'd dealt with a slippery heaving deck, a gale force wind, and rain and darkness. Aiming the gun couldn't have been easy. They got to him in seconds, and one of them held him down while the other closed the hatch. Then they picked up the injured man by his armpits, hauling him back across the transom and up the stairs to the entrance of the mess hall. They violently threw him through the door. A big wave hit the port side of the ship knocking one of the pirates off-balance. His mate grabbed his elbow in support and they turned around and wrenched the hatch-door closed against the resistance of the wind. Meanwhile, their new captive was painfully crawling to the communal bench leaving a trail of blood behind him.

"Shawn, are you alright? What'd those sons-of-bitches do to you?" One of the men on the bench then changed the direction of his protestations towards his captors, "Hey, come on! Let me loose! There's a first aid kit under the counter over here." Hands tied, he frantically nodded at where it was. "Let me free so I can help him, damn it!"

One of them was named Victor, the most sociopathic in the bowl of mixed-nuts, and he stared down at the handcuffed man with contempt. In Vic's head, everyone on that bench was responsible for destroying the world. Why should he be worried about the well-being of the man he'd just shot? Of course, not all the eco-terrorists were quite that chilly. His cohort chimed in.

"Come on, Vic. We can let him bandage it. It doesn't matter to us either way."

"If you think we should let him free, you better ask Harris first. He's got to be done with the captain by now. I don't know why we haven't heard from him yet."

Captain Zack was brooding over the glowing radar display. The southern jog hadn't worked. The squall tailed them towards the equator like a lap dog. He was half-heartedly listening to radio chatter coming out of the speaker above his head. He had not heard gunfire, and he didn't hear the door behind him open either. Harris struck Zack on the head with the grip of his gun quite energetically, and the captain slipped off his cushioned chair like pudding. He ended up lying face up on the floor, and Harris didn't want to turn the unconscious man over on his back. Using the plastic restraints he had in his pocket, he tied his wrists together in the position he was in. It didn't matter. Facing down or up, there was nothing he could do to stop them anymore.

Before the mission, Harris learned everything he needed to know to navigate the freighter without help from anyone. Opening the navigational charts on the counter behind him, it only took him five minutes to find their bearings. The ship was no longer going to Japan, but they couldn't get to work in the teeth of this storm. Glancing over at the radar, he calculated the quickest track he could find to get out of it, and then he turned back to the charts again. This nameless monster was barreling due south, so he needed to go west-northwest. They should be out of the worst of it in twelve hours, and Harris typed in the new coordinates into the auto-pilot. The Ocean Swan would stay on its new path without any more of his attention, and he deftly nudged the levers next to the captain's chair. He increased their speed by a hair. Bending over, he checked the pulse of the mound of pudding on the floor. He saw some color in his face, and his eyelids were fluttering slightly indicating he'd probably wake up soon. He answered the ongoing buzzing coming out of the radio on his belt.

"This is Harris. It's over and done. The ship is ours. I assume your objectives were completed without incident."

Victor responded to his leader's statement with cold composure, "Yes, everything is done. The crew is in the mess hall, and you're right, the boat is ours."

"Hey, what about letting me see to Shawn's leg, you assholes!"

Harris could hear the screaming in the background.

"It was only a flesh wound, boss, just a nick. I had to stop him from getting to you and the captain. No worries."

Harris knew about Victor's disregard for anyone who didn't understand his idea of the truth, and he probably wasn't telling him what was really wrong with the guy.

"Vic, let him take care of the injury. Think about it for a minute. Our prisoners will be more compliant and less aggressive if we give them a little bit of leeway. I'm ordering you to be more-easy going, okay."

And he abruptly cut the connection, and leaned back in the captain's chair. Staring through the safety-resistant windshield into the black turbulence surrounding the ship, Harris stayed in that position for a very long time before he ordered two of his men to transport Captain Zack to his own quarters. Traveling along the thin corridors and down steep steps before they got to his cabin, the captain hung there as dead weight between them until they tossed him onto his cot. They attached plastic restraints on his ankles, looping a small chain between them to anchor him to the leg of the bunk. In consideration, they gave him just enough play in the chain to get to his privy on the other side of the tiny cabin. Then they left him still unconscious on the bed. Coming to forty-five minutes later, he found himself cuffed and chained to the leg of his cot. Why he was in that position was a question he couldn't answer, no matter how hard he tried. Why would anyone want the poisonous crap he was hauling around? The ludicrousness of his plight didn't change the fact he had to act. There was a threat to his life and those of his crew, and he had to get his boat back. He began to think over his limited choices. Tied up in his cabin like a calf in a rodeo was not something he would tolerate. The so-called cuffs were only plastic after all. The motherfucker who'd knocked him out must have been pretty stupid, because his expensive lighter was still nestled in the back pocket of his jeans. Getting off the cot, he stayed on his knees and twisted around and rubbed the pocket against the edge of the wood under the mattress. The lighter popped out onto the cot. Turning around, he grabbed at it, and when he snagged it, he flicked it on with his thumb. He angled the flame towards the thinnest part of the plastic around his wrists. Some of his skin was very close to the ongoing heat, but he had no choice in the matter. He'd deal with the discomfort. He needed to be free. After three hours of stopping and starting with second degree burns on his left wrist and part of the pad of his right thumb, he'd finally stretched the plastic out enough to get his left hand out of the cuff. It was easy to undo his ankles without any pain or needed patience. With the extended length he had with his arms free, he'd been able to reach his footlocker. It was in the small closet in the far corner of the cabin, and he knew there were wire cutters in it. After two powerful snips to the heavy plastic around his ankles, Zack violently kicked the chain and the cuffs across the wooden floor. Still boiling with frustration, this small freedom wasn't even close to his ultimate goal.

On a high shelf in the locker next to the porthole, were an array of different sized bandages and the EPIRB. All commercial crafts are instructed to have the *Emergency Position-indicating Radio Beacon* on board. It was mandatory. The one on the Ocean Swan was the size of a paperback book. There was nothing on it but a red button and a small light. Zack took it off the shelf and instantly hit the button. As the light lit, so did his hopes. The instant signal he'd started was bouncing off a satellite to be picked up by any coast guard station or military base within a thousand mile radius. A hail from an EPIRB is a dire one; screaming out across the wild and salty as far as it can go: *The ship was grievously damaged and she is probably sinking.* Getting the digitally advanced radio message, the military bases automatically send the stricken craft's coordinates out on a single-sideband wave to any vessel in the immediate vicinity. Hearing that reintroduced hail, those within range tried to get there as fast as they could.

Hitting the panic-button, Captain Zack knew the cavalry was on their way, yet that hadn't been enough to calm him. He didn't know how far away the closest ship might be, and he curled up on his mattress to worry and wait for help. With a collection of fervent prayers from the bottom of his heart straight to heaven, the hours crawled by like slugs 'till they stopped in their tracks and died. As he pled to God that their rescuers would show up sooner than later, he was terrified it was already way too late.

On her new west-northwest journey, the Ocean Swan kept bucking thirty-five foot waves. It took her twenty-four hours, not twelve, to reach the tranquility the eco-terrorists needed for their project. As soon as he realized it was finally flat enough, Harris lowered their speed to five knots, and he left it there; didn't want to use extra fuel if he didn't have to. Just enough to remain stationary in a sea with waves cresting at ten feet, and they'd face those waves and maintain that relationship for as long as they needed to. It's time to get to work. Well, almost time. It was three hours until dawn, and he wouldn't use the hydraulics in the dark.

When the sun seared above the horizon, Harris woke up his team, and sent them all out on their respective duties. Wilson, who had experience with on-board hydraulics, place himself into the metal seat welded to the deck in front of the controls. He started by opening the oversized hatch doors in the middle of the main deck. Looking through the large window in the wheel house, Harris knew the other men were busy arranging a web of steel around one of the casks inside the hold itself. They wanted to toss all three of the containers into the Pacific, and then escape, believing this absurdity would shock the world into stopping the dangerous practice of shipping radioactive waste across the Atlantic *and* then the Pacific... only to go through the entire trip all over again. In their badly disjointed reality, they didn't think they were hurting anything. They believed the lead containers would remain impervious down there on the bottom forever, and none of the radiation would ever leak out. In this ridiculous forecast of theirs, 'real' terrorists might commandeer a freighter just like this one and free the glass rods inside the casks to poison a city with them *or something.*

When their heroic plan was done, they'd get away from the Swan in a dinghy to rendezvous with a larger boat waiting for them a couple of miles away. Harris had been updating the captain of their escape-boat about their changing location on the sideband, and he had just ordered him to come in close as they were about to escape within the hour. It was time for the final act, and after that definitive communication, he shut all radio contact with the rest of the world down.

In the beginning, Zack hadn't wanted it. He hadn't wanted to move that poisonous junk. However, he was going belly up financially, about to lose everything, including his ship. Since, the power companies were eager to pay through the nose, offering him an exorbitant fee, what was he supposed to do? Either he did it or he would fold.

Looking out of his porthole, it was getting brighter outside. He couldn't figure out why the hatch-doors were wide open. Why would they want to get to the casks in the middle of nowhere? Whatever the reason, it seemed he had no way to stop them. He had no gun. Nobody on the Swan did. As he watched, the winch rotated over the hold, and he actually cringed. They'd set up the metallic net around one of the casks, and Zack's fists clenched with frustration. Besides the physical danger they were in, a more terrible truth made him feel even worse. He'd be sent straight to the poorhouse if those bastards stole his transport.

And things were getting worse by the second. Now sweating bullets, he looked out towards the horizon, and he noticed an itsy-bitsy speck out there. Was it what he was waiting for? Stepping over to his locker, he grabbed his binoculars. His hands were trembling, and it was hard for him to get them in focus, but when he did, he smiled. It was a frigate...military. Couldn't read her name on the bow, but he guessed it was American or British. It was the help he'd triggered the EPIRB to bring, and it was almost there. It would knock those dopes right on their asses. Flatten them in a New York minute, and this sudden optimism gave him the courage he needed; the mettle to go into action and work alone. He'd stop what they were doing...or slow them down anyway, before the hammer falls. It was obvious the whole group was very busy, so when he slipped out of his cabin and down the passageway, no one noticed. Besides, he needed to hold onto to his radioactive gold, and he'd come up with a plan to do just that.

Harris's attention was glued to the main deck, and he was blind to the small blip on the radar screen behind him, nor did he acknowledge the speck slowly growing on the horizon line. It was a Navy frigate, and it was bearing down on them at thirty-seven knots. Not the fastest clip the USS Nickolas could truly do, but it was adequate for the circumstances. At the moment, the eco-terrorists didn't know they only had forty-five minutes left before everything they were doing would end abruptly.

Wilson was controlling the hydraulic winch, and Harris was on a personal intercom with him, while the rest of the men helped by giving him last minute advice. After fifteen minutes of their careful coaxing, the nine ton barrel, wrapped in a steel cradle, hung twenty-five feet above the deck by a thick cable coming from the crane. In this particular part of the transfer, Harris had to make sure the freighter remained stable in the unpredictable appearance and height of the waves. The ship was still on auto pilot, but one of his hands stayed on the jog lever. A sudden shift in the wind or the arrival of a rogue wave would call for an instant course correction.

Captain Zack was silently opening the wheel house door behind Harris, wanting to return the same thing the bastard had done to him the day with gusto. He was holding a book about piloting in his hands, and it was a big book. Those extra twenty pounds would help him to seal the deal. He'd gotten so close...inches away, when the asshole twisted around and ducked, and punched him hard in the belly. Harris was twenty years younger than Zack and that gave him an edge. However, the captain was bigger and he had a lot more experience under his belt in hand to hand combat, and at that point, he also had a lot more adrenaline in his blood stream. Balancing the factors involved, it turned out to be an even match, and the men wrestled back and forth across the small room. In way too close, their punches had little effect. Harris shoved Zack against the closed door, and he'd leaned backwards and raised his right hand for a killer blow into his opponent's thorax. He'd used up half-a-second to get the distance he needed, leaving a chink in his defensive armor, and Zack used it to push him backwards like a human piston. Harris was then off-balance, and the captain aimed his own punch at the bridge of his nose. And then the ship lurched over a ten foot wave, and Zack missed, hitting him in the throat instead. It also threw Harris straight into the jog lever, and the boat rudders were instantly wrenched twenty degrees to port. After being punched hard in the gullet, Harris's head crashed into the shelves behind him with so much force he was out for the count, falling unconscious to the floor. The ferocious fight had ushered in the exact opposite of his previous diligence in stabilizing the Swan. The freighter had plunged sideways and an even bigger wave hurtled into her broadside, tilting the deck in a steep pitch. The tension on the cable holding the cask in the air increased as the downward slope had turned into a tighter and tighter angle.

And then it snapped. The thick steel of the cable lashed across the deck as if it was alive, and the lead cask bounced off the starboard rail and into the ocean as if it was made out of papier-mâché. After an extraordinary recoil like that, the container sank so fast it didn't look natural. The Ocean Swan had been moving sideways across the surface of the water, and in the first millisecond of the cask's descent, the stern of the ship had raced right over it. One of the ship's swirling props, edges sharp as a razors, had sliced into the lead of the cask like a hot knife in butter. It was only a small wound, but the cut was certainly deep enough to matter. The prop had gotten in. It had nicked the glass skin of one of the twenty-eight rods packed tight inside the barrel. As it tumbled end over end to its resting place on the bottom of the Pacific, the small scratch in its side would be the last ingredient to generate something; awaken and animate an unknown force remaining hidden in the vast depths for years. Now, it didn't matter whether the poisonous rods stayed where they were in the lead-lined cask or somehow got completely free of it, to somersault the rest of the way down to the sandy bottom like oversized radioactive toothpicks.

His fight with Harris was clearly over. Captain Zack had his wheel house back, for the moment anyway. Using the jog lever, he turned the Swan back into the waves again, before checking Harris out on the floor. He was knocked-out cold. Zack was confidant the outlaw was out of the running for a good long time. Re-setting the autopilot, he left the wheel house. He'd really screwed things up royally for the pirates, and he was happy he'd stayed in one piece in the process. Nevertheless, it seemed prudent to hide again, and he squeezed himself into a crawl space in the short corridor coming out of the wheel house with the intention of stay there until soldiers from the frigate had gotten on board.

Three of them had been standing on the deck, while another two crouched in the hold when everything went nuts. Wilson was in the chair welded to the deck, slack-jawed as the cable snapped and a clump of frayed steel threads sprouted out of the end of it; a snake's head moving wildly above their heads. Ducking out of the way of the cable, Victor tried to get Harris on the radio, but he'd gotten no answer. Seconds later, Wilson was tossed out of the chair, and in the process of getting back on his feet, he was bowled over again in a different way. He saw the USS Nicholas closing in, and it was maybe only ten miles away. He knew they'd be on top of them in half-an-hour, and he whistled to his cohorts and pointed to the northeast. They all saw it too, and it was more than likely their goose was cooked. They'd pick up their skirts and run anyway, and Vic came up with new orders to his cronies in the hold.

"You guys get to the chain locker and get our wet suits. We'll meet you at the stern as soon as we can. Something must have happened in the wheel house, and I'm going up there to check on Harris."

Wilson and the other men on the deck, followed Victor to the wheel house. Being in a hurry, wasn't the correct description of their frantic demeanor as they burst into the room. Panic was already skittering through their eyes when they saw Harris motionless on the floor. Victor kneeled and checked his pulse. He tried to wake him up with a very brisk slap, but their leader stayed dead to the world. Vic looked up at the others, shaking his head and a mournful expression took over on his face. There was no time to revive him, and they couldn't bring him along as dead weight. Since there were no other options, they left him behind to continue their frenetic race to meet Billy at the stern of the ship. They had to put on the wetsuits, inflate the dinghy and use their own small beacon to signal the getaway boat exactly where they'd be when they got into the water.

"Sir, I still can't get anything out of them on the radio."

The communication officer turned around on his seat, relaying the news to Captain Peterson on the bridge of the USS Nicholas.

Another officer scanned the entire length of the Ocean Swan with a pair of binoculars, "I can't see anyone on any of the decks and I don't see anybody in the wheel house either. They're running at five knots into the waves, so it's got to be on autopilot. What are your orders, sir?"

"Rustle up a copter for us, Lieutenant. We'll know soon enough what's going on over there if we drop six men on her in battle gear."

The USS Nicholas had three SH-60 Seahawk helicopters on board, and only eleven minutes elapsed after Peterson's order before heavily armed soldiers shimmied down ropes from the belly of one the copters hovering over the main deck of the Ocean Swan. Whatever control the eco-terrorists may have had on the ship was clearly washed away at that point.

Three of the soldiers un-cuffed the crew in the mess hall, and the others went to the wheel-house to find Harris on the wooden floor. Captain Zack appeared in the doorway, hands up, and he told them who he was and what he'd done to the man in black unconscious at their feet. He went on to tell them he had no idea where the rest of the violent lunatics had gone, suggesting that when they do find them, they should simply throw them over board.

The officer who'd come along with the men from the USS Nicholas radioed Captain Peterson telling him what they'd found out so far. He was ordered to search the rest of the ship; *top to bottom*. Flush out whoever might be left. Peterson got off the line with him, and connected to the helicopter pilot, telling him to grid-search the water around the freighter for the rest of the criminals. The pilot quickly located the remaining eco-terrorists.

They'd been floating just seven hundred feet away from the freighter. The poor sods had pulled the cord and inflated the dinghy. They got into it and paddled away as far as they could, knowing it was already over and they really wouldn't get away. A motorized launch holding more armed men emerged from the Navy ship to collect them. None of them picked up a gun or raised a hand in protest, knowing what would happen to them if they did. They were tossed into the brig on the lowest deck in the frigate, while their still insensate trail-blazer lay chained on a cot in the clinic.

Bouncing off the steel-rail of the Swan and into the ocean, the grievously punctured cask tumbled downwards to end up sitting on the edge of a volcanic rift, one hundred and seventy-five feet wide and two and half miles deep. And it lay on this gently sloped sand for six hours before its impressive weight began to make a difference. It started to slowly slide closer to the nearby abyss…inch by inch.

Peterson quickly learned about the fate of one the casks that had been stored in the hold of the Ocean Swan. He deployed their unmanned submarine to search for the lost container. The cameras on the small sub relayed information to the screen on the bridge of the frigate, and someone was watching the ongoing feed. So far, it was nothing but grainy static. The purring motor of the sub propelled it over the bottom for hours before they saw it, and it looked fine. They assumed it was unblemished. Why shouldn't it be? The damaged side of the cask was squashed into the sand, nevertheless, not knowing about that abysmal problem hadn't diminished the worry hounding the Captain. The container was sitting on a volcanic rift, and the blurry image of the situation did not underline the gravity of it. The sonar of the bottom did, and Captain Peterson wanted to retrieve it as fast as he could. He wanted to put it back into the hold of the Ocean Swan, and send the freighter on its merry way back to Japan. Mulling over how he might achieve that goal, he remembered what had happened when the EPIRB had gone off on the Swan. A research ship called the Equinox, had been racing to her coordinates. He'd turned them away, assuming they could handle the emergency without any help…and ninety-nine times out of a hundred, his decision would have been the correct one. How on earth could he have known this was to be the long shot? The cask was three miles down and they didn't have the equipment to bring it up, and the Equinox did, and that vexed him. He was about to ask them to turn around and come back. It would take at least two hours for them to arrive, and he didn't think anyone had that extra time.

The instant the Equinox got there, The USS Nicholas gave them the exact coordinates. Their science team quickly sent the drone to the bottom to scope things out. The images coming up were extremely informative in a bad way. *There was nothing there.* An empty hollow pressed into the sand elongated to a wide track ending at the edge of the rift. There was no way to get to it now. The radioactive glass rods were forever out of reach.

During its second unlucky voyage, the lead barrel rebounded from one side of the narrow chasm to the other, radiation flooding out of the gash in its wall in a nonstop flow. The cask ending up wedged between two stony outcroppings jutting eight feet over a volcanic fissure. The devilishness of its position was so awful it almost refuted the concept of coincidence as an ongoing plume of scalding water jetted out of the crack right below it, passing over the curved metal of the container like affectionate fingers from hell. Magma bubbling just under the earth's crust at that particular section of the ocean floor was responsible for the ongoing infernal level of heat. The spent fuel rods would hang there forever in those lightless depths. Nothing could unseat it but an earthquake. Any molecular relationships in this upwelling boiling river would begin to warp out of true, and that abnormal deformation would expand and reach hundreds of miles of the Pacific Ocean.

On the surface, Captain Peterson came up with a different list of things to do, beginning with a call to an Admiral he knew for guidance. An older and wiser oracle, he hoped the man would help him with a logical assessment of the facts, and how he should deal with it. With the input he got during the call, he then explained to the liberated crew of the Ocean Swan that they'd be paid for three casks when they got to the nuclear plant on the coast of Japan. The American government would take care of the discrepancy, and the Japanese authorities don't care what happened to the missing cask. They would remain tight-lipped over its disappearance, and the crew and the captain of the Ocean Swan would be just as reticent. They didn't want this to go public, afraid that the ongoing transport of nuclear waste over the oceans may stop. Officers at the highest tier of America's military would simply skew the story, permanently removing any evidence of what had taken place, and slickly re-write the historical truth. If no one knew about it, what had gone wrong hadn't really happened. Everything would be fine. Right as rain.

Walter's camouflage had worked. He'd lived through hours of isolation, nibbling on some of the provisions around him and creeping out of the pantry and into the head on the other side of the galley when he really needed to. When he heard a helicopter engine, he'd hoped it was a sign they were about to be saved, and when the door of the pantry slammed opened minutes later, he peeked out from behind a bag of potatoes. A man in a Navy uniform was towering over him, and Walter wriggled out from his pile of bags with his hands up and a smile on his face.

Navy officers interviewed everyone in the crew while they scoured every inch of the freighter to remove anything that would support what had taken place. After a day and a half, their job done. The USS Nickolas disappeared into the distance, and the Ocean Swan resumed her trip to Japan. She was a little bit lighter…and maybe a few feet higher in the water, but everyone on board forgot about why that was. Zack was more than thankful that his payment was going to stay the same.

On the second morning of their renewed voyage, Walter was leaning against the jamb of door leading into the mess hall, drying his hands off with a work towel. He'd just served a sedate meal to the men, and he was enjoying the sunlight beaming in on him, and then he looked up. There was only blue sky up there, occasionally dotted with a cumulous cloud. It was supposed to stay tranquil for the rest of their trip to the coast. He could hear them babble as they ate their meal, and they sounded giddy, yet their optimism couldn't help him. Walter's spirit was in turmoil, and lowbrow humor and calm seas wasn't enough to soothe him. Only the men on the Navy ship had known exactly where the Swan had been at the end of the debacle. At 37' N 145' W they'd been right in the center of the stagnant eye of the Northern Pacific Gyre in its slow migration north, and what difference would that make?

Even though Walter hadn't known about that possibly devastating trivia, things weren't lining-up properly in his head nonetheless. As if a bad moon was rising, his powerful premonition would not go away; an unspeakable thing would soon be let loose on land and in the sea. Of course, it was only a feeling, and he kept on trying to ignore it as hard as he could.

7:15PM Tuesday November 15th, 2006 Arlington, Massachusetts

Eric and Vera Adler were escorted to their table by the maître d', of course, they hadn't had enough time to sit completely down before a young man wearing an expensive suit sidled up to Eric. Politely nodding to Vera, he whispered into Mr. Adler's ear as he gave him a business card. Eric stared at it. ***The Blackmore Coalition***. He'd heard of them. It was a legal firm most people wouldn't want to tussle with. Agreeing to the man's tête-à-tête at the bar, he told Vera to be patiently. He'd be back shortly, and he walked away with someone he didn't know.

Another man waited for them at the bar, and he stood up and shook Eric's hand.

"Hello Mr. Adler. I'm Michael Chandler, and this is my associate Steven Boone. We're here to ask for your help. A couple of months ago, someone in our group dropped-out and we also had an influx of new cases at the same time. We're a bit short-handed, so we looked you up, checking on your work history and your character. We liked what we saw, and we are offering you a position in the firm. Don't worry, sir, you have time to think it over. If you're interested, or if you have any questions, just call. You can make an appointment at the main office in Chelsea on Monday."

"Well, this *is* a surprise, sir. Thank-you for the grace period to consider the offer," Eric said. Boone slid a thick manila envelope towards him across the bar.

"This has all the information you need to know about our practices, including our list of clients. If you do come on board, we don't mind if you stay with your current customers until their cases are resolved. However, if you are currently in contention with anyone on our list, you'll have to shut those cases down immediately."

"Alright, Mr. Chandler. I'll look it over. The wife is waiting, and I must get back. I'll give you an answer in the next couple of days."

"You can call me Mike. I'm optimistic we'll be spending a lot of time together very soon."

He smiled and tilted his head as Eric went back to his table.

9:30 Monday December 6th, 2006 Chelsea, Massachusetts

His briefcase was stuffed with all the cases from his own practice, and shouldering his way through the double doors leading into his new office wasn't easy. It was Eric Adler's first day at his new job at the Blackmore Coalition. After meeting those scouts in the restaurant, Eric had gone through their list of clients the instant he got home, and there was only one customer on their list that was also on his own. *Carnelian Cruises.* He had a client suing the line, and if he was going to work for Blackmore, he'd have to withdraw from the case. Normally, that wouldn't bother him in the least, however he'd just unearthed a solid clue to support his client's claims about her brother's disappearance. He was about to call Lyndsey and make her day, however it he wasn't going to do it now. He wanted the cushy deal they were offering instead. If that meant he had to be a heartless mercenary and drop her like a hot potato, he's going to have to rearrange his feelings to accommodate that.

Lyndsey's brother vanished on a cruise with his fiancé six months ago on a ship called the Caprice owned by the Carnelian Line. She wanted justice for whoever was responsible for his disappearance. If she can't have that, she wanted a reasonable explanation for his being gone, and she'd hired Adler to sue the corporation in an attempt to get either of these results satisfied.

Sending her a dismissive letter explaining he could no longer represent her, Eric was relieved when he got no response at all from her. After this cold and abrupt legal departure of his, Lyndsey would to have start the entire process up over again from ground zero. He couldn't even give her the file, nor the information he'd just found. Dumping her like yesterday's trash, he *assumed* he wouldn't deal with any repercussions from her in the future; a supposition grounded in her ongoing silence. No phone call, no email on his site, and she hadn't shown up in a tizzy at the office. Being a very busy man, trifling things like scorning young women wasn't important enough to warrant anymore of his energy than drafting up the letter to do it in the first place.

He hung his jacket over the leather chair behind a large mahogany desk, and he sat down at his new perch, linking his fingers behind his head. Noticing an invitation in the center of the desk, he leaned forwards and snatched it up and opened it with movements echoing an oversized bird. The bulbous end of his nose didn't interfere with reading this missive, and a smile bloomed upon his lips. The firm was giving him and his family an all-expense paid vacation on the Carnelian Day Dream Cruise sailing out of San Francisco on January third. It was a yearly tradition for the firm, and almost everybody goes. They'd be out at sea for twelve days.

The rest of the day passed comfortably enough. He began to build friendships with certain well-placed individuals. It was a little after five when he looked out the window of his office to see a red Mustang convertible screech into the parking lot outside with Tiffany at the wheel. Back at home, he knew his wife was cooking a congratulatory dinner for him, and it would be cruel of him to ignore that, but emotional brutality had never been a problem for him. His own idea of having fun that evening was a little bit different than Vera's, and he slipped the invitation into his suit pocket. He'd come up with an excuse to smooth her feathers when he gets there. Too late for dinner, that's for sure. Leaving his wife out to dry, he'd tell her he'd worked late, and then he'd describe the cruise to her; a perfect palliative to make her feel better. Everything would be fine.

Eric really shouldn't have called Tiffany about his first day in Chelsea, however he'd been way too excited to hold himself back. Hearing his voice on her message-machine, Tiff put the bottle of nail polish she was holding back on the bedside table, and she'd picked up the phone. Her nails could wait, and her right hand slid between her legs for some self-appreciation. Tiffany mimicked Marilyn Monroe in her appearance and her gestures, yet she knew she'd never get the perks the real star had enjoyed if she kept on working as a receptionist in a dental office. Eric had to leave his wife and use all his attention…no, all his *money* on her.

Putting his jacket on, Eric grabbed his briefcase. Walking through the main office, he waved goodbye to anyone still in the room, and he took the elevator to the first floor. Stepping out of the building, he went over to the Mustang gleaming like a cherry in the late afternoon sun. The car engine purred, and the top was down, and Tiffany looked up at him with a leer. She leaned over the center console and opened the passenger door for him. In Eric's mind, this temptress had taken away any choice he might have had to do the right thing, and he got in, and they drove away. He didn't make it home that night until after midnight.

4:48PM Monday **December 6th, 2006** **Somerville, Massachusetts**

Wearing a dark blue sequined top and beige slacks, Vera Adler dropped the cook book on the counter, and she took the turmeric out of the spice rack on the wall. She was religiously following a starred recipe to make Jambalaya. Filling a crock pot with tomatoes, celery, rice, and three different kinds of meat, she had plugged it in and turned it on hours ago. She was trying to create a heavenly taste in her mélange with a hodgepodge of spices. Eric had not made it home for dinner once last week, but since today was his first day in the new office, she'd congratulate him with a celebratory meal. One she'd never cooked before.

Years ago, in her previous career as a psychologist, she'd dreamed of motherhood, and that drive had goaded her into retiring after her marriage to Eric. Her only pregnancy ended in miscarriage, the following months silently padded by her like melancholy ghosts. She thought about going back to her career, but going through the rigmarole to renew her license hobbled her efforts. Instead, she played tennis with an instructor. She did volunteer work, and scads of exercise classes. Of course, none of it fulfilled her. None of it fed her soul, and her relationship with Eric was disintegrating. She barely saw him. When he was there, he could not help her out of her growing malaise.

Vera's mouse-brown hair was now streaked with grey, and she didn't dye it. It appeared the forty-seven years she'd lived on the planet were dragging her down, but it was just another symptom of isolation. She remained muscular and thin on the powerful metabolic system she was born with. Vera's weight hadn't changed much since she'd left high school, and it didn't matter whether she went to exercise classes or not.

The Jambalaya had been simmering for a long time, and the smell coming from her new experiment was incredible. Vera was pleased. Looking up at the wall clock, she saw it was almost five. Eric should be home by six. She prayed this new job in a new firm would be an ignition. It would heat things up between them again.

Setting the dining room table with care, she placed two servings of butter lettuce and radishes at both of their places. At seven, she put the pot of Jambalaya on a wooden tray in the center of the table, and then she filled two wide bowls with generous dollops of her masterpiece. Putting the ladle back in the notched rim of the pot, she sat down and poured herself a glass of Chardonnay from the bottle resting in an ice bucket on a small stand next to the table. She swallowed it down like water, and then she refilled her glass. Staring at the food on her plate, Vera didn't move for two and half hours. The candles she'd lit were gutted out by the time she sipped her second glass of wine. Eric had not even called her to cancel.

The forty-three muscles of her face were slack and her eyes were glassy, and the vacuous on her face did not bode well for the marriage. Frozen next to the congealed dinner she'd slopped onto her plate hours ago, the dark bud inside of her finally opened and began to slither into life. It started with a rebellion within Vera's already uneasy morality, and civility was the first to fall. Like a line of falling dominos, this cascading effect on her psyche signaled a dangerous transformation. It would have been a lot better if she'd tossed her full set of fine china on the parquet floor beneath her feet, and watch it shatter into pieces instead.

11:00AM Monday December 6th, 2006 O'Hare Airport

At five eight, Lyndsey had won awards in gymnastics in high school. After graduation, Ms. Delft had quickly found work as a stunt double, and it was an easy gig for her. Light brown hair cut in a shag, her green eyes glittered with intelligence and humor, and she enjoyed her job. She'd been on a movie shoot in Quebec since November 28th, and when the director was finally done with her, it was time to go home. She walked out of O'Hare and got to her car she'd left in long-term parking. She drove eleven miles to Watertown, and she picked up her mail on the way.

Twelve months ago, Lyndsey had tried to put the brakes on her brother's marriage. She didn't think his fiancé was what she seemed to be, but her earnest attempts hadn't worked. The happy couple skipped up the gangplank of a cruise ship to celebrate their engagement. As soon as they got on board, it seemed that Byron instantly skipped out on her, however Sheila hadn't told anyone he was gone. She assumed he was hanging out with some other girl…just like she was. After forty-eight hours, she began to get worried, and there was a search with no conclusion. He wasn't anywhere on the ship, and Lyndsey had been more devastated about his ongoing disappearance than Sheila was.

Carnelian Cruises did not have a stellar reputation, and Lyndsey went on the warpath, paying a private-eye to find out what he could. The guy found zilch. Then she hired a lawyer with a reputation of winning most of his cases, and his name was Eric Adler. She wanted to stretch the cruise line over a barrel, and things were starting to get more difficult for Carnelian. Lyndsey was optimistic that they were about to tell her what had happened to her brother. Having been stuck in Quebec for three weeks, she was looking forwards to some positive news from Eric somewhere in the pile of backed up mail she'd picked up and put in a plastic bag. The second she got inside her condo, she threw her keys on the coffee table and dropped her luggage on the floor, and then she got the bag that had been held in her teeth in her hands. She spilled it upside down, and everything scattered out on the kitchen table. Pawing through it, Lyndsey quickly found his letter, ripping it open with anticipation. It had to be the good news she was waiting for!

Mr. Eric Adler ESQ.
247 Midway Road
Arlington, Massachusetts 48776

Dear Lyndsey,

I regret to advise you I can no longer provide you with legal representation. My upcoming employment with the Blackmore Coalition creates a conflict of interest. In accordance with the prescribed actions in the matter of Delft vs. Carnelian Cruises, I will file a motion for leave to withdraw as counsel. Pending the court's approval of the motion, I will continue to serve as your counsel of record until the motion is granted and then our relationship as attorney-client will end.

I apologize for the unforeseen circumstances guiding me into this action, and I wish you every success in your future endeavors in the case.

Sincerely,
Eric Adler

Her fingers had gone numb as she read it. The dreadful piece of paper fluttered to the floor, and Lyndsey slumped on a kitchen chair, holding her head in her hands. Eric Adler had never thought very seriously about Lyndsey's real response to recusing himself out of the case. Still reckless in his actions, the lawyer had just stepped on another time-bomb as the tears currently falling on Ms. Delft's cheeks would soon dry.

2:18PM Thursday **December 14th, 2006** **3000 feet above the Pacific Ocean**

Davis Reed and Brady Shultz were tracking the direction of the gyre in the northern Pacific. They were in a reconnaissance plane owned by the University of San Francisco. The science department sent the plane out every six months to visually record the deleterious effects going on in the center of what is sometimes called the Trash Vortex. It has grown dramatically since their last overview, and Brady was scanning the surface through binoculars. Most of the flotsam was hidden under the chop, yet there were still a lot of larger pieces easily made out on the top. He was surprised by that. His mild astonishment was replaced with curiosity when he saw something very odd in the distance. There was a strange color in the water, and he nudged Davis who was piloting the plane. Directing his attention, he pointed to the east. The bottom was riddled with volcanic fissures, and Brady suspected it could be a bloom of some kind or perhaps another chemical spill. Davis banked the aircraft. He would get them closer. Five minutes later, they were staring down at what looked like an abstract painting spanning miles of ocean water.

"Have you ever seen anything like that before? It's gotta be coming from a rift, but I don't know how all that detritus could make it to the surface. The bottom around here is about two miles down," Brady said.

"It's a doozy, all right. It's purple. It is purple, isn't it? I'm not seeing things? And there are streaks of green and blue in it too...and...and... Brady, do you see that? That milky looking stripe bubbling over there to the left. This thing is huge. Fifteen miles wide, at least." Davis was stunned.

"We've got to call it in. We don't have the equipment to get really good pictures of it, and I think it should be documented. They should send the research ship out."

Brady picked up the radio.

"Recon one to base."

"Go ahead recon. How are you doing out there?"

"Well, it's certainly not boring that's for sure. We're flying over an anomaly, and it's important to get some more definitive pictures of it. The grainy crap coming out of the cam on the outside of this plane isn't going to be clear enough. We need to send out Primus Time to coordinates 37' N 145' W. The instant they see it, you'll send the research ship out here too, and figure out what the hell it is."

The second plane got there twenty-three hours later, but the mysterious phenomenon had dispersed.

9:00AM Thursday December 14th, 2006 The Aspersion's Foil

The Aspersion's Foil was owned by the Heinem Pharmaceutical Corporation. At three hundred and seventeen feet in length, she was big enough to hold the star-studded benefit set up on her that evening. From the Captain all the way down to the janitor, the entire staff was working hard before the guests arrived. Ms. Donnelly had lined-up a lot of stars from Cher to Clapton to support her in her benefit, and G. E. Smith would orchestrate an eclectic back-up band for them in a seamless production.

Things in the galley were humming along well enough. Gus, a young helper, was peeling a pile of potatoes in the corner of the room. When he thought over what Holly was doing, he wanted to donate a little of his own money to the cause, hoping it wouldn't be too late. As his mind drifted off, he cut his finger on the peeler, and he had to go over to the small closet to get a Band-Aid. He watched two guys enter the galley. They were wearing the same uniform he had on, a white jacket and pants, and they tramped over to Vince, who was the head-chef of the ship for directions. Gus heard him order them into the cooler to bring out more stuff, and he was surprised. Ms. Donnelly usually doesn't need extra help. Maybe she wanted to speed things up this one time for the benefit. Of course, his silly guess was way off the mark.

In a phone call earlier in the afternoon, someone had told Vince his employer had engaged extra help in the galley just for a few hours right before the event. He thought the information was given to him by Ms.

Donnelly's assistant, but the person on the phone had tricked him by mimicking their voice. In reality, those men were not kitchen help, and they were about to do something that had absolutely nothing to do with food.

9:00AM Thursday December 14th, 2006 Washington DC

Getting out of his helicopter in Dulles International Airport, Attison Korybante was on his way to a meeting with the Ocean Conservancy. The next day, there was going to be a congressional hearing to address the problem of pollution in the five ocean gyres, and Attison intended on being there. He was a very powerful man. Besides being an international commercial lawyer, and the head of the board of trustees of the Hienem Pharmaceutical Corporation, many of the other things he did remained hidden behind the curtains. Only a few people knew the wide influence he had. When Holly Donnelly's entire family was murdered during their Thanksgiving reunion on their estate on Bass River in Massachusetts last year, she became his charge. She'd turned thirty a couple of months ago, ending the legal link he had to her. However, the emotional and spiritual connection between them had deepened, and he kept on advising her.

It had been a pointless consultation with the Conservancy, and he hailed a taxi to the capital building. Getting out of the cab, he climbed the stairs to the pillared entrance, and the two hundred steps didn't bother him. He actually increased his speed. According to his driver's license, he was over fifty years old, however anyone meeting him would not have believed it. How could cosmetic surgery be responsible for erasing so many of those years right off of him? Attison looked naturally young. It was yet another of the many mysteries he held back from general knowledge. His dark hair was long, without a single strand of grey, and his features were compelling. Standing over six feet, he was trim and muscular, and his classical beauty was hypnotizing. Walking into the halls of power, he'd intentionally muted that part of his physicality. He didn't want to confuse the politicians or the industrialists with unnecessary information. It was extraneous, and he wanted the logic in his upcoming presentation to win the day. Of course, his words would probably not be enough, and the other more controlling options he could invoke would not work on the hill.

The day before, twelve men had met in a briefing room off the main lobby of the same edifice. Three lobbyists, a representative of the Ocean Conservancy Group, three congressman and four CEO's from manufacturing companies responsible for most of what we use and then throw out...and Attison. Lincoln Douglas, the owner of Aspect Forge, a conglomerate of bio-engineering firms, was a big commercial voice in that mix. They were having a discussion over host countries paying a tax on effluents coming out of factories from other nations they'd allowed in, and the input ping-ponged around the large conference table. Attison and Lincoln were both silent. There was a different kind of interaction going on between them. Attison was sitting across the table from Lincoln, and a female intern had given him a personal note from the mogul a few minutes ago. The CEO of Aspect Forge wanted Attison to have this update as quickly as possible.

Att. Mr. Korybante;

You have a relationship with the titular owner of Heinem Corp. My employees informed me that Ms. Holly Donnelly will not be at her benefit this afternoon, and I worry for her safety. Perhaps you should simply take care of any repercussions of this hazard by letting the steering committee know you won't be at the lectern to address congress tomorrow. These august representatives don't need to be irritated by a bugbear, and Holly would go back to her fundraiser. I know you will do the right thing, so the entire matter can be dropped.

Attison glared across the table at Lincoln, anxiety woven into his courageous front. Lincoln Douglas had to believe the threat he'd outlined to Holly was real to him, and even if the man's criminal bullying was actually nothing but humorous to him, he must keep on looking nervous before he caved under his frightening threat. He stalled a little longer than he should have, but the rest of his off-the-cuff reaction to the letter had been perfect, and Attison believed his acting had been superb.

Korybante had every intention to persuade everyone at the meeting in congress the next day that his dire warnings were true. They must harken to his advice and stop tossing effluence into the earth's oceans. His chances of denting their indifference or their greed were bleak. At least Mr. Lincoln Douglas had just inserted a bit of levity in this gloomy forecast, and Attison instantly pushed down an elfish smirk trying to come out. He must remain solemn for the moment.

3:00PM Thursday December 14th, 2006 The Aspersion's Foil

After most of guests got on board, Holly had given the order to leave port. The Aspersion Foil cruised three hours before she anchored on the east side of Catalina Island, twenty miles off the coast. Keith Fischer had received his own invitation to this star-studded benefit a month ago, and Holly had scribbled a personal note for him on the back of the card.

'Looking forwards to talking over the strange lands you don't always want to visit. Sincerely, Holly'.

It was important for her to meet him as the connection between them was getting stronger. Keith had felt the same invisible tug, and he too realized its importance. There was no way he could ignore it.

That morning, he'd met a Greek shipping magnate in Northern Los Angeles to talk over an installation of revamped LRNs in his tankers, and Aspersion's Foil was gone when he showed up. In finding another way to get out there, he remembered an acquaintance who owned a cigarette-boat docked only three miles away. He called him up, and he was more than happy to ferry him out there, and Keith walked up the gangway and onto the lower deck of Holly's ship in under an hour.

The elegant design of it impressed him. The designer had used minimalist precision to create a muted splendor. The pool was shaped like a wing in the center of the deck, and an optical illusion in the azure feathers painted on the bottom made them flutter under the water. The band was supporting Tom Jones as he sang 'Rolling down the River' on a small stage in the starboard corner of the deck. Holly had pulled out all the stops, and Keith really hoped the donations would follow her in kind.

Looking up, he scanned the rail of upper deck fifteen feet above his head. Crowded with jeweled and silk-wrapped politically connected individuals, he saw Holly. It was easy enough to pick her out. She was holding a glass of champagne and she was smiling, and he'd seen her pictures in magazines and newspapers. Of course, her physical presence out-stripped any of those pictures. At 5' 8", she had the muscles and litheness of a dancer. She'd left her black hair loose, and it hung in wonderful chaos as a diamond clip held it away from her face. The sleeveless bodice of her gown was light beige, dusted with glitter, darkening to black at the hem. Eyes tinged with violet, Holly dropped her remarkable gaze to the lower deck, and she saw Keith standing there. She waved at him, but someone touched her shoulder and whispered a question in her ear, and she turned away as the revelers closed around her. Keith sauntered over to one of the open bars and he asked for a bottle of beer. Picking up some tiny sandwiches with cucumber on them, he walked to the stern of the boat. He decided to wait a few minutes before slogging through the crowd to get to her.

Vince had sent a message to Ms. Donnelly and his emissary was nervous relaying it to her.

"Good evening, Ms. Donnelly. The chef asks for your presence in the galley for a moment. The Bourbon Chicken is almost done…and…and he's hoping for your approval before sending it to the dining room."

"Thank-you, Susan. Tell him I'm on my way."

There were five decks in her floating palace, and she'd installed two elevators; one for the day to day use and a service elevator to transport staff and supplies in and out of the large ship. Excusing herself, she left the deck and walked into a corridor ending in front the oversized service elevator. She got on and hit a button, and in seconds she got off and walked into the galley.

Tasting the sauce surrounding the chicken, Holly smiled, "I just gave you a few ingredients, Vince. I couldn't have created anything like this.

You are what you are. Whatever I gave you was overwhelmed by genius. Next week, I'll be in Massachusetts, and I don't think I'll enjoy Bass River the same way. I'll miss you, and what you create. Yes, send the Bourbon Chicken up to the dining room!" And she hugged him with real affection.

"Thank-you, Ms. Donnelly. It's nice that you give me so much leeway with my recipes. Working on the Foil is like living in a fairytale."

"I'm happy you're happy...oh dear, I'm sounding ridiculous. Listen, I've got to go back to the party."

Louis and Reeves were contracted to kidnap Holly Donnelly. They had been cutting up celery sticks and carrots and they'd been doing it clumsily. All their attention was directed at Holly while she talked to the head chef. It had been a very short conversation, and they watched as the last of her in the form of the sparking hem of her gown vanished through the door. Then they sidled away from the cutting board and followed her into the hallway.

Waiting in front of the elevator doors, Holly seemed unaware of the men silently sneaking up behind her. Reeves had already poured chloroform on a rag, and he reached around and pushed the wet cloth over her mouth and nose. He held it tightly in place. His other arm was around her waist, and he lifted her right off the ground. Her struggling ended in under a minute, and her head drooped and the rest of her upper body went limp. The female tycoon hung like an over-cooked noodle in the arms of her attacker, and Reeves tossed her over his shoulder like a sack of flour. The elevator doors opened, and he got in with Louis at his side, and they took the car to the lowest deck on the ship. When the doors opened again, they ran for the loading platform at the stern of the ship, and the burden Reeves held felt very light. Louis was using the radio he'd had with him to signal their compatriot who was out there at the wheel of their escape boat just two thousand feet away from the Aspersion's Foil. It only took him four minutes to get here, and they could hear the engine of a sixteen foot Whaler chug into the loading dock inside the ship. Holly was starting to revive, and a muffled groan came out of her. Reeves off-handedly used the same rag he'd put in his pocket over her face again, and he'd left it there. He had to be positive she'd stay docile for at least the next ten minutes.

The kidnappers ripped off their white jackets and aprons, tossing them behind a metal pole in the corner of the loading area. The surly looking man behind the wheel of the Whaler gave them flannel shirts and fishing caps. New camouflage. They hurriedly put it all on. Louis grabbed Holly's feet and Reeves took her shoulders, and they put her between two seats on the Whaler, curling her up. The guy behind the wheel was named Stu, and he dragged a tarp out of a foot locker behind him to cover her body. Louis and Reeves sat down on the rear seat, and Stu dropped the engine into reverse, slowly backing out. As soon as he got about twenty feet away from the Foil, Stu sped up. But not by much. The mercenaries were now holding fishing poles, wanting to look innocent until they got farther away. After there was over a mile between them and the ship, they put the poles down. Stu pushed the throttle to the limit, and in the beginning, it looked like the small boat was racing straight out to sea. However she suddenly veered to the left, and disappeared behind the other side of Catalina Island.

Ten minutes later, they roped the Whaler to Wonderland, yet another oversized yacht. It wasn't as massive as the Aspersion's Foil, but at one hundred and forty-five feet in length, it had more than enough space for what her owner had in mind.

Vince glanced over his shoulder. The extra help he hadn't needed had been in the corner of the room cutting things up and now they were nowhere to be seen, and he couldn't even remember their names. Incorporating morels and diced garlic into a reduced wine and chicken broth simmering in the bottom of an oversized steel pan, he didn't care about their sudden absence. Probably lollygagging around somewhere. He wasn't sure if Holly had told that silly paper-pushing Martha Travis anything about anything, but Vince didn't want to interrupt Ms. Donnelly's evening with trivialities like that. He'd give Martha a piece of his mind the next day, instead.

Keith swallowed the last of his beer as he looked out at some impressive mansions on the coast of the island. He could faintly make-out the unmistakable slide guitar of Bonnie Raitt coming to him from the party, but there was no one at all at the stern of the ship. He found peace in the momentary solitude. Staring straight down, he saw a small Whaler with three men close to the hull of Aspersion's Foil. It seemed they were fishing, but something seemed off-kilter to him. And the green plastic tarp lumped over something on the deck between the seats bothered him even more. Already conflicted about his upcoming meeting with Holly, he certainly didn't want to be sidetracked by non-essential psychic white-noise. Popping the last sandwich in his mouth, he sauntered back to the party.

His earlier fame as Kevin Fielding had died out soon after his disappearance. Having changed his name, he began a new career as a marine technician, yet a different kind of celebrity reappeared with his uncanny speed, ingenuity and inventions. Some of the guests were sidling up to him with questions, and Keith enjoyed this happy banter, yet Holly was not around. He looked at his watch, and it was almost 6:30. It was almost dark. His tension over meeting her was changing to foreboding, and he nodded politely to the people he was talking to, but he told them he had something he had to do. Checking every single section of the ship that was open to the public, she must be moving around like a jack-in-the-box, or she'd retired to her cabin. *Maybe.* He walked into the dining room, way too distracted to be drawn towards the smells coming from the buffet table, and he stepped over to a window. In the distance, he saw four different vessels. One of them was small, and it looked like the Whaler he'd seen near the ship. A feeling was growing on him. Staring down at his sneakers for a second, an awful certainty slammed into his head. What he'd felt earlier had not been white noise. It had been a real warning. Keith straightened up and sprinted through the dining room like an Olympian, suddenly understood what, or more precisely, who was under that tarp and it hadn't been engine parts or coiled rope.

Holly's captors were doing guard-duty in front of the door of a small cabin on the lowest deck of Wonderland.

"It's getting late and I'm starving. Come on, Louis. We can eat in the mess hall right now. That scrawny thing in there isn't going anywhere," and Reeves jerked his thumb over his shoulder towards the cabin. "You put so many loops of metal twine around her wrists and ankles, it was like tying up super-girl or something," and Reeves threw his hands up in frustration.

"Charlie wants us to stay here. He doesn't want us to leave cuz' she might find a way to make noise or something while someone was walking by the door."

"Nobody *ever* comes down here, and even if they did, they all know about Donnelly. I mean, there's gonna be a session with her later on. What could really go wrong? It's locked with a dead bolt and we have the only key, and remember, she was zonked out when you roped her to the chair. Even if the door was wide open, she still couldn't go anyway!"

Louis at Reeves. He was hungry too, and his partner had a point.

"What if you go up there and eat and then come back, and then I'll go. If Charlie shows up, I could tell him you were in the can, and you could do the same thing for me."

"You're kidding right? That stupe never leaves his office."

Reeves stood up and shrugged.

"Okay, let's go. It'll only be about ten minutes, and we'll feel better when we come back."

Louis got up too. He used the key to open the cabin door. He wanted to ease his mind. Holly was tied to a straight backed wooden chair wedged between the beds, and her chin was resting on one of her collar-bones. Seems as if she'd passed out again. Reeves was right. They shouldn't worry. Bringing her up to the conference room later on would be easy as pie. No problem-o.

He'd never been on the Foil before, but Keith used his general knowledge about vessels to get himself to the loading area in sixty seconds, especially since he knew exactly what he wanted. A twenty-six foot Donzi was nestled in a cradle six feet away, and he stepped over to the control panel on the wall. Instinctually, he flipped the right switch, and a hydraulic arm went under the boat, shifting and lowering the craft into the small channel. He released the cradle and it lifted up and out the way. Next to the panel was a line of keys hanging off a cork board, and Keith picked the ones that had white tape right above them with the name *Donzi* printed there.

Hopping behind the wheel, he turned the ignition key and the engines started right up. He didn't have the time to let the MerCruisers warm up, and he dropped the transmission into drive and slowly moved through the channel. Reaching open water, he pushed the Donzi to her limit. It wasn't going to take him long to get wherever he wanted to go. At fifty knots, the boat skipped across the surface like a bird. When he got to the other side of the island, the mystery about where he was going go was glaringly answered. The Wonderland was anchored on the ocean-side of Catalina, and he bee-lined straight towards her as his internal voice told him that Holly was on that ship. Five minutes later, he tied the boat to a cleat near a diving platform. He jumped on, and climbed a metal ladder to the main deck, staying in the shadows. He'd been lucky. No one had been around, and he ducked into a hatch. As if he was following psychic bread crumbs, he raced down the nearest stairs to get him two decks lower. Trotting past a line of cabin doors, he stopped in his tracks. Keith felt her presence on the other side of one of the doors. Of course, it was locked, but that wouldn't stop him. He'd dressed for the benefit fairly formally, but he could never forget about practicality; ergo the sneakers. Digging into the back pocket of his silk pants, he took out the Swiss-army knife he'd put there. He flicked out the long thin probe and he angled it into the key hole on the knob. Rushed by his concern over Holly's safety, he used a smidgeon of telekinesis to aid him in picking the lock, and the bolt quickly slid back into its slot in the wall. As the small door opened, he saw Holly tied to a chair five feet away from him. He switched the tool on his knife to the largest blade, and he began to cut the metal twine off her wrists. Keith hadn't noticed the expression of flat-out anger on her face. It seemed the normal 'saving-the-damsel-in-distress' thing wasn't really happening. And then Reeves clogged up the entire doorway with Louis standing right behind him. Keith moved towards him, geared up to knock them both out…one way or another, but a very strange noise halted the action on both sides. Kicking her left calf forwards with so much speed and force, the twine around her left ankle popped off like thread, and then Holly freed her right ankle in the exact same way half-a-second later. And then she wrenched her hands down and forwards. The remaining twine on her wrists snapped off with the same unnatural ease, and she got out of the chair. Holly then casually nudged Keith out of her way.

"You should both sit down on those beds right now, otherwise we're gonna…" but Reeves enthusiastic pronouncement was interrupted by a slap to the side of his face so powerful he simply slumped to the floor unconscious, and his partner didn't have much of a chance either. Using ungodly swiftness, Holly followed her dynamic back-slap with a gracefully pirouette, giving herself more momentum before she faced Louis. A roundhouse powered by her frustration was illustrated by her tight fist crashing into his temple, and it was delivered by a hurricane she no longer had to hide. No time to attack *or* defend himself, Louis became another lump on the floor. Holly turned to Keith, her gown sparkling, as she began their first introduction with exasperation.

"Why are you here?"

"I thought we were just going to sit down have a drink and get to know each other on your ship, but I saw what was happening, and I had to help. Perhaps rescue you? When I realized you were in the fishing boat, I didn't think anybody could reach you faster than I did. Obviously, my silly idea that you might be trouble was ridiculous, but how was I supposed to know you have a black-belt in everything and you're immune to chloroform?"

Keith could smell the chloroform splattered down the front of her dress, and the inference that she'd been dosed with it clearly hadn't affected her speed nor her accuracy in her sudden attack on the men who were twice her size. Knocking them both out in a trice, she may be more than she appeared to be, and he was getting even more apprehensive. Being 'in good shape' doesn't really explain what he'd just seen, and Holly could be beyond his ken, nevertheless he held onto his hope that she still might be just a gifted person and that was it.

"I'm sorry, Keith. I've been waiting to meet you, and these odd circumstances took away my manners for a moment. I've been looking forwards to meeting you, and what you did was honorable. Most would find what you did impossible to achieve. If I didn't have the ability, I know you would have overpowered those thugs and tossed me over your shoulder and we'd escape on the Donzi…I assume you took the Donzi? It's wonderful to meet you sir, even in this difficult situation. Again, I'm sorry I was a little bitchy. I wanted to find out exactly who was behind this. After I got the info, I would have called the captain of my ship to send over a boat for a ride back. I'm sure he would have used the Donzi too, but of course that plan can't happen now."

"Ms. Donnelly, I don't think it matters whether you're gifted in the art of defense or not. We should just get the hell out of here. I don't know who owns this boat, but he or she is not very friendly. Let's beat a retreat *right now,* and we can talk about anything you want when we get back to the Foil, okay?"

Keith gently put his hand on Holly's elbow to guide her over the kidnappers she'd just flattened, however, when they got into the corridor, she stopped.

"First; call me by my first name, and since you've screwed up any chance I might have had to figure out who was in charge and what they'd wanted, you can give me enough time to get the hull identification number out of the engine room. If I have that, I can find out who owns the Wonderland, and right now the only thing I do know is that it's not going to be an heir of Charles Dodgson."

Holly crouched and unsnapped the hunting knife in a sheaf on Louis's belt. Taking it out, she quickly weighed it in her hand, and then she moved away in the wrong direction, according to Keith.

"Go to the Donzi and wait. It'll only take me a minute. No time at all," and Holly pronounced these orders over her shoulder.

"Why did you take his knife instead of his gun? And don't you want the pen on the desk in the cabin behind you. Wouldn't that help you remember the extremely long pesky number you're supposed to find?"

Holly had turned the corner at the end the hall, and his questions just hung there, unanswered. Keith raced back to the loading platform to wait, as he'd been instructed to do. He wasn't very concerned about her solo trip, having seen her in action, and Keith didn't think anyone on the ship would be able to match her.

Getting closer, the sound of Wonderland's diesel engines intensified. Holly wanted even more speed in her stride, and the length of her gown and the high heels slowed her down. She ripped two and half feet from the hem of her dress with the help of the knife, and after that she stepped out her shoes and left them behind. Seeing a metal door with **SERVICE** printed on it, she stepped into a very thin passage and walked another twenty feet until she reached a much larger hatch leading her into the engine room itself. Two diesel engines sat on either side of the walkway, almost as big a VW's. Huge exhaust manifolds rose out of them and she also saw hydraulic lines running along the ceiling. At the end the short catwalk, she reached over her head, and used Louis's hunting knife to cut both of the lines, and hydraulic fluid began to spray onto the very hot manifolds. That dousing would go on until the end. Steam was already hissing out of the drops, and she knew that would soon change to smoke. Holly hadn't really gone there to find the number. Not really. Attison could easily look up the owner of Wonderland for her if she asked him to any time. Rotating on her bare heel, she sped up her return trip to Keith and the Donzi, and at that point, no one would be able to stop her. It was just as well no one tried.

Keith watched her fly down those thin metal stairs like a circus acrobat. She'd torn off the lower part of her dress and he enjoyed the vision of her muscular bare legs flying along. He'd already started the engine, and as soon as Holly jumped on board, he untied the Donzi and hit the gas. Checking his watch, he saw it was a little past nine, and they could actually get back to her ship to appreciate the rest of her benefit. Moving that fast, he needed to look out in front of the boat like an eagle, and he was careful. Holly was sitting on one of the benches behind him, staring back at their wake. Well, more precisely, at Wonderland herself, and she saw a wisp of smoke coming from one of the lower port holes. Seconds later, flames accompanied the smoke.

"Did you find what you were looking for? You must have been in a hell of a hurry, getting rid of your shoes and your skirt." Unable to turn around, he threw the question at her over his shoulder.

"Not exactly. Something else came up. I don't think I'll have any more problems finding out who owns the Wonderland. My guardian is…."

Keith saw the reflections of the flames on the surface in front of bow of the boat. He slowed them down, and Holly's answer to his question was suddenly overwhelmed by a deafening boom. Keith put the Donzi in neutral, and he turned around. An enormous ball of fire was ascending to heaven while the burning carcass of the Wonderland began to sink beneath the chop. Holly's hands were clasped. She leaned demurely towards him, and she looked sheepish. She was responsible for the utter destruction of the yacht and everyone on board, and she knew he would know that.

"That's why you wanted that knife? It wasn't for protection at all was it? *I can't believe you set that fatal fire!* There's a good possibility you've just killed innocent people who were on that ship. Did you think about that? Or is it all collateral damage, an acceptable parameter in your violent plans? Human life is negotiable to you? What the hell controls your moral compass, woman!" And her bright devastation burned two thousand feet away from them, and Keith remained dumfounded.

"It's still pretty early. We can hear James Miller and Warren Haynes when we get back, and I'm starving. Couldn't we talk this stuff over later when we eat?" Holly smiled, as if she really hadn't blown up fifteen people to their graves on a huge yacht seven minutes ago.

"You know, that sounds thrilling, my dear! I can't wait!" Keith tried to sound like a sycophant, and then his voice went back to normal. "Come on, Holly! You sound like a politician. You can't side-step my questions again. Give me your motivation behind this deadly action right now!"

"Okay...okay, alright! You know, if you hadn't shown up, this wouldn't have happened, and I would have known a lot more about them. I could have used that knowledge to destroy them commercially, or something, I don't know. Anyway, that screwed-up my attempt at being sneaky not violent, and what was I supposed to do? Someone attacked me. They might have killed me, and you don't think I should fight back? There's a lot at stake on the world stage, and they need to understand that attacking me will *always* have consequences."

Keith scowled at her, and then he turned back to the wheel. He knew that Holly didn't have a lot of experience, and he was hoping that her childlike reactions would temper. He hoped that scruples would soon root themselves in her soul to tame her wild abandon. Piloting them back to Aspersion's Foil, he kept on shaking his head. Another explosion went off behind them. It had to have been the second fuel tank in the ship.

9:00AM Friday December 15th, 2006 Washington, DC

As the hearing over the status of the earth's oceans was taking place on the floor of congress, Lincoln Douglas and three of his toadies were sitting ten rows back from Attison Korybante, whispering like teenagers.

"Why is Korybante still on the list of speakers? I thought we'd got him off?"

Mr. Marshall was Lincoln's senior advisor, and he was a go-to guy. He'd directed his question to his boss, but Mr. Forsey, who was sitting on his left, was the one who answered it.

"It was too late for them to reprint the list. You heard what he told Lincoln on the intercom last night. He wasn't going to talk to anyone today, and he wouldn't use any leverage to change what we do in the construction trades…and he also said he wasn't going to address congress either, if you remember."

"Yeah, yeah," Lincoln hissed, "so why is he even here?"

"Maybe he wants to support Hartmann, that crazy zealot," Forsey chuckled.

"Well, it doesn't matter. He's not going to do anything at all, worried about getting his little girlfriend back. This is ridiculous. They're clapping through Hartmann's two cent rant like he's a knight in shining armor, but you know he's not gonna get any real votes out of that fake adulation."

Attison remained subdued quietly in his seat. In the conversation he'd had with Lincoln Douglas the night before, he'd tried hard to make him think he was terrified for Holly's life. He'd do *anything* to save her, anxiety dripping off his words like syrup. And it seemed to have worked perfectly, yet he remained pessimistic. A dark miasma hovered over DC. Normally, finding any resistance to certain ideas he was, shall we say, insistent about, he'd simply sculpt certain individuals as if their emotions were soft clay in his mental fingers; gently channeling their actions like a hypnotist, yet he not could persuade the politicians in the room with that approach. Attison Korybante may be a lot more powerful than a hypnotist, but his unusual talents don't hold any weight on the hill. Unable to get a handle on the disposition of a single elected official he'd met thus far, he was facing an insurmountable problem.

An ethereal snow storm of nullification had frozen their humanity, and white noise swept around psychic mountains of nothingness towering within the politicians around him that day. In denial, they didn't know they were spiritual floating over a bottomless pit, and they remained content. Some could hear a duplicitous voice, telling them they would sit next to God when they died, while the rest only believed in financial and physical power in the material world. Congressmen and senators on the hill worked together like ants in a dangerous colony. Ignoring the wishes of those who had voted them in, they responded only to an internal call from a demented queen who sits on a throne made from the bodies of lobbyists. Attison knew he had no control over the atypical force vibrating behind their eyes, but he wasn't going to give up on his more difficult attempt to reroute their dark voyage later on in the day.

Brenda Conlan, a young intern, had slipped into the main room of congress through a door right behind Lincoln Douglas and his staff. Breathless and aroused, she was upset about giving Lincoln the news she was about to impart to him. Face flushed pink, she bent over and whispered in his ear, and then Mr. Douglas leapt out of his chair with a scream.

"What! It blew up last night? That can't be right!"

Twisting around in their seats, people nearby were irritated by the volume of his words, shushing at him, but Lincoln ignored them. He was already running up the aisle, disappearing through the same door Brenda had just emerged from.

Attison had not been surprised by the ruckus a few rows behind him, and there was a trace of a smile on his lips. Lincoln Douglas shouldn't have prodded at Holly. Kidnapping the helpless heiress to silence him in the hearing might have worked on almost anyone else, but being a bully is a dangerous hobby. Odds are, the victim may someday be stronger than you are, and it seemed that Holly had struck back with devastating effects. Lincoln should lick his wounds...and stay out of the way forever.

10:30AM Tuesday December 7th, 2006 Somerville, Massachusetts

"I am sorry about last night, Vera!"

Walking into the kitchen, Eric kissed her on the cheek. His wife kept on sipping her coffee and she stared out of the dining room window as if he wasn't even there.

"It was the first day in a new office, and I was way off kilter. They hauled me into a complex meeting about a difficult case, and I know that's not an excuse and I'm really sorry I forgot to call you. I feel terrible about it. Can I take your mind off this with some good news? The firm is giving us a mid-winter cruise. We'll depart from LA on January third, and we don't have to pay for a thing. Twelve days out at sea," and he tossed the tickets on the kitchen table. "Here!"

He really thought it would even out his latest gaff.

Vera looked up at him with a blank stare. She picked up a spoon and stirred her coffee. Those seconds of silence seemed to build into time without end until the stillness roared. Finally she responded to him, but didn't even sound like her voice.

"I'm not going anywhere with you, Eric, and I don't care if you have a great cruise or the boat sinks and you drown. I'm not going to be on it. Your marriage with me ended years ago, however I've found the energy to legally support the truth. I'll be on the phone to a divorce lawyer tomorrow, and in the meantime, you need to find a place to stay. You have to get out of this house by the end of the day."

Eric moved into his swanky men's club at the golf course, and Vera began the divorce proceedings haphazardly. With no schedule in her day-to-day existence anymore, her mind was slipping, however that problem would change very soon. Lyndsey, also furious at Eric, was a lot more coherent in her quest to destroy him. Two days before Christmas, Vera got a manila folder in overnight mail, and the return address on it was bogus. Opening the envelope, there were eight glossy pictures with dates printed on the back of every one. The first had Eric and a young blonde locked together like hormone driven teenagers squeezed between the bucket-seats of a red mustang. In the next, they were entering an apartment building. Vera's favorite of the series was the last one. Eric was naked in bed, screwing the same bitch doggy-style. Leaving the pile on the dining room table, the images remained in her head, and with Lyndsey's help, Vera found the get-up-and-go to start a brand new project of her own.

5:45PM Sunday **December 17th, 2006** **Bass River, Massachusetts**

The donations from the benefit had only been a Band-Aid. It was way too late to stop the approach of what had hatched out there, and Holly knew something wicked was coming. Its magnitude frightened her. She'd jetted out of California the day after the party, retreating to her family's estate on the shores of Bass River in Massachusetts. It was a childlike thing to do, but she did it anyway. Now, three thousand miles stood between herself and its lightless cradle in the Pacific Ocean, and Holly held onto this illogical premise. The truth was unpalatable. Taking her mind off of things, she distracted herself by working on her computer game. It was a fantasy world far away from reality. She knew Attison Korybante was going to call her within the next few hours, but she kept on negating the inevitable. The upcoming conversation with Attison wasn't going to happen, and concrete reality could go away and stay away.

Sitting at Latham Donnelly's desk in the office on the second floor, she was staring at the computer screen in front of her. Latham, and the rest of her family had died at the estate during their reunion in 2005, and Holly had spent weeks in the hospital overpowering the same deadly toxins in her own turkey dinner. She ultimately survived the trauma unscathed, and she had become a medical miracle.

She was busy building a new layer in her environmental quest for the 'Golden Fleece'. It was a revised version of the old fable in an interactive computer game. The gamer had to go out into the real world and get a picture of a certain item. It was a material key to reach the next level.

Whether it was the fount of a mountain stream or an orchestra-sized harp being played at the moment of the snap shot, the images can't be faked. The player is drawn into adventures in getting these pictures as fast as they can in a digital odyssey to find the golden answer and fuel the planet Opaline. The phone on the desk rang, and Holly frowned. Then she wriggled. There was no way out. If she did not pick up, he'd show up at the front door soon enough, and that might be worse.

"Hello, Holly."

"Hello, Attison. I don't want to talk you right now. Can't we have this discussion in about a month or so?"

He laughed. "You used to enjoy our conversations…aah…I think I know what your problem is. Our options are whittling down to only one answer, my dear, and it's getting late in the game."

"One? You're kidding right. Can't we just slowly reverse what's wrong? It'd turn the tides in ten or twenty years and that should be fine. That would do it!"

"Political maneuvering to clamp down on the pollution isn't on the docket today, I'm sorry Holly, and even if we could, it's way too late. You know why I'm calling you, and I can only advise you. I have no right to order you into anything. I have a feeling you'll cleave to the real task in front of you, and it's not a computer game. The sky is really falling, Holly. How can you run, if you know? Not facing it, your own beautiful gilded ceiling will eventually crash on your head too."

"I closed my computer as soon as the phone rang, and right now I'm rolling my sleeves up. Of course, you're right. I know what needs to be done, it's just I have a bad feeling about the whole thing."

"I can feel the power behind it too, but it is what it is and that's that. You have a compatriot to help you with the scientific part of it, and someone else to help you with herding the dredges you'll need."

"You're talking about Keith Fischer aren't you?"

Attison did not answer that question.

"Put your game aside. Forget about everything else, and get the tools you need to exorcise this demon. I hate to say it, I really do, but I advise you to get back on your plane and fly to the west coast and set up another meeting with Keith. If you have any problems trying to find the weakest link in our enemy's armor, *just call me.* I'll try to fill you with any information you might have overlooked. I foresee drinking champagne with you on a cruise ship in the Pacific next year toasting our triumph."

10:17AM Monday December 7th, 2006 La Jolla, California

Joe Matya was hung over at his job in a data-retrieval center of the National Oceanic and Atmospheric Administration near San Diego. He was drained from a date he'd had with a wannabe starlet named Susan Barnes the night before, and he was almost asleep in his chair in front of a wall of monitors. He grabbed the cup of coffee on the counter in front of him, and started drinking more of it. The caffeine had to perk him up.

NOAA was using two kinds of satellites to acquire information. One orbits above the poles, five hundred and forty miles above the ground, while the 'geosynchronous' satellites stay where there were twenty-two thousand miles up, able to incorporate a wider range than their orbiting cousins. Using these tools, one of the things NOAA does, is to update weather stations throughout the country about upcoming storm tracks and variations in the jet stream. They also monitor the oceans as the massive fronts continue to collide above them.

Joe had got up and refilled his cup. Having spent minutes spacing-out, he had every intention of getting back to work. That included looking at all the monitors, and he instantly noticed something coming from a satellite flying over the northern Pacific at coordinates 37' N 145' W. Normally, there's nothing usual in that part of the ocean. His eyes were blurry from the extravagances he'd gone through the night before, and he swatted at the black spot in the center of the screen. He thought it was a fly. His attack had not worked. The smudge was actually inside the image. Joe stood up and got a lot closer to the monitor. He tried to figure out what on earth it could be? What could be responsible for a splotch like that in a remote part of the Pacific? When the tiny spot grew, his bloodshot eyes widened. It had reached almost an inch in width. It had to be made up by like millions, no, billions of things flying in a swarm of some kind...and...and...then it scattered in a thousand directions all at once, and the frightening blemish was gone. There was nothing left on the monitor but a uniform grey-blue. Shaking his head, he stared down at the swirl of milk in his coffee.

And Joe was the only person who'd seen it. By the time anyone sees the recording, it won't matter. With no explanation, he stayed tight-lipped about it. It was much easier to accept what he'd seen as fuzziness from the four Mai Tai's he'd drunk the night before, than to think about what it really looked like...an alarming birth of some kind way out there in the open ocean.

10:00AM Tuesday December 19th, 2006 Marina Del Ray, California

Bryon had ferried him out to Aspersion's Foil a few days ago, and Keith had also accepted his invitation to stay in his house for as long as he'd like. He'd been ironing out the kinks in the installation of hardware in his Greek customer's tankers, but at the moment, he was dozing on his friends couch.

Getting back to the ship in the Donzi that night, Holly had picked up her duties as hostess with the speed of a lightening stroke. They hadn't had the conversation he'd wanted to clear the air, and Keith had no intention of going back to Exeter until it was resolved. Walking away from being a marine technician was turning out to be a different thing to do. With a large fan base, he couldn't change his name and fly away like he did before. Right now, he had a few technicians taking his place back home if something went wrong on one his devoted customer's boats on the east coast. His mobile phone was *on* and with him at all times, and the peaceful moments of tranquility he was enjoying on Bryan's couch were about to be the last he'd see for a very long time. And it began with the ringing. The ringing of his phone.

He checked the ID. *Captain Frank Gabriel.* Aaah. He'd repaired his shrimpers here on the gold coast a few years back, and they'd gotten to know each. Hanging out at a bar frequented by commercial fisherman and charter boat captains, it was called the Castaways and it was on the inlet leading into the marina at Long Beach. It was the same place Bryan docked his speed boat.

"Hello Keith. Didn't want to bother you, mate, but things are so off-whack, it seemed important to give you a heads-up."

"It's great to hear from you, Frank."

"I'm sorry about the reason for this call. I won't waste time about how Charlene is doing, or the rising price of diesel, because things are disintegrating in a really weird way and I can't figure it out. You're the only person I could think of who might be able to help me…but forget about that. Maybe you could come up with something to stop whatever it is. Maybe use your gift to repair anything and save the day," and Frank then laughed with hollow emptiness. "Right now, I have four boats in the fleet, well…I did. Two days ago, I had to leave Deejay at the dock. Not enough men to take her out. Half my crew is sick. I guess."

"You guess? What does that mean?"

"Barney is one of my captains, and he told me a story about what happened to them last week. They were seining, and the Hotshot was moving slow. A horde of flies dove onto the boat, and attacked everybody on deck. Barney called them Borg flies. I know it sounds ridiculous, but I kid you not. He said their tiny bodies reflected the light as if there were pieces from black metal or hard plastic, or something, as part of them. I don't know what they are…a new breed of insect, but I do care about the health of my employees. Everyone swatted at them, but they wouldn't go away until Mick put the power-washer on full, blowing the entire horde off the deck. Ben, Charlie and Stan were bitten, and even though they went back to work, something was wrong with them. They weren't able to move fast enough to keep up, and it got worse. They went down to a crawl. Barney asked 'em what was wrong, and they said they were fine. That was strange. He called me on the radio, and I told him to go back to the dock and drive them to the hospital. I thought it had to do with the venom from the fly bites, and the doc would take care of it with an antidote, but that didn't happen, Keith. They couldn't find anything in their blood, and so they couldn't do anything. Right now, the guys are stuck at home, cuz I can't run a shrimp boat with zombies…oh, and they kept on insisting there's absolutely nothing wrong with them, yet they get slower and weirder every day. No one has the faintest idea what's wrong with them, and I can't replace them. Deejay stays at the dock. I use the men from the smaller boat to replace them on Hotshot. And there's more to the story," and Keith could hear real torment in his voice.

"There's more? I'm already stunned, sir."

"Emily Rose is in dry dock right now, and I have to come up with the money to replace her prop, the shaft and most of her stern. Yeah, I told you about what took place on Hotshot, but what happened to the Rose is just as bizarre. Maybe even odder. It must have been a whale…or a nurse shark, and it had come straight up from the depths, I mean *straight up*. Like a bullet crashing into the stern of my shrimp boat. I thank God, over and over, no one was standing there when it happened. The crew said it had been the nose of plane, and that sounds ridiculous. There weren't any pieces in the water to support that idea…just expensive pieces of my own boat. Whatever it is out there, has sent a third of my work-force home and two of my boats out of commission. I'm getting more than worried. I can tell you stories just like my mine from a lot of other fisherman having the same problems. Things are getting dicey out there, and it's getting harder and harder make it out there without getting scratched."

Keith's phone had started to blink. Someone was trying to call in, and he saw it was Dimitri Kalpakis, the Greek Tycoon.

"Sorry Frank, I have another call coming in from a customer. I'll call you right back, the second I get off the line with him okay?"

"Sayonara, chief."

Frank hung up, understanding his friend's priorities well enough. Keith touched his screen, crossing over to the other call.

"Dimitri, what's up? You're calling to tell me how wonderful the world is, and everything on all your ships is going fine, right?"

"Ciao, Fischer. Listen…listen…I'm seven miles out and I don't want to call the coast guard. I know you can fix it, you can fix anything real fast. We've lost our auto-pilot, and no one has any idea what could have possibly gone wrong. Can you make it out here? I'll send a copter and pick you up at Long Beach. It's possible? Isn't it possible? You've got to help me! I can't be late to this meeting, I don't want them to think I'm weak."

"No worries. I'm pretty sure I can get out there on my own. Just give me your coordinates."

Dimitri was on the Zephyra, his own personal yacht. At one hundred and eighty feet, it was as modern as anyone could get within the technological parameters currently available for marine vessels. Of course, that doesn't matter in the least. Murphy's Law will throw a curve ball at anyone, even if they are richer than Croesus. The Zephyra was a complex ship, and this glitch could be part of a larger problem; the tip of an iceberg hidden below the surface. A more serious problem could be unraveling somewhere else in the system.

Writing the information he needed to get there, he got off the line with Dimitri and instantly called Bryan for permission to use his boat again. And he got it. Keith got off the couch, and grabbed his leather jacket and his heavy tool box he'd brought with him from Exeter. Out the back door he went, on his way to the speed boat at the dock.

It didn't take him long to get to the Zephyra, and when he got onboard he found the problem in under fifteen minutes. The ship's engineer told him they couldn't get the thrusters to turn hard-to-port when the auto-pilot was engaged, and Keith suspected a failure in the rudder feedback unit. The part was four inches across with an attachment connected to the rudder. It looked like the head of an over-sized duck, and it was in the lazarette where the rudder-shafts are. It was a closed section in the rear part of the ship, and he'd gotten there through the engine room. As soon as he saw the complex plug, he was curious about what had really gone wrong. The electrical connection responsible for transmitting information to the auto-pilot had been in his hand, and he followed the thick wire leading out of the main assembly to the plug he guessed was the culprit. Uncoupling the connection, he saw something he'd never seen before during years of experience in the trade. Immersion in, or around salt water triggers oxidization. He expected to see the usual furry looking white corrosion on the prongs. It wasn't there. Half-an-inch of metal from the ends of the eight steel prongs was gone, and tiny bubbles were scarred on the useless nubs. Looked like they'd been dipped in hydrochloric acid. Or maybe a puddle of lava. Salt water does not dissolve steel in that way, and he shook his head while he cut off the destroyed plug. He soldered the open wires onto the new plug he'd gotten out of his tool box, and the job was over. Wrapping the new connection in a blanket of electric tape to seal the repair away from the elements, he no longer knew what was on that list anymore.

Zephyra's auto-pilot should work perfectly, but Keith didn't feel any better. What had eaten part of the steel of the prongs had begun another enigma on his growing list of mysteries. The ongoing incomprehensibility was starting to really bother him.

Squeezing himself out of the lazarette, and through the engine room, he had lots of grease on his clothes, and on his hands. It was even on his face. When Keith appeared on the main deck, the black smudges all over him meant nothing to Dimitri. He came over to him with a cup of espresso, praises, and a check for thirty-thousand dollars for the off-the-cuff save, and Keith got back on the cigarette boat. Giving Dimitri a salute and a smile, he untied the boat from the gunnels.

The wind was calm, and the sea spread out in front of him like glass. He began his trip back to shore on a day that was perfect for racing-boats. A day for just about anything, and he slowed the vessel down as soon as he was miles from the Zephyra; miles from everything, and he stopped the boat and shut off the engines. He got out of the front seat and laid back on one of the cushioned benches and he relaxed. Staring out at the horizon in a stolen moment, nothing but the comforting sound of the water lapping at the side of the boat came to his ears. What Frank had described to him on the phone, didn't go with the endless blue lake he was bobbing on at the moment. And he unwound, falling into a deep meditation, yet the wonderful rejuvenation he thought he was going to get did not happen. Alien thunderheads were rolling along on his own internal horizon, outriders from the same premonition he'd had a year ago. This time, the clouds looked worse…and they were bigger and a lot closer.

Badly startled, he'd wrenched out of Alpha-Theta and sat up. It was warm outside, but he had begun to shake. He'd been sucked into a rabbit-hole too dark to stay in, yet returning to normal consciousness wasn't helping him that much. His knowledge of recent events nibbled at him. He couldn't get the memories and snippets of stories out of his head. There really was no way out.

He had to uncover the enemy, drag it out into the light, and he took his mobile phone out of his jacket. Finding Frank's number, he hit the speed dial. He wanted to go back to his conversation with the Captain before he does anything else.

"Hello Frank. It's Keith. Forgive my extended interruption, but I had to take care of a strange situation, and I told you I was going to call you back, and I meant it. You're right. There is something going on around us, and it's getting treacherous, about to rip everything into shreds. Your uneasiness is a normal response. I feel the same way, only maybe worse."

"Hey, Keith. Great to hear back from you. What you're saying makes me feel better. Look, I have more to tell you, stuff you absolutely need to hear. Two weeks ago…" But Keith Fischer cut in on him.

"Wait, Frank, wait a second. It's almost five o'clock. We should meet at the Castaway, like we did when I worked on your fleet. I can get there in about thirty minutes. We'll have a beer and a burger and talk these things out. How about it?"

"Sounds fine. I'll see you there."

Frank had gotten to the bar first, and he picked out a booth in the farthest corner of the room with a window overlooking the inlet. He didn't want anyone to overhear them. A long-legged blonde trounced over to him. She wearing a name-tag spelling out *'Ingrid'* on her blouse.

"Hello, sir. What can I bring you to drink?" She tossed a menu on the table.

"Hi…Ingrid. A pint of draft beer...scratch that, bring me two."

Keith was standing right behind her. He'd gotten there as quiet as a ghost. Ingrid nodded and turned around, and almost bumped into him. Apologizing, she went off to get the order, as Keith sat across from Frank with curiosity in his eyes.

"Hi, Frank. What's up? You know I gotta know the rest of the latest story. You gotta tell me the weirdest thing you've heard or seen, so far," and he planted his denim covered elbows on the table, propping his chin on the palms of his hands.

"Well, you're full of surprises. You didn't seem that interested this morning."

"Oh, I was interested, I was seriously interested, Captain Gabriel, however something came up. Believe it or not, what broke on this guy's ship was bizarre too. I've never seen steel burned off like that before, and whatever got to those prongs destroyed them completely. Oh yeah, I was very attracted this morning and now I'm hooked. Come on, come on...give me everything you've got."

Ingrid reappeared with two mugs of tap beer, putting them on the table, "Need anything else, boys?"

They ordered cheese burgers with bacon, and the flaxen haired server sailed to the kitchen.

Captain Gabriel stared at Keith, and he took a very long breath. He was about to start talking, but he stopped and drooped a little bit and a long sigh came out of him. At 60, his hair was completely white, and he was wearing silver-wired glasses on the bridge of his nose. His blue t-shirt had a message on the back: *Your paycheck won't shrink if you eat Sherwood Shrimp, the tasty pink gold of the sea*. His hands were cracked and calloused by years of pulling nets on a string of work boats, until he finally got enough capital to start his own fleet. He'd been in charge of it for twenty years, and he didn't want to tell his companion a story so awful, he wished it was a nightmare. It would be so much better, if it was a dream. There was nobody else out there that could find a handle on *any* of it, and Keith was the only person he could think of. Pushing himself, he had to get past this hesitation. Well, okay then. His friend said he wanted the worst of the worst, but Frank sighed one more time. It was actually going to hurt to go through this tale, but if there's a chance he could do anything at all...

"You're right. I didn't want to get into the crazy stuff on the phone. What I'm about to tell you could be lethal if you say it to the wrong person, but I know you. You can keep things to yourself." He kept on sounding apprehensive, and his voice was no longer steady, but he kept on nonetheless.

"About a year ago, Danny Nescott, one of the men working for me, had gotten real sick. He was a great guy and a hard worker, so I went over to his place with some antibiotics. I tried to get him back on his feet. He was staying in a small house with his brother, but Foster, his brother, wasn't around at that point. He'd gone out on a freighter shipping stuff from here to the coast of Japan, and he would disappear for weeks. Anyway, I gave him the pills. I wasn't too close to him, I mean I left a lot space between us, and I didn't touch anything while I was there. I felt so bad for him. I hung around for a few more minutes to help him take his mind off things, and Danny was grateful for that. He liked talking to me, even when he'd gotten a little bit delirious. And then he started to tell me what his brother had told him in confidence, and I don't think he would have told me, if he felt a little bit better. He was really spaced-out and lonely."

Frank looked pale, and he stopped talking for a few seconds to sip at his beer. Keith stayed silent. He was waiting.

"Foster had told Danny the military had wanted it to stay under wraps… forever. Shit. That should have been a joke. Way too many people were involved. I'm surprised there weren't a lot more fatal accidents resulting from flapping lips, but I guess the honchos were not that worried about it. They didn't think anyone would believe it. Of course, there were some assassinations at the outset, but then they gave up. I've even heard versions of it coming out of the rumor mills, but those versions could not touch what Danny was telling me that day. I don't think anybody can control this…or fix it either. Not even you, Fischer."

The waitress arrived with their food, and Keith ordered more beers for them. He'd already lost his appetite, and when he heard about what had happened on the Ocean Swan in 2004, his unstable belly turned sour. Danny's brother had been part of the crew that winter, so what Keith had just listened to had only been retold by two people. It was only slightly distorted from a living witness's account. Of course, Foster had included an awful possibility in his slant on what had gone down. Nobody else had considered it. He'd found just enough length in the rope to get his head through the nearest porthole in the mess where the pirates had tied them all up, and in the chaotic seconds after the cable holding the cask had snapped, he swore to Danny he'd heard a quick grinding sound coming up from the water. It was so loud, he thought one of the blades of a prop had put a hole in the side of the barrel. He thinks the lead cask on the bottom of the Pacific is leaking radiation, and Danny told me his brother was getting really bad dreams about the entire thing, and they won't go away. I'm impressed that Foster still has the fortitude to go on the same trek, doing the same thing."

Keith looked calm throughout the story. At least, he'd appeared that way, drinking his beer and nodding once in a while. When the story was over, he asked the captain a question.

"I don't suppose Foster knows the coordinates of the place where this fiasco took place, and if does, does Danny remembers the numbers?"

"I was hoping for the same thing after hearing this horror story. Well, we're blessed or cursed by getting exactly what we both asked for. For some reason, Foster burned the coordinates into his brain, giving them to Dylan like he was confessing to a priest. I have a terrible feeling that whatever happened out there at 37' N. by 145' W. is getting closer to us every day."

Keith hadn't touched his burger and the fat that had sizzled out of the bacon had congealed into white droplets on the plate. He'd drank his third beer with nervous concentration. The restful sleep he'd had on Bryan's white leather couch was likely to be the last he'd have for quite a while.

10:19AM Monday December 9th, 2006 Los Angeles, California

He was a librarian in the public library eight miles from his condo in Venice, and James Martin was twenty-eight years old. His shift didn't start until twelve that day, so he was sitting on his veranda on the third floor, sipping coffee and basking in the sun. His view overlooked route 22, with the ocean on the other side of the road.

It was a balmy day, and his income was acceptable. He had a comfortable circle of friends, and James's family was not in the turmoil he heard about from everyone else he knew. He was actually quite happy. The sunlight soothed his skin as he quietly read an article about antiques. Lost in the complexity of very old farm equipment, he didn't notice an oversized fly buzzing around him. He had shorts on, and the insect didn't spend much time trying to find a good place to land, biting him hard on the calf. Yelping in sudden pain, James swatted at it, hoping for lethal results. He'd been way too slow, and as the black marauder flew off, he looked down at his leg. Rubbing at what was soon to become a very large red bump, he went back to reading.

12:45PM Tuesday December 19th, 2006 LAX, Los Angeles

Attison Korybante's attempts at chiding Holly into action on the phone two days ago, hadn't been for naught. Her apprehensiveness about dealing with this upcoming conflict, held her down for one more day. She kept staring out at Bass River from the second floor windows of her sprawling mansion; a temporary truant to an allegiance she could not escape. The power of her own integrity forced her out of sleep at four in the morning as if she'd gotten a belly cramp. And she tried hard to go back to sleep. Trying hard to throw out a future she did not want, her rebellion was nonetheless subjugated, and she stayed awake. Tossing her sheets and blankets into the air with angry surrender, she then got on the speaker phone and arranged a flight to California. It was time to return to the battle lines. Getting dressed, a lump of fear crept up her esophagus and into her mouth, and it tasted like reflux. She stopped what she was doing, and dropped her panties on the bed. She had to swallow that fear, no...no, get rid of it completely. Cowardice would affect her performance in the future, so she had to burn the idea that she was unmatchable into her quick like a branding iron sizzling ownership into the hide of steer. She shrugged. It was the best she could do, and she went back to putting her clothes on.

Deplaning in LAX eight hours later, her Lear jet rolled off to park in one of the back hangers, and Holly walked into the private lounge. She was wearing a beige rain-coat and wraparound sunglasses, and she looked like an undercover spy in an old black-and-white movie. Stepping over to the counter, she asked the attendant to check on where her helicopter might be. The small building in which they stood began shaking as a helicopter began to land close enough to be annoying, so he hadn't needed to answer her question at all.

She got out of the copter on the landing pad on the highest platform on Aspersion's Foil an hour later. Running down the stairs leading into the bridge, Holly was finally home. The Foil had already become her real center of operations. She said hello to the captain and the rest of the bridge crew, and she kept on going. It was only 3:00PM, and she wanted another temporarily escape. She went to her bedroom and changed out of her traveling clothes, believing her nerves would be appeased if she trotted along the beach in the Dockweiler State Park. Holly knew a section of the shore was usually deserted, and that solitude was calling to her. Wriggling into a pair of jeans, she put on heavy boots and a pea-green jacket over a thin sleeveless t-shirt, and she left the bedroom in a rush. The elevator would be too slow, and she took the service stairs to the area holding the smaller boats. Using the same control panel Keith had used, she hit the same button, and the Donzi was lifted out of its cradle and dropped into the eight foot wide canal of water in the center of the hangar. She pushed another button, and the rear hatch opened, giving her a view of the horizon; freedom to leave the mother-ship. Holly could have ordered one of the mates to set the Donzi up for her, even start the engine and park it next to the gangplank, but she hadn't wanted that. A self-contained force, she'd rather do it on her own, and most times it worked out faster. Stepping into the Donzi, she turned the key. The engine rumbled into life, and she eased the boat out into open water. Holly had the eyesight of an eagle, and as the prow lifted out of the water, she started her journey towards a part of the coastline she wanted to be. It didn't take long before she was docked at the public pier at the state park. Done with tying the Donzi up, she quickly jogged past the more populated areas of the beach.

3:45PM Tuesday **December 19th, 2006** **Dockweiler State Park, California**

Rachel Ruchman had gone through hoops to finally get permission slips from the parents of her fourteen students in her Earth Science Class to go on a field trip to Dockweiler State Park. How could the children understand the real fragile balance between two environments without hands-on experience? To actually physically see what happens. She worked for Los Verdes Oreja, a private school in Santa Monica. The grounds weren't far from an undisturbed stretch of forest owned by the State Park. Rachel knew there was a section where the trees dwindled and the beach took over. A wonderful tool to explain the interaction. She'd enlisted Linda Merrick, a young women attempting to get her own certification. She'd help her during the trip. Most of her students were nine years old, besides Melinda and Damien, who were respectively, eight and ten. It was imperative to have another adult on the outing to make sure the kids were constantly supervised.

A week ago, Rachel had called for a variance to allow the school van to be able to park near the trail leading into the woods and onto the beach. Public parking would have been too far away. The children wouldn't have had enough time to get to the trail and then back to the van in the two hours allotted for the field trip. Expecting the usual red tape would make her wait for months as they reviewed her request, something in the heavens must have moved those bureaucratic mountains. They told her to go right ahead and do it. She could pick up the waiver at the office the next day.

Everybody unloaded at 2:15. Rachel and Linda guided the children down the path, and farther into the woods. Rachel would pause and describe and explain the erosion on a ledge to their left or that the trees slanting in the same direction had grown that way because of the prevailing wind. Everything was going great until they tramped out onto the beach, and at least the first fifteen minutes out there were alright. Wind calm, and sun bright, Rachel was inspired. She'd decided to orchestrate a moment of oneness with the earth. Ponytail hanging down the back of her mustard colored corduroy shirt, she beamed out a smile large enough to crack cement and her brown eyes were dancing. She instructed her young audience to sit in a circle with her on the warm sand and hold hands, and she nodding to Linda. She'd be included too.

"Hundreds of years ago, people here would pray to the gods of the sea and the sky, honoring them and pleading for their help. One of their prayers has survived, and I've learned it, and I think we should say it together for a couple of minutes. It'll be our way of asking for peace on earth and to support all the good things we'll do for Mother Nature."

Rachel began to recite the old Indian prayer, starting slowly, until she got it swinging back and forth. A singsong lullaby, *'cha hala gata woti, cha hala tasi...chaaa hala woti, chaaa hala tasi.* Around and around it went, working like a charm as the students mimicked her the best they could. Melinda, the youngest in the group, removed her hand from the girl sitting next to her, to push her bangs away from her eyes. She noticed a man traveling quite rapidly towards them across the beach, and at that point, he was only half-a-mile away. He was closing in. Still hadn't bothered her at all, and the child went back to holding hands and chanting.

Rachel's position in the circle faced the ocean, and of course she hadn't seen the approaching stranger yet. When she finally did, flickering her sight over to him, she too, ignored him. He had on a brown rain jacket, and its hood covered his head, concealing most of his face. Crouched over, he was prodding at the sand in front of him with a long stick as if he couldn't see what was in front of him. The posture indicated an old man partially blind, yet as he scrabbled towards them, he continued to stay in a straight line with a lot more alacrity than an older person would ever be able to muster. It was a public beach. Rachel kept on ignoring him. If the screwball wanted to wobble past them, he certainly had the right to do so.

The wind picked up from the west as if something had flipped a switch. And then it suddenly changed to the east, continuing to change directions like a merry-go-round. The only thing that remained the same was the power of it. Some of the gusts crept close to gale force strength, and the blue sky was now invaded by thunderheads. Rachel's tenuous circle of light and meditation was crumbling. Three kids were crying, and two more wailed while the ladies tried hard to hold on to some kind of order and get the students off the beach as fast as they could.

The odd-looking man had tapped his way on top of them and a swarm of black flies swirled around him as if he was rotten meat. Some of the oversized glittering bugs peeled away from him and into the students. Melinda was running up the beach, and the girl she'd been holding hands with was following her. Four others were climbing the side of the steep dune at the edge of the beach, trying to escape into the woods.

In shock themselves, Rachel and Linda had lost their handle on things. The old man waving his dangerous stick, was inexorably closing in on the children who had remained as a group. Swatting at them, he hit one boy on the head. The child fell face first onto the sand. Not knowing exactly what to do, Rachel instinctively ran towards the monster who'd just hurt one of her students. She had to stop him in his tracks somehow! Stop him from hurting anyone else, yet even though he was only twelve feet away from her, the wind held her back. She couldn't quite reach him.

One hundred and fifty feet up the beach, Melanie and the other girl had cowered down behind a ridge in the sand and they were hugging each other. Eyes closed, tears streamed down their faces, gusts of wind tugged at their hair so hard, they were afraid it would be pulled right out by the roots. A fly had somehow found purchase on Melanie's shoulder. She hadn't know it was there until its nasty bite gave her burst of pain.

And the wind strengthened. Squalls punched out with invisible fists in haphazard fits, and the crazy man kept on flailing his heavy staff in a chaotic circle in the center of the kids. The flies had somehow found a way to stay around him against the increasing push of a gale that should have logically blown them away.

More children would certainly get injured in the swirling circle of his wooden staff, but Holly had come out of nowhere, sauntering up to him cool as ice, and she was about to end that possibility. Easily ducking under one of his endless sweeps with aplomb, she stood right in front of him for a second. Appearing to be a casual slap, she backhanded him across his cheek, but the weird guy dropped his heavy stick and fell to the sand, out cold. He would stay that way for quite a while.

It had been simple enough to stop that part of the threat to the children and the teachers, yet Holly's violet-grey eyes were tinged with blue as she stood over his unconscious body and absorbed the rest of the abnormality of what was going on. A fly landed on the back of her hand. It was trying to bite her, however it couldn't pierce through her skin. Holly crushed it flat with her other hand and then she put the tiny corpse in a small pocket in her jacket. Staring out at the rest of the flies with a withering glance, she teleported them forty feet up in the air. The wind stayed in one direction. Straight out to sea, and when Holly raised her hands, the entire horde was blown out to the horizon. She lowered her arms, and the sudden gale abated.

The students were already getting back up on their feet, and those who'd tried to escape over the dunes, returned. Rachel checked on the boy lying on the sand. He was recovering nicely. She trotted up the beach to collect the two girls, and Linda stayed behind, restoring order in the shocked ranks. Neither Rachel nor Linda had seen what Holly had done exactly, and they hadn't had any time to get over to her and thank her. Since the menacing clouds were gone and the sun was coming out, the easiest thing to do would be to forget the entire thing. A bad dream quickly forgotten. Busily getting the class together to walk back, Linda watched Holly pick up the awful madman, and toss him on her shoulder like he was nothing but a pillow filled with feathers. Then she ran off down the beach and disappeared. Rachel reappeared with the two runaways, and the entire class started their short trip to the van.

Holly had only been able to enjoy fifteen minutes of her solitary walk, before seeing what was happening farther up the beach. It would be all good and well to save the children, but the upcoming interaction was also going to give her more information about the uncanny deterioration in the over-all state of the environment, and so she ramped up into an Olympian dash. Taking care of things quickly enough, she decided to bring the culprit and his stick to a different section of the beach and interrogate him. No point in talking to the two adults. She knew they didn't know anything, and any clues to the deepening mystery might be hidden in the head of the unconscious burden on her shoulder. Yes, she'd get any information he did have out of him in the next few minutes.

After leaving a mile and a half behind her, she dropped him on the sand. It was far enough to avoid any prying eyes. Taking off her jacket, she stretched the kinks out in her shoulders. Holly took the insect out of her jacket pocket, and opened her hand. It glittered in the sun just like a Borg fly from that Star-Trek movie. Microscopic circuits and metal or polymer pieces intertwined with biology, and it puzzled her. She couldn't imagine where this flying detritus had come from, and even more problematical, Holly knew that evolution hadn't had a damned thing to do with it. Putting the fly back into her pocket, she turned her attention to the man at her feet.

She kicked him in the ass and nothing happened. Then she kicked him in the ribs. Zip. Crouching down, she peered into his face. His eyes were closed. No one was home. She ripped the guy's over-sized rain-coat off, and it turned out he was a young man in good physical shape. Wearing beige pants and a white long-sleeved shirt, his clothes looked new, and it seemed he'd been clean as a whistle when he'd dressed himself that morning. Holly flipped him over on his back, and she grabbed his shoulders and shook him like a rag doll with still no results. Holding his head up with one hand, she slapped his face more gently with the palm of her hand. Then she tried talking to him.

"Come on, you dolt. *Wake up!* I need to talk to you and it would be in your best interests to respond...*now!*"

So far, nothing had worked. Sagging in her hands like a dead thing, her patience ran out. Leaning forwards, she whispered something in the young man's ear, and whatever it was had been powerful enough to instantly open his eyes. He was coming back to life and the rest of his body shuddered. Holly let him go, and he fell backwards on the sand. The concussion she'd given him could be responsible for the incoherent mumbling coming out of his mouth...or maybe not. She had to know what was pushing him, and she started her questions in a voice that was precise and even tempered.

"What's your name? Hello...*what is your name?*"

"Hmm....a."

"What did you say?"

"Hmm...mm...James...James Matin...Martin, I mean Martin."

"Tell me what you were up to today?" Holly said.

"Why did you have to hit me that hard?" And he wiggled his jaw to see if it was broken.

"Can you remember where you were and what you were doing? If you can remember that, then you'd know why I did what I did."

"Well, um...I had the day off work," pausing, he lowered his head and winced, nervous she'd wail into him again. It didn't happen, and he went on. "I work at the public library in Venice, and I decided to go out for a walk on the beach. I'd heard a forecast on the radio that there was a chance for rain, and I grabbed the raincoat and put it on...wanted my hair and clothes to stay dry. After parking over there," and he waved vaguely behind him, "I walked out on the beach. I found a cool looking stick in the dunes, and I thought I could carve things into it when I got home, and I decided to use it as a walking stick and sort of play with it in the meantime."

Holly was disgusted. Picking up his precious branch, she rested it on her thigh and snapped it in two, and then she tossed the pieces into the ocean. One of the weird flies had returned to circle James's head, and tiny glint of blue flickered in her eyes. After a faint pop, the insect was no longer there.

"It didn't look like you were playing a game when you hit that boy on the head...*James*." Holly's tone was frosty.

"I didn't hit a child! Are you nuts? I hit a dog, it was a feral dog. There was a pack of wild dogs up there, and I didn't want them in the park. I was trying to get them out of here. I don't know why they didn't attack you!" He straightened up, arms and hands gesturing with sincerity. Holly was frowning.

"What day of the week do you have off?"

"Don't you know what day it is today? I told you, it's my day off."

"Today is Tuesday, so I guess that's it."

"But it's not! Today isn't Tuesday, it's Sunday."

And then he got to his feet in defiance. Well, sort of. He was still cowering a little bit. He really believed the wrong day was a delusion of hers. Things would soon get clearer for her.

"Are you also going to tell me you had that wrinkly piece of dirty-brown rain coat in your closet?" Holly said.

James didn't answer. He looked down in silence.

"Where did you get it? Just tell me...*right now*."

"It wasn't in my condo, you're right, but I can't remember where I got it. It was important to stay dry, is all."

She saw a scab on his calf probably left by a bite from one of those aberrant bugs a few days ago. Holly postulated that the venom of one of the Borg-like flies had changed a competent librarian into a dangerous freak, no longer in-tune to the real world. Holly watched him as he tried to stand straight, and as he wobbled there, she watched a thin stream of drool leak from the corner of his mouth. Shaking her head, it was obvious she was going to have to restrain him somehow. Resting her fingers on his forehead, she telepathically instilled a powerful directive: *Go home and stay there. If you run out of food, go to the market and buy some. After that, go home and stay there.*

Not sure how long her mental Band-Aid would hold, she didn't have any more time to build a more permanent solution. There's a pandemic building fast, and she needed to figure it out and stop it. The young librarian was just one infected individual, and she needed to stay on the case like a bloodhound.

She took his shoulders and gently directed him to the parking lot. James (or whatever he'd become) lurched away from her, and she hoped he'd go where she'd told him to go. The entire incident had been riddled with absurdity, but Holly was not laughing. There was an undercurrent that scuttled any humor, and as she watched what had once been a healthy young man vanish down the beach, a sorrowful groan came out of her.

Returning to the ship, she showered and changed. Attison hadn't told her much when he'd called her, just something about getting ocean dredges. He'd been very vague, but there was something badly wrong out there in the Pacific, and she had to hunt it down. Hunt it down and destroy it.

Holly had inducted Dwight Wyndham, a gifted financier, to take her place as CEO in Hienem whenever she's otherwise disposed. His older brother was a five star general in the Navy, and she'd met him in Washington at a benefit. She'd use her coincidental connection to him through his brother as starting point for her highly driven investigation into what was going on. Or more precisely, breaking down. A general would be able to fill her in concerning the nastiest, illegal and dreadful secrets the U.S. military locks up in its secret vaults. In a conversation she'd had with Dwight a couple of months ago, he'd off-handedly mentioned his brother relaxes in his mansion in La Jolla when he wasn't in Washington or at the Pentagon. Holly picked up her phone and speed dialed Dwight, and he answered her call in the first ring and then he answered her questions just as fast. His brother was currently at home, and he gave Holly Carl's personal phone number. A number only his closest family members and the pentagon had. Mr. Dwight Wyndham worked extremely closely with Holly, and any allegiance he might have over any information he considered secretive would not withstand Ms. Donnelly's inquiries.

And then she called the General. He agreed to meet her the next day. His wife was on a sabbatical in Europe digging up evidence to support the idea that crop circles were created by interstellar visitors. Her absence would give Holly more psychological leeway in their upcoming conversation. They'd both be able to be more open. He told her they should have lunch at one at his house. Whatever she was looking for inside the General's head, was going to be even easier to unearth.

10:15AM Wednesday December 20th, 2006 Coastal Highway 101, California

Leaving the Foil that morning, Holly docked the Donzi at the public dock. A company car waiting for her there. The driver dropped her off at a parking garage Heinem owned in downtown LA. Her personal vehicles were stored there. Entering through a side door, she took the elevator to the second floor. Riding to La Jolla in the back-seat of a Rolls Royce driven by a chauffeur was always an option, but driving there by herself in a sports car was more appealing. Taking the keys out of her clutch, she walked past the Harley and the Kawasaki Ninja. Showing up on a motorcycle would have been impolite.

She'd take the Ferrari. It was olive green with thick gold flake shimmering in the depths, and the power under the hood would sustain the wild child in her. Glancing at her watch, she had more than enough time to get to Wyndham's estate without breaking the speed limit even though she'd break it the entire way there. A blue velvet skirt was tight on her body, yet the spandex in the fabric let her move freely. She had on silver heels, and a dark blue sleeveless satin shirt with nothing but a mesh of small chains draping across the open back. A rope of diamond chips held a sapphire between her collar bones. She'd had it on during the Thanksgiving reunion in which the entire family had been killed, and she had been injured, yet she hadn't linked any sentimentality of that horrendous event to the necklace. It was just jewelry.

Driving along US 1 in a twelve-cylinder beast, she passed an unbroken line of houses on her left. The buildings became a blur, and on the right of the highway, a cliff dropped abruptly to a sandy beach. From there, the Pacific Ocean stretched out to the horizon as an azure backdrop. Sea and sky and speed.

It didn't take her long to reach his hide-away. Tall hedges marched away from either side of the entrance, hiding the property from public view. It was 12:15 when she pushed the call button on the intercom installed on one of the two granite columns that bracketed the driveway. Someone answered, and she told them her name and gates opened. She drove along the extended driveway through fifteen well-landscaped acres he'd surrounded himself with. This lush barrier was loaded with colorful fruit trees and flowers, and the house was elevated, positioned to face the sea. Holly parked and walked over to the front door and rang the bell, and the General himself opened the door. He was dressed in blue pants and a blue shirt, and at the age of seventy-three he was still only semi-retired. The Pentagon had not cut him out of the inner loop yet.

"Hello, Miss Donnelly. Not only did you arrive early, you left a real beauty parked in my auto-court, and I love to invite splendor to my door. Please, come in."

General Wyndham bowed to her, compliment well deserved. Like most meeting Holly Donnelly for the first time, he was slightly taken aback by her beauty.

"Why thank-you General. I'm grateful for your invitation, sir. It seems as if you would have offered it up, even if my urgent plea for your help had not inveigled you. I'm sure we'll have a wonderful lunch with a conversation I don't think you'll be able to forget."

Holly glided into the man's home, her forearm elegantly resting on his own.

"Would you like something to drink, Miss Donnelly? Coffee or something stronger?"

"A glass of sherry would be nice, and please…call me Holly."

A maid hovered in the back of the room, and Wyndham waved to her and she bustled off, quickly reappearing with a glass of sherry and a dry martini for the host. They sat on some over-sized cushioned chairs arranged in front of a window overlooking the ocean.

"And of course, you must call me Carl," and he chuckled. "I'm more than pleased to meet you as my curiosity is peeked. What on earth do you want to see me about? Why you would have any interest in our military endeavors, past or present. Your pharmaceutical business is in a completely different world. Please, tell me why you want my help."

Wyndham picked up his martini, smiled and drank. Holly had paused, eyes narrowing. She looked over at him, thinking over what to say. *Could truth be a possible option?*

"Well, I've heard some rumbling about an environmental problem coming from an upheaval of some kind in a particularly contentious part of the Pacific. I don't like bothering you Carl, but if anyone knows the real down and dirty behind the speculation, you would."

Holly decided to start out by telling him the truth. There was a chance he might answer without duress, and she had nothing to lose. He might actually answer her...he might.

General Wyndham groaned. He swallowed the rest of his martini in a gulp, and he got up and made himself another at the bar. Holly waited patiently, gazing through the window as she watched clouds travel along the horizon until the General returned to his chair.

"I'm sorry, Holly, I truly am. I'm sorry you're concerned about something that is ridiculous on one side and depressing on the other. I've heard those stories myself. The Navy has no idea what could be behind any of this. We've brought experts in to figure out what could really be responsible for this crap."

"Really? What did they come up with?"

"Not much, I'm afraid. Pollution is reaching dangerous concentrations in all the oceans, but they can't link any of that to the metrological anomalies or the sudden abnormalities showing up in the natural world. It has also affected a percentage of humans as well."

"So it's a mystery to you? I'm not sure what you just said was actually true, Carl...oh, I'd like to have another sherry before we have lunch."

At that point, he did not respond, and in the ongoing silence, the uniformed maid walked across the living room with a tray holding a glass of sherry and a martini. The martini was a double this time. She placed the drinks on a small glass table next to the chairs, and she took away the empty glasses. Surprised by her foreknowledge and timing, General Wyndham stared out at his employee's back as she walked off. Picking up his drink, he made a condescending retort to the non-answer he'd already given Ms. Donnelly. He was gearing up for even more loftiness. Holly kept on smiling at him, and he was blind to the flickering blue rising in her eyes. He began scolding her, edging his voice and putting volume behind his pronouncements.

"Is there a bee in your bonnet telling you that I'm lying to you? I have no reason to hide anything from anyone. I've invited you here to tell you exactly what I *do* know...and you should...ah..." He faltered, and then he stopped talking. The mild irritation on his face drained away, replaced with a blank slate. Sitting back in his comfortable chair, he looked out at the cumulous clouds in the sky. Wyndham sipped at his very dry martini, as if Holly was no longer in the room.

Entering the general's home, Holy knew he had the knowledge she was hunting for, and during their short discussion, she could almost see it clearly on the surface of his waking mind. Those nefarious secrets were just glowing there. She'd giving him the option of telling her on his own, but it seemed that wasn't going to happen. She would have to dig them out on her own. Taking control over the entire room, Holly instructed Emily, his housekeeper/maid to bring them another round of drinks without saying a single thing. She plowed through the feeble barriers Carl had put up in his mind to avoid the painful event, and she absorbed what she wanted. It was a very blurry vision of what had taken place years ago in the center of the northern gyre in the Pacific, and his version of it had been hobbled together by many different sources.

"So something did go badly wrong out there," as Holly waved at the picture windows, "and there's nothing you can do to fix it. The experts you called have given you dire forecasts without any options, and the other higher-ups at the Pentagon are nervous about the secret you can't or won't divulge to anyone, right?"

"Yes, you're right. I can't tell you about it, Holly, and I don't even want to remember it myself."

He was quiet as he spoke, and then the General smiled, "Can't we talk about *your* company, or maybe which sailboat we could charter for a trip to some island instead?"

"No, Carl, I'm sorry. You're going to have to tell me what you can about this predicament…here and now."

Holly was hoping vocalization might add another slant to the story.

"Okay, alright…aah…shoot," but it took him a second to get his bearings, gulping back his revulsion in explaining something he wished had never happened.

"A commercial freighter called the Ocean Swan had been crossing the Pacific…"

Listening to him speak did shave off a lot of the fuzziness she had to deal with in his consciousness. At the end of the tale, he valiantly insisted the Navy doesn't believe there's radiation leaking out of the cask, even if there were doomsayers popping up in their ranks. According to Wyndham, it really doesn't matter either way. It had tumbled way too deep, and there was nothing they could have done about it then…or now.

"Give me the coordinates, Carl. Maybe I can reverse this whole thing, or somehow put it back to normal."

"I won't forget the numbers for the rest of my life, Holly. I think the devil himself burned them into my brain. *37' North by 145' West,* and I really hope you do have the power you say you have and get us out this very hot water."

Holly let Carl and Emily go, and she wiped the past minutes out of their memories. The excavation had been successful. She spent the rest of her time with him talking about sailing and the best places to go, wanting to make the rest of her luncheon there more peaceful for General Wyndham, having pushed him into something he truly didn't want to do. Leaving the estate, she sped back to LA on the same road that hugged the beach. Holly looked out at the horizon for a second and she got a chill down her spine, triggering her into calling Keith. She arranged a meeting with him the next day.

4:45PM Thursday December 21st 2006 Aspersion's Foil

Climbing the gangplank for the second time, there was no one around and Keith was fairly sure Holly would not disappear on him this time. If, by some fluke, it happens again, he'd leave it be. Holly can certainly handle herself with mundane things like kidnapping without him. Their connection got deeper as he walked across the deck, and climbed the stairs to the higher deck, and then saw her staring out into the distance. Her elbows were on the rail, and she looked like the mistress of the wind; tendrils of her long hair rising up in the air while her thin skirt ballooned behind her in the steady breeze.

Holly had heard him coming, and she spun around. The obvious apprehension on her face instantly blew his silly vision to pieces, and Keith had a very good idea what was generating her nervousness. He felt the same way. There was a deep transformation going on worldwide, and the magnitude of what they were up against was, to say the least, disconcerting. Holly walked towards him, smiling, hand out in salutation, yet hiding her misgivings from him was impossible. They could read each other's thoughts almost as clearly as they do with anyone else but Attison.

"Hello, Holly. It's been hard to get a meeting between us together hasn't it?" He shook her hand.

"Hello, Keith. Well, it's important we do this, as there are quite a number of things we've got to go over. Maybe we should go inside, it might be more comfortable," and she hooked her arm into his. They walked through a hatch leading into one of the viewing rooms.

"Are you hungry? Would you like something to drink?"

"Well, right now my belly isn't quite stable, but I'd enjoy a beer, thanks, and if you don't mind, you would crush three or four tranquilizers into it before you serve it to me."

Holly sent a restrained smile at him, while they sat at a table in the corner of the room. A blonde woman in brown slacks and a white t-shirt stepped over, and Keith asked for a Foster. Holly ordered Absinthe in a remembrance of her mentor and the words he'd spoken to her in her family's garden over a year ago.

"You've done some digging on your own, haven't you? I assume what you found had to have been a bit uncomfortable. You wouldn't be stressed out, otherwise. Am I right?" Holly said.

"Well, we were trying to find the source of this strangeness, so I did what I could to hunt it down. We need to pierce the heart of this mystery." Keith lowered his voice. "We have to figure out a way to squash it, and then put things back to normal somehow. You've been working on something too, otherwise you wouldn't have that haunted look in your eyes."

The server dropped off their drinks, and Holly looked up at her, "Thank-you, Wendy."

"You're welcome Ms. Donnelly. I hope you and Mr. Fischer will let me know if you want something else," and then she went back to the galley.

Keith told Holly the story about the metal plug he'd repaired, and the upsetting revelations from Captain Gabriel and what he thought it meant. In return, Holly described what had taken place in the state park as well as the unsettling answers she'd gotten from the young man who'd been at the center of the disquieting event. Keith had seen Holly go into hyper-drive during her kidnapping, but that glimpse of her physical power hadn't included the mystifying things she was casually reporting she'd done on the beach that day. Then, she told him about her encounter with the five-star general in La Jolla. Almost done telling him everything, Wendy reappeared, and they asked for more drinks and porter-house steaks with mash potatoes and peas. Keith was feeling better, and his stage-fright over meeting Holly was gone. He really believed he had a powerful ally in a battle that was getting more nightmarish by the second, and for the first and only time in his life, he could communicate with someone who truly understood what he could do. She could even commiserate with him on subjects that had always been taboo for him to talk to anyone else about. They were enjoying the second round of drinks, until Wendy and another girl brought their food out on two trays.

"I guess there are benefits in being a CEO of the Heinem Corporation," Keith said. He was impressed by the lavish meal.

"And that is off-set by an endless list of responsibilities I didn't want, and you should think back on why I ended up with all this monetary power."

"Isn't that an echo of our current dilemma? Neither of us wanted to be front and center in the middle of this mess, but there is no way out of it. We have to find out exactly what it is, and then come up with something powerful enough to defeat it, and shooting clay pigeons in the back yard isn't going to save us. Whatever our strategy is going to be, it has to be death-defying and I know we won't want to do it. It's not gonna matter how we feel, we have to keep on going. If we stop, the end result isn't going to be pretty, like the world ending and stuff."

Keith put his fork down, apparently done eating and talking at the same time and he burped at the end of his last sentence with a polite 'excuse me'. The following silence swelled with an odd certainty while Holly and Keith stared into each other's eyes like besotted lovers. Of course, that certainly wasn't the case. The actual explanation for their ongoing gaze came out as they both blurted 37' North by 145' West at the same time, and then their shook their heads, laughing at the synchronicity.

"So it looks like we need to get there," Keith said.

"And we are in a good position to reach those coordinates fast. Do you have any current responsibilities to hold you back? Can we just go?"

"I can come along if you want me to. I need to go back on shore and pick up my suitcase at my friend's house. I'd feel much better if I change my clothes once or twice during the voyage."

"Take the Donzi."

"Well, your offer may be the fastest option."

Keith got up, wanting to get his luggage as quickly as he could, and Holly went back to the bridge. She told Captain Walker to begin preparations to reach these coordinates, and she and the captain and the navigational officer went over the best routes to get them to nowheresville, yet Holly's uneasy feeling grew. For some reason, open water out there in the ocean had become a lot more menacing.

11:35PM Thursday December 21th, 2006 La Jolla, California

General Carl Wyndham turned off the light at the end table near the edge of his king-sized bed. Almost eleven, he quickly fell asleep for about fifteen minutes until his cell-phone rang with a more disturbing tone. It woke him up right up. No one called him that late unless it was an emergency, and he sat up. Unconsciously, he ran his hands through his hair for a second before he got on the line. Wyndham didn't say a single thing at first. The mesmerizing sound of Holly Donnelly's voice slithered into his head until the end of her instructions. At that point, all she needed was vocal acceptance out of him before ending their interaction, and that was exactly what she got.

"Uh-huh, alright. I'll take care of it…right down. *Yeah, right now,"* and the general emphasized the last bit. His line went dead, and he got out of bed and walked into his office, and sat down at his desk. He called the pentagon.

"Hello, Brian. Something's come up. Can you transfer me to research."

The operator knew exactly who it was, "Hello, General Wyndham. No prob, I'll connect you."

Wyndham heard some weird whistles and clicks until the connection got him to the supervisor of scientific research wherever he was in the vast five-sided building.

"This is Captain Prescott."

"General Wyndham here. I have a request, but I don't want any scuttlebutt to get out about it, okay?"

"Yes, sir. Mums the word," the captain said.

"Call 32nd Street Station in San Diego, and order them to send their fastest research ship to 37' N 145' W in the northern pacific. Use my name if you have to, and they can also call me on this number for conformation. I want the best men they have to man that ship. I'll give the boys on board more information when they're on their way."

9:32AM Thursday December 21st, 2006 Somerville, Massachusetts

Vera parked on the street near the drugstore, and she got out and went inside. She went to the section where the hair dye was, and she stared at the endless boxes of different colors, quickly realizing she wouldn't be able to create a new slick-version of herself on her own. Not buying anything, she went back to her car, and it was a little after ten when she was back home. She picked up the yellow pages opening to 'beauty salons', and she randomly picked one from of the long list. The owner of the salon on route 48 told her she'd just had a cancellation that very afternoon, and Vera was pleased, as she wanted to get everything done as fast as she could. The woman on the phone asked her for her name so she could write it in her appointment book. 'Adler' hung on the tip of her tongue, but she found the power to replace it with *Burrows*, her maiden name.

Her dark shoulder-length hair was colorless with only streaks of grey to accentuate it. If Eric's despicable behavior hadn't ignited her, she would have probably left it untouched until she died. However, after her personality had been transformed, she walked into the beauty salon for a full makeover without a second glance. Five hours later, another step closer for lift off, she walked out onto the street, and her burgundy hair shone in a modern cut to supposedly sustain her new aura of personal power. The sculpting layers accentuated her jaw line, and a small tail of hair was left to hang down the nape of her neck, a hint she might have a tinge of a pixie in her. It was clear that Mrs. Adler was gone, and Ms. Burrows had taken her place. Getting into her Enclave, she drove to the nearest shopping center two exits south on the interstate. Parking, she went into Macy's and bought herself an entire new wardrobe, beginning with the sultry foundation of lingerie. Vera had lost another nine pounds since she'd thrown Eric out, and she had to cover her svelte form with a new palette of come-hither clothes, and when she was finally done, twelve thousand dollars had been charged to her credit card account.

She hadn't seen Eric since he moved out, and she would not pick up any of his phone calls. There would be no more personal interactions between them, and she didn't want him to know anything about her activities. He could call her lawyer. If Mr. Tuthill did not have the information to any question he may ask, then neither would he. She wasn't sure whether or not Tuthill had gotten the divorce papers done to give to Eric, but Vera really wanted him to be served before the cruise.

Ten days ago she'd called the Carnelian Cruise Line and booked a cabin on the same cruise the Blackmore Coalition was also going on. Her cabin would be on a high floor with an outside porch. She used a credit card that had remained in her maiden name to pay for the trip. The complexity of changing *all* her cards to his name when she got married, had gotten way too much to deal with, and it seemed that past difficulty had become a blessing in disguise. Eric would have no idea she'd be on the same cruise, and she wanted it to stay that way. She wouldn't have been surprised if her ex-husband didn't remembered her maiden name at all. Either way, they would not live together under the same name again.

The back seat and the trunk of her car were loaded with bags. It was getting late. It was almost ten as she sped up and got onto the interstate. A clear night, Vera leaned forwards and looked up for a few seconds. She wanted to see the stars through the windshield. Feeling wonderful, perhaps even exalted, everything she'd done that day had vindicated her motivation. As the miles rolled by, she thought over what her first name was going to be in the beginning of her implacable campaign out on the roiling seas.

7:30AM Monday December 25th, 2006 Trash Vortex

The second he woke up, Keith left his cabin. It may be Christmas morning, but he was not concerned about that. The night before, Holly had told him they'd reach the coordinates by dawn the next day. Lying in bed, he mulled over how they'd decipher anything without a single tool to do it, but he wanted to get straight to work on something anyway. Keith thought they'd left LA way too fast, and it was starting to look like a pretty stupid mistake. Aspersion's Foil could certainly get them there, but she didn't have a lab or any implements to collect any samples. Were they supposed to psychically *know* by staring down at the surface of the water? Maybe Holly had arranged a candlelight reading from an Ouija board in the bridge. He chuckled. His concern over what was a serious deficiency was ramped up. He'd have a talk with the queen right away. Being rich as Croesus, she could take care of this problem…even if they had to wait a few days to get it lined up.

Moving up the corridor and climbing a small set of stairs, he emerged on the lower deck. He took more stairs to the next level, and then he walked over to the port side of the ship. It was a brisk day, and he could see for miles. Gazing down at the water lapping at the side of the Foil, it was murky and grey, and unnamable things floated on the surface. He tasted bile rising at the back of his throat, and so far, he hadn't gotten anything in his belly to stabilize himself against morning visions like that. He walked over to the dining room, and that was when he saw the Cutaway.

Only half-a-mile away. She was off the starboard side of the Foil. A research ship from the United States Navy, at two hundred feet in length, she was sleek and professional, and she reflected the morning sun like a dream come true. Opening one of the glass doors leading into the dining room, Keith was shaking his head. He'd put Holly's resourcefulness out to pasture and it was obvious he should not have done so. How did she finagle that vessel out there *so fast* without the necessary rigmarole? And then he remembered her story about having dinner with the five-star general in La Jolla, and the answer came to him. She'd tweaked the poor man into actions he normally would not have done. Well, at least this last mind-control was done for a very good cause.

Three people in white lab coats were sitting at a corner table eating English muffins and drinking coffee. They were talking with real animation. He'd never seen them before, and he assumed they'd come over from the Cutaway. Holly was by herself in the middle of the room, genteelly cutting up Eggs Benedict, and Keith went over to her and sat down.

"Good-morning Keith, hope you slept well."

"Good-morning, and I slept and that's enough for now. Why didn't you tell me about it? I was going nuts when I woke up! Have they done any tests yet? Oh, and by the way, why didn't you tell me about it?"

"What about Oatmeal? We have fresh fruit to put on it. Strawberries, or maybe Peaches?"

Holly smiled, and ate more of her eggs. Teasing Keith was a nice morning perk; his curiosity, a toy.

"Come on, come on…fess up, girl!"

She kept on eating, looking into his eyes with a twinkle. Silence remained supreme.

"Alright. Okay. You want to play like we have tons of time to screw around, *fine,*" he said. "I love oatmeal. No, no, I adore it! I'll order a double serving of it for breakfast, right now."

The same girl who'd waited on them the day before had come over.

"Good-morning, Wendy," Keith said. He was staring at Holly as he politely ordered. "Please, I need the biggest bowl of oatmeal you have with peach slices on it and a pitcher a maple syrup on the side. Thank-you…*and will you please open up!*"

"What it is you'd like me to open for you, sir?" Wendy said.

"Sorry, nothing thanks. That's it. That last was directed towards the lady in charge."

Wendy filled his cup with coffee and went off to get his breakfast, while Holly smirked. Sitting back in his chair, frowning, Keith raised his arms in a gesture of defeat. Soon enough, Holly decided she was done playing around, and she put her fork down on the plate.

"They got here late last night. We've been on the radio with them until it went dead a few hours ago. Now we can't hail them, and we don't know why."

"Okay, that sounds bad. Wanting to know is turning out to be a bummer. It's already souring my belly."

"Hmmm. Aren't you the one who stated that this was going to be a difficult venture? Holly paused, looking sorrowful. "It doesn't matter how you feel, Keith. It doesn't matter at all. We have to get over there and figure out what's wrong and it's important for us to do this locked and loaded. Stop flipping out. This could be dangerous, and I know you can defend yourself quite handily and you aren't stupid...and you'll have me at your side," her smile reappeared, and she put her palms up indicting an upcoming success.

Placing steaming oatmeal in front of Keith, Wendy walked away, and he looked down at a breakfast Holly had instructed him to have. It smelled great, and he did like oatmeal. Whenever she was made out of star-dust or not, adding her abilities to his, does give them quite a lot of clout. Nevertheless, he was concerned about her arrogance, and the well-used saying 'pride before a fall' came into his mind as appropriate.

"Alright, alright. I'll slop this down my throat and we'll get over to the Cutaway and see what's up."

8:45AM Thursday December 21st, 2006 '32nd Street' Naval Station, San Diego

The fastest and most well-equipped research vessel the Navy had on the west coast, the Cutaway had been christened only twelve months ago. Fifty knots was her limit, yet that was a concealment. She could do quite a bit more, if she's pushed. The hull was a FSF (Fast Sea Frame), and it was surprising light having been forged out of aluminum. A catamaran, she was able to support a platform wide enough for two helicopters. There were twenty-five modules bracketed in her hold, and they could be taken out and reinstalled depending on the possible needs foreseen in her next mission.

General Wyndham had called the Naval Station the night before. He had ordered the officer in charge to oversee the instillation of three modules into the Cutaway, designed for deep water retrievals and collections as well as a range of tools and implements for dissection and categorization. They would collect evidence to be later examined in their onboard lab. The Cutaway wasn't going out to fight, so it didn't need weapons modules, nor did she need a helicopter to scout anything out. Normally, there were twenty-two people in the crew, but Wyndham had instructed that they would include three more people: an expert on bio-quantum theory who was currently working at the university in San Diego, plus two of their own marine scientists.

He was a respected General. His orders had been followed very quickly and to the letter. A bit past nine the next morning, the Cutaway glided out of the harbor and into open water. She had everything she needed for the upcoming investigation in the center of the gyre. Two GE LM2500 turbine engines, and two MTU 16Volt 595 TE 90 propulsion diesels, as well as four Rolls-Royce 125S11 water-jets propelled her onwards. The Cutaway was ship-shape and everything was where it needed to be, and the men and women in the crew even had good water pressure in their showers.

Captain Aaron Moran was trying to get the Cutaway to her destination in a hurry. Every order Wyndham had given him was lined up in his head in a logical list. He was staring through a pair of binoculars, and there were no sailboats or dinghies nearby, and there was nothing on the radar. They'd started out fast, but he ordered the helmsman to push it past fifty knots. Having been told to get to the coordinates with dispatch, he was following his orders precisely, and two plumes of white water got wider behind them. Told not to communicate with anyone else, not even military craft, Moran was avoiding other vessels. He veered away from traffic out there. Once there, he would wait for Aspersion's Foil. He would collaborate with them on examining the water and the atmosphere of the surrounding area in a battery of tests, and he'd been told to start on the tests, even before the other ship arrives.

After two and half days, in the early hours of the day before Christmas, Captain Moran instructed his helmsmen to slow down. Putting the ship on auto-pilot, the Cutaway remained in a four mile wide oval. She was moving at a sedate 4 knots. He got on the radio to Aspersion's Foil, and he got an instant response. Her Captain told him they'd be there in the morning.

The temperature was seventy two degrees outside and the sea was calm. No wind at all. He ordered his crew to unbox the research tools in the modules. After that, he gave anyone who didn't have current duties the freedom to relax and do as they wished…it was almost Christmas after all. Leaving the bridge, he proceeded to the residential section of the ship. It was time to wake-up his tagalong scientists; time to put them in gear and get to work. Captain Moran began knocking on their cabin doors until they had all responded with groggy acceptance.

Then he gave himself a break. Walking out onto the deck, the sky was a powerful ultramarine blue, and the sun blazed down onto his head. Of course, the surface of the water was not reflecting anything. It didn't look right. Far from it. What the Cutaway was cruising through at that point, was something he had no memory of seeing before in his many years of looking out at the Pacific Ocean. His self-imposed short relaxation began to evaporate. And then it was gone.

He should not have seen what he saw on the horizon, and it was busily getting closer by the second. A mysterious looking black cloud was wheeling to the left and then the right, and then sweeping to the surface only to shoot straight back up again. He trotted to the bridge to snag the binoculars. The darting cloud was magnified into a swarm of flies. He couldn't understand how or why they were so far out from land. As far as he knew, there wasn't a single bug able to fly that far out on the ocean, however these oversized flies were energetically sweeping across the deck of the Cutaway nonetheless. Whoever had decided to go outside to enjoy the free time they'd been given were ducking away from the insects. In their ultimate escape, all of them went back inside the interior of the ship. Of course, some of the diligent swarm had used the seconds between the opening and closing the hatches to follow them in.

The three scientists were having breakfast in the mess hall and they were talking over the project. Things looked okay until one of them looked out the window. His mouth had dropped in astonishment, and his mealtime companions followed his gaze to find their own disbelief.

After four minutes of dive bombing, the horde lifted away in a series of aerobatic lunges before disappearing into the distance. The Borg-like flies had done well. They had bitten almost the entire crew. Deceived into thinking the whole swarm had flown off, they didn't understand some had stayed behind...inside the Cutaway to complete the job of infecting *everyone*. The remaining flies were hunting down anyone still virgin to their peculiar venom.

Captain Moran was in the bridge, when it happened. He slapped at his neck, and minutes later he went to the head to inspect the damage. A red boil rose over his jugular vein, and he gently touched it. He started to get a very funny feeling, and he wished he hadn't been bitten all.

9:45AM Monday December 25th, 2006 The Cutaway

Holly and Keith were sitting on the front seat of the Donzi with semi-automatic handguns holstered to their hips. Bringing along extra fire-power, two other crewmen sat silently on the back seat with machine guns strapped across their backs. In the wake of the Donzi, two more heavily armed men followed in the dinghy. They tied both boats fast at the stern of the navy boat, and then they quietly climbed up the metal gangway, guns drawn, senses on high alert. When they all reached the deck, they spread out, everybody looking in all directions. Apparently, there was no one home. *No one.* Just an unsettling silence pressing in on them.

The gray walls of the navy ship weren't mottled with mold. No Spanish moss hung over the rails or anything like that, yet they still felt as if their boats were now roped to a desert island. The Cutaway didn't feel like the military research ship she was, and the unnatural atmosphere was haunting. The entire boarding party was getting badly disconcerted. They thought they'd walked into a trap. As if an invisible force was staring at them waiting until it was time to…to do something ghastly to them. Climbing up to the next level of the ship, Keith was leading the way to the bridge. When they got inside, no one was there either. No bodies, and no evidence of a fight or anything else that might have happened.

"We're going to have to search the entire ship." Holly's words were muted by the heaviness in the air.

Keith was handling this creepiness the best he could, hiding the waver in his voice under a layer of honey. "You know none of this is right. It's doesn't jibe with what *should be.*"

"I'm not disagreeing with you," Holly said, "but it is what it is, and we have to take care of this. There's no time to try to figure it out…we have to just keep on going."

"Of course, you're right. No one should go anywhere by themselves, so we'll pair off. Neil, you and I will go to the lower decks on the port side of the boat, and Holly, I think you and John should go to the starboard side and do the same thing. Will and Steve can check out the rest of upper sections of the ship."

They knew the Cutaway had had a full crew a day ago, and standing on the bridge of the same military ship, suddenly abandoned in the middle of the Pacific Ocean was unsettling everyone. Even Holly was creeped out, and Keith wasn't going to let any crewmen into the bowels of the Cutaway without himself or Holly by their side. It was likely that guns weren't going to be the correct defense if defense becomes appropriate.

5:15PM Sunday December 24th, 2006 The Cutaway

The bite on Captain Moran's neck continued to swell. Looking over at the communication officer sitting at the radio, he saw the same kind of bite on the back of his hand. Those flies had to have been rapacious. Captain Novak, the communication officer, had already sent their position to the Aspersion's Foil the night before, and they'd estimated their own arrival back to him. Currently, there was a new message from the Foil coming in, but no one heard it. Novak, Moran himself, and the other two men on the bridge, *did not hear it.* Swiveling his head around, the captain was caught off-guard. A glint of sun reflecting off of something many feet above his ship speared into his eye, and he was stunned by the almost magical appearance of two military helicopters proceeding to land on the Cutaway. They hadn't called in, and no one had reported their approach. Barreling out of the room, he raced up the stairs to the landing pad. While the pilots shut off the engines, Captain Springer climbed out, and he was dressed in full regalia. He stood in front of Captain Moran, and saluted. Returning the standard acknowledgment, Moran actually knew him. He'd met him at boot camp, and they hadn't seen each other for years.

"Hello, Captain Moran. General Wyndham has gotten a heads-up from Aspersion's Foil…the ship you're supposed to meet here in about 12 hours or so. It seems they'd found solid evidence about a gas bubble rising to the surface in this area, and they had told the General to evacuate the Cutaway right away. You can leave the ship on auto-pilot until the poisonous fumes dissipate, and in the meantime we can air-lift you out of danger. We can bring you back when it's over."

"I guess it's not so good to see you after all those years, Barney. Are you sure there aren't any other options…okay, okay. I'll start the evacuation, but I have twenty-five people on this vessel, and those copters can accommodate just eighteen of my crew. I can't leave seven people behind."

"Don't worry, my friend. Another bird on the way. After everyone we can pick up is onboard, we'll lift off and she'll land and get the rest you."

The two officers were returning to the bridge, and Captain Springer was moving fast. He left Moran behind as he was leaning heavily to the right. And he was stumbling, as if he was tipsy. He was trying to keep up with his companion, and it seemed very odd to him that Barney never looked over his shoulder to notice his tardiness.

Entering the bridge, Captain Moran got on the intercom letting everyone know about the emergency. In fifteen minutes, he'd assembled the entire crew for transport. Well, almost everybody.

Wesley Palmer was the only civilian on board. A bio-quantum mathematician from San Diego, a representative from the navy had called him and asked for his help. He was already worried about the environmental abnormalities popping up world-wide, so the thirty-six year old accepted the invitation. Rescheduling his appointments, he packed a bag and they flew him to Los Angeles and he got on board the next day.

After the memorable breakfast watching a swarm of flies darting around on the deck, the scientists retired to the lab. They had begun setting up tests for the water and air, and they were arranging all the tools they would need to collect whatever might be still alive in the center of the Trash Vortex. Wes was attaching a chronometer on the side of a metal vat to regulate the timing of the dose of something they'd give to whatever could be clamped inside of it, when he felt the first inklings.

Might have seasickness left over from the bumpy ride he'd endured in getting him there, or perhaps he was allergic to something he'd just eaten for breakfast, but a cramp slammed into him, and he doubled over. The pain got worse fast. The poor man was quickly chained to the tiny toilet in the claustrophobic cubicle in the corner of his cabin for the rest of the day.

Captain Moran had oversaw the evacuation. Of course, he had no intention of leaving his ship in the first excursion. After all of the scientists, and most of the crewmen were lifted off, he'd finally escape on the third chopper.

Professor Palmer was a real problem. He wouldn't come back to the landing pad with the other scientists. At first, he kept on insisting there weren't any helicopters sitting there. What drivel! He kept on with the same statement over and over again. *'There's nothing on the landing pads....nothing at all'*, he'd screech, waving his hands in the air. What a namby-pamby little girl. His crazy rants must be coming out of a deep-seated fear of flying in a copter. That was it. Too flipped-out to fly. The Captain watched these hysterics until he couldn't stand it anymore, and he ordered one of his men to restrain him and simply put him into one of the helicopters. At that point, the professor bolted through the closest hatchway he could get to, racing off the deck like a rabbit running for his burrow. Nobody had been able to get their hands on him since then. Moran's first attempt to save Wesley Palmer, wasn't going to happen, and his future plan to get him into the third helicopter wasn't going to happen either. That last copter would never land on the Cutaway, however that fact was only a small part of a reality that would soon undermine the Captain's folly.

Moran, three officers and two crewmen returned to the bridge. The Captain sent the crewmen out to hunt the professor down and bring him back. The navigator, the communication officer, the helmsman, the other two crewman, himself and the scientist would wait there to be evacuated. Apparently, the final phase was taking a lot more time, and minutes piled up into a half-an-hour. Everyone's attentiveness was drifting, and their concern over the rising bubble that was supposed to emit toxic gas began to fade from their minds. Virgil Marquis, the navigator, was the first to leave the bridge, floating lackadaisically through the door. He was on his way to his cot, and when he got there, he laid down to stare straight up at the bottom of the cot above his face. Closing his eyes, he replaced the grey plastic with a vision of a sunny island, and he was on it, and a very pretty girl was fawning over him. Yes, the previous danger was gone from his head. The other officers also wandered off soon after his departure, listlessly wandering to different locations on the ship. Captain Moran could be found swaying along a corridor like wax dripping down the side of a candle. His last orders to the two other crewman had been ignored. They hadn't located the professor, nor did they return to the bridge.

Wesley Palmer slowly opened the utility closet door. He'd been hiding there for the past forty-five minutes, and he didn't want to make any noise at all leaving the closet. He'd decided to see what was happening, and he started down the corridor. He certainly wasn't getting on invisible helicopters. When Carey Dickinson, the helmsman, suddenly stepped in front of Wesley at the end of the hall, he was about to race away from him, but the expression on Carey's face gave him pause. Wistful and distracted, it was clear that the officer was not about to drag him anywhere. Walking closer the Navy man, the professor had drummed-up enough courage to ask him a question.

11:20AM Monday December 25th, 2006 The Cutaway

Holly and John went through their side of the lower decks of the Cutaway, and that had included the expansive laboratory. Impressed by it, she hoped that Keith and the other technicians would still be able to use it. The uneasy feeling she'd had was gone, and her mind was free to come up with new strategies. Yet, that hadn't happened to crewman at her side. He was pale with dread, and Fischer himself, in a different part the Cutaway, was also flustered. Ms. Donnelly had found the necessary kernel of concrete to banish the ghosts, returning to the shore of serenity even under a mysterious threat emerging from the extraordinary disappearance of the entire crew of the Navy ship.

And then she sped up. Holly wanted to be done and over with the search. Quickly opening the oversized door that led into a storage area, she and John were surprised by the sight of Wesley, the navigator, the helmsmen and one of the crewman sitting around a folding card table. They were playing a game of crazy eights. Oddly, their appearance had not interrupted the game, and the players kept staring at their cards as if she and the crewman weren't even there. Until Wesley started talking.

"It's about time somebody got here! I don't know what happened or what's behind this mess, and I don't know what's wrong with these guys. They don't seem to be..." However, the helmsmen interrupted him.

"Wes...Wesley, I think I'm about to win. I think I can put down all my cards and win the game!"

"That's great, Carey, but right now we have guests, and it's important to find out what they want. Doesn't that make sense? We'll play the rest of the game in a couple of minutes, okay?"

He looked down at his cards, and he stayed in that position and he didn't say anything else. The other players mimicked him like a strange freeze frame; three wax figures in a museum display. Wesley's previous experience as a substitute teacher in a kindergarten class years ago, had helped him to gently herd these badly compromised men away from doing anything disastrous.

And Holly absorbed the whole thing in a glance. She also saw a fly buzzing around her own crewman, and she watched it land on his cheek. Moving inhumanly fast, she stepped over to him and swept the insect up in her hand and then she crushed it flat. She dropped what was left on the steel floor, and its attempts to do anything were over.

"Your shipmates aren't interested in much these days," Holly said, unconcerned about what their response to her stellar appraisal of them would be, yet she put urgency in her next statement. "Right now, there's a very dangerous puzzle we have to solve as fast as we can. Please, it's important to tell us exactly what went on, and where's the rest of the crew?"

"You have to be from the other ship...the one we were supposed to meet out here, right?"

Holly nodded, "Yeah. Yeah, we're from the Foil. If you don't mind, tell me what happened...hold on. Wait a minute."

Picking out two folding chairs from a stack held in a bracket welded to the metal wall behind her, she set them up fifteen away from the other men. She gave Wesley some privacy from the others. He followed her over, even though he remained agitated.

"Look, if you want me to go ahead and tell you where everybody went, I'm afraid you're gonna think I'm bat-shit crazy."

"*Wesley, please.* I assume you don't mind that I'm using your first name, but stop worrying about that right now. I'll accept your story as true. The whole situation has already bounced right out of bounds. Everything here, or not here, has already become impossible. Forgetting about the short expanse of time that was involved, how did the men on this ship disappear? We're talking about hours here. There's no way you can come up with an invention any stranger than the real one."

Holly had put a soothing calmness in her voice…as well as a slight push; a mental hook to draw him out. His indecisiveness should now be gone. In any other circumstance, Holly wouldn't have done it. She could have waited a few minutes for Wesley to open up on his own, but they were running of time. If they can't defend themselves against an enigma, they can forget about attacking it. It was imperative for them to glean every single bit of evidence from any source found so they could build a picture of the enemy and decipher its weaknesses. Wesley had been badly drained. He didn't have much energy left. His voice was soft as a whisper as he began his tale, and it seemed Holly's gentle paranormal pry-bar had been exactly the right thing to do.

Minutes later, Keith and Neil entered the hold, Captain Moran in tow. When Wes saw the Captain, he cringed, but he continued talking. Holly turned around and put her finger to her lips, indicating he should not be interrupted…

"Before I went to my cabin yesterday, we watched a swarm of bees that had come out of nowhere dive-bomb the deck while we were having breakfast. And that was weird. I don't know how many of the crew out there had gotten bitten by them, but they all raced inside to avoid them, and then the crazy looking bugs flew away. After that, Chris and Steve and I began to set up our experiments, but I started to get sick. I wanted to stay in the lab with them, but there was no way, I had to get to my cabin and stay there on the toilet. I don't remember what time it was when I heard the alarm and the Captain's orders on the PA system telling everybody to go the helicopter landing pad. We were supposed to be evacuated by helicopter 'cause a bubble of toxic gas was about to reach the surface of the water and poison us. Something like that. I was feeling a little bit better by then, thank God, so I made it up there…to see what was happening, and I felt sick again. I guess they were all hypnotized into thinking the helicopters were really there, thinking they'd be lifted away from the danger. The stuff about the bubble had to have been made up too, anyway, I tried hard to shake them out of it at first; telling them they were hoodwinked. I started screaming my head off, but it didn't matter. Nothing I did or said made any difference. I'd watch them crouch down, as if the blades were really swirling above their heads as they carefully climbed into the passenger section of a craft that was not there. It was miserable to watch. They'd just step off the edge of the pad and plummet sixty-five feet into the ocean. None of even screamed! How damned deep into it had they been? They couldn't see the water rushing at them? I thought I was living in a nightmare, and I could not wake up. When Captain Moran ordered one of his men to grab me and put me into one of the helicopters, I had no choice. I ran. I hid in a utility closet for a while, praying they wouldn't find me. The whole thing sounds ridiculous, I know, but it's true. I swear to God. It was awful watching them die like that…and there was nothing I could do to stop it."

"It's okay Professor, everything will be taken care. You need to rest on my ship for a day or two, and after that we'll talk things over again. I've read your treatise on quantum mathematics. You have a real cool slant on the biological component in the universal equation. You have some revolutionary concepts in your head. Yup, I think it's important we get together after your recuperation. Thomas, if you please: guide Professor Palmer over to the Aspersion's Foil, and take him to the infirmary. Use the Donzi. After he's situated, come back here, alright."

"Of course, right now, Ms. Donnelly."

The young man walked over to Wesley and took his arm, and he helped him out of the storage area.

"Wesley's story is true, isn't it Moran? Everybody did jump to their deaths in the ocean? *Why would you do something like that? Why'd you do it?*" Keith said.

"I had too! I had to get everyone away from the gas. And they are safe now, but…but we're still in danger, and I'm worried. The last helicopter should have gotten here by now. We...we should get to the landing pad right now and..." Holly quickly interrupted him.

"Don't concern yourself about the problem anymore, Aaron. The gas has dissipated. In a radio transmission from the 32nd Street Station fifteen minutes ago, the officer there confirmed it. No more worries, sir. Everything will be fine. The men you have saved are in a briefing at the station."

And she glared over at Keith with irritation. He shrugged. He was checking on Moran's emotional state, wanting to see if there would be a physical response to reflect what he'd telepathically made out in the Captain's mind. Holly put her arm around the captain's waist, guiding him through the door.

"Keith, please round up everyone left in the Cutaway and get them all in the mess hall."

"Okay. You want the rest of us there too?"

"Everybody."

He got on the radio and told the crewmen he'd left on the top deck to meet him in the mess hall. Then he and Neil led the rest of the survivors up there. The men from the Cutaway could not stay focused on anything, and an overall stupefaction was getting more prevalent in their behavior.

When the last of the remaining crew sat silently at one of the dining tables, Keith looked over at Holly. She looked straight back. Nodding towards the motionless group, he bowed slightly in her direction. He wanted her to take the reins over their disintegrating psyches. No time to mull over a job either of them could do, and Holly understood his quick deferment. Captain Moran had just stood up, instinctively trying to take control. He was trying to give them a direction he no longer had within himself.

"The up-coming danger from the poison gas needs to be handled... and...and we were supposed to meet the other ship, Aspersion's Foil. We were supposed to work with them and..."

Holly cut in on him again, this time with a glint of blue shimmering in her eyes.

"No, no, Captain Moran. The poison is gone. *The danger is gone.* All of you will be working with people from the Foil during the next few days. In the meantime, there are more tests to be done before we can even start that project. Like I said, the danger is gone. You and your men can relax. You need to an onboard-leave for yourself and your men to recuperate. There's no reason left to worry about anything. *You will remain at peace.*"

The powerful resonance in those last words had calmed all of the injured warriors at the table. She'd sent the short command deep into their subconscious minds with a mental heat intense enough to burn it into their essence. Neither Keith nor Holly wanted harmful outbreaks popping out of them during the next week, while they try to set up defenses against something they barely understood.

Thomas had dropped Wesley off at the infirmary on the Foil, and he zipped back to the Cutaway as he was told to. Keith had radioed him about the all-hands meeting at the mess hall, and he'd walked in just as Holly finished with her preventive work on the poisoned Navy men. Already on his feet, she requested him to shepherd the rest of the addled men.

"Tommy here, will lead you into the galley, and you can make some sandwiches for lunch. After that, you can go back to playing cards again or maybe have a cat-nap."

And Holly whispered into Thomas's ear, "*Stay alert around them. If anything unusual crops up in their actions, let me know, immediately.*"

Nodding, he did lead the docile men into the galley, and Ms. Donnelly sent the remaining three crewmen of her own out on the deck to wait for further instructions. Keith was already out there. He was leaning against a rail, staring out at the horizon.

"Listen Keith, I squashed one of those flies buzzing around us in the storage area. I'm concerned there may be more inside the ship. I may be impervious to them, and you might have your own protection too, but I can't let that dangerous possibility of getting infected by this crap go on for anyone else. I won't let my crew or the technicians be poisoned by them, and all I need is twenty minutes. Make sure no one opens a hatch, and nobody goes back inside until I'm done. I'm about to make solid sure the *entire* inside of the Cutaway is utterly free of them."

"Please, go ahead and take care of it, Holly. It's got to be the first thing we need to do to defend ourselves. Oh, what about Tommy? He's with the other guys in the galley. I'm assuming the surviving crew from the Cutaway are already infected, but should we be worried about leaving him in there?"

"I checked the galley and the mess hall as soon as we got there, and since I'm about to get rid of the problem faster than they can eat their sandwiches, Tommy will be fine. In a few minutes, he'll be able to go anywhere on the ship without that dangerous possibility….for now anyway."

"Okay. I'll see you in a…."

But Holly was gone, having sped up into a blur and then she left that behind too. Zipping through every single corridor, cabin and closet in the Cutaway, like the fictional 'Flash' from the Marvel comic strip, every single Borg-like fly was hunted down. She had eradicated two, and imprisoned two more in a beaker for future study and dissection. No stragglers left behind. Nothing else buzzed free anywhere on the Cutaway.

The center of the gyre was badly unstable. And treacherous. They understood that, but even after the terrible forecast in which most of the crew of the Cutaway had perished, *they could not leave.* They had to find the source behind the global-wide upheavals and defeat it, and if that meant they had to endure more enigmatic attacks; so be it. Evidence anchored them there, and they knew their crusade wasn't going to get any easier. However, unlike the decimated population of the science ship, Holly and Keith would be more difficult to overcome. Tricking them, and by extension those around them, would be almost impossible, and they would also fight back with a vengeance. Something else the monster had not encountered yet.

Holly remained uneasy. Nebulous shapes in a divination she was trying to ignore had appalling silhouettes, and even though Keith didn't skip out quite that far, he too felt apprehensive. As if reality was being replaced by a mirage, and a thunder cloud that didn't rain nor blow away was hanging motionless over their heads. The searing blue sky above the Foil and the Cutaway that morning hadn't helped them in the least.

Stepping out on the deck, Holly told the men it was okay to come back inside, and she sent two to the wheel house to be on watch and make sure nothing else was coming towards them in the sky. Then she ordered John to take the Donzi over to Aspersion's Foil.

Keith had stayed at the rail while she was gone, and he didn't say anything when she came over and leaned her elbows on the metal bar next to him. She sighed for a moment. Taking her phone out of her pocket, new priorities had risen to the top of the list. Her first call was to Captain Egan Novak. At forty-eight, he had an exemplary career in the military under his belt, and she'd picked him for captaining Aspersion's Foil. Seconds before her call, he'd been standing on the bridge in a perfectly pressed uniform. He was trim, and his green eyes shone with the depth of a mountain stream and lucidity of mind.

"Heads up, Captain. We have a problem over here. There's no bridge crew in the Cutaway. Well, actually there's no crew at all. The few survivors aren't mentally fit. Please tell, Stevens, our first mate, and the navigator, to pack an overnight bag and take the Donzi back over here. We need them on the bridge right now. I'm leaving one of the crewman I brought along here behind. Pick out six more replacements to work with our scientists in the Cutaway during the next day or two. The quantum-biologist, Professor Wesley Palmer, who's resting in the infirmary right now, will also give us a hand deciphering this stuff when he feels better."

"Yes, Ms. Donnelly, I'll take care of it right now. Excuse my unasked for input, but things are looking a little dicey out here. Maybe we should alert the pentagon. They could send out a battleship, or some tomcats to fly over and check things out. Considering the strange disappearances and injury to the Navy crew, I wonder if they wouldn't toss us all into the brig if we don't alert them," but he chuckled at the logical conclusion he'd come up with anyway.

"No, no, Egan, no. None of that is going to happen. Don't worry. I'm going to take care of this predicament with one more phone call. I'll be back to the Foil by eight or nine. We'll have a better handle on the situation by then, and we can talk over our plans to be more careful in this, shall we say, erratic location. I compliment you for overviewing the extenuating possibilities."

"Thank you, Ms. Donnelly," and he automatically bowed politely to the compliment even if she couldn't see him.

Getting off the phone, Holly looked over at Keith, and her eyes narrowed in concentration. She was already building up kinetic energy for the upcoming call she was about to have with General Carl Wyndham. She knew it was going to be a difficult task; the man was hundreds of miles away and she had to guide his actions to safeguard their position. As she and her cohort stepped into the mess hall, they sat down at one of the tables, and Keith leaned back in his chair. He waited patiently.

3:00PM Monday December 25th, 2006 La Jolla, California

Hannah was carefully applying eye-shadow, huddling over inches away from her make-up mirror on a vanity in their bedroom, and General Wyndham was staring through a window at the sea. He was sliding a silk tie under the pressed white collar of his shirt.

"You know we're supposed be at Brook's estate at five thirty. He lives only five miles away from us, so I don't know why we're going over there so early?"

Hannah tossed the question over her shoulder. They'd been invited, again, to the annual Christmas pageant of a party at Brook LeBron's mansion nestled in ten acres of perfectly groomed land. LeBron had been responsible for an innovative adaption of magnification in plastic and glass, and he had grown into a billionaire. A loyal supporter of any of America's military efforts, he could care less where the dogs of war go. The ongoing conflicts, wherever they are, would pours gold into his coffers and that was a wonderful thing. To honor Christ's birth at the designated holiday, he would always invite three hundred or so guests to his lavish spread.

"We're getting there early because I have to spend a couple of minutes with him personally before everybody arrives, my dear. There are a couple of items in next month's acquisitions we need to discuss and…"

This irritating answer was interrupted by his phone ringing and Hannah's instant retort, "Well, what am I supposed to be doing while you talk? You should leave me behind. I'll just show up later on, and why is it so important that it can't wait until *after* the party? Or maybe you could talk to him tomorrow instead?"

"Hold on, Hannah, I have to answer this call, like *right now*."

Wyndham waved her off, and he left the bedroom. He walked along the hallway until he found himself looking down at the great room on the first floor.

"Hello Holly, Merry Christmas. I have a terrible feeling it's not turning out to be a very merry one for you, otherwise you wouldn't be on the horn with me right now. I really truly don't want to know what the real reason behind this is."

"And Merry Christmas to you, General Wyndham. I hope you and Hannah are well. I assume you're on your way over to LeBron's festivities."

"Hmm…yeah, and we're fine, thanks. Yeah, we're going to the party. Come on, come on, Holly, what's wrong? Something happened on the Cutaway didn't it?"

"Well sir, you're on the money. Something disastrous did take place…oh, by the way, you've been doing a great job in making sure our arrangement stays under wraps. In the meantime, things out here have gotten hazardous. Almost the entire crew of the Cutaway was killed by a huge swarm of flies…"

But Wyndham was furious, and he cut in on her, "***What!*** *What are you telling me?* I've got go to Washington and drum up some help. Have you gone completely insane! We can't leave things like that running rampant and unchecked. It's time to get the big guns in here, and…"

As he went on railing at her, Holly's eyes lit up into solid bright blue. When *she* interrupted *him,* there was now a peculiar nuance in her voice. She had to have utter control over the General instantly, and she prayed the lasso of an echo reverberating out of the vowels in her words would be enough. It had to be.

"Listen to me Carl. Listen. Relax and calm down. Everything out there is under control."

Her statement was far from true, yet she was ready to do or say almost anything to get what she badly needed out of him, and she needed it right away.

"Make sure there won't be any reconnaissance out here in the sky. We don't need jets dropping bombs or battleships battling anything either. Any kind of military presence of that kind would be a devastating mistake. We don't want any more men dying, and there's nothing floating around in the center of the

Northern Pacific Gyre tangible enough to explode. Make your friends in the Pentagon forget all about the Trash Vortex. Keep on keeping the lid on this. Okay?"

His anger was gone, and the General was suddenly calm again. Able to make him composed, the rest of her commands were also working just fine. Wyndham had leaned against a marble pillar at the far end the hallway like a teenager trying to look cool.

"Alright, Holly. I have no idea how you're going to get anything done without any help. It sounds like you're hell-bent and I can't stop you."

"Well, you are wrong. I'm heaven sent and I have help. A lot of it. Civilian help, and another kind of support you don't need to know about right now. Nevertheless, I still need your help. Tomorrow morning I'll give you the names of the five survivors that you'll later transport back to the onshore medical facility, and you must also tell the families of the fallen soldiers about their loss...but you just can't tell them quite yet. Their reaction would turn attention to what we need to remain secret for a little bit longer. Oh, by the way, there aren't any bodies. They drowned before we got there. Look, I know what I'm about to ask for is a difficult request, but we absolutely have to replace the entire crew. I'm optimistic you can get them out here very quickly, and I assure you...no, *I promise you,* these replacements will be guarded twenty-four seven. I'll be on site indefinitely until the job is done. Whatever we're up against is gonna have to go through me and Keith first."

Telling him that she had full control over the entire area was just a fairy tale. Her last proclamation was a bit more realistic, but she's not God. There was a chance bad things could happen in an ongoing battle that was apparently ramping up to an apocalyptic war, but it was the best she could offer him.

Even though Carl Wyndham was certainly under Holly's thrall, he wasn't a drone. He had a grasp of what she was dealing with, and he knew it was dangerous. In his soul, he felt she was dealing with the situation in a positive way, that she would protect the men he was going to have to send out to the Cutaway. Down deep, he could sense her extraordinary power, and he hoped it would be enough to get us out. The Navy ship had been out there alone for almost a full day before Aspersion's Foil's arrival. If Holly had been there, she would have stopped the attack somehow. She'd sounded upset about their deaths, and resolute about never leaving them without security again. He wasn't happy about sending more men out there, but her words had soothed him a bit, even if he had no choice in the matter.

"Alright, Holly. I'll get on the line and send them out. I guess you know whatever Christmas cheer I might have is gone now. You have wrecked it completely. Thank-you for your exquisite timing."

"Just rise above this stuff for a while Carl, and enjoy the party."

Holly abruptly cut the connection to the General's cell, and the half-smile on her face vanished so fast, it didn't look like it had ever been there.

10:45AM Wednesday December 27th, 2006 Port of Los Angeles

Nine members of the Blackmore Coalition ascended the covered gangway onto the Caprice. The companionable group would spend the next two weeks together to enjoy the lavish bonus the company offers in an annual retreat on the high seas. Standing on line with the other company men, Eric felt vindicated, relieved, and complacent. He'd invited his mistress to come along, but she hadn't been able to get the extended time off her job at a dental clinic. Fending for himself without her was just as appealing.

Entering the body of the ship, a uniformed female directed them towards their cabins with an engaging smile. The Carnelian Caprice had been built in Italy in 2002 by Fincantiera, a company that manufactured nothing but cruise ships. The business, and the vessels they produced had both expanded over time. With 3,852 passengers, and 1,500 crewmen and laborers, the Caprice was one of the biggest ships currently working commercially. Her cruising population could fill a small town, and that was the perfect milieu for Vera. She imagined zeroing in on Eric in full-sight, yet she'd still remain invisible to him; using different foliage and feathers of a different shade. She dreamed of that final moment. She'd be only an arms-length away from her ex-husband. Vera wanted to be close enough to kiss him goodbye forever, while he'd be none-the-wiser until the awful truth lit up in his eyes; a ruinous revelation.

While the ongoing boarding of thousands of passengers went on, Adler and another Blackmore lawyer got to their cabins at the same time, coincidentally next to each other. Stowing their luggage that had been dropped off next to their cabin doors, they went up to deck eleven and walked into a bar. Ordering Bloody Marys, they picked up their icy cold drinks and strolled out on the promenade to look down at the last of the passengers shuffling slowly up the gangway.

"We're gonna have a great time this year. You haven't been on one of our cruises before have you? I'll clue you in. We *all* play while the cat's away."

His name was Joel Rosario. Their forearms resting on the rail, he turned to Eric and smirked.

"I left my wife behind. Most of us do. In my case, it was easy as pie. My mother-in-law fell off her bicycle last week, and the fall pulverized her left leg. Put the whole thing in a cast and Mildred wanted to stay and help her out. Even though we set up a live-in nurse to take care of her for the first two weeks, help her to the bathroom and stuff, my better-half could not accept that. It wasn't enough," and a shit-eating grin bloomed on his face as if he'd won the lottery or something.

"Well, I'm separated, so I'm already free, but I agree with you. This cruise should to be a hoot. I'll probably never want to come back to earth again. I'm gonna just relax, lie in the sun, get a tan and get fatter. I read some of the reviews on line about the restaurant food on this ship, and they were raving about it. Four stars."

"Look Eric, I'm not impressed with your idea of getting fat. Wouldn't it be more fun to eat entrees that can wiggle? And let's stay on the subject a little bit longer. We should really…wait…wait a minute. Can you make-out that redhead down there at the far edge of the dock?"

Joel had just picked Vera out of the crowd. Her burgundy hair and an over-sized bronze medallion around her neck were both shining like beacons in the sun. At forty-three, Joel's penchant was cougars, a difficult hobby for him. Older women on the hunt would generally want younger lovers. Nevertheless, he did pretty well at breaking through. Vera was wearing a purple dress so tight it looked like paint, and that was another flag drawing him towards her. No, he didn't like younger women. They were too flighty, grabbing at his wallet…or wanting to get married or something. Vera's orchestrated transformation had certainly landed her right in the middle of his parameters. She was exactly what he was hoping for. Eric followed Joel's pointed finger. At a distance, she seemed strangely familiar, but that was all. She had sprouted plumage he could not envision coming out of his x-wife, and Vera was hiding perfectly in broad daylight.

5:36PM Friday December 29th, 2006 The Carnelian Caprice

The ninth deck of the Caprice was transformed. It was carnival night! The activity director had ordered his workers to build a line-up of different games, as well as small versions of some of the regular rides that were general found at carnivals. There was a Ferris-wheel, a merry-go-round, and even a tilt-a-wheel with teacup seats, and they held center stage in the widest part of the deck. Hotdogs, cotton candy, funnel cakes and fried Twinkies were fresh, there for the taking, as staff stuffed into blue top-hats and red and white shirts were taking care of everything with smiles planted on their faces like crazy glue.

A family with three children wove through this spectacle, ending up at the rail. And they stayed there. One of the workers was swirling spun sugar coming out of the holes in a metal bin to make cotton candy, and she looked over her shoulder, noticing them standing there. Twenty minutes later they were in the exact same place. Dad was wearing green shorts and a white T-shirt, holding hands with his six year old daughter. In a bright yellow sleeveless dress, mom stood next to her son who was holding a toy train on a long leash behind him. This stationary line-up ended with the oldest son, and he was nine or ten; tall enough to put his elbows on the rail like his parents. None of them said a thing. They looked like a wax display, or maybe an ad.

It was after ten. The deck crew was breaking down the rides, putting everything used in the carnival extravaganza back in the packing boxes… as fast as they could. The Cotton Candy Girl was folding the banner that had been fluttered above her booth during the entire day, and just for a second, she looked over her shoulder one more time. The family was gone. She'd been way too busy to have seen them whenever they'd finally departed, and she offhandedly wondered where that strange family might have gone. She giggled. A picture popped up in her head in which they'd reset themselves on a different deck, continuing to enjoy their vacation as potted people plants.

Everyone in the Blackmore Coalition was stuffed like a flock of Thanksgiving turkeys. They had dinner at one of the restaurants, and they reconvened at a lounge on the tenth deck. They watched as the Carnival Night was being dismantled on the deck below them. It was the first week of their vacation, and they wanted to spend part of it together telling each other about courtroom hijinks with accompanying gales of laughter. The frequency of those happy outbursts had increased with their growing drunkenness. By eleven, most of them had gone back to their cabins to sleep it off. Eric Adler, Charles Penny and Joel Rosario were still there. The diehards.

The cocktail lounge they were in was called *Sail Away,* and the designers had done a great job in mesmerizing the customers to order one more drink. And then order another, and just keep on going. Food, regular drinks, and the sight-seeing trips and the rafting and surfing expeditions lined up when they got to Hawaii were all included in the first steep ticket price. *But not the alcohol.* The Carnelian Line made a lot more money on bar bills, so it would make sense for them to line up lots of events that would take place in the lounges. Of course, the members of the Blackmore Coalition weren't worried about their mounting bar bills. There wasn't a teetotaler in the group, and the rest of them played hard every year. On the last day of the cruise, the astronomical bill reflecting their liquid extravagances would arrive in an envelope at their cabin doors, and they would pay it without a hint of regret.

Even Eric and Charles were beginning to fade. They'd had a little too much sun during the day. Joel Rosario smiled goodnight to them both, continuing onwards to follow his dream. He thought he still had a chance to meet the right lady as it was not even midnight yet! Checking out who was staying around to the last, he ordered a Moon-trap; a deadly concoction made with pineapple and mango. This tropical saccharine slush was about to carefully disguise double shots of rum into his gullet. When the bartender put the drink in front of Joel, Vera Adler sat down next to him at the same time, and Eric, who was walking out of the lounge, had turned around.

"Good evening, miss. I'm Joel, Joel Rosario. I haven't seen a wrap as fetching as the one you have on right now today, or perhaps it's not the clothes. Maybe it has to do with who's wearing it? Can I buy you a drink?"

He was beaming at her as if the sun had come out in the middle of the night, and he'd been right about her dress. It was lovely. The forest green at the shoulders fading to light green at the hem, and the gradating color accented the reddish-purple in her hair. She had truly evolved into a magnetic temptress.

"Thank-you sir. I'd like a seven and seven," and she put her hand out to shake his. "I'm Yvette, Yvette Payne and I hope you're going to be able to answer a question I've been trying to figure out the entire day." Vera smiled coquettishly at him.

"And what of earth could this difficult question be, my dear Yvette?"

"I can't curl up at eight and crochet like my fuddy-duddy girlfriends. I need an adventure of one sort or another. My question to you is whether I can find the excitement I'm looking for or not?"

Eric had stopped in the entrance, watching Vera and Joel flirt. He wasn't very far away from the woman he'd been married to for years, but those one hundred feet were enough. Vera had redone herself so completely, he still could not place her. The same faint familiarity he gotten when he'd first seen her on the dock came back, but that was all. In his mind, Joel was about to be bamboozled by a gold-digging floozy. He shook his head and turned away. It's a free world, and the guy can do what he wants, and Eric got on the elevator to his cabin on deck seven.

4:45AM Saturday December 30th, 2006 Carnelian Caprice

Harry Curtin was on night shift. After everybody was curled up in their beds, he'd get up at midnight and brush and floss his teeth, and then he'd put on his uniform. Leaving the tiny cabin he was sharing with Donny, a dishwasher, he went straight to the cafeteria assigned to the crew. And when he got there, he guzzled three cups of coffee. On that particular morning, he wolfed down French toast as if the ship was sinking. In his current rotation, he was assigned to the ninth deck. Done with his meal, he walked over to the service elevator, got in and hit nine on the panel. The doors opened, and Harry went over to the nearest utility closet, and he used his universal key to open the heavy door. Rolling out a garbage pail on wheels, he filled a grey bucket, also had wheels, with hot water from the sink in the corner. He poured in the proscribed amount of anti-bacterial soap into the bucket, and then he picked up a mop and dropped it in the pail. Holding the door open with his elbow, he kicked the bucket out on the deck next to the garbage pail, and the door slammed hard behind him. He stood there for a moment deciding where he wanted to start. There was no one around, and that was normal. Harry stared out at the empty expanse, and for a second he felt like he was stuck on an abandoned ghost ship. Someone had forgotten to remove the multi-colored lights from the Carnival display off the stair rails leading up to the tenth deck. They were still blinking. Whistling softly, Harry rolled his two containers onwards. He'd start at the bow, and move towards the stern on the starboard side of the Caprice where the whirlpool was. Picking up the mop, he dropped it on the deck with a squishy slap, but he paused. Someone was still in the whirlpool at this late hour. It's usually teenagers or love birds. It's never older men by themselves. This guy was wearing blue speedo swim shorts, but he certainly wasn't swimming. He wasn't doing anything at all. He floated there like a dead thing. Harry was getting the heebie-jeebies as he stepped closer to the hot tub. Seeing the pallor in the man's face with eyes glazed over by a thick white film, he himself started to move away from him as fast as he could.

Leaving the pail and bucket behind, he ran to the nearest emergency phone under the colorfully lighted stairs. The operator transferred his call to the medic, and Harry wanted him to pick up the phone like yesterday. Looking around with real dread, his earlier feelings of being on a haunted ship had returned. Of course, finding what had looked like a dead body in the whirlpool had certainly given the concept a lot more weight and substance. His uneasiness jumped front and center and it stayed there.

Things on the Caprice were actually going to get worse, so his reaction was spot on. The cruise wasn't going to be quite right for anyone for quite a while.

The medical system on this floating island was comprised by fifteen officers with differing levels of ability. There was a clinic and even a morgue, and there were two certified doctors on board. The medic who'd answered his call, quickly arrived at the scene, pronouncing the man dead. He told Harry to get off the deck with a stern warning not to tell *anyone* about the incident. Harry was more than happy to roll away his equipment and himself, while the medic called one of the docs. Lester Mallory had been on the rotation, and when he picked up the phone and got the news, he got out of bed, got dressed and arrived at the whirlpool in short order.

"Who found him, Arthur? Was there anyone around when he died?" Doctor Mallory asked.

"The night porter, Harry Curtin, found him. He doesn't know *anything,* and I let him go. I don't know if anyone was around or not, but maybe we should just get him to the morgue. It would be easier to identify who he was and what happened to him there than here, and I don't think it's a good idea to have him here any longer. We don't want to flip-out any of the passengers seeing this."

The doctor nodded in agreement. Getting a phone out of the large pocket of his white jacket, he called for a gurney ASAP, and then he notified security. Twenty minutes later, Joel lay on a cold piece of steel in the morgue. The whirlpool had been drained, and neon yellow tape saying **"UNDER REPAIR"** was draped over temporary barricades that had been erected around it. Sidney Nugent was the head of security and he and Doctor Mallory had been talking until quarter to two in those dismal morning hours. Nugent had told the Captain about the dead body in the hot tub, letting him know he'd update him with any developments.

They were in the clinic and the morgue was in the back of the large room. Nugent had taken a picture of Joel's face, and he'd inserted the image into the ship's registry. There was a likeness of everyone on board in the program. In thirty seconds, the question over his identity was solved as a name popped up on the bottom of the screen. *Joel Rosario.* Nugent then checked to see if he had family members with him on the cruise. Coming up with zip, he wasn't done yet, pulling any information they had linked to the purchase of his ticket. A lot of businesses go on junkets, and he was relieved to find a connection. He was in the Blackmore Coalition out of Massachusetts, and there were nine members on the trip. Of course, there's just eight left to enjoy the rest of this wonderful voyage, and he didn't want to wake up the president of the Coalition at three in the morning, but there was no way out. It was the only option he had.

Back in the morgue, Doctor Mallory had rolled Joel into a refrigerated drawer. He was trying to imagine what killed him. Could it have been a stroke? He got back on the phone to security, requesting that they search through his cabin for medication of any kind. If they find anything, they must bring it to him at the clinic. Directly to him.

Between the sundrenched hours he'd spent on the lounge chair plus the many drinks he'd had with his cronies at the Sail Away, fifty-seven year old President Steve Boone was in a sleep so deep it was close to coma. The phone next to his bed rang endlessly, but it certainly wasn't enough to wake him up. Chief Nugent had sent one of his underlings to knock at his door. Of course, knocking hadn't been enough either. The young security guard was forced to pound on Mr. Boone's door so hard it shook in its frame. The ongoing ruckus finally broke through, and he got out of bed and answered the door.

"I'm so sorry Mr. Boone, but there has been a tragedy. It's important that you come with me to the clinic and talk to Doctor Mallory."

"Alright, alright. Give me a second to get dressed, and I'll meet you in the corridor," and the President closed the door.

Steve Boone clumsily put on a hodge-podge of miss-matched items. He had on a Hawaiian shirt with the silk black pants that were supposed to be part of a formal suit. Oblivious to everything, he stepped out into the corridor behind the guard, and he had remained half-asleep.

"Thank-you for coming, Mr. Boone." Doctor Mallory had a solemn expression on his face as he held out his hand. The two men shook hands. "I'm sorry for your loss, especially since he was someone you worked with.

I know this is very difficult, but I need the necessary identification. I'd also like to know if you have any idea what Mr. Rosario had been doing last night, and did he have any physical problems that might be responsible for his demise?"

Boone had leaned back against the counter. He remained mute, and he was shaking his head for a minute or two until he found his voice.

"Thank-you, Doctor for your careful professionalism under the circumstances. Perhaps we should take care of the worst of it first. If it's not Joel, we can stop wasting our time. I assume his body is in the morgue? The ID may put nightmares in my head forever, but I should probably get it over with."

Doctor Mallory walked him into the small room designated as the morgue, and he pulled out the drawer. The President looked down at a grey memory of a man he had just laughed and drank with the night before. Giving Mallory a nod, Boone abruptly left the windowless chamber, trying very hard not to puke. Stopping next to the entrance of the clinic, he slumped against the wall, and the doctor came over and put his hand on his shoulder for a second and then he backed away. He still had those other questions that really needed to be answered.

"Again, I'm sorry things worked out like this, but I have to ask you for a little bit more information about Mr. Rosario. I'm hoping you can draw on your own personal knowledge about him. Was he sick? Did he eat or drink something last night he might have had an allergic reaction to?"

President Boone sighed, and his next breath was drawn very deep in his lungs. "No. As far as I know, Joel wasn't sick. He had a great day and great night. I left our get-together at the Sail Away around ten. He'd been the last in our party to have the stamina to keep on forever it seemed. He was telling a joke when I left, and he looked healthy as a horse. He'd had surgery on his heart last year, but I don't know about the particulars. I'm not sure if there were restrictions on his diet or not. You're the MD. You probably already know that anyone over forty isn't supposed to put anything down their mouths but water and grass, and that green stuff better be organic," and he chuckled very softly. It seemed the man was tempered by shock. Before Doctor Mallory could answer him, a security guard burst into the clinic holding plastic pill bottles in his hand.

"Excuse me, Mr. Boone," Doctor Mallory said, as the uniformed man dropped the bottles into his hands. He instantly read the ingredients, and it was clear that all three medicines had been prescribed for a heart condition. A pretty dangerous one at that.

"Well, now it seems that Joel was living on the edge; enjoying his vacation a bit too much. What these bottles in my hand are telling me is that his indulgences could have been his downfall. I'm guessing he ate a heavy dinner and he kept on drinking way too much liquor, and it's possible he topped all of that with some kind of aerobics exercise…or maybe the hot water in the whirlpool triggered the catastrophic event. I'm not positive, but it certainly looks like he died from a heart attack."

Steven Boone went back to his cabin feeling bad. But not *that* bad, and he went back to sleep in two shakes of lamb's tail. He'd tell the rest of the Blackmore contingent after he wakes up again later in the morning. Doctor Mallory called the Captain again and told him his assessment, and Captain Walker got off the line with the doctor. He called the central offices of Carnelian on an emergency number open twenty-four hours a day, and his advice to them was to keep it quiet. There was no reason to upset everyone else on the cruise, or end their vacations, and it would be a financial drain on the line. Getting off the phone to the main office, who had agreed with his opinion, he called Chief Nugent and ordered him into his office. The corpse would remain cold and forgotten and it would stay that way until they got back to Los Angeles. Captain Walker wasn't worried about how the rest of the lawyers in the Blackmore Coalition were going to feel about the death. Under the circumstances, they would appreciate the rest of their time on the ship and try hard not to mull over the death of their coworker.

6:35PM Saturday December 30th, 2006 Carnelian Caprice

Congregating at a large table on the promenade, the lawyers from Blackmore commiserated. Eric Adler had stepped away from the table to gaze out at the horizon. The setting sun was underlining some cumulous clouds, and normally the sight would calm him, however it didn't have any effect on Adler's current mood. He'd been getting to know Joel. The news of his death had been depressing since he thought their budding relationship was going to evolve into a real friendship. The last time he'd seen the man, he'd been nuzzling up to an older women. He'd been on his cougar hunt. Eric had no idea who the good-looking red head he was flirting with was, but it looked as if Joel had been in his glory right before the end.

2:35PM Sunday December 31st, 2006 Carnelian Caprice

Vera Adler was in her suite on deck eight, and she was unzipping a suitcase she'd previously tossed into the closet. There would be a lot of New Year's Eve celebrations throughout the ship, and she could use the holiday as another backdrop. But she needed more camouflage. Hadn't decided whether or not she'd change her name, and that was going to be a last minute choice. The opened bag on the bed was empty, and she flung it over her shoulder with frustration. Vera unlatched the next one on the pile, and she exhaled. There it was, curled up in the corner of the bag like a sleeping Chihuahua. It was a wig made with long blonde hair.

She'd seen it in the window of a beauty salon as she walked along main-street many weeks ago. Looking so real, she'd entered the business and bought it; a future prop in her upcoming assaults. And she molted. Her burgundy hair was tucked away in a professional cap, thin and tight, and she aligned the wig to be centered correctly on her head. Taking a slip of a dress out of the small closet, she stepped into it and wriggled it over her bony hips. There was a revealing seam starting at her belly button. She found the necessary patience to clip the endless run of metal hooks of it together. Done, she sat down on the edge of the bed and wriggled her feet into a pair of six inch black heels. Checking herself out in the full-length mirror, she wanted to make sure the rear was keeping up with the front. Satisfied, Vera was telegraphing exactly what she wanted the world to think she was offering.

But her plans were fluid. The prize she would be trolling for was not. She knew exactly what she wanted, and that certainty was made from ice.

Frozen harder than that, and it was encrusted with blood. Opening the top drawer of the bureau next to the bed, she took out a pair of handcuffs with jewels on them and she dropped them in her purse. Snapping it close, Vera was done. She was content in her latest disguise, and she was optimistic that things were going to veer in her direction, and that they would fall under her dark finesse.

In the daily list of happenings on the ship that was always left in the plastic holder on the wall next her cabin door the night before, she'd noticed a wine tasting on deck six at four that afternoon. She was intrigued. She knew that Charles Penny, one of the lawyers in the Blackmore firm, was a wine connoisseur. Sparkling white wines would be highlighted, and the Carnelian Line hoped that those going to the event would also buy bottles of champagne. New Years was a good inducement for people to pop the corks from their newly bought bottles of champagne while they watched the fireworks that were scheduled to go off at the aft of the ship at midnight. Vera had a good instinct that Mr. Penny was going to be at that tasting, and she was hoping to entice him into a more personal meeting with her later on. Or perhaps in the early morning hours of the brand new year.

Her forecast was fulfilled, and Rita Quinn and Charles Penny sat at a table next to the pool while the announcer who'd been on a TV series in the late sixties as a member of a fake rock-band called the Monkeys orchestrated a guessing game. A waiter wearing a tux with a white napkin over his forearm was moving from one table to the next, freely pouring imported champagne into the fluted glasses of the audience. Charles loved white wine and blondes, and he was drawn to Rita's luxurious hair. Vera's well-executed flirtation had hooked him deep, and her age had not skewed the deal in the slightest. Artfully opening her purse to give him one of her business cards, he was greeted with the sight of her jeweled handcuffs. This carefully inserted jolt of mystery had channeled his interest away from the taste of the wine and closer to eroticism, and brand new flavor in their ongoing flirtation.

"The last one I drank was the best so far. What do you think, Charles?"

Rita slid a business card over to him high-lightening the name of her enterprise. ***"Designing your World"***. Miss Quinn was a home-decorator, or at least Vera wanted Charles Penny to think she was.

"I'm not sure, my dear. It was a bit too sweet for me, but here comes another one. Let's see how you feel about this one."

Rita sipped the wine, and giggled.

"Oh, you're right. Of course, you are! This one has to be the star of this entire tasting...you know, I think I'm getting woozy. Maybe I should nibble on some more cheese and crackers, or something." Smiling entrancingly over at Charles like a pitcher plant, she wanted him to fly in on her charms on his own.

So far, they'd had four 'tastes', and each one was three to four ounces of wine. Charles himself was getting tipsy, and he laughed in commiseration.

"I'm afraid I'm getting lightheaded too. Perhaps we should eat something and stop drinking for a while. Oh, and have you made up your mind about where you're going to go to ring in the New Year tonight?"

Rita wore no wedding ring on her left hand. There wasn't even a blemish on her skin indicating she could have taken it off just hours ago. That was a good sign for Charles.

"Well, I'm in a group of ladies from Monterey. We got ten percent off this trip! There's going to be a celebratory dinner tonight. I can't remember what it's about, but I *should* be there anyway. I'll be free as a bird after nine-thirty or so."

"Would you like to meet me later at the stern at that big open dance floor? I'll buy us a bottle of the tasty wine you picked out, and we can drink some of it and watch the fireworks at midnight. Does that sound feasible?"

Vera Adler dripped her 'yes' in honey, and she sent it over in a hypnotizing smile to seal the deal.

After watching the fireworks, Rita followed him along the carpeted corridor to his cabin. At thirty-eight, his mouse-brown hair shouldn't be so sparse. At least he cut it well. Wearing a long sleeved blue shirt tucked into a pair a khakis, he had fifteen hundred dollar loafers poking out from the hem of those pants. They'd drank the entire bottle of the champagne during the display, and Charles had invited her to his cabin for some fireworks of his own. Hot and bothered, Vera was looking forwards to it. Slipping his card through the slot, they entered his three room suite, slightly larger than hers. She sidled over to the bar, and two glass decanters were standing in wooden braces to avoid being broken in a rough seas. The golden liquid in one of them had to be brandy, and she poured two double shots of it into the glasses she'd slipped off a bracket above the bar. Stepping over to Charles, she gave him one of the glasses, and then she bent over and whispered in his ear…

"Do you know what you want in your life, sir? I don't think you do. It's time to let go, utterly and completely," and her free hand dropped to the bulge under his belt-buckle.

When Vera had met Charles at the fireworks, she'd brought along a larger bag. Tossing her brandy down her throat like water, she put the glass down and led him to the bedroom, still stroking his erection. Her larger bag was over her shoulder, and when they reached the bed, she dropped it on the satin comforter, instantly removing some of the items within.

"Oh, Rita, you have no idea how much I love letting go. Every day at work, I put myself into three piece suits and I don't want to put them on and do as I'm told. And…ah….that feels so good….and…and when I get to court I have to direct everything perfectly as if I'm the judge. Yet, I'm not….and…and…if I don't do it right, whoever is really in control could throw me under the bus. And I get yelled at by Boone, and…oh, Rita! I can't explain any of this right now. Where you're sending us doesn't have much to do with changing my screwed-up life style."

His breathing sped up, and he was scrabbling at the clasps running down the front opening of her dress. She grabbed his wrists and pulled his hands away.

"Hold your horses, Charles. You're in my court now, and you have to do more than relax. I'm ordering you to let go. Release it all, and give *me* all the power. I'm gonna put you on a ride you've never been on in your life."

Vera was swinging the sparkling handcuffs back and forth in her hand. Charles nodded with acceptance, eyes wide with excitement. Trusting a stranger wasn't something he would ever do, but Vera had short-circuited his logic with the tantalizing idea of sexual domination…and being half-soused was helpful too. That last double shot of brandy had cut the last link of a chain connecting him to self-preservation.

"Yeah! Let's go for it, girl. You have the reigns….and…and," but he was too distracted to end the sentence. Vera tore the clothes off his body with ferocity as if she was on fire. Charles hadn't seen the extra pairs of handcuffs on the corner of the bed, nor had he noticed the stretchy rubber tubes… or the lump of black vinyl. And leather things with metal studs. Vera had stayed in her black dress as she gave him oral sex, and Charles stretched out like a cat in ecstasy. Pausing, just for a sec, she reached up and gently locking a handcuff around one of his wrists. She was in the process of binding him up as her wandering tongue, lips and fingers made the process wonderful. He didn't want it to end.

When it was done, Charles was truly trussed up. Vera snatched her pile of unmentionables on the bed, and Rita giggled in delight. She disappeared into the bathroom.

Splayed out on bed by four sets of handcuffs, his wrists and ankles were firmly secured to the four bed legs by the long rubber tubes. She'd knotted those tubes to the other cuff that didn't hold a wrist or an ankle. The unbreakable rubber reached the bed posts on the floor, and Vera had tied them like a sailor. Mrs. Adler had needed to find cuffs that would fit the ankles of a normal adult male on the web. It had certainly been worth the effort. The vision she had for this project was a pleasurable one for the new and improved version of herself, and the cuffs were not all she'd ordered.

Closing the bathroom door behind her, she took off her dress and bra. Leaving her six inch heels and her crotch-less black panties on, Vera put on fingerless leather gloves with steel knobs on the knuckles, as well as a tight vinyl hood, covering her face completely. Her fake blonde hair poked out of the back of the hood, falling between her shoulders. Picking up a short leather crop with tassels with bits of metal at the ends, she went back to the bedroom.

Charles looked up at Vera's new appearance. Glossy blankness replaced her face. She stared at him through pin holes pierced through the mask, and all he could make out was a sudden flash of light reflecting off the wetness of her eyes. Vera was standing above him, and he looked at the studded black gloves on her hands…and the short whip she held. He started to get worried, with maybe a tinge of fear. And that was good. A good emotion to push him closer to the final release.

She slapped his leg with the crop *hard*. The metal nobs broke through his skin, and the countless small holes began to bleed. Wriggling onto the bed, Vera planted herself on him, knees pressed down on each side of his chest, and Charles heaved into her. Vera tightened and released the muscles of her vagina as she moved seamlessly along with him. No reason she couldn't have some fun on her twisted way to the inevitability end. Her body was heating up, and the hottest part of that warmth was focused between her legs. Things were reaching overload. Vera was about to fly over the rainbow with everything Eric had stolen from her in her marriage back in her hands. Looking down at the man she was conjoined with, she knew he was having a good time inside her body. She smiled and she stopped massaging her own breasts. The hidden viciousness coiled inside of her was suddenly free, and Vera leaned forwards and grabbed an oversized pillow nestled under the comforter as if it had been under the devil himself on his throne. And she pushed it over Charles's face, quickly changing the position of her hands to increase the pressure on his nose and mouth. It really looked like she'd done this kind of thing many times before.

And her sexual partner began to buck. He was trying to breath. His own mortal survival overwhelmed everything as he kept straining to save himself. Bouncing as high as he could in the length of his restraints, it was became a paralytic fit. His hysteria had sent Vera straight into an outer-this-world orgasm, and her pulsations slowly receded in harmony with her victim's increasing weakness. Of course, she had no intention of letting the pillow go until Charles had stopped moving completely. When that finally happened, she fell forwards on his sweat-drenched chest, feeling as if she'd gone along with him to the other side; a terrible allegory, considering the situation. Vera kept resting on her second trophy allowing herself a few minutes to get her bearings back. Filled with satisfaction, she wanted that contentment to stay inside of her forever, like it was an addicting drug.

After half-an-hour, she got up and showered, and put on her clothes. She looked at herself in the mirror and smirked. Rita Quinn's life was going to be a short one, and at that point, it was almost over. It was two in the morning, but she felt like she'd slept like a baby the whole night. Vera was rejuvenated by the slaughter, having given her newly born soulless vengeance free reign. Picking up her bag, she left the hood, the whip, the ties and the handcuffs behind. She even left one of Rita Quinn's business cards on the corner of the bed. Strolling out the cabin door on those six-inch heels, she swept silently away like poisonous smoke.

4:25PM Tuesday January 2nd, 2007 Carnelian Caprice

The Rock of Ages was a Broadway play performed on different nights on the ship's theatre; a fine diversion in the already abundantly stuffed vacation package. It was Tuesday night, and the show would start at eight. Passengers who'd seen it were impressed. How did the Carnelian Line make the show so professional?

Actors and the stagehands don't get to the theater until six. Between performances, the place was empty. Three times a week, housekeeping had two workers go there and vacuum and dust and clean the entire theatre. Up and down the aisles and the seats, and even the stage. And behind the stage where gadgetry is used during the production itself. Floe had been ordered to the theatre for one of the weekly cleanups, and she was sweeping the floor behind the second curtain when she noticed a paper cup sitting on a coil of rope nearby. She stepped over to toss it in her rolling garbage pail, and she was moving fast, worried they wouldn't have enough time to be done before the players got there in fifteen minutes. Tripping over Garret Layer's dress shoe that was poking out from beneath the curtain, instantly erased her concern.

Vera used a sand bag as homicidal ballast, and it landed on his head with precision. Floe pushed the curtain back to look down at a pool of blood plus some weird stuff sitting in the blood itself. The pool was obviously leaking out of what was left of his head, and Floe turned into a wailing fire-alarm. Her co-worker was vacuuming the space in front of the stage itself, and he jumped up on the stage and ran over to her. Seeing the body, he hugged her and gently moved her away. With his phone appearing in his hand, he was also calling security.

The play was suddenly cancelled for problems in the electrical system, and management graciously told the dejected audience about another show added to the next night to support their reservations. The Carnelian Line itself and a very small amount of people on the ship really knew what was going on, and they wanted to continue to hide the truth. *Forever,* if possible. Sweep this bugbear under the carpet until the ship docks in LA, as it wasn't a good thing to panic people densely packed in the middle of the ocean.

Doctor Gaynor, Doctor Mallory, and Chief Sidney Nugent were standing around a metal table in the clinic on which Garret's body lay. Currently, the dead body between them had been utterly forgotten in a confusing and heated debate between the three of them. Captain Walker, leaning against the wall in the corner, remained silent as he watched the ongoing quarrel. They weren't sure what the right thing to do would be, and the correct action got more confusing as their mulled over their dwindling options.

"It's got to be a madman or madwoman running free on the ship," Chief Nugent said. "Three members of the Blackmore Coalition have been murdered. Got to be a vendetta against them, and right now, we don't know why. We don't know anything. It's possible..."

Doctor Mallory interrupted him, "And what am I supposed to do about these bodies!?!" Mallory looked over his shoulder and directed his next sentence towards Walker, "Captain, we only have three drawers in the morgue. If someone else gets murdered, where can I put them?"

Doctor Gaynor chimed in, "We're supposed to check his blood for poison or drugs or whatever, but we don't have a lab equipped to figure anything out, so we won't know for sure what killed him," and then he turned his attention to Officer Nugent. "Isn't there a way to decipher most of the chemical tests without using those huge machines anymore? Don't they have that new technology in hospitals dedicated to research?"

"Does any of that matter right now, Philip? Passengers are getting killed, and I don't have the resources nor the knowhow to find this maniac. More to the point, doc, if I can't do anything about it, what's looking pretty squirrely to us right now, is gonna probably get worse!" Nugent was shaking his head.

"Oh...I see. How they get slaughtered doesn't matter in the least? We'll scoop them up like yesterday's dinner and toss them in the corner of the clinic like rubbish. Oh yeah, and we'll remember to toss ice cubes on the growing heap. Sounds okay, Sidney. If physical evidence doesn't concern you, then you are hundred percent correct. You'll never figure out anything."

The medical man and the security officer stared at each other with irritation. Nugent was about to wade back into the fray, but Captain Walker ended their bickering.

"Stop it, both of you. What we can do or can't do is no longer a theoretical detail to argue about. We need to quickly decide on the best action in all respects. Sidney, I hate to mention it, but you're going to have to alert the rest of the members of the firm about the ongoing threat. Wait a minute, there's another call coming in for you, and it seems you must pick it up *right now*."

Nugent answered the transmission on the radio clipped to his belt. Everyone in the room stopped talking, and they all watched Chief Nugent go white listening to the latest news. Things had gotten worse. Much worse.

"Yeah….yes, ah ha. Alright. No, don't call a medic or a doctor. Bring them both to the clinic, *and don't say a thing*. If anyone asks you a question, tell them they are too drunk and you're helping them to their cabins."

They'd had dinner with the group, and then Victor Tillman and Robert Cameron had gone off to play a game of chess. As soon as they sat down at the table, a hostess glided over wearing a name tag announcing her name was Yvette Payne. Asking them if they'd like something to drink, they told her to bring them a carafe of coffee. Yvette came back with what they wanted… and a little bit more. Playing for fifteen minutes, Robert had been gaining ground on the board before he passed out. Victor attempted to get help for him, but in the process of standing up, he only made it halfway out of his chair before he slumped back and lost consciousness as well.

Victor and Robert hadn't known the waitress didn't work for the ship, and Yvette Payne wasn't her real name, and that ignorance stopped their hearts. The lethal concoction Vera had swirled into their tasty brew had done its job exceptionally. A few minutes later, a middle-aged matron had walked past the murdered lawyers, and she'd assumed they were inebriated. Irritated, she called security to clean up the mess.

And then there were five. More bodies that didn't fit in the morgue anymore. They'd find space for them. They had to, and Captain Walker stayed calm. These ongoing tribulations couldn't overwhelm him as he began to calculate how he would save the cruise. Ordering the doctors to do whatever they could to give him any input on the murders, he then took Mallory to the side. He told him to get on the phone to the main kitchen, and clean out one of the smaller freezers…and no, they didn't need to know why. Tell them, you have the captain's say-so. They can call him if they want to. Sending the Chief of Security off to relay the terrifying update to the surviving members of the Blackmore Coalition, he also informed Nugent to tell them that there would now be security around them. The Carnelian Line would protect them.

The captain would also invite the president of the Blackmore Coalition to his office immediately and personally tell him the dreadful news. And he'd rectify the situation, and calm his fears. He'd find a way to hunt down the perpetrator; stop the bloody campaign before the serial-killer wiped out the rest of the coalition.

It was ten-thirty that night, when Steve Boone walked into Captain Walker's office. He was terrified. When another crew member knocked on his cabin door, he was wide awake. Things had changed dramatically since the last summoning he'd answered, and since it was fairly late, it must foretell something he does not want to hear.

President Boone shook the captain's hand, before sitting across from his desk. Walker told him about the casualties and the ongoing security they'd employ to save the rest of the members. In the middle of trying to reassure him by describing his next plan, Boone interrupted him.

"This has got to stop, Captain. We can't allow this lunatic to keep on running out of control, and I know your security on the Caprice doesn't have the right tools to handle an outbreak of this kind."

"Chief Nugent is our head of security, and you're right, sir. He never learned how to deal this kind of criminality. I was about to tell you that I was going to call the main office and insist they send out the kind of help we need. A well-vetted investigator as quickly as possible. I know he or she could tie the whole thing up, and the animal preying on us would be in the brig without any more bloodshed. In the meantime, armed men will be an unbreakable barrier for yourself and the rest of the men of the firm. You'll be taken care of."

"Your reaction to this situation is professional, Captain, and I thank-you for your own resolve in trying to stop it, but I have a different approach… that perhaps could be more expedient. Blackmore's base is in Massachusetts, and there's a good chance the source of these attacks comes from a nasty kernel out of someone's personal history. We generally deal with commercial law, but that doesn't mean we've never faced the violent side of things…I'm sorry, sir. Give me a moment." Boone took a handkerchief out of his pocket. He had to mop the sweat on his face, and his hand was shaking badly as he did so. "I have an ongoing relationship with the chief of police in Massachusetts, and I'm fairly sure I can get one of the most notoriously best detectives to fly out here and take care of things. His home state is coincidentally Massachusetts, and I'm sure the Chief will help us under these extraordinary circumstances…if you can accept my offer. I'll call him right now, if you okay it? With any luck, and it's time for us to have some, this individual could be helicoptering out here in a day or two."

Captain Walker assumed what President Boone had told him was a real option. The head of a powerful law firm can usually pull influential strings. The guy he wanted was certainly better than what Carnelian would have come up with, and he nodded to him.

"I bow to your judgment, sir. Please, make the call."

9:30AM Wednesday December 27th, 2006 Aspersion's Foil

Holly was naked, and she was inserting one foot into the leg hole of a one piece bathing suit, and after she got it on, she dusted the rest of her skin with baby powder to lessen the drag of neoprene. She was about to wriggle her body into a full-length wet suit, and dive into the eye of the gyre. The only individual able to withstand the hazards in the water around them, she would collect as much evidence as she could. Her sat-phone was on the top of one of the bureaus flanking the door of her suite on the Aspersion's Foil, and it had started to buzz. So far, just one of her legs was in the wetsuit. At that point, it was simpler to take her leg out and leave the flexible rubber in a pile on the floor. Since only a few people knew that number, she would always answer.

"Hello Holly. I don't mean to interrupt your endeavors out there, but something quite unpalatable is being cooked up in hell's kitchen, and extremely dangerous repercussions may evolve out of it, if we don't restrain it. Nip it in the bud. It's logical to ask you for help. It would only take you away from the main project for no more than a day. Possibly two."

"Hello Attison. I'm getting the feeling that when you call me these days, it's never a 'what's up' kind of response. Everything is in a non-stop disaster and sentimentality has flown right out the window."

"Let's be reasonable, my dear. The natural molecular order is off-whack, and things are racing out of control. It sounds like you're missing the old days in which you could put the puzzle back together with glue. Right now, there aren't many who could reclaim the prize, so no, I'm not calling you to gossip with you about your computer game or tell you I adore you," and the tinge of humor in his voice didn't naysay the gravity.

"Alright, alright. You have an unpleasant and crappy point. What or who do you want me to destroy?"

"His name is Wilfred Gorman with a PHD in geology. Years of experience in the field, something bad happened to him. It's possible one those insects bit him, but whatever it was, we have an upcoming problem. I know he's about to drive sixty-five miles north of Los Angeles to build a bomb in his friend's basement. Actually, I'm afraid he'll be working on more than one. This well-educated professor also knows *exactly* where the San Andreas Fault is, and he also knows about a cavern running next to the most unstable part of it. He wants to place those bombs in certain sections of the cavern, and then, using a remote control, he'd ignite them. The pressure waves from the explosions would almost certainly trigger the terrible earthquake everyone is hoping won't happen from the increasing tension building between the two tectonic plates. I'm afraid his own forecast is right, and I don't want a catastrophe like this one to happen. Do you?"

"Of course not. I'll take care of it, but I worry they could be attacked again out here, and I'm not sure if Keith can defend himself and everyone without me."

"I understand your apprehension, but relax. I know they can handle things until you get back. The next couple of days will leave them free from swarms of flies or weird weather or odd singularities of any kind. If I tell you that forecast, you should bet on it."

"Alright, Attison. I'm putting my traveling clothes on as we speak. I assume you've ordered a helicopter for me, so I won't call for it."

Attison sighed. Holly could have easily intuited his actions on the helicopter, but it's more likely she'd already known about it. Apparently, she knew him too well, and it was unsettling to have anyone peek under his cloak of concealment.

"The copter will land on the Foil in about fifteen minutes. I advise you to get ready and make your farewells".

10:45AM Saturday December 30th, 2006 The Cutaway

After one day in the infirmary, Wesley had perked up, and his previous seasickness had turned out to have been a boon. Stuck in his cabin, the swarm hadn't gotten to him, and the few winged soldiers left behind had missed him in the following hours he'd been walking around the ship. Currently, he and Keith were perched on stools in front of the counter in the lab on the lowest deck of the navy ship. Shoulder to shoulder, they peered into a small dish holding sea water, waiting for the murkiness to clear; waiting for the transformation. Soon enough it did, and they smiled even if it was too early to know for sure. Wesley picked up a slide and a dropper as the clarity did not actually mean a thing. Putting a drop of water on the slide, he swiveled around and slipped it under the microscope.

Holly had been gone for close to three days. Keith and Wesley had kept on working on halting the molecular mutations raging through the entire marine environment. They'd been going at it as if the house was on fire, and besides a few short breaks to get their breath, and brew another pot of coffee and wolf down some sandwiches, they just kept on. The odd happenstance linking the men together had been fortuitous. Wesley's innate creativity in quantum physics and bio-chemistry interweaved with Keith's ability to mold the material world with his mind was becoming a powerful combination. There wasn't another team out there that could crack this impossible nut any faster than they could. Be that as it may, they both wanted Holly to come back. She had different gifts of her own, and they believed she could help them get to the answer even faster.

The replacement crew had arrived in a transport the day before, and the new captain, navigator and communication officer relieved their counterparts. It was clear the few survivors couldn't do their jobs. Captain Moran and the other officers and crew men were gently urged to go back to the transport ship. They quietly agreed. Taking them back to the base for medical evaluation, the doctors there would treat them the best they could. Captain Russell Gates was the replacement, and he was courteous to Keith Fischer. He gave him full access on the Cutaway. It seemed that General Wyndham must have briefed him about the strange situation.

Of course, Holly had left right before she was about to dive, and Keith had to come up with an alternative. He'd gotten a remote-control submersible out of storage in the cargo bay, and he sent it into the contaminated water. They were on the bridge staring at a screen, and the feed was coming from the rotating cameras on the sub. Nothing of any interest appeared in the small floodlights beaming out of the small craft. They directing the vessel deeper. Zilch. The inky depths of the center of the gyre was empty. Opening the collection ports, Keith trapped water samples at different depths. Then he brought the sub back to the small canal inside the ship where they removed the containers holding the retrieved sea water. After that, they retreated to the lab, putting the new samples under the microscope, and then the much larger electron variety.

Keith didn't know much about of micro-biology, and it was Wesley's forte', but utter bafflement was planted on both of their faces as they looked into the lenses of the microscopes. Keith could remember pictures of molecules and atoms in the science books he'd had in high school, yet the geometric shapes he was staring down at were not the same. Connected together like an abstract painting, to Wesley, the normal phytoplankton and diatoms who lived on the light of the sun, and the algae responsible for photosynthesis on the surface of the sea weren't there. What was, did not have much to do with the word 'normal'. The particles had machinelike qualities; as if some gifted micro-designer in Asia had built them for a backdrop in a techno-music video. The infinitesimal mutation in the atomic fabric in the natural world was making him cringe. Keith had already dealt with some of the repercussions of it, and he knew this ongoing distortion wasn't going to go away. In fact, it would probably develop and multiply. Wesley was shaking his head, unable to say anything for a moment or two. The concepts he'd learned as a basic format were bouncing around in his head like super balls in a theoretical pin-ball machine that was replacing logic. When words did come out of him, they poured out like diarrhea in a spurt of adrenaline. He had to find the stake to send this molecular vampire back to the grave as fast as possible.

"Do you remember the embryonic cells Holly said were in stasis in this lab? Maybe we could use those stem cells? Any other biological material can't help us, but there's a possibility these adaptive cells would be able to interact, maybe twist the double helix on that tetrahedron DNA. You know…the rotaxane over there in the corner, the one that looked like a dumbbell. I know you can see it. A lot of those cells appear so mechanical. They look like nanomaterial, and I can't fathom how they could have ever been formed…."

After five more minutes of his scattered rambling, Wes finally sputtered out. They tried the stem cell idea. It didn't work. The artificial looking helix of the tetrahedron DNA latched onto those amorphous human cells like hungry sharks, swallowing them like wounded prey. Back to the drawing board, they went. Then he reversed the mutated force by interlocking it with the small amount of neutral material still left in the oxygen-deprived Pacific water. No go. And even if the stem cell idea had worked, it probably wouldn't have mattered. They'd likely revert to the wrongness after a short time of being 'right'. Keith and Wesley were praying for a miracle. What was alive on planet earth was all going to be blasted into distortion in short order, and they had to find a way to deflect this evolutionary disaster. Very shortly, they'd be up the creek without a paddle as the process of deformation would soon reach a tipping point. At that point, even God couldn't put the humpty-dumpty back together again.

Wesley was telling Keith about phytoplankton; they needed sunlight and oxygen to survive…they also needed minerals and vitamin B, nutrition usually driven to the surface by water plumes ascending from very deep water. Obviously, everything in the eye of the gyre had changed, and even though the rising columns were still riddled with matter, it was no longer material to build chlorophyll. And the final kicker for them was finding the inexplicable presence of radiation. Estimating the level of the radiation, they saw it got stronger the deeper they checked.

Ultimately, they agreed on a possible salvation. They would dissolve this poisonous chameleon by using filters. Large ones. In the beginning of their idea, they thought of a filament stretched across the frames of these filters, but they quickly realized it was conceptually impossible. The gravitational attraction between solids and liquids would screw-up the process. Instead, they foresaw just waves bombarding the water in a wide-ranging potential, *if they could find the right combination*. Then, they'd find a way to generate these important beams inside the frames of the filters themselves.

To defeat this caustic monster, they had to find the correct ratio to blend the necessary forces, but they weren't even sure if there really was a sweet spot like that to reach. The rub was finding it, and that rub was getting painful, wearing their minds and their bodies down.

Closer to a checkmate in this apocalyptic game, the pressure began migrainous, as Keith and Wesley had combined their efforts in this maddening race. They were elevated to a plateau, one more step higher on the ladder. In an experimental mockup arranged on a large table in the laboratory, they'd combined certain radio transmissions, UV light and ultra-low vibrations, and it looked promising. Wesley's mathematical applications and Keith's profound knowledge of electronics had been used in tandem, and their 'filter to be' was almost working correctly. Keith's crazy nest of circuitry surrounding a small dish holding the test water, did change the twisted particles back to normal, but it didn't stay that way. It kept reverting back to being wrong. Keith was fidgeting while Wesley stared into the eyepiece of the electron microscope, worried that what had happened before would happen again.

"Damn it!" Wesley said. "It's disintegrating again. The quantum size effect keeps on interfering with the electronic properties inherent in the particle size, and there's also something weird screwing with the neustonic polymer molecules. It's decaying the particles we just altered. God, Keith, this is getting ridiculous. We're so close, yet we might as well be on Mars for all the difference the end result turns out to be. It's making me fucking nuts!"

Keith wheeled over to him on the stool. The water in the Petrie dish was as clear as a mountain spring. He hadn't understood exactly what Wesley had just said, but he got the gist of it. The clear water won't stay that way. The unblemished water in the container would get grey and murky in about six hours, and the unstoppable fiend with long sharp fangs will come back smiling.

Wesley stood up, and stepped away. Keith looked into the microscope himself, and he saw none of the awful techno-looking molecules he remembered being there before, but he knew that Wes had made out a more subtle hint reappearing in the water.

"Come on Wes, cheer up. I mean, I know you're right. We are almost there. We'll get a solid connection real soon."

Wes ignored his upbeat remark. He stamped out of the lab, slamming the outside door as hard as he could. Keith groaned, knowing he had to follow him and calm him. He went outside, and stood next to his partner on the passageway.

"Leave me alone, Keith…and you're wrong. We aren't any closer. It's like I'm standing next to the Grand Canyon flapping my arms and it doesn't matter whether I flap them fifty times or fifty thousand, I'll never make it to the other side. The biomaterials, the nanoparticles involving double atoms, and the radiation and another electrical component are all mixed up in my head. A confounding equation. What we set up should work! It's should! We're just wasting our time, and there's no answer for any of it. *What the hell!*"

Clutching his mathematical notes in his hand, Wes was holding them over the rail. He was about to let them go. He wanted the pages to seesaw back and forth in the gentle wind, broken-winged doves to drown thirty feet below in the polluted water. A poetical moment in a graphic illustration of his final defeat.

Of course, his destructive childlike theatrics weren't going to take place. Keith's hand had closed over his, a tenth of a second before he released his notes. He was just as exasperated as Wesley was, but his reaction to high levels of stress was not the same. Keith had lived his entire life fighting the odds, and he'd never let go for hell or high water. Having taken the pages out of Wes's hand with gentle force, he quickly put them in his back pocket. He then grabbed Wesley by the shoulders, and turned him away from the rail.

"For God's sake, you have to accept our position, Wes! Things look pretty damned dim right now, my friend, but we have to fly straight across that canyon or get crushed on the valley floor in the attempt. I'm sorry, but we can't give up!"

"Let me go, you idiot. I told you to leave me alone. If you think we can now solve this fucking thing because you want that to be the right answer on the test, then we will hug and make-up, if not," and he forcefully pushed Keith away from him, "we should pick up our marbles, and go home."

Wesley shoved Keith so hard, he stumbled right into the rail. Quickly getting his balance back, he put his palm squarely on Wesley's chest, propelling him backwards five feet. Soothing his friend was not working, and it seemed they were about to start punching each other instead.

"*I won't and you can't!* It might look impossible right now, but the situation we were in from the beginning has remained the same. We have to get on top on this problem. There's no one else but us. We have no choice; we have to keep going, Wesley. *There's nobody else out there!!*"

Thirty seconds of silence reigned besides the faint susurrus of ocean water slapping against the side of the Cutaway. Wesley stared at Keith, and his lips had compressed to a thin line, right hand clenched. The pressure was mounting between them, about to erupt into a flat-out fight. Suddenly, a soft voice blew their anger to the winds.

"But there is, Keith, there is. I'm back, and I'm not going anywhere until this definitive battle is won or lost."

Keith pivoted around with surprise, and Wesley's eyes widened for the same reason. Just eight feet away from them during the entire time they were there on the walkway, somehow they hadn't noticed her. Holly Donnelly looked relaxed, as if she'd been on a holiday in Belize, not defusing and then permanently derailing a madman. Intentionally oozing cool composure, she wanted to defuse things for them. She wanted to become safe harbor in their dejection.

When her mission was over and the threat neutralized, she got back to the center of the gyre as fast as she could. A Hienem Corporation copter had dropped her off on Aspersion's Foil thirty minutes ago. Changing out of her machine-greased pants and bloodied shirt and into some soft clean jeans, and a satin top, she put on a leather jacket, ready to get over to the Cutaway. She had to get over there. There wasn't much time left, and she'd get her breath back later on.

Keith and Wesley hadn't heard the helicopter, nor did they hear the Donzi engine as she transported herself over to the Cutaway. She knew they'd be in the lab, and when she saw them burst out onto the walkway, she'd simply crept on behind them. She'd watched them argue until it was time to step out of the shadows.

"When did you get here? Why didn't you radio ahead and give us a 'heads up'? How did it go…are you alright? It looks like you were vacationing or something, you look great," Keith blathered.

And of course, Wesley was talking to her too, "It's great to have you back here, Ms. Donnelly. Did you take care of that awful problem? Of course you did. It had to have been done, otherwise you wouldn't be there, would you? Listen, we've reached a brick wall, a brick wall made out of light and maybe…."

"*Both of you zip it!* I can answer only one question at a time."

They both shut-up. Then, staring over at Wesley, Keith began again.

"Okay, Holly, alright."

He came over and gave her a hug, and she hugged him back with a squeeze to let him know the simple gesture meant a lot. The psychic link between them had gotten emotional, and their ongoing independent swagger in front this frightening onslaught was a necessary act. But it was an act. Uneasiness haunted their hearts from the beginning, but as the unwanted ghost of worry flickered around inside their heads, the weight of its chains had gotten heavier with the arrival of dread. Neither would talk about this internal upgrade. And acknowledging a more dismal forecast wasn't going to help anything. More likely weaken them instead, and the passing hug was the limit of any remonstrative support they would accept under the circumstances. They could hear the apocalyptic timer counting down.

"Let's start again, alright. How did it go?" Keith said.

"Well, the lunatic is now in prison, and I've set up a barrier. If anyone else gets the same idea, they won't be able to get to the same place." Part of what Holly had said was a lie. The geologist was actually six feet under, however she didn't want to tell them about that. Not necessary to stir up more images of violence instantly ascribed to her right now.

"That's old news, guys. Where are we right now! How close are we getting? Can I help you? Do you need anything?"

"Well, we're crazy close, but we have a recurring problem. Can't quite make it over the top, and since you're a wild card in the mix, maybe you can come up with the unanswerable answer we can't find…and it would be nice if you can do that right away, okay? Keith smiled over at her, and Holly grinned right back.

Wesley told her the specifics about what they'd put into the filter they'd created. Keith didn't understand everything that was pouring out of him, and he sulkier thought Holly wouldn't get it either. But she did. Everything single drop of it. Like Wes was telling her how to play tic-tac-toe. As he went on, Keith took the lab notes out of his back pocket, and he gave them to Holly.

They all went back into the lab, and she looked through the microscopes, and then she stayed on the stool to speed-read Wesley's notes. Not saying anything, she didn't move for over an hour. Wesley and Keith leaned against the counter on the other side of the room, and just stared at her. They couldn't help themselves. Holly's eyes were closed, immune to their irritating curiosity, intent on finding the impossible.

Her eyes opened and she asked Keith to set up the same experiment all over again. She wouldn't talk about what could be a powerful insight that had come to her, afraid she'd jinx it or something. With this gut-response propelling her, Holly believed the dead end they were in may be over. Keith quickly placed another container with more of the tainted sea water in the middle of his multicolor collar of wires and circuitry. He nodded at Holly, flicking a switch to power the whole thing up, beginning another trial.

Holly had walked into the lab a little over an hour ago, and her companions thought she'd need hours to understand the situation before doing anything. They had been wrong. Hovering over the ongoing display, a bluish light had risen in her eyes. It seemed that Holly was about to put her own shoulder to this complex wheel, believing she was going to get it out of the proverbial ditch.

Having dosed the water with the combined rays for ten solid minutes, plus Holly's new mysterious influx, Wesley put the water on a slide and he guided the sample under the microscope. Holly and Keith watched as stress wrenched his shoulders to his ears. Wes stayed like that for the next five minutes, finally relaxing. He pushed away from the metal table and stood up, and he reached out and gently grasped Holly's hand and then he bowed. Dropping to his knees, he kissed her hand. In his mind, Holly must be forged from quicksilver as it appears she'd just solved the irresolvable.

"I don't know how you did it, but from what I can make out it's done! Considering the period of time I've watched it, and the particular kind of atoms in the water are still in the water, it seems you've given us the cure. If this water remains clear after six more hours, you two won't be able to tell me I'm wrong, and we can start manufacturing those screens." He'd sounded like he'd won the lotto, and Holly smiled.

"You know it didn't come to me as fast as I would have liked. Using concepts entrenched in western and eastern cultures to guide me into finding what I was looking for, I started to see the connection in the... *Wes, stop that and stand up! I won't talk to you until you stop this groveling.*" Holly took her hand away from him, and she waved him up off his knees. Keith was already laughing at him as Wes looked up at them like a simpleton. As if his overblown reaction was the correct one. Since he wanted to know what she was about to say, he got up and sat on one of the stools. Nodding curtly, Holly went on.

"We needed more clout in the wave distribution already there. Persistence in one form or another, and part of the final answer came to me in the image of Yin and Yang. I didn't have to do much. The hidden glitch you had to deal with was continuity. I realized I had to banish the cataclysmic reflection the intelligence behind all of this deformation was using. I *inferred* a repeating recharge in negative space. Like an ongoing and apparently not needed pounding of a boxer already out for the count, lying unconscious on the canvas in the middle of the ring. Our enemy found an escape hatch out of your one-punch attack. I just changed the interval. I don't think it can dodge the insertion of ongoing cross-fire anymore. Every two seconds, in a short span of a hundredth of a second, I put a stop on the radiance coming from the filter. The Nano-like mutations had been reviving by turning a slightly angled face in their oddly built composite against the ongoing wave. Now, they're being tricked over and over again for a blink, and in those tiny blanks, they don't have a care in the world. Blasting our wave attack in a machine-like repetition is probably going to be too much for it to adapt to…oh, and even better, the intermittent blackout can be technologically mimicked. Wes is right. We won't need my intervention to make the filters work correctly in the future. We'll just install the crazy stop and go control over the waves."

"I can certainly set up pulse modulators in a digital system to do exactly what you've just done in a couple of days," Keith said, and he had started to smile. "Holly, don't you have a machine shop in Bakersfield? It's not very far from the coast. Maybe we should use that factory to pour the frames we need, and it's possible we could use another section of the building to install the rest of the filters."

"I do have a factory there, and it sounds like a very good idea, Keith. We can certainly use part of the warehouse for the project. How many filters do you think we should make? How many do we need to alter the right about of water in the time we have left?"

"I'm not sure. None of us do. We also don't know whether this restored water would have a domino effect of the tainted stuff around it. If that works, we'd be in better shape."

Wesley sat down in front of the microscope again and he came back with a happy update, "The sample is still fine. Not turning to crap, and I don't think it's going too!" And Keith put his hand on Wesley's shoulder in support, while he kept on talking to Holly.

"When we know about that, we'll have a better idea about how many filters to build. We should probably go back to Aspersion's Foil and sit down with a computer model and estimate the best we can. We have nothing to gauge this project to, since nothing like this has ever been done before."

Twelve hours later, having checked one more time on the water sample to make sure it had remained normal, Wesley, Keith and Holly had reconvened at a dining room table in the Foil. Scattered on the glossy top of the table were notebooks, pencils, pens, a printer, a Mac PC, and three oversized coffee mugs. A steward appeared every half-an-hour to refill their cups, and that kept on going even though the meeting went on way past midnight. Sent into hyper-drive, they could feel the hot breath of the four horseman of the apocalypse feathering the backs of their necks, while the vibration from the hooves of their steeds got more substantial by the second.

Reading the last results, everyone was relieved. The changed water apparently could transform a proscribed amount of the corrupted sea water after it was reintroduced to the environment. To a point, losing its strength after thinning out farther with the rest of the water. They had to find a way to increase the outflow of the restored H2O back into the eye of the gyre. The larger the amount, the longer it could have this transformational ability. Perhaps if got bigger enough, it wouldn't dilute at all...just expand. Of course, these uneasy collaborators weren't sure about *anything*, gambling on the limited results garnered from their ongoing tests.

They decided to make twenty-two, and it wouldn't take long to fabricate them. Nevertheless, they reached an impasse. They weren't sure how they were going to get the sea water through the large metal frames and then back into the Pacific Ocean.

"Why don't we build a platform like the ones surrounding the oil-rigs off shore?" Wesley said.

"Ah huh. Well, it would certainly give us stability, but we don't have the time to construct anything like that," Keith said.

"Yeah, but we really don't have a lot of options to pick from, guys. Since we solved the impossibility for the filters, we should be able to iron this out too? Should be a snap."

As if she already knew the answer, as if they all did, the subtle insinuation behind her next words had a lot of weight. "It has to be dredges," and Holly's voice was soft.

Keith stared across the table at her, instantly understanding, and he chimed in, "The biggest ones out there. Look, I know most of the captains, and I wouldn't be at all surprised if you didn't know some of them yourself,

Holly. I think we can finagle ten or eleven boats to stop whatever they are doing and race out here. Some are up north in the Netherlands, others may be working on the China Sea…or off of Singapore. I know that most of these ships are on the other side of the world, and it's probably going to eat up a month to get them all here, but it's still the best option I can think of."

Holly lifted her coffee cup and sipped at it, before saying anything, and Wesley was looking over at her, not saying anything either. And then she broke the silence.

"I have a feeling things are already speeding up. Have you ever talked to the Captain of the Essayons? I flew over her a couple of weeks ago as she's at the commercial dock in Los Angeles. At least that ship is close. She's in the Army Corps of Engineers', but there's still a very good chance they'd let her help us."

It was way too late to call anyone on the phone, and Keith and Wesley had to have some shut-eye. It was time to call it a night.

Keith was back in the dining room pouring more coffee into the glaringly white bottom of another mug. It was ten in the morning, and he'd only had about six hours of sleep. Breakfast was set up from six to ten every morning for the crew and the guests on board, and he was also filling a plate with scrambled eggs and sausages off the buffet table. Holding his plate and cup, he went over to a table near the window. There was no one was around while he wolfed his food down. He had to charge himself up for what he was about to do. It was going to be a very important phone call. One of the ship's satellite phones was discreetly concealed in the wall behind one of the chairs at that table he'd picked out, and first he got out his own phone out of his pants pocket. In between putting another fork full of food into his mouth, he started to scroll through his contacts. When he saw Captain Stewart Martin's personal phone number, he wrote it down on a scrap of paper. He was a captain in the Army Corps of Engineers, and few years ago, he'd called him for help in rewiring the depth sounder on the Essayons and he'd formed a personal connection with him. Holly's off-handed mention of the Essayons triggered an uphill battle of his own to help round up these ships. Keith knew about that dredge's sister ship, the Yaquina. He was optimistic he could get both of these over-sized dredges into service for the cause. A great first step. Keith wanted to call Stewart on the Aspersion's Foil's phone, thinking that link would give him a little bit more 'oomph' in his upcoming pleas to the Captain. Might make the man more likely to believe his crazy story, even if it sounds like a fairy tale made up by a madman.

"Hello, Captain Martin. Long time, no see. I pray things have been going well for you, sir. Listen, I wish this call was only an invitation to come fishing with me, but it's not. Far from it, actually."

"Hi, Keith. Great to hear from you, and I feel the same way. It seems that things are really slipping right off the wheel. Last week we were supposed to dredge out a harbor in Santa Barbara, but some nut poured gas on the abandoned bicycle factory and set it on fire, and the factory was right on the beach there. We had to help douse the flames. Yup, it's getting weirder and weirder. What used to be alright doesn't stay that way anymore."

"Well, Stewart, believe it or not, I'm trying to put the overturned apple cart back on its legs, and my strange efforts have to do with a problem in the northern Pacific. Now, this is going to sound preposterous, but just hear me out...." But the Captain interrupted him.

"I already know about the whole thing. We'll get to your coordinates in five days. It makes no sense for us, or the Yaquina, to get there unless you have the filters, and you haven't even started production yet. So that five day estimate should work out. We'll just wait at the dock, until it's time to motor out there."

First surprised by Stewart's reaction, Keith quickly assumed Holly had called him before he woke up. And he felted jilted. *Does that woman ever sleep?*

"Alright," Keith said. "It seems as if someone else has got you on board with our plan, and I'm relieved. Look, I'm sort of in a bit of a hurry. Mind if I cut this call short? I'll get back to you as soon as I have more updates."

"I've got my own long list of duties too, my friend. Ah, if it weren't for these god-awful circumstances, seeing you again would have been a blast. Sayonara for now, Keith. See you on the flipside."

Putting the phone back in its cradle behind his head, Keith stared out at the empty dining room. Wesley and Holly coincidentally walked in through the entrance next to the buffet table, and they kept on going, disappearing onto the deck using a door on the other side of the room. He could hear them talking over wiring diagrams; how to incorporate everything inside the frames, and Keith got up and followed them. He wanted to thank Holly for their first connection. The first in the flotilla of dredges they are going to need, but all he got was an off-handed nod. Her conversation with Wes hadn't even burped. Maybe she hadn't heard him. The two of them went down the stairs to the loading platform. Holly looked over her shoulder, and told him they were going over to the Cutaway, and Keith just stood there and shook his head. He went back inside the dining room and poured himself more coffee and grabbed himself a croissant. He sat back down, and thought over who he'd call up next?

Cristobal Colon. He knew her captain too. Her home port was in the Netherlands, but the ship could be anywhere. It was going to take weeks to get her here. Maybe he'd be able to get Leiv Eriksson, her own sister ship, to come over too. Nothing he could do to speed it up, but start the ball rolling. Returning to the menu on his phone, he found Ian's cell number. This next appeal was going to be more difficult. He'd have to use every trick he had up his sleeve to inveigle the man into the voyage. And after that, assuming he'd found a way to get the man to believe him, he'd also have to ask Holly to *'persuade'* the owners of the dredge to believe in the importance of this mission, and it's good that Ms. Donnelly's appeals can get more intense than his own.

"Good morning, Captain Hanson. I hope the swells aren't too unsteady out there in the North Sea," Keith said.

"It's great to hear your voice, Keith! I've been waiting for your call over the past couple of days. We're on our way to you. We should be waving hello in about a week and half, depending on the wind and the currents."

Captain Ian Hanson's voice was conversational. He sounded composed, and Keith was baffled.

"I can't believe what you're saying! The whole crazy spiel I had in my head to tell you is no longer necessary. Why on earth would you pinpoint nowheresville in the middle of the Northern latitudes of the Pacific Ocean, and pull up your anchor and get over here? Did it look like an off-the-cuff lark? My head is spinning. I mean, I'm happy you're on your way, but you're going to have to explain this, please!"

Captain Hanson was laughing, knowing that Keith was still in the dark. He'd been told to enlighten him.

"Two months ago someone called us, and he wasn't screwing around. He had enough capital to change our schedules and our minds, but he was also honest. He explained the danger waiting for us all, and the owner and I agreed to take the risk, realizing the entire shebang is about to come straight off the hinges if we don't do something to stop it. Our lives and our riches became secondary in the wider scheme of things, especially if those things are in the balance anyway. He also paid a king's ransom for the trip, and that certainly didn't hurt the arrangement."

Keith hadn't told anyone about the coordinates. Neither had Holly. Only one other individual could have had that unattainable information. Someone who would send a dredge out to the center of the Trash Vortex in the Pacific.

"I don't suppose his name was Korybante, Attison Korybante, was it?

"That was it, you got it! I thought you knew him. Anyway, he was adamant about giving you the entire list, wanted you to know about the other dredges. They're on their way to the same place we're going. Considering their different home ports and where they'd been when he gave them the option to go, Mr. Korybante was careful about setting up their trips. He wanted all of us to get there at about the same time. Anyway, the list is right in front of me. I've added the names of the Captains too, since you'll be dealing with the lot of us. Well okay, Keith, here we go. Oh, wait a second. Want to write it down, or would it be easier if I just send the file over to you."

"Pop over it into my mail. Do you have the address?"

"Yup."

"Then that's the fastest, Ian."

Moments later, the list arrived on the small screen of his IPhone:

Essayons Captain Stewart Martin.
Yaquina Captain Richard Marks
Geopotes 15 Captain Dover Sodano
Orisant Captain Paul Herring
Ham 318 Captain John Donlin

Eagle 1 Captain Addie Corbin
Vasco Da Gama Captain Emanuel Constantine
Queen of the Netherlands Captain Suter Copenhaver
Breughel Captain Alexander Novick
Leiv Eriksson Captain Peter Kromer
Cristobal Colon Captain Ian Hanson

Having read the list, Keith was impressed. He really hadn't thought much about Attison; forgotten that he was a pretty powerful force moving around behind the curtains.

"Well, thanks, from the bottom of my heart. I gotta get off the line and digest what you've told me…and where you got it from. I'll call you back in a few minutes. We'll talk things over a little bit longer."

"If I don't dive into the ocean, you know I'll be here and nowhere else, sir."

Moving in slow-motion, Keith put the phone down on the table, and frowned. So it had been Attison. He had started the whole thing months ago, way before he and Holly had that kind of information, and he kept thinking about the conversation he'd had with Ian Hanson with more deliberation. He hadn't even met Holly when Attison went into gear, and he certainly hadn't met Attison Korybante face to face, either. So far, what Holly had told him about Attison and her unusual relationship with him had been circumspect and hesitant. Keith thought he was her legal guardian, and that had evolved into a real father-figure for her. He was also deeply involved in the Donnelly's financial empire, and Korybante had to have been a trustee in the Hienem Pharmaceutical Corporation. For all he knew, he might have been the Chairman of the Board, and it's possible he may still be there. His curiosity was peeked, and he pinpointed his power straight at Attison. Keith had the idea he could delve into him; that his gentle psychic probe would give him more knowledge about the man. And it didn't work. A pointless endeavor. There was so much interference surrounding his aura, it looked like white noise. There was no way he could refine his attempts at getting any closer, and he shrugged and gave up. Whoever or *whatever* Attison Korybante may be, Keith was extremely relieved that he was fighting on their side of the battle!

The chronological squeeze-play in getting the ships where they needed to be quickly, would not have happened without Attison's surreptitious intervention. Right now, almost all the dredges were in transit. Getting all the ducks in a row, they may still overcome the odds and actually win this war. Maybe.

Holly reappeared through the same door she'd walked out of minutes ago, and she walked briskly over to Keith's table.

"What are you working on, Kevin? It looks like you're not doing anything. Looks like you're sitting there like a bump on a log burping." She sat across from him, smiling.

"I've been trying to set up the dredges, and what an eye-opening surprise it has been! Oh, and by the way, why are you dredging up dead history using a name I no longer use? Attison may be able to travel through time, *but you don't need to.* Let's be in the moment and work on future plans, hmmm? I guess you don't remember the 'thanks' I gave you for setting up a dredge to come out here?"

"I'm sorry, *Keith,* no, I was distracted. I don't remember what you said. Tell it to me now, as you have my full attention. If you want Kevin to stay forgotten, forgotten he will remain. And what did you mean about Attison's time traveling?"

She hadn't heard him. She didn't know that a fleet of dredges was already in transit, and her thanks had been specious. Telling her the good news might restore part of her equilibrium, knowing that Attison's hidden support would give them a better chance. Holly's pale skin had whitened to alabaster over the past few days, and when he looked in the mirror that morning as he shaved, Keith could make out a tinge of paleness in his own face. And an uncomfortable feeling in his guts that wouldn't go away. Faith had always anchored him like a rock in the past, but it seemed it couldn't sustain him quite as well out here in the eye of the vortex.

Their concern over getting the ships out there in time was partially relieved, and they'd come up with the best weapon they could think of. Things were lining up okay, but their apprehension grew. Overwhelming an ecological tidal wave was a very large order. Natural laws kept bending farther and farther away from true, and their current path looked like it was already carved into stone; as if they had no way out. They didn't talk about the four horsemen galloping towards them or the awful possibility that the hooves of their plague-ridden nags may soon leave terminal bruising on their skin.

THE TWELVE DAYS OF CHRISTMAS

Day One: Christmas Day

6:55PM Monday December 25th, 2006 Cedar City, Utah

Kimberly Crail and her eight year old son, Kenneth, sat under their Christmas tree. Kimberly heard the timer, and she rushed off to get the blueberry muffins out of the oven. They had to cool down before she could took put icing on them, but she opened the fridge and took the bowl holding the creamy stuff out anyway. During this grace-period, she rinsed off the dishes and put them in the dishwasher, however in the middle of doing this simple task, she was startled by an awful howl coming from the living room.

Kenneth had wriggled out of the pile of wrapping paper to look out the picture window. Their house stood on a rise right next to a shopping center, so at first all he saw was a parking field linking Walmart, King Kullen and Best Buy together.

The Grebe was an aquatic bird, smaller than a Mallard Duck, and it had elegant black and white markings. Every fall, the Grebes would migrate to Mexico, and they flew over Utah to get there. What Kenneth was about to watch happen, had taken place before in the exact same way, in the exact same place, but not quite as severe.

The clouds were hanging low, very low. And they were reflecting the manmade light in the lot in a very duplicitous angle. Normally, the Grebes would spend the night on the surface of a pond or a lake, however, currently, a large flock was about to land on that asphalt parking field, tricked in by a mirage. Five thousand birds thought it was a calm glassy pond. The density of the huge flock dropped the amount of waning sunlight coming through the living room windows, and that sudden darkness had drawn Kenneth over.

He watched as hundreds of birds died when they hit the asphalt. There were some that were badly injured, and they were dealt a more painful exit. A percentage of them had stumbled through a landing their species was not created to handle, but it was a small amount. The tinge of yellow in the tall lights beaming down on the lot made the blood coming out of them black as pitch, and the macadam got darker and darker and…wetter.

Kimberly rushed into the room, and she too saw the devastation going on outside. She placed her hands over the boy's eyes, as if she could take back what he'd already seen, and he won't see anything else, and her heart broke. The devastating landing kept on for two more minutes.

Kimberly dropped Kenneth off at her sister's house in the suburbs of Cedar City, the next day. Kimberly's husband was a trucker, and he was out of town on a job, and there was no way Ken would be able to help with the volunteer work she was about to do. Her sister would baby-sit him for her. Lots of folks living near the shopping center had chipped in to help the fire department and the cops to clean up a fluttering field of dead and injured Grebes. 2,000 had died, and many others had broken wings or broken legs. And even the few unhurt remained earthbound as they had to have water to get airborne. Everyone worked on trying to transport the shocked survivors to the nearest waterway in vans and trucks, and there was a good chance they could heal in time to get away before the final freeze.

Kenneth began to have nightmares in which he was at the bottom of a well or he would watch the flock crash-land all over again, and again.

Day Two: Wren Day

11:00AM Tuesday December 26th, 2006 Binkley Cave, Indiana

Gary Roberson was twenty-eight, and Theresa Cayden was twenty-six, and they'd met in a gathering of cavers. The old moniker 'spelunker' was no longer used in modern vernacular. Their friendship blossomed into love, and they would marry in a church in Corydon in the spring. It was hard for Gary to picture her in a wedding dress, or for that matter, the vision of himself stuffed into a penguin suit. At five feet nine, he had brown hair and brown eyes a bit too close together. He wasn't ugly, just humdrum, and his stocky frame matched Theresa's perfectly. With a soft wilt in the curve of her eyelids, she appeared placid. She'd tied her blonde hair in a bun. It's very important to get it out of the way during the adventure they were about to go on. Hunter-orange helmets with halogen lights strapped tightly on their heads, they also wore five millimeter thick wetsuits plus gloves and thick soled Neoprene boots as they fearlessly plodded deeper into the unexplored section of the cavern. Any ingress of the thirty-five mile length of Binkley Cave was on private land, and Barry Packard was one of the three owners holding the land in question. He was also Gary's first cousin, and Packard had given him the green light; permission to explore the cave. At dawn, the love birds drove their Jeep down on a dirt trail disappearing into the woods behind Barry's house. After three bumpy miles, the track petered out next to a hole in the ground bracketed by blackberry bushes. The cavity gaped as thorny twisted vines and blocky pieces of granite that mimicked off-kilter teeth beckoned at them gloomily. Setting their backpacks and the rest of their equipment down, they quickly got ready for their adventure, oblivious to the creepiness of it. Most people would be queasy standing right next to that lipless black mouth sucking at the air, but they were experienced cavers. It was only easy access, and that was all.

They'd trekked almost four miles inside the cave. There were a lot of streams and rivers running through the entire cavern, and they'd just passed a large lake. They were slogging across a stream that was rushing towards a subterranean pool, and they were very happy the current was not too strong. Looking to the right, they guessed the confluence of the stream they were crossing was about eight hundred feet away, and since they didn't know how big the pond it was about to flow into was, they'd feel better when they got out of it on the other side.

"Gary, don't you remember what Jake told us last week about the bones?"

He was two feet in front of her, water mid-thigh on him while she pulled along in his wake.

"Of course I do. I just can't remember exactly where he said they were. I gotta' say it sounded crazy, going on and on about tons of skulls, peccary skulls and piles of long bones glued or stuck in a mud wall right over him. Wouldn't it be cool if we could map out a find like that?"

"They'd name one of these streams or lakes after us, or...."

But Theresa abruptly stopped talking. Her silence went on for three long seconds until a sky-high glass-breaking scream exploded out of her, rebounding off the rock walls with echoing strength. Gary wanted to put his hands over his ears, but instead he twisted around and grabbed her, and then he hugged her tight.

"What's wrong? What is it, sweetie? Tell me. Are you okay? Did you step on something?" He tried to speak to her calmly, and ease her fear. He had always been a down-to-earth kind of guy, but even so, a touch of her mysterious and sudden terror nevertheless crept through the thick Neoprene around his torso. Theresa had begun to hyperventilate.

"You didn't see it, did you? I've never seen anything like it before in my life! And there aren't any pictures in any book anywhere that looked like what I saw...and, and it moved like lightening and there were three saucer-sized eyes on the top of its head, and down there where it's always dark," she was pointing at her feet, "it shouldn't have eyes and it was all white. Tube-like things were coming out of its head and along its side and...and then it flipped over. I saw long teeth coming out of its mouth and if that thing got its mouth on me, I'd be ground up like fish food..."

"Wait, Terry, wait a minute," Gary wanted to anchor the woman he loved. "You gotta slow down and relax. You know we've pushed ourselves too hard today. It's possible you might not have seen what you thought you saw. Maybe it had been an odd reflection on the surface, and the sight fooled you. There's a good chance there's nothing out there."

Theresa wriggled out of his arms. She pushed him at the far side of the stream they were crossing with anger.

"Yeah. Uh-huh. Okay, Mr. Skeptic." She was shaking, "And I put psilocybin mushrooms in my omelet this morning too, so there's no problem at all. I'm just hallucinating everything. Shit. *I don't care what you think. We need to get out of here, right now! Get the hell out of this current.*" Terrie began to move as fast as she could, and she hooked one of her hands under one of Gary's backpack straps in order to drag him along with her.

"Alright, alright. Let go of me. I can make it on my own, but we're gonna have a serious talk when we get out of the water!"

Gary sped up, easily passing her. Getting to the other side, he got out. She was three feet away, and he waited impatiently for her to get there. He reached out and grabbed her hand, helping her climb over the uneven rocks at the edge of the water. She slipped on them anyway, at least, he thought she had. That had not been the case however.

A thick white tentacle had encircled her ankle with the clenching power of a boa constrictor, and it had instantly tightened on her like a vise. Gary lost his hold on her hand, and Theresa was violently dragged away straight towards the open water. Alarmed over the unwanted destination she was about to be deposited into at the end of her short voyage, he ran along the uneven surface next to the stream, trying to grab onto her again. He needed to stop this horrifying ride. Theresa had returned to hair-raising screams, as the nightmarish journey sped up even faster.

They both had utility belts around their waists holding tools anyone exploring the subterranean world needed to have to survive. One of the items carefully secured on her belt was a coil of rope. As Theresa bulleted down the channel, the bright beam from her helmet swept chaotically across the black surface of the water. Gary was frantic. Theresa really believed she was about to reach the possibly fatal deep water in thirty more seconds… until she jerked to a halt. So abruptly, her scream was cut off at the same time.

The coil of rope at her hip had luckily hooked on an outcropping of rock, yet whatever was twisted around her ankle hadn't quite given up on its dinner. It started to slowly crawl up her leg. Gary crouched down and grabbed her hand, sure he could pull her right of the water, but it didn't happen. Racing over ideas to save her, he let go of her hand and unclipped his own rope from the steel bracket on his belt. He looped it around a boulder behind him, and then he bent down again and snaked more of the same rope under her shoulders to anchor her more securely where she was. The current and the tenacity of whatever was pulling at her had become two opposing forces against the ropes holding her back. That ongoing tension had stretched her body lengthwise only inches beneath the surface of the water. Theresa's breathing had turned into a series of rapid puffing, and her eyes had bulged out, pupils zigzagging back and forth in absolute panic.

Gary snatched the knife strapped to his calf out of its sheaf. He stretched across the rocks, and gave himself as much length as he could...without falling into the water. Ignoring her incoherent mumblings, he angled the light on his helmet into the stream to make out the tentacle coiled around her left ankle. And it was creeping up higher on her leg. In desperation, he used the blade in a demonic fury, slicing at the mottled flesh as if he himself was a monster too. Stabbing and carving with gusto, blood blossomed out of the injuries he was inflicting. He was trying to cut through the tentacle itself, as the hold the entity had on her appeared unbreakable. Finally, his ongoing attack became bothersome to it, and it let go; sliding off into the blackness from whence it had come.

Gary lifted her out of the stream, and they hugged each other and sobbed. After fifteen minutes, the shock abated enough to let them think again, to consider what their next move should be in the long and short future cast. At first, it seemed they didn't have any evidence to support their ridiculous story until they both looked at the lower part of her injured leg. The thick wetsuit had been ripped off right below her left hip bone, exposing fifteen circular wounds on her skin. Besides the blood leaking out of them, there was also a brownish-green glop coagulated in some of the deeper gouges on her leg. That looked like physical proof, especially if a doctor saw the rings and then he'd send out some of that weird goo to a lab to be tested. Terrie felt sick to her stomach, and she wasn't sure whether it was just shock or if the poison had gotten into her bloodstream and that was the reason for it. Gary picked her up again and walked her back to the wider part of the cave. This time, even farther away from the lake. She was getting groggy, and Gary leaned her up against a boulder. Scrabbling through his backpack, he took out a bottle of water and some smelling salts. It had become extremely important for them to get the hell out of the cave since the shadows no longer looked like shadows, and they were afraid anything at all could suddenly come alive. Nevertheless, they still waited an entire hour on the uncomfortable rocky ground before she was stable enough for the trip out.

Gary supported her during what had turned out to be an escape. They had to re-cross the stream. There was no way to avoid it, and as they splashed along the air around them appeared to get darker, but nothing else interrupted their limping retreat. Their wish to find a discovery in the Binkley Cavern had certainly been answered, however the idea of linking their names to what had happened to them wasn't something they wanted anyone, including themselves to remember.

Day Three: St. John the Evangelist

3:30PM Wednesday December 27th, 2006 Portland, Ohio

Next door neighbors on Old State Road near the city hospital, Adam Vega and Wayne Morgan were spending the afternoon exploring the area on their bicycles. Adam was eleven, Wayne thirteen, and their vibrant curiosity had driven them up and down the alleyways and abandoned lots like jet fuel that powers the young. The weather report called a snow/rain event at dawn the next day, but that didn't mean a thing to them. At fifty degrees out with no wind to speak of, these were perfect conditions to scout things out. Even though they were only a mile and half away from their houses, the upkeep and the tidiness of the dwellings had suddenly fallen-off in a remarkable way.

Wayne's flaming red hair was pointing in every direction over his pale face, and Adam was a dark counterpoint to him with dark skin and glossy black hair. The two had stopped in front of an abandoned building foreclosed on years ago, windows and doors nailed over with sheets of plywood, but it wasn't the creepy old house holding their attention. Adam had heard a howling noise and he hadn't been sure where it had come from. When they both heard another strange outburst, Wayne turned around and looked a few feet behind him at a storm drain under a steel curb protected by a metal cover. The sound had to have come from that drain. Adam was backing up, and he was getting pale, yet Wayne's white cheeks were blushing in excitement. Not afraid of whatever was making those noises, he really wanted to see it face to face. The mysterious entity that was somewhere in the sewer tunnel had started up again. It sounded like it was keening for something it had lost an ululating howl. And after that faded, growls were intermixing with bubbles popping. Adam stared at his friend with anxiety painted on his features like a neon sign. He wanted to get on his bike and ride away, ride anywhere. Anywhere but there. Wayne looked back, oblivious to his friend's reaction. He dropped to his knees, and put his ear to the metal cover wanting to hear the ongoing sonata from hell more precisely.

"Come on, Wayne. Let's go. There's nobody at the park right now, and we could go to the hideaway and no one would see us. We could work on it…whad'ya think?"

"You're kidding, right? Don't you want to know what's down there? *This is so cool!* I can see handles on the wall inside there, and they're made out of metals," and he was pointing through the small rectangular opening just under the curb. "See. See them? There's no one around here either. We can pick this grate up and climb down and find out what this crazy thing is. I know you want to see it."

"*No, I don't!* It could be a rabid animal down there, and…and it might be poisonous. Nobody should go down there. You sound like you've lost your mind, and I think we should…"

Wayne was already lifting a corner of the iron grate up and out of the lower setting in the asphalt all by himself. Adam stopped talking, stunned his friend was about to go down there by himself! Then Wayne put his lower back against the metal curb and used his legs to push the grate farther out, able to make it into a feasible access even if it was a very small one. Good enough, if he can actually get through, and it really looked just fine.

He wasn't very big himself. Meanwhile, Adam was getting more and more upset.

"Wayne! Hey! Wait a minute. Let's be serious. You have to hold on… wait. We gotta talk about this for a minute, I mean, maybe we can go down there, but right now we don't have any flashlights. How can we see anything down there without a flashlight? How 'bout we come back tomorrow with the stuff we need. How 'bout that?"

Wayne had been peering down into the drain, and he stood up with concern on his face. Of course his friend was right; they had to have flashlights.

"Forget about tomorrow. We can go over to my house and borrow my Dad's flashlight out of the garage. We can get back here in five minutes. What about that?"

"Yeah…that sounds okay, but you know this drain isn't going anywhere. Maybe we should go to the park instead because it's empty right now. This place is always deserted, and we'd be able to go down here any time. We could come back here tomorrow."

Adam was trying to wheedle his buddy into getting out of there. He had no intention of going go down that drain, whether his friend invited him to do it right now, tomorrow, or next year. He was truly worried about Wayne. He was gonna' do it with him or without him, and he couldn't figure out why. Busily scouring his brain to come up with yet another excuse to stop him for a little bit longer, circumstance intervened. Adam hoped it was going to be enough to stop him, maybe even save his life.

A beat-up green Civic had stopped in the street right next to them, and the red headed driver lowered her window. It was Wayne's mother Glenda. Seeing her freewheeling son, she decided to stop and order him home. She wanted him to salt the driveway and the sidewalk as there was a storm coming. Wayne had to bike home, and then he was tied up with a long list of chores for the rest of the day.

It was after eleven, and Wayne was in bed, but he was too wired to sleep. He still needed to know what had been making those noises coming out of the storm drain, and he put his clothes back on again. His bedroom was on the first floor, and it was a snap for him to open the window, take out the screen and sneak out onto the yard without waking anybody up. He crept into the garage through the side door, and he picked up Dad's flashlight before quietly rolling his bicycle through the same door. Pedaling across the grass, he avoided the crunching salt crystals he'd thrown on the driveway that afternoon, and he vanished into the night like a ghost.

It would be easy to stifle his devilish curiosity. The answer waited for him a little over a mile away...under the road. Whatever had gotten under Wayne's skin, was starting to seem almost as unnatural as the sounds themselves. Why on earth would he want to climb down that storm drain alone in the middle of the night? His best friend's instinctual reaction to the hair raising howling was normal. He wanted to get away and stay away.

Dropping the bike on the sidewalk, Wayne stepped over to the drain. No one had noticed that he'd opened the grate, so it had stayed that way... waiting for him. Turning the flashlight on, he squeezed himself into the gap. He held the metal rungs that had been soldered to the cement wall of the drain during his trip into the sewer system of the city. He'd stuck the braided cord coming from the base of his father's flashlight between his teeth, since he had to use both hands while he climbed down thirty feet to the bottom. Hopping off the last rung, he stood in the middle of the circular drain and nothing greeted him there but silence. That didn't matter. Wayne had faith. He knew he'd meet this curious beast, and he started to wave the flashlight around. And he saw a tunnel, six feet in diameter, running east to west. It had to have been built to relieve any flooding by transporting the overflow away in a storm.

When the tiny hairs on the back of his neck stood up, Wayne suddenly wasn't very courageous anymore. He was about to climb back out of there, when he heard it. It was coming towards him in the tunnel, and it sounded as if it was traveling from a very long distance. Frightened, he jumped onto the ladder as fast as he could, but it hadn't been fast enough. The answer to his question had been loping along with an uncanny speed. Emerging into the drain itself, Wayne had only a second or two to decipher what it was, but that hadn't been close to enough time to be able to comprehend what was suppurating next to him on the concrete floor. For a moment, he glimpsed glistening scales, tentacles, and a beak hidden in twisting folds of flesh parroting those of an ocean faring squid until the light was violently knocked out of his hand. The flashlight shattered on the floor, and the forgotten sewer system was instantly sent back to its normal gloom. In the concealment, the monster tore at the young child with a hungry eagerness, and Wayne quickly passed out. He hadn't had to deal with the pain for long.

In only a few hours, dawn slithered in and it had begun sleeting. By noon, Adam was being pummeled by questions, repeated over and over by everyone. His whole family had congregated at his friend's house, and they'd brought him along. 'Where on earth is Wayne?' and the mantra went on and on like a broken record. He tried to tell them. He tried to tell them what he guessed could have happened, but of course they ignored his insight. And the nonsensical interrogation just kept on going until they heard knocking at the front door. Wayne's father found two cops standing on his stoop, staring solemnly at him.

"Are you Mr. Morgan, sir?"

"Yes, officer, yes, I am. What's going on? I called you guys three hours ago, so you must know where my son is by now! Tell me where he is!"

"I'm very sorry, sir. A passerby noticed a young child unconscious on the front yard of an abandoned house on Willow Lane about six blocks away from here. We've ordered an ambulance for him. He'd had…he'd… ah," the uniformed man paused, and then he gulped. He didn't want to go on, but he had no choice. "We assume he is your son, but it seems he has endured quite a lot of trauma. I would wait until he heals a little bit for the identification."

Adam raced off the kitchen chair, weaving around everyone in the room to bolt outside through the side door. He had to see his friend. He'd get there on his own…but forty feet down the street, he stopped. In his tracks. An ambulance, lights on and siren howling, zoomed past him in a grey curtain of frozen rain. After that, Wayne went back inside. He knew it was way too late for him to do anything.

Neither the doctors nor the detectives could explain what might have inflicted Wayne's injuries, nor could they find an antidote for the poison in his system. He died two days later, leaving Adam alone with his own conjecture over what really happened. Knowing that they'd found Wayne comatose on the frozen grass right in front of the empty building, he could not have climbed those rungs by himself, and Adam couldn't get rid of a particularly horrible speculation over how he had been tossed out of that storm drain.

Day Four: The Feast of the Holy Innocents

1:00AM Thursday December 28th, 2006 Montauk Point, New York

The young men sleeping in their cots in the Coast Guard Station at Montauk Point were awakened by an alarm coming out of an EPIRB on the Peconic at one in the morning. At one hundred and twenty feet in length, the Peconic was a commercial fishing boat with a crew of five, and they'd been off-shore fishing for cod when something went wrong. Getting the emergency call, those on duty had started up the engines of a cutter named The Nomad. She was their fastest rescue boat, barreling through just about anything to reach the destination at about thirty-five knots. The commander of the station had ordered a helicopter into the air for additional support. At coordinates 40' N by 68' W coming out of the radio beacon, the copter could get there faster than the Nomad. Having heard nothing on the radio from the wheel house, speed had become a priority. Normally, the captain of the Peconic could tell them about the disaster, but all they had was the signal. They had to assume the worst. In under two hours, the helicopter began to circle the location, but there was nothing there. They expanded their search, as crewman used heat-seeking binoculars to scour the heaving surface of the ocean below. After three hours, they had to go back to the coast to refuel, but they returned at dawn to keep on trying to locate the ship. The Nomad arrived at mid-morning. At that point, the future of the crew of the fishing boat was very bleak. Inching close to futility, they would soon have to give-up. The captain of the Nomad conferred with the pilot of the copter by VHF, and they'd agreed stop the search at 3:30PM.

Twenty minutes later, and twenty miles to the west, a trawler radioed to the Coast Guard that they'd seen the Peconic on their radar; even seen her out on the horizon as well. Of course, the missing ship hadn't been on any of their screen displays before, and they were baffled by its sudden appearance. As if she'd materialized out of thin air. Be that as it may, the captain and the navigator of the Mandela had heard about the emergency announcement from the Coast Guard the night before, so they'd charted a course straight towards the stricken boat. When the Mandela called the Nomad, they had revised their location of exactly where the Peconic currently was, and the Coast Guard told them they'd meet them there as soon as possible.

The helicopter was about to return for more fuel, however the aircraft had veered off her course for a few minutes to check out the state of the finally found lost ship. Hovering over the stricken Peconic, they signaled to the crew that help was minutes away. They got no response. And they didn't have any more time to hover. The pilot turned the copter home and on the radio, he told the Nomad that they hadn't seen anyone on deck. It looked as if the ship was adrift. No one heard him say *'and it looked like a ghost ship'* since he'd whispered that under his breath.

Nomad had reached the Peconic well before the trawler did, and the captain radioed back to the Mandela. They didn't need their help anymore, and they were happy for their help so far. The trawler swung around and returned to work.

Brian Casio was the captain of the Nomad, and he would stay on board with the navigator. He would send the rest of his crew onto the fishing boat to reconnoiter. At nineteen, Niles was the youngest of the group, and he'd only been in the Coast Guard for six months. He didn't have a lot of experience to draw from. He did have the gift to sense things with a higher degree than most, and when he jumped onto the deck of the Peconic, he instantly noticed the boards under his feet. They were grey. And the metal in the rigging over his head was rusted, and the rest of it was rotten. It looked like the boat had been out at sea for years, but he knew that wasn't true. He was getting nervous. Maybe more than nervous, yet telling the others about his intuitions hadn't always worked out very well…

"This whole place doesn't seem right, guys. Maybe we shouldn't split up our search yet. Stay together as a team until we go through the entire ship?" Niles was trying to sound reasonable and professional.

Hamilton was their leader, and he'd snapped around and stared at him and then he laughed.

"Look to your right hip, my boy. Think about that, okay? Your little friend there should make anything on this old scow scatter if they see you coming." Then gestured at the closest hatch, having crushed Nile's suggestion with ego-driven relish. "Get going, get inside. One of you to the bow, the other check the sleeping quarters. I'm going to the wheel house. We'll regroup back out here as soon as we've checked it out."

With a grim expression on his face, Nile nodded as Gary, the other member of the team, stepped right past him and through the hatch into the tack room. He kept on going into the small galley and mess hall, and Nile followed him in. He had no choice but to climb some very steep stairs to the bunk room. He didn't hear anything but water lapping against the side of the ship, and the occasional creak of wood or steel. It has stayed calm for the past two days, very good news for the Peconic. Without a crew to stabilize her, she could have easily capsized.

Niles's uneasiness grew into full-blown apprehension. Was he really on a ghost ship? So far, no one had a clue what had taken place on this vessel, or why she was apparently deserted. He'd looked inside both of the two bunk rooms, and they'd been empty. Going up the stairs, he heard knocking coming from one of the cabins, and he climbed back down. He walked along the short passage until he stood between the two doors, not sure which cabin the sound had emanated from. He slowly opened the door on the port side of the ship. There's a fifty-fifty chance he'd be right on the first try. Not wanting his mates thinking he was a fraidy-cat, he didn't want to ask them for help, so his heart was pounding with apprehension. The one he'd picked seemed to be empty, and he was leaving to re-inspect the other cabin when he heard some weird wheezing. It was coming from the tall chest that was anchored to the wall in the corner of the room. Taking his gun out of the holster, he released the safety, and raised it chest high and then he quietly stepped over to the chest.

Hooking his left hand around both knobs of the two doors, he wrenched them open with powerful slam. There was a scrawny guy coiled up in there. He sprang at Niles like a snake, or a jack-in-box; crazy fast, and he was smiling as he plunged a fillet knife into his shoulder. Niles hadn't had time to defend himself, all he could do was to try to push this lunatic away from him. He wasn't fast enough. This glassy-eyed monster had already taken the very sharp blade out of his shoulder, and then re-angled his knife in a blur. He would cut Nile's throat as if he was nothing but a piece of bait. And he would have done it too, if Hamilton hadn't showed up. He'd been standing in the doorway, and he'd sent a bullet into the man's forehead, saving Nile's life by a hair.

George Neely had been the only one on the Peconic. Putting his body through a barrage of tests during his autopsy, they tried to figure out why he'd acted the way he had during the last moments of his life; hoping for a clue about what happened to the rest of the crew. It would have been nice if they'd found an exotic virus, or maybe an unusual poison in his cells, but all they found was lots of magnesium in his blood, and under the electron-microscope the platelets in his blood were deformed. With no other bodies to dissect, the evidence was perplexing and undecipherable. The mystery could not be solved.

Why the EPIRB was floating miles away from where the Peconic had really been, or why she was so weathered, were two more questions on the long list of puzzles that can't be answered. And the entire thing was heart-breaking.

The fuel tanks of the Peconic had been empty, and Captain Casio had ordered a tug boat to drag it back to land. Meanwhile, he felt dejected. Getting off the radio, he went out on the deck of the Nomad, and he gazed out to a limitless horizon, not wanting to think about the five families of the lost fishermen. After years of recues under his belt, this one didn't sit well in his mind, and it's possible it might take the prize as the most egregious of them all.

Day Five: St. Thomas Becket

9:45AM Friday **December 29th, 2006** **Wheeling, South Carolina**

Caleb Mulligan had been working for the Miller family for over ten years. They'd left for a vacation in Florida for over a week, and he'd been taking care of their four acre estate on Hyatt Road during their absence. After a long day, he relaxed in his cottage, imagining the family sipping cocktails on their veranda, watching the sun set behind the sycamore trees on the other side of Ravine Lake. At times, these visions would expand, and his eyes would close for at least half an hour.

The Millers go to Key Largo every year for their vacation, and Caleb always wanted to spruce the whole place up before they got back. This year, he'd found a way to get that done without losing too much energy.

Caleb was in his sixties, and he wasn't much to write home a lot. His grey hair was long and unkempt, and he had small brown eyes and a small mouth with diminutive lips. He'd never had a shit-eating smile on his face ever, and he didn't smile much anyway. Living alone in the guest cottage six hundred feet away from the main house, that morning he'd put a brown bamboo hat with an oversized brim on his head, and then he covered the rest of his lumpy body with overalls. As he began to diligently weed the flower beds near the front door, Caleb mulled over the list of things he wanted to get done before they would arrive later on.

A day or two before the Millers had left for Florida, Caleb had been drawn to the old well in the back yard. Town water is now piped to the property, but for some unknown reason he was attracted to the ground water still sloshing at the bottom of the well. The color of it, green as the moss on the well's stone walls, had gotten even more intense. And there was a different smell wafting up. He thought the well-water had to be infused with nutrition, and instead of using the garden hose, Caleb had been watering all the plants around the house with well water. He'd even started to drink it himself!

Honoring their grandparents, the Millers had left the old wooden bucket in the well, and it still cranks up and down and scoops up the water by a new nylon rope they'd installed. The old bucket had held on. It didn't even leak. Everyone in the family were way too flustered right before their departure to notice Caleb's watering system. Jim and Melanie and their two sons hadn't seen him roll the bucket up and down endlessly, as if the house was on fire or something. In reality, there was nothing wrong with the house itself. Ten years ago, they'd had an infestation of termites, but they took care of that. After that, they contracted a commercial company to apply a coat of yellow paint with preservative in it on all the outside wood, and then a layer of lacquer. Their three story colonial shone with an inviting glow. Boston ivy had grown over the shingles on the south side of the building, however the vine's normal endless creep had stopped fifteen feet off the ground. Whether it had been a chemical change in the pigment of the paint, or maybe there was different glue under the tarpaper, but whatever it was had retarded the vines progress. Coincidentally adding another layer of coziness in the visual appeal of the house. However, quite a lot has changed since the family had left for Florida, and Caleb was happy about all of it. For one thing, the Boston ivy had wildly broken out of its previous boundaries, climbing three feet higher in only four days. More problematically, Caleb had kept on drinking more of the well water, and his own internal boundaries no longer held him back. What had always been a muted disposition was now free from any constraints, and he too was getting wild with the rest of the greenery.

Driving in, the kids were hopping up and down like rabbits in the back seat, and Jim and Melanie ignored them as he parked the car in front of the house. They'd only been gone for seven days, but the shrubbery and the plantings around their front door was telling them a different tale. They all sat there, stunned by what they saw. The most baffling sight was the ivy. It had made it to the third floor of the house, and there was even a tendril slithering into the rain gutter...and it had also grown sideways. It was almost at the front door! Caleb stood on their stoop, and he was holding a bouquet of flowers in his hands. After minute or two, the Millers got it together, and they opened the car doors and piled out.

"Caleb, you need to explain this! It looks like some kind of weird radiation had beamed in here. Nothing can grow that fast, nothing!" Of course, Jim's amazement had blocked out his politeness, and 'Hellos' had been sent out to pasture.

"Well, you're right, that's true in most cases, sir. Oh, here are your flowers. I think they are exceptional. Usually we can't grow them this time of year," and Caleb graciously bowed, giving the bouquet to Melanie, who was standing next to her husband. She accepted the flowers, but her numb fingers were dropping snapdragons and mums on the flagstones. She couldn't accept what had happened, what had expanded all around her house.

"Please, Caleb! Tell us what happened? What is this?" Melanie pleaded to him.

"Okay, okay, you guys. You've got to relax, it's really no big deal. I've been watering the plants around the house with well water over the past two weeks. I had a really good feeling it was gonna to be a wonderful jolt for them. A lot better than town water, that's for sure. I wanted things to bloom and grow for you, so I could surprise you when you got back from your vacation."

"*Surprise* doesn't cover it, Caleb. It's closer to dumbstruck, or maybe flattened. I think we should check out the well together, right now. It seems I'm going to have to have a better handle on things from now on. Oh, and by the way, we're going back to town water for the moment, alright?" Jim said.

Caleb didn't understand. They should be thrilled by these results, nevertheless he obediently followed his boss around the side of the house. The rest of the family went inside. Jim drilled him with questions for another half-a-hour, and he kept staring into the old well shaft. Unable to understand any of his caretaker's answers, he wasn't happy about the uncanny growth. But he was tired from the long trip. He wanted to put his feet up and stretch out. Giving Caleb a stern warning not use anymore of well water, he retreated into the house, assuming he would deal with this crazy stuff tomorrow after he got some rest.

No one wanted to talk about what they'd seen outside. They all wanted a peaceful night to recharge. After a simple dinner of spaghetti and meatballs with ice-cream for dessert, Jim and Melanie sent the boys to bed, before dragging themselves up the stairs to their own bedroom on the third floor. They watched a couple of hours of TV, and then they shut the lights off. It was a peaceful night outside. It wasn't cold or windy; perfect for sleeping… and hunting too.

Caleb hadn't slept much when he started drinking the well water. That insomnia had become worse every day. He'd been wide awake for three days by the time the Millers had gotten home. After Jim and Melanie and the kids had fallen asleep, Caleb was sitting on his couch in his tidy cottage with no REM sleep in over seventy two hours to sustain his sanity. Having slipped into hallucinations, he could actually *see* the things he wanted. Mostly they were things he couldn't really have, but at three in the morning, he came up with a plan to solve that problem. And it was also the perfect moment to put this new plan in motion. He got off the couch, and he put on his old ripped grey sweater and walked outside. Moving sedately down the path from his cottage to the garage, he went inside and picked something up. Caleb ambled over to the main house, and he let himself inside since he had his own key to the front door.

Jim and Melanie had been sleeping soundly when the main lights over their heads had burst into life. Melanie had managed to sleep through the change, but the sudden brightness woke Jim right up. Done rubbing his palms into his eye sockets to get rid of the sleepy-bug stickiness, he saw someone in the doorway holding gardening shears with very long blades. It took him a second to realize it was Caleb. His trustworthy caretaker, in an abnormal surge of speed, raced straight at him as he lifted the cutting shears over his head for a lethal downward thrust.

Day Six: St. Egwin of Worcester

6:30PM Saturday December 30th, 2006 Garden Grove, California

Officer John Logan was answering incoming calls that night. His precinct included a good percentage of Orange County, including Garden Grove and Cypress while Los Alamitos and Stanton were served by other divisions. A lot of neighborhoods in the county were fairly new, tract houses built over the last forty-five years. The cookie-cutter houses were lined up for inspection like wooden soldiers on precisely groomed streets and their uniformity was the norm. An ocean of sameness rolled out to the horizon, a similarity supportive for some, but also the only offering held out to most.

Logan himself owned a three bedroom ranch in Los Alamitos. Besides the fish tank, a white angora cat and a terrier, his wife and three children lived there with him as well. Most of the officers in the precinct had houses in the neighborhood, and they weren't worried about break-ins or robberies. The congestion of blue in the area was something a criminal should avoid.

Tapping his fingers on the desk, Logan stared out into space. He should be going through paper-work, but it had been just a peaceful weekend, he was using this unlikely respite to relax for a moment. Surprised by the lull, it seemed they'd been teleported to Mayberry. One head-on collision on the freeway and a domestic disturbance in Cypress, and that was it. He couldn't remember a weekend this quiet. It could be the quiet before the storm, and he did feel uneasy. And then the phone rang.

"Hello…um. Could you guys help me? I mean, we had her on the lease outside and the back yard is fenced in, and Crystal's a gentle dog, and…and she loves us and we love her and it looks like somebody must have gotten in and kidnapped her and…"

The Officer Logan interrupted him, "We need your address and your name, sir."

"Oh…sorry. Yeah. I'm Stephen Griffith. We're on 1800 Grand Avenue in Cypress. Now, you should know that she's a collie, only two years old. You should send out a car and check things out. I mean, I'm about to knock on my neighbor's door and see if they saw anything and…"

Logan interrupted him again. More lines were lighting up, and he needed put him on hold or transfer the call.

"Yeah, okay Mr. Griffith, I'll send a car over. The officer will talk to you and see what they can do. There's another call coming in sir, and I need to go."

"Thanks, officer."

He hung up and picked up the next call.

"Hello, please hold …" Covering the mic in front of his mouth, he yelled over his shoulder to the other dispatcher behind him to send a car to the address in Cypress about the lost dog. Then he took his hand off the mike.

"Hello."

"Hi. My name is Tommy Morton, and we live at 12 Shorewood Lane in Stanton. He's gone, Officer. I couldn't find him when I got home from work. My niece was in the house and she can't or won't explain what happened. He's called Shadow, he's a shepherd, and I won't let her leave until you guys gets over here. We can both grill the truth out of her together, cuz' I think she sold him. She doesn't think I'm paying her enough…."

"Hold on, sir. I'm transferring you to an officer who can help you."

The computer screen in front of him had lit up like a Christmas tree. Shaking his head, it seemed as if it was feast or famine. His own personal cell was buzzing in his back pocket while he juggled the sudden avalanche of calls. Apparently, his earlier premonition had been spot on.

Logan stole thirty seconds to check on the text left from his wife. *'Link is gone: Help!'* Their terrier was gone too? Nothing he could do about that at the moment, since every other dog in a twenty-five square mile area had also vanished. The ones in the town kennels were gone too! The disappearing act had affected forty-five thousand homes, and three police precincts are dealing this uncanny disaster the best way they could. For many families, the way they felt towards their pets could match how they felt towards each other, and the authorities in the affect communities were beset by a massive influx of shock and pain. The owners wanted them to find their pets and release them from anguish, or at least tell them where they were!

But the police couldn't do it. They couldn't free them. They couldn't come up with any kind of surcease from the pain.

A frantic search for the canines began and it expanded and continued. Using heat-seeking glasses flying in helicopters above acres of wild woods, abandoned lots, and ravines, they found nothing. On the ground, search parties would march across the same empty land while others knocked on doors. Five more days of going through this pointless enterprise had left them stymied. Not a single clue was found. No hair snatched on a branch, no whimper and no faraway bark. In teary-eyed confessions, those who had been robbed whispered over the possibility a government crew had stolen their dogs for experiments or perhaps an alien invader landed on Saturday and snatched every pooch in Orange County.

A week after the mass disappearance, John Logan's nine year old son was sitting on the back-step of their ranch on Penny Lane. He was tracing lines in the dirt with a stick, and he didn't want to play with his friends. Once in a while, he'd stare out at the back-yard. Mom and Dad had already gotten rid of the blue and lavender dog house, but that hadn't helped. He still imagined Link snoozing away in it. Billy wanted his furry side-kick, to come back. The white cat, Hector, rubbed up against his leg. He off-handedly rubbed his back, but Hector had never been that close to him. In his mind, that puff of white cared more about treats Mom gave him than anything else. Fifteen more minutes went by until the back gate behind him opened, letting him know Dad was home from work.

Officer Logan crouched down and looked into his son's face. Billy turned towards him and hugged his knees. John knew he'd been hit harder than anyone else in the family by the terrier's disappearance, and Logan gently released his current hold so he could sit on the step with him. He hugged his boy, and Billy embraced his father again, and his small hands ended right above his handcuffs and gun holstered on his work belt. He dug his fingers into his father's jacket holding on as if for dear-life, and then he began to cry.

"Why Dad? Why isn't he here? What happened? Where did Link go? Why can't we find him?"

John Logan couldn't answer him, and a small tear leaked out of his own eye. Neither of them knew that the ultimate clarification was percolating in the center of the Trash Vortex in the Northern Pacific.

Day Seven: Hogmanay

8:19AM Sunday December 31st, 2006 Lake Tahoe, Nevada

Twenty-two miles in length and twelve miles wide, Lake Tahoe drained into Truckee River, and from there the finally stop was Pyramid Lake in Reno. The bottom of Lake Tahoe was a thousand feet deep, and in a few sections it dove another seven hundred feet deeper. It was the second deepest lake in the United States, and a lot of legends about phantoms and monsters surrounded it. There was a well-entrenched tale involving a casino built on its shore. In the 20's, it was rumored wise guys tossed squealers and schemers into the lakes secretive depths, and so hundreds of well-dressed corpses should be floating down there perfectly preserved in its glacial cold water. Besides that over-told story, there had been sightings going back over a hundred years in which a slinky beast, reported to be fifteen to sixty feet in length swum through these waters. Descriptions similar to the ones chalked up to the Champ, another mysterious reptile-like creature supposedly inhabiting Lake Champlain in Vermont, experts in cryptozoology loved to use these sightings as a true indication that an extinct dinosaur; a plesiosaur or possibly a basilosaurus still exists. The length remains in question, but almost everyone insisted it was black or a very dark green. Locals had named her Tahoe Tessie.

Glen Singer and Peter Harrison were students at the Sierra Nevada College only five miles away from the lake. At six feet, Glen's blonde hair framed a handsome face, yet his friend and co-producer of their independent film was not quite so well endowed. Too thin and gangly, and at six feet and four inches, Harrison's height could be a distraction. At least he had beautiful white teeth and a wonderful engaging smile.

On winter break, they were using their free time to film a documentary on Tahoe Tessie. Glen's parents had died when he was three, and his uncle, Virgil Singer, had stepped in to raise him. Virgil was wealthy. He'd given Glen an open-ended charge account to bill *anything* he wanted or needed to make his film. With support like that, Glen and Peter could make the production into a stunning jewel. They'd rented a thirty foot long boat as a working base as well as a sixteen foot Boston Whaler. Both boats were anchored at the commercial dock on the southern coast of the lake. The larger boat had been used for filming recreations of some of the tales about Tessie. Since Peter was skilled in scuba diving, he'd done most of the camera shots himself, and almost all of the underwater scenes were in the can. The most complicated shoot, the grand finale, had been planned for the 31st. The weather was working with them perfectly. It was fifty degrees, and the wind was slight. It was uncommonly balmy for December. They'd hired two commercial divers for the extra help they'd need in one of the shots. Glen planned to drop them off near to the Whaler holding a mockup of Tessie's head, neck and body in rubber and plastic. There were even handles inside the construction to hold it where they wanted it as they swam sideways or up and down. After dropping them off, Glen motored a thousand feet away in the work boat, leaving Peter in the Whaler in a fishing cap and wearing a hunting jacket over his wetsuit. They've clamped a fishing rod on a holder at the stern. Peter was supposed to look like a lonely fisherman while the larger boat got closer. Glen would be filming him, as he got surprised and then fearful. After this simple acting job, Peter would use a handheld camera to record the paid divers swimming the fake Tahoe Tessie up from the depths of the lake. Glen would have gotten close enough to record them from another direction as they pushed the creature to the surface with gusto.

By mid-morning, everything was in place. Peter Harrison was calmly 'fishing', and Glen had started filming, having already dropped the divers into the water near the Whaler as planned. They'd explained to Glen that getting the cumbersome thing down to the depth he wanted was going to use up ten minutes before they could swim straight back up. Glen was talking to Harrison on the walky-talky during this short waiting period, instructing him to add some loathing to the fearful part of his act. Turning over his shoulder, Glen asked the captain to slowly get them closer to the Whaler as it was almost time for the larger cameras on the work boat to also record Tessie's upcoming attack. Of course, he certainly didn't know that one of the divers was having problems with his regulator. They were actually swimming back to the work boat to get to their bag of tricks. They had a replacement there just in case something like this comes up on a job.

In the meantime, Glen and Peter were patiently waited for Tessie to rise out of the darkness below. Peter was staring down into the seemingly bottomless lake holding a digital movie camera in one hand and a powerful waterproof floodlight in the other. So far, it was nothing but flickering blue that faded to black, and he was excited about the upcoming scene. Normal daylight lit up the water to only twenty feet, and they wanted to record images farther down. The extra floodlight would add the necessary lumens and deepen the view. Besides, it could paint dramatic shadows on the up-coming star of the show. And then Peter's rather extended wait was abruptly over.

It was enormous with white skin mottled with beige, racing at him through the cold lake water like a missile. As if an invisible hand pushed him backwards, he was jolted backwards in surprise. Getting closer by the second, it moved like quicksilver, and then it flipped over on its back. Peter saw a circular mouth the size of a manhole cover ringed with long inward pointing teeth until it flipped around again. Hitting the surface, the creature hadn‘t given him any time to get away. It had used its back to summersault the fishing boat bow over stern and then straight into the air. It ended bottom up on the surface. Peter was tossed out of the Whaler, and he landed a few feet away. He was waving frantically for help, but thirty seconds later, Glen and the Captain watched him being jerked eight feet forwards. His signaling had stopped, and his face had gone slack until he was sucked under the surface, and he never ever came up.

"Can't you get us there faster, Enzo? We need to help him. You saw that thing right? I'm not going crazy right?!"

"I'm pushing this engine as hard as I can, sir, and of course I saw it breach. It looked like a nightmare, so abnormal it didn't seem real."

They quickly got closer...only one hundred and fifty feet away from the last time they saw Peter. Scanning the surface with his binoculars, Glen's fading hope had suddenly soared. It had to be his friend floating thirty feet away from the work boat! Yet his flicker of optimism changed to shock instead and his pulse rate raced even higher.

Oh, he'd seen a body alright, but the sight of it hadn't remained stable, and it morphed into yet another unbelievable event. The one body had been joined by hundreds of corpses that had been weighted at the bottom of the lake for years. Popping to the surface like ravioli in a pot, and they were perfectly preserved. Most were men in pinstriped suits with an occasional female usually adorned in a sparkling gown with glittering beads still roped around their necks like a flappers, a fashion in the 1920's, and it looked like they'd all drowned fifteen minutes ago. The commercial divers were climbing on board behind Glen and the captain, leaving the recreation tied to a cleat in the water. They had no idea about what had just transpired, and Glen rushed through the story as fast as he could. Things were still going on; he waved towards the lake so the divers could see the two hundred or so bodies floating out there in the faint chop.

Glen decided to look right over the gunnels of the boat, and he wasn't pleased when he saw the hide of the dappled behemoth rushing along *right underneath them*. A mix between a giant squid and an extra-terrestrial mistake, it was over a hundred feet long. Then it broke the surface again, very close to the hull of the work boat. In a flash of adrenaline, Glen screeched to the divers to cut the line that was holding the mockup, and in the same breath, he ordered Enzo to turn the boat around and get them out of there as fast as possible. Staying alive trumped curiosity hands down. The unanswered mystery about what was zipping along beneath them, or why bodies were now surrounding the boat, would be addressed at a later date as Enzo tried as hard he could to move his wide-bottom clunker into a much higher gear and he was also on the radio to the authorities.

Peter Harrison's body was never found, and the secret behind the preserved bodies was never answered. Whatever had been in the water that day had probably eaten Peter before it jetted off to Tattler River, or instead curling up on the bottom of one the deeper ravines. No one saw anything in the upcoming search.

A molecular change in the lake water in 2004 could be responsible for the appearance of this deformed creature, and it's possible that the powerful action of one its over-sized flippers dislodged the corpses from their frozen tomb. Either way, it certainly ended the debate. It seemed the wise guys had really thrown their unruly stool-pigeons into the lake after all.

Day Eight: The Solemnity of Mary

3:35PM Monday **January 1st, 2007** **Verbena, Alabama**

Chester was barreling down county road 59 on his way to a great place to polish his skills as a marksmen. With an unnecessary burst of speed, he veered off the road and onto a dirt track hidden behind a juniper tree. It was a back way in, and hardly anybody knew about it. Now he was jolting hard down the trail while the back wheels of his broken down pick-up spun dust behind him like a smoke screen, and he was right on the edge of crashing. His mouse colored hair was short and buck teeth held back his smiles. A twelve gauge shotgun was clamped across the back window of the cab of his truck, but that was not the tool of the day. There was a Remington 700XCR in an expensive case that had jumped off the passenger side of the seat and onto the rubber floor mat. Ammunition for it was stored in the glove box.

The largest recycling center in Chilton County, it was on the outskirts of Clanton, and Chester was almost there. He still called it a garbage dump. According to him, if it looked and smelled the same, why shouldn't he call a spade a spade? He knew the gates closed at five, but he also knew that they'd keep on using those oversized machines to move mountains of crap around until it got dark, *but not on Monday.* There was a poker game at the foreman's three bedroom ranch in Marbury, right off the county line, and it always happened on Mondays. After Chester heard about that, he knew no one would be around, and right now, there'd be another hour of light left.

Exploding out of thick foliage, Chester hit the brakes. The rough track he'd been on ended on a thin ridge overlooking the northern edge of the dump, and he was looking out at acres of rubbish. The final four hundred feet of the trail zigzagged along this dirt cliff. For the first time in his trip, Chester slowed down, inching the truck around the very tight corners on a very steep path until he finally rolled out onto the paved part of the site. Now, he found himself in a human valley and mountains of filth surrounded him on all sides.

The idea of target practice had come to him a year ago, and doing it at the dump seemed to be a simple option. In the beginning, he'd line up cans he'd find in the clutter and at first, he missed most of them. Refining his grip on the gun and angling the rifle nestled on his shoulder with an altered degree, his proficiency increased. Inspired by his increasing ability, he bought himself a new rifle; an expensive one. The technology built into his pricey toy gave him another edge, and he quickly got a lot better. In only weeks, he hit all the cans most of the time, and that was cool, but soon, those tiny explosions of metal shards were leaving him wanting more. The idea of a moving target came into his head, and he instantly thought about the scurrying possibilities out there in the rubbish. Another level to hone his skill. The coincidental camouflage the living targets could dive behind was an interesting asset, making it more difficult. Chester had begun this new phase about six months ago.

He got out of the truck, and walked over to the passenger door to get his rifle. The sun was dropping, and the shadows were stretching out. Day was darkening to dusk, and night was creeping in, but that didn't bother Chester. More than enough light was left for his plans, and he quickly unzipped the rifle out of its leather case and then he loaded it with ammunition. He walked easy slouch over to a section where the public was told to drop their old refrigerators, washing machines, old water heaters and televisions. Finding a comfortable perch, he rested his elbows on the side of an old Frigidaire, and his Monday hunt began with an echoing boom. His first shot had blown the tail off an over-sized rat that had been diving behind a pile of trash bags to avoid his attack.

Taking the same sneaky way into the dump as Chester had, Morgan Whittaker knew about his friend's hobby of shooting at stuff on Mondays. He wanted to surprise him. They'd been buddies since high school, and since Chester's thirtieth birthday was coming up the next day, Morgan wanted to give him a six pack and two front row tickets to a concert that headlined Joe Taylor and the Howling Gators next Saturday in Birmingham. He wanted to give these things to him the day before his birthday, and he too had stopped on the overlook watching his friend work hard at his craft. The birthday boy-to-be was fifteen hundred feet away, and Morgan's eyesight was far from perfect. Seeing the old truck and Chester himself in an orange windbreaker, when he heard another gunshot, he assumed it was another casualty, but he didn't know for sure.

Something weird happened on the parking field below him, and Morgan wasn't exactly positive what it had been, but that's okay. He was good at filling in the blanks. It had to have been a bulldog, and it must have been a rabid one, leaping out of that pile of rusty metal boxes right behind Chester. And the dog slammed into the back of his friend's head. It was clear as a bell he hadn't known about its airborne landing, as Morgan watched him drop his gun and fall face first on the ground. Apparently stunned, he couldn't get control of the situation, and Morgan was horrified when this mongrel began to drag Chester deeper into the jungle of trash with his jacket collar in its teeth. Morgan jumped into his own truck, and he wobbled his way down the narrow trail as fast as he could to save his friend.

The ride used up three long minutes before he finally parked next to Chester's truck. He got out and ran to the last place he saw him, however he wasn't positive which direction he'd been dragged to. He slowed down. Hearing some gnawing sounds coming from the left, they weren't very far away, maybe ten feet tops. Probably on the other side of that pile of hot water heaters. Morgan trotted towards the noise until something else erupted behind him, and he whirled around to face whatever it was.

He'd been wrong about the bull dog. It hadn't been a dog of any kind, and what he'd blurrily seen in the distance was now standing five feet away from him. But there were a lot more than the one he'd seen drag Chester away, and the only thing he did get right was the size. Darting at him on mass, he stared into their beady red rodent eyes, and he realized he'd never hear the heart wrenchingly beautiful songs Joe Taylor was going to play at that concert unless he can meet him in heaven.

Day Nine: St. Basil the Great

3:00PM Tuesday **January 2nd, 2007** **Dixie National Forest, Utah**

Bruce and Charles Malone-Feldman married on Christmas day in Cedar Rapids, and Charles had arranged a three-day jaunt on the Christmas Train. Leaving Hutchinson, Kansas, the train would roll along the rails all the way to San Francisco. A perfect honeymoon. Since it was late in the year, the trips would only take place if the forecast was solid as a rock. Morley Rails Incorporated owned the luxurious holiday train, and they accepted reservations only with this inherent proviso. They would refund everyone's money if they had to. This year, the weather report for the next three days looked fine. A stint of perfection for the revelers; clear, calm and warm. Two hundred and fifty people were signed up, looking forwards to crossing vast stretches of majestic and undisturbed land. After climbing through the Raton Pass in the Rocky Mountains and into La Junta, it would then enter the Glen Canyon National Resort to continue onwards in the Dixie National Forests in Utah.

The Christmas Train's departure time at the brutal hour of eight on Monday morning had inveigled the newlyweds into spending the night in a hotel in Hutchinson on Sunday. Holding their suitcases, they got on board on time, and an elegantly uniformed stewardess with endless legs and a smile to die for, greeted them. She gave them a coupon for fifty percent off the price of a steak dinner at Rainbow Wells, a restaurant in walking distance from the station in La Junta. There were red and green bunting on the sides of the sliding doors between the cars, and decorative lights were draped everywhere, frantically twinkling. The energetic decorators had also put presents in the center of all the tables in the restaurant car holding mints and chocolates. Duly impressed, Bruce and Charles entered their private compartment. They left their bags behind, and locked the door. They went up the aisle and through some cars until they reached the curved windows inside one of the viewing cars.

They used the coupon on some rib-eyes during the four hour stop-over in La Junta, and after a peaceful night of uninterrupted sleep, they ate a large breakfast in the restaurant car. In only two hours, it was time to have lunch. The seats in the viewing cars were designed with relaxation in mind, so after they were done slurping up the last of their lobster soufflé, the newlyweds burped their way back to those comfortable recliners. And they stayed there, digesting like beached whales. The train was flying through the Dixie National Forest in Utah, and Bruce and Charles gazed out at mother-nature in her untamed glory...without moving a muscle. It had started to snow lightly, and five minutes later, it got more intense. That was odd. They'd been no report forecasting a single flake.

Scott Palmer was the engineer of the Christmas Train, and Butch Kaye, his co-pilot. From the beginning of the trip, things had been peaceful behind the four inch thick windshield of the control car, and there were only three or four of the endless dials and gauges on the panel that needed intermittent attention. Periodically checking on the internal temperature of the diesel engine, the oil pressure and the hydraulic pressure throughout the train, they'd just seen the numbers minutes ago. Everything was fine, and the internal systems were working like a clock made in Switzerland.

And then it started to snow. The flurry escalated into a white out, and Palmer got on the radio to Gorton, the next station coming up. Since they were only eighty miles out, this unexpected precipitation shouldn't interfere with his radio call. But it did. Palmer and Kaye stared into each other's eyes as the previously calm and balmy transmuted into the unexpected.

"Right now, we're gonna get an inch every ten minutes, bud," Palmer said.

"Yup. I think you're right. Something like that. Shoot. Where did this thing come from? Do you know?"

"Not a clue, but it's giving me the creeps."

They had been going at fifty miles an hour, but the young engineer put his hand on the throttle and cut their speed in half. The mechanic was asleep in the car designated for crew members, and Palmer called a steward and told him to wake the guy up and get him dressed and on-call. He ordered three wait-staff to tell the passengers not to worry: the situation was under control (whether it was or not). He wanted everyone to remain calm. Thirty minutes went by, and he was still able to plow through what was falling on the tracks, yet both of them were getting more worried by the second.

And then the snow stopped, and their anxiety vanished. Six inches had fallen, and Palmer was able to speed up to thirty-five miles an hour. But not for long. The forest had been crowding the tracks for miles, however the tree line retreated as soon as the rails straightened out after a mile long gentle curve. A blinding glare bounced into the windows of the viewing cars reflecting off a snowy field. Only a few shrubs and one wind-crumpled tree interrupted that whiteness, nevertheless the engineer dropped their speed to a crawl and he engaged the hydraulic brakes until the Christmas Train ended up dead on the tracks. The passengers had no idea why they'd stopped in the middle of nowhere, but they hadn't seen what Palmer and Kaye were staring at through the windshield. Fifteen hundred feet away, piled in the center of the tracks, was a large pile of twigs and broken branches, as if someone wanted to start a bonfire. It was too big for the train to burst through it. In the beginning, the pile appeared surreal, however the longer they stared at it, the quality of it began menacing. It was not supposed to be there, and its presence was *wrong*...frighteningly wrong. Palmer decided go outside and move the wood off the rails, instructing Kaye to follow him. He had to do his job...even if he doesn't want to.

The newlyweds had fallen into a deep sleep after their ongoing stint of gluttony. Those sitting next to them had accepted the gentle harmony in their snoring, and they hadn't woken them up. The blonde stewardess had walked by, and soothed the nerves of the passengers with knowledge she didn't have about how everything was okay. Moving along the corridor, she told people the snow was about to end, and when it actually did, she was surprised. The nervousness tugging at the riders evaporated, but when the train slowed down and stopped, everyone in the viewing car got up and stared through the glass. Chit-chat ramped up into nervous questions, musings and explanations for the stall. The ongoing hubbub finally woke the honeymooners, and they too got up to peer through the window.

A thick cloud floated over the sun, making it harder to make things out. Nevertheless, it was impossible for anyone not to notice them as they loped towards the train like black water pouring out of the tree line in the distance. There was over a hundred of them, and their black fur displayed an effortless approach against the white snow. Slightly smaller than wolves, their faces did not mimic their larger brothers perfectly. Noses blunted, they had large eyes and ears, and the length of their teeth was uncanny. Besides a minor resemblance to wild dogs who roamed the savannas in African, their general originality did not support an easy explanation.

Two guard dogs were lost in the same area three years ago, and that mistake could have something to do with it. If those dogs had lived, and then bred with each other or a member of the wolf population inhabiting the Dixie National Forest, the molecular alteration in the water could have warped the DNA and RNA in the cells of those unlikely whelps. It's possible that degradation could have started a domino effect resulting in the anomalies that had run out of the woods and across the field. It was a lot more likely that the domesticated dogs had died under the usually extreme conditions during the winter.

The passengers were stunned by the wolf-like pack's approach to the train, however when they saw the engineer and his assistant dragged out into the pasture and torn to pieces, their feelings crystalized into a block of dread. The snow surrounding this travesty became a rich scarlet red, and then the electric lights in the car went dead. Bruce hugged Charles, and they both started to cry.

The Christmas Train never made it to Gorton, their next station on time. A local meteorologist noticed the intense storm hanging over a short section of the tracks in a satellite display, and the information prompted him into calling the company who owned the train. Morley Rails sent a helicopter out with a medic, and a county sheriff on board. By the time the pilot finally found the train, the storm had vanished. The sky was clear, and the moon had risen, and when they looked down, the train appeared dead as a door nail motionless on the rails below them. Landing near the long line of cars, the sheriff was the first person who got out of the copter, gun in hand. He stamped through the snow and got on board.

Climbing the metal stairs, he entered one of the viewing cars, and he found passengers and crew huddled away from him badly frightened. Many had hypothermia, and they all tried to forget what they'd seen hours ago. Oh, they'd heard the helicopter landing, but nobody would go out there. The train had become their harbor in a world gone mad.

And by the time they'd been found stuck there, the pile of wood on the rails was gone. There weren't any bodies out there either. Not even any pieces. Just very long streaks of blood in the snow trailing off into the trees. Of course, the authorities combed through the forest to find Engineer Palmer and Butch Kaye, but during their intensive search, they saw no wild dogs or wolves or any supernatural version of either anywhere. No evidence of a large pack of any kind in the woods either, nothing to support the witness's accounts besides the paw prints in the small amount of snow surrounding the train. It had quickly melted, and they hadn't had equipment to get an impression of those ghostly prints, only a blurry picture before the elusive confirmation dribbled away. The crowd of official investigators grew, patiently listening to the stories coming from the passengers and the crew. Hours whittled by. There were no sounds coming out of the wild woods. No howls nor barks, only a feeling of imminence. Everyone held their breaths. The company mechanics were busy getting the train back in running order, and the guy in charge had announced it would be ready to roll in an hour or so, but in the meantime it felt as if something was still out there…circling them, and no one really felt safe.

Day Ten: The Feast of the Holy Name of Jesus

9:55AM Tuesday **January 3rd, 2007** **New York Harbor at 116th Street, New York**

Yolanda Pollack called the precinct at eleven. Stanley hadn't made it home for dinner, and she was worried. He'd gone out that morning with his cousin to get their thirty-two foot yacht out of the water, and she hadn't gotten a phone call or anything else from him to explain his very late non-arrival. The boat ramp was a mile and half-a-mile away, and he'd kissed her on the cheek that morning, saying he'd get the Sea Bandit out and onto the hitch on the back of their station wagon. It wasn't going to be a problem. Stanley, and his friend Blake always used this annual job to get the boat into storage until the spring as a wonderful excuse to disappear for most of the day. Quickly hitched to the station-wagon, and parked it in the yard, they'd walk over to the strip club across the street and hang out and get plastered.

Yolanda gave the cops the nearest cross street next to the ramp, and she thought the boat was probably still in the water. A patrol car went out there and checked it out, but the officers didn't see anything besides the station wagon parked in the lot looking abandoned. The water at the edge of the dock was thirty feet deep, and one of the patrolmen took out a flashlight from of the trunk of the car. He walked over and pointed the beam straight down. There it was. At least the fly-bridge anyway, and the patrolman's guess that this sunken vessel was the Sea Bandit was true.

A rescue boat with a salvage team got to the sunken boat in the morning. Two police divers wearing seven millimeter thick neoprene wetsuits with thick boots and gloves and hoods, had tanks of air strapped to their backs. Extremely seasoned divers, they'd been beneath the surface of many of the harbors and waterways around Manhattan Island, and those waters are considered to be the most dangerous on earth. No contest as the strangest. Their latest orders were to discover, if they could, what had sunk the boat, and see if there were any bodies on it, in it or near it. Human or otherwise, and then bring the whole thing up.

Being a sunny day was helpful. Any extra light is always appreciated. The halogen lights from their hoods, and the lanterns in their *hands* might be enough to make out what was going on in the tangled confusion near the ramp. Bennie and Virgil had been partners since 1996, and they'd seen some pretty bizarre stuff. Four years ago, a dredge was hung up on something near the mid-town tunnel, and they were told to fix the problem and when they got down there, they saw that the excavator was caught in the breast bone of a giraffe. That sight was added to their list of individuals they'd never imagine meeting at the bottom. Oh yeah; it would take quite a lot to ruffle them.

Stepping backwards off the diving platform of the rescue boat, they flippered to the Sea Bandit's keel. The vessel was tilted slightly to port, having shifted six feet deeper into the unstable muck. Stanley's corpse was posed in a surreal tableau. The glass in the windows of the cabin was gone, and the fingers of his left were curled around one of the metal bars that used to hold the plates. He was also standing on his own right for some unknown reason next to the wheel. The divers assumed the floating bundle behind him was his cousin's body, but it was too murky to make that out for sure. It was unsettling, and the whole thing didn't look right.

Virgil gestured to Bennie. He'd begin the process of getting Stanley out of there and up to the surface. While Virgil swam over to the entrance to the cabin, Bennie noticed that one of the corpse's fingers that was curled around the metal rod had begun to move. Seconds later, the illusion that they'd been Stan's fingers vanished, and a more vicious reality slithered in. It had been white tentacles covering his dead hand, and as soon as they let go, the body slowly drifted off towards the back of the cabin. Virgil was very close to the body when it began to let go, and it was extremely unfortunate Bennie hadn't had enough time to warn him. A much larger tentacle, mottled with beige spots and suction cups, had insinuated itself through a hole where one of the windows had been, and it was undulating tentatively towards Virgil. The second he saw it, he unsnapped the knife at his calf. A normal defense move. He'd never seen anything like it before, at least the part he saw, anyway. The body of this creature could be anywhere. Under the blackness stretching back beneath the dock, or on the other side of the sunken fishing boat, or…or…anywhere in this floating murk.

More tentacles, thicker ones, were snaking out of nowhere, latching onto Virgil's arm and tightening on his upper legs. He sliced at them, and Bennie was shocked at what was happening to his partner twenty-five feet away. Swimming over there as fast as he could to help him, a torn metal grill of some kind protruded out of the cloud of silt, and it tangled him up and slowed him down. Madly pushing away from it, he kicked his long flippers harder than ever until he was free from the blasted thing, yet it seemed he hadn't gotten any closer to his friend; looked more like he was frozen in place like a fly stuck on flypaper. He quickly realized nothing would have mattered in the end. Things were taking place to Virgil way too fast, and in the foggy darkness, that speed had become secondary to an increased intensity. He'd been madly stabbing at the tentacles around his legs, but what had then rushed around the hull of the sunken fishing boat as nothing but a blur was about to negate any effort Bennie ever would have tried to do to save him. The tentacle was two and half feet wide, barely able to squeeze through the hatch. It swept around Virgil's waist, and the smaller tentacles now oozing black glop from the many slices he'd gouged into them, let loose and disappeared into the gloom. *Play time was over.* In this new embrace, he was wrenched backwards as if he was on a carnival ride in a nightmare come to life. Bennie watched as the light clamped on his head became dimmer the farther away he got, until he glimpsed the last of it before it blinked out. His partner…no, *his friend* had been dragged so far under the dock he'd never be found.

Bennie hung there transfixed by shock. Another mid-sized tentacle wormed its way around the hull, sinuously creeping towards him as the remaining diver. Self-preservation shook him out of this dangerous standstill, and he flippered up to the surface, waving desperately at the crew on the rescue boat. Didn't take him long to get on the ladder, and usually it's an easy climb; three steps up and out. He was on the last step when he felt a hell of tug on his left ankle, and he lunged forwards on the dive platform as the drag got more intense. Two officers jumped over to him, and they hooked their arms under Bennie's armpits. They were pulling hard, and all three men were fighting the unbreakable hold slowly dragging him back to the water. Bennie unsheathed his own knife, and he plunged it deep into the coil of tentacle around his ankle...and, thank God, it was the last straw. Finally letting go, it lazily slipped off the platform like chum. The officers on the boat were momentary speechless as they watched Bennie tear his diving mask off his face and crumple on the deck wracked with tears.

Day Eleven: The Feast of Saint Simon Stylites

12:30PM Wednesday January 4th, 2006 Benton, Arkansas

Raymond Walton and his nine year old son, John, always went to the kite competition behind the Sharon Baptist Church on 402 Shenandoah Road. Twenty acres of empty land behind the church were perfect, and there were no telephone pole wires to entangle the strings. The first twelve acres had no trees at all. John was on a holiday break from school, and most businesses also shut down for the event. Mr. Walton worked as a nurse in the health clinic downtown, but he reserves these days months in advance. He crossed his fingers there wouldn't be a pile-up on the interstate to drag him away from his role in the event.

With an entrance fee of ten dollars whether you fly a kite or stand and watch, the winner gets five thousand dollars: second prize, a thousand and third, five hundred. The local Rotary Club had started the whole thing four years ago, and it had swelled into a giant. All the profits were given to a charity; The Last Chance, an animal rescue group. The judges included the mayor, his wife and two business owners, and they would pick out ten from all the entries, and after that, the crowd would vote on the winner and the runners up. It was named *Flying the Rainbow,* and the only criteria you needed to enter was a ticket and an original kite that had to actually fly. This year, the lot next to the church was full by 10:30, and the rest of the cars were parking on the grass behind the building. The competition was slated to start at twelve. By 11:45, fifteen hundred people had accumulated with four hundred and fifty-seven entries. The judges had perched themselves on their plastic chairs in the middle of an open field surrounded by hot-dog carts and vendors selling everything from fresh cookies and funnel cakes to glass beads and posters. Port-a-potties were lined up next to the church, and everything was set up and ready to go. A brisk wind out of the south was gusting to twenty-five. Perfect for the contest. Kites were going up in groups of twenty-five to fly for ten minutes. That allowed the judges time to cull the best out of the pack. That part of the competition went on for two and half-hours, and then it took another hour for the crowd to vote the winners out of the ten flying over their heads. The competition ends in a ceremony in which the three medals would be hung from the necks of the winners like in the Olympics.

Raymond and John Walton were in the last viewing as their last name was near the end of the alphabet. At forty-two, Ray's curly brown hair had receded and there was a balled spot on his head. Twenty pounds overweight with black-horned eyeglasses, he was never going to be a social butterfly, but it didn't make any difference. After his wife's death five years ago, he'd supported his son through the trauma like a super hero.

They'd done a remarkable job on the kite. Their ideas for it had combined into a dolphin with angelic wings sprouting from its curved back. John had the eye of an artist, and he'd helped Raymond arrange the color gradient in the wing feathers. At a distance, the dolphin looked real. Wearing blue-jeans and a red windbreaker way too big for him, John had angled the kite away from the other entries in the group, hoping the judges would be able to make-out his kite without the distraction of being too close to the others. His bangs were blowing into his eyes and he had to push them away with one hand off the controlling string just for a second as the judges singled him out for the final viewing. John was excited. Having been picked out of this first group, he was going to have a chance win in the next one!

It was four o'clock. The ten finalists were flying their kites over the eastern edge of the grassy field in the final viewing and they waited for the ultimate choice from the popular vote. The area behind them was crowded with other contestants and their kites who hadn't made it. Some of the contraptions were quite large. The creator of a twenty-six foot long Chinese dragon kite was undoing its supports and packing it all away while an eight foot wide paper Thunderbird car nearby had been forgotten on the grass during the final moments as that kite's owner was waiting with the rest of the crowd for the results.

The south wind had shifted to the east and picked up. With no forecasts connected to any precipitous events that day, those in charge kept on with the ceremony. After all, the breeze had been perfect...and it should stay that way. The ten kites up there were magnificent, and at the moment, the last votes were about to decide whether the flying dolphin or an octopus would be the winner of the festival.

Dad was close to his son, only fifteen feet away. John was suddenly having problems holding on to the kite. They'd put the string around John's waist to make sure the kite wouldn't get any higher, but the wind was building and Raymond was getting worried. In a sudden jolt, a rogue gust reached fifty miles-an-hour, however it hadn't been a gust at all. That dangerous level of speed stayed there. Reaching his son became a real struggle, as John got dragged across the fescue grass by a wind that had turned into a gale. And the kite itself pulled him along too, since the string around his waist was strong, and it did not break. John couldn't let go, and he didn't have the weight or the strength to pull the dolphin out of this crazy weather squall. The rest of the other finalists were quickly dragging their own entries down as fast as they could. Meanwhile, all four of the judges were knocked off their plastic chairs, and they stood up and ran to their cars with everyone else. Raymond was sprinting behind John, and he was trying very hard to get to him. In the last second before his son would be lifted out of reach, he desperately snatched at John's sneaker laces. If he could hitch on to him, he'd be able to anchor him with his own girth...but he missed, and the hoary adage 'give 'em an inch and they'll take a mile' careened into his head while he kept on leaping towards him even though it was pointless.

At sixty-five MPH, almost everyone had left the field and found shelter, but John was tossed head-over-heels into a pile of kites that had been blown up against a fence erected at the western end of the open field. His over large wind-breaker had hooked onto a sharp piece of metal coming from a kite that looked like an eagle, and that other creation was also free like his dolphin to lift him even higher. The string around his waist had already got him off the ground. The eagle had completely dislodged itself from the hurricane fence, and its extra lift had pulled John almost straight up at a hard angle. The wind was creeping to seventy miles per hour, and an off-duty police officer grabbed Raymond by the arm, dragging him back to the parking lot. Ray stumbled badly during this terrible trip, looking over his shoulder to watch his son's flight preposterously attached to an eagle and a dolphin. In despair, he saw John rise higher and higher through the air like Mary Poppins and her umbrella.

No one else at the competition had been injured. John Walton's body was found six miles away from the Church, three days later. A local farmer had noticed something red fluttering thirty-five feet up at the top of the old elm tree in his back yard, and he'd called the searchers. Showing up in a fire-truck, they had to use extensions on the longest ladder on the truck to reach him. Apparently, the highest limb of the tree had broken off in the wind storm, leaving a sharp point behind at the top. As if some sarcastic deity had decided to end John's innocent life as human shish-kebab, the fireman who'd had the wherewithal to climb up there, found the nine year old impaled on the pointed branch. The two kites were never found.

Day Twelve: Saint Julian the Hospitaller

1:00AM Thursday January 5, 2007 Tannersville, Florida

In the master-bedroom on the second floor of their farmhouse, Dallas Holbrook snored along with his wife, Cassandra. Usually, he enjoyed eight hours of uninterrupted sleep, however something outside had gotten loud enough to wake him up. The intrusiveness of the sound had broken through that thick window glass, ungluing his sticky eyelids. The middle-aged farmer sat up, and planted his feet on the carpet while Cassandra slept on, untouchable. He could blow an air-horn into her ear for all the difference that would matter.

As the bread winner of the family, he was always on edge. The federal government had knocked on his door again last fall with another deal, and the experimental crop of corn he was growing for them was supposed to grow to maturity without a flaw. He was going to make-out like a bandit in using their latest miracle seeds. *Just take care of this stuff,* the man said, *and we'll harvest it for you, and we'll triple the highest price anywhere on the market.*

Couldn't say no to that. Currently three weeks away from harvest, the government corn was growing on forty acres near the house, and the only thing Dallas wanted to hear out there were those corn husks rustling in the breeze. Instead, there was a high-pitched drone with a metallic tinge, and he shuffled over to the window and opened the curtain and raised the blinds. Looking out, his heart skipped a beat.

There was no moon out there, and Dallas wasn't able to make things out as clearly as he'd like, but he did make out a quick moving cloud flying around this particularly important corn. Had to be insects, and it seemed they were diving in and out his very expensive crop. It was this swarm that had woken him up. Almost running to his closet with questions crashing in his head like a logjam, he snatched a jacket off a hanger and slipped it over his pajamas. Haphazardly stuffing his feet into some lace-less sneakers, he grabbed the flashlight on his dresser and trotted out of the bedroom. He was on his way to the cornfield, trying to figuring out why those bugs were there. Dallas was in hurry to get there; afraid the insects were eating his nuggets of gold. And what were they anyway? Locusts? Bees? The awful noise coming from the swarm kept on in his head, and when he saw a greenish glow radiating out of the same place, he got even more upset.

Inheriting a thousand acre farm from his father, he'd done physical labor throughout his life. At 52, he had some extra poundage on his old bones, but besides that, he'd been holding on pretty well. Leaving the main house through the back door, his stride was long and panic stretched it out even farther. He had to get to the bottom of this problem right away. His brown eyes were still twenty-twenty, yet good eyesight wasn't going to be enough to help him figure this one out. Standing in the middle of corn field, he looked up at the irritating insects. They were flying just over his head. Inches away from his nose, seeming to taunt him. That close, it was obvious they were flies of some kind. He had no idea how long they'd been out there before he woke up. Chilled by the robotic ticking and clicking behind their drone, it sounded as if tiny pieces of metal or very hard plastic had to be a part of them. Minutes later, the enigmatic horde surged away into the night, weird rattle helpfully leaving with them.

Dallas had remained just as frightened. He walked through the sections where the mature stalks had been squashed flat, and the radiance he'd seen from a distance was faintly glowing up from the ground itself. Were the injuries to the stems of the bended plants have anything to do with the greenish light? He couldn't figure out how any insect would be able to flatten corn plants down like that, but the proof was in the pudding.

Dallas didn't know that the green pudding was toxic. He started to feel sick to his stomach, and he walked back to the house and tried to go back to bed, but he could not get back to sleep. He had decided to call Andy. The man worked full-time for the local growers, since he had his own helicopter. Yup. He'd call his friend up, and ask him for a fly over. Of course, he couldn't bother him at two in the morning. Squeezing his hands together tight, he started to watch the clock. At seven, he got up and went downstairs and picked up the phone.

"Hello Andy, its Dallas. Look, I know it's early, but something really wacky happened in the middle of one of my fields last night, and I need a fly over to see how much of my crop has been destroyed. You gotta let me know when you can get me into your schedule. This is important. A lot of my plants were crushed and I need to know how extensive the damage is."

"Good morning to you, Dallas. Doesn't sound like things are going very well for you, right now. Look, I gotta' go over to Harrick's spread right now. It's about sixty miles north of here. I have *no* time at the moment, since you called when I was halfway through the door. How about if I get to you right before sunset? I can even pick you up, so you can see what's up for yourself."

"Okay, that sounds fine, thanks. Around what time should I be looking out for you?"

"Ah...'round five or so, I guess."

"Looking forwards to it. See you later, and thanks again. I'm really in a fix."

Dallas fidgeted throughout the day. He tried calling some of his acquaintances for succor, but it didn't work. Telling them what happened, they suspected he was drugs or that he'd lost his mind completely. Their advice was useless and irritating. After these pointless calls, he made himself a lavish lunch. He didn't eat any of it, and he walked back outside and drove his pick-up truck as close as he could to the affected field. Parking, he climbed onto the bed of the truck, and rested his hands on the top of the cab, teetering on his toes to lift himself a smidgeon higher. The plants were still hundreds of feet away from him, and his idea of looking down on them from the truck was ridiculous. All he could make out were indistinct shadows in the swaying rows. When he heard an engine in the distance, he jumped off the bed and back into the cab, and he drove like a madman to the pasture he knew Andy would use to land. Getting there early, Dallas watched the copter slowly lower to land. When the aircraft was just three feet from the grass, he crouched down and ran towards the copter. Reaching the ground, Andy didn't shut his engine down, opening the passenger door for Dallas instead. He smiled and tossed a headset over to him so they could circumvent the engine noise during their conversations. When Dallas was belted into his seat, Andy lifted the bird straight up, the fastest express elevator in the county.

"I certainly understand why you wanted me to get here, after I saw it four miles out. I don't know why you don't have a crowd up there already." Andy sounded happy, as if it had been really cool.

"What are you talking about? Why would the destruction of my crops from a swarm of flies be interesting to anyone? I can't imagine why flattened plants would be fascinating to anyone?"

"Maybe you should shut-up, my friend, and look down. It's something you need to see, and it's spread out like butter on bread."

Dallas did as he was told, and the sight shut him right up, closing his mouth before opening it up again in surprise. It was a crop circle, a big one, and it was complicated too. The devil-born insects had destroyed thirteen acres of his experimental crop, and he started to worry about what the secret arm of the governmental GMO nuts were going to do to him.

"How the hell could they make anything like this, Andy? Its nuts. I've never seen or heard of a crop circle this far south. Ah…shit! There's nothing I can do about this. Nothing. God, this thing it going to get a lot of attention, and I'll have crowds of tourists and press and…and…"

"Dallas," it looked like his passenger was having a coronary, "you need to relax, and look at the flip-side of things. Maybe you could sell tickets or have a festival of magic acts or something."

Andy didn't know about the possible repercussions connected with that particular part of his friend's crop of corn, and Dallas wasn't listening to him. His misgivings waxed as the sunlight waned, and paranoia started to buzz into him; a new swarm of worries needling straight into his head.

"Can you see what's wrong, Andy?" Dallas was pointing down at the circle, "It's getting dark, so you must be able to see that the entire symbol is lit up. See it? Can you see it?"

"You're right. What do you think it is? Could it be radiated?"

"It has to be, and that glow was there last night, when I first saw the flies building the damned thing. I've been ignoring the way I've felt since I went out there, but I wouldn't be at all surprised if I don't have radiation sickness."

"You do look sort of crappy, and that might be a feasible explanation. Maybe there is something wrong with this. Shit, maybe the circle is poisonous."

Andy dropped him off, and flew away. The ghostly radiance coming from the cornfield got more intense, beaming brighter through the shroud of night. Dallas got back in his truck and drove to the main house, and he was juggling ideas about what he should do in a situation he couldn't understand. Should he call someone? And who exactly? Walking into the house, he began to screech Cassandra's name, now concerned about her own well-being under the circumstances. He found a note on the dining room table, letting him know she'd gone to a hairdressing appointment. After that, she'd written out that she'd be going to Sarah's house for dinner. She'd be back around ten or so.

Already after six, it was almost dark outside. Then he heard what had to have been the engines of smaller planes flying over his farm, more precisely over his crop circle. And his house phone started to ring. Ah. Of course. An onslaught of messages for interviews with him, and the whining over his house got louder as the ringing inside, kept on; a droning fly he could not swat. The circle crop had become a magnet, and its unmatched southern placement had made it even more appealing. Nothing had ever appeared below the thirty degree latitudinal line anywhere else, and that made the appearance of the circle in southern Florida remarkable.

Dallas was getting physically sicker by the minute, and day-to-day normalcy was quickly unraveling way too fast. He had to decompress then and there. He walked over to the liquor cabinet in the living-room and poured himself a shot of bourbon, and then he poured himself another one, praying it would be enough to stabilize him. Sitting down on the couch, he waited there like a directionless lump needing more information, feeling like he was fading away. Overwhelmed, he dozed off and he didn't wake up until nine-thirty. Surprised by only silence surrounding him, he turned his head slowly to the right and then to the left. The phone wasn't ringing, and the planes weren't flying overhead anymore. What could be behind this latest transformation? Dallas had lost any drive to figure that out. Another cryptic mystery on the lengthening list. He wished the whole thing was nothing but a dream, and he hadn't really woken up yet. He wished he was about to watch an old movie with Cassandra when she gets back home in a few minutes. The comforting vision lulled him back to sleep.

The very loud knocking on his door came to him like a scream coming out of nowhere, and his brittle peace was shattered. He had not answered the front door fast enough, and the awful knocking changed to pounding, and the bell began to chime so endlessly it sounded broken. Dallas wobbled up and stumbled to the front hall. By the time he got to there, the heavy oak door was shaking in its hinges.

"Jeez. Hold your horses, whoever you are. What do you want?"

The pounding was replaced by a man's voice.

"Mr. Holbrook, it's imperative you open this door right now! We're here to help you, sir. My name is Collins. I'm a captain in the National Guard and you and your family are in danger from the radiation coming from the field near your house."

"Well, it's about time you guys got over here…" And Dallas unlocked the door, quickly sliding the safety chain out of the hasp. He hadn't really had enough time to actually open it completely when the door slammed at him with a lot of force. He fell backwards. They weren't really the National Guard, and they were in uniforms he'd never seen before. An off-shoot of the US Air Force, they had no intention of helping him. Two grunts picked him up by his armpits rushing him out to a military RV parked in his driveway. They'd been waiting impatiently for this extraction, and all they'd wanted was for him to just open the door.

Project Blue Book was a department in the United States Air Force that used to investigate evidence on U.F.O.s, and they would interact with the public in a minimal way. Scrapped in 1970, they'd been replaced with more secretive one called Variant 9. No one knew anything at all about it, and that reticence was so overwhelming a large percentage of the Air Force itself didn't know about it either. Having seen his crop-circle on a satellite feed, individuals in Variant 9 had been sent out in a helicopter to look at it up close, and then other agents had been ordered out to pick up the Holbrooks. The belligerence in the symbols stamped in the corn in Florida, as well as the radioactivity coming out of it, had motivated them into containing the entire thing. Muzzling the media, they sent out a cautionary proviso over the entire farm. No more fly-bys. The airspace above the farm and the outlying land was heavily restricted. Their own scientists would decipher what they could, and that included the questioning of the farmer and his wife. Of course, before they were let go again, they would certainly be branded with a threat of grievous injury if they ever utter a single word about the circle or what was behind their ongoing silence. A few days later, Andy went through an interrogation from Variant 9 as well. Dallas recovered fairly well from his low grade radiation poisoning as someone in the department found compassion to treat it.

TWELFTH NIGHT

The twelve days of Christmas are crowned by a fulcrum in Christian religion. On the end day, they commemorate the miracle of holy-spirit manifesting itself in the physical form of a mortal man. Named Epiphany, it's generally observed on January 6th, and the last twelve hours on January 5th is observed as Twelfth Night. In the middle-ages in Tudor England those hours were filled with humorous wantonness. Like irreverent children, everyone, including the royalty, ignored the proper rules in the twelve hour countdown, emotionally believing that God's eyes were about open a lot wider at 12:01 in the resurrected gaze of Jesus Christ.

From the humble taverns to the castles of their overlords, and even in the court of the king himself, the powerful would change places with the lowest. In a madcap juxtaposition, the scepter would be held in the hands of the lowliest of the low, and that individual was called the Lord of Misrule. He would be in on the throne for the next twelve hours; the carefully proscribed hours of madness on twelfth night. During the scandalous hours of the Lord's reign, things in general were also topsy-turvy. Handmaidens wore papier-mâché crowns, while the countess and her husband would serve wine into crystal glasses held by the brigands who usually muck out their stables.

Twelfth night isn't commemorated in the same way anymore, however there are exceptions to the rule. A few individuals have clung to the old traditions. The Cleves were wealthy and very English, and after migrating across the pond ten years earlier, they'd built a castle on Martha's Vineyard. And it really was a castle, even if they called it a country estate in conversations.

Their ancestors had lived in the King's court during the Tudor age, and they would not forget that heritage. As King Henry the Eighth casually ordered a river of blood to flow through the divot on the side of the chopping block outside the Tower of London as the heads of those who'd vexed him fell, their forebears had been wise. They had survived his duplicitous whims.

Katherine and Felix Cleves were bubbling with the excitement of teenagers. She was forty-eight and he'd turned fifty-three a week ago. They were re-creating the ancient twelfth-night celebration that used to take place hundreds of years ago in their ballroom in the east wing of their stone bastion. They'd installed a custom throne in the very large chamber, and it stayed there as a staple for the yearly event. The over-sized mahogany chair had gold filigree and semi-precious stones installed into its wood, and it sat on a platform covered with purple carpeting. Whoever ends up sitting in it, oversaw the room. Every year, the Cleves send out invitations to friends and family in England and the United States, and at least over half of their guests would fly in from Europe.

Sallie Evans was Katherine's first cousin. Marrying an upcoming screenwriter named Robert Bertram thirty years ago, Sallie's husband's talent was discovered in a big way. He was revered in Hollywood, and Sallie herself had a life-long friendship with Daniel Craig. She'd saved his life when they were teenagers swimming off the coast of the French Riviera, as he'd almost drowned, but she'd dragged him to the shore. The familial connection to the rich and the famous drew Katherine and Felix into a love affair with the performing arts. Their social circle included actors, directors, screen-writers and producers. Ennui can easily replace oxygen in the upper atmosphere of the ultra-rich, and practical jokes and pernicious back-biting gossip is a soothing salve for this unpredictable crew. Felix drew on that penchant to expand on more unconventional events during his party every year.

At the beginning of their twelve hour long celebration, each male guest would pick out a token from a bowl situated next to the arched entrance of the ballroom. After everyone was seated, Felix would instruct his favorite niece from Surrey to grab another corresponding piece from a different glass bowl sitting on the table in front of the throne. The ringlet-bearing maiden would then announce the number printed on the one she'd chosen.

Whoever matched it would be the lord of the evening. Felix would then get off the throne and remove his tasteful gold crown off his head, and graciously place it on the head of the winner. After that, he'd sit down next to his wife. On a regular chair. The Lord of Misrule, whoever he was, would climb the dais to the throne and rule over the twelve hours of drunken merriment. Felix and Katherine and many of their extended family would wait tables in their makeshift court, pouring wine and bringing food to their guests as serfs. Of course, the antics would vary every year. Who would put a lampshade on their head or start a food fight was up for grabs, but all the revelers would certainly be hammered by midnight.

Lydia, the English girl who usually picked out the number every year, would always be escorted out of the ballroom by her nanny by three in the afternoon. Any other youngsters were also dragged away at about the same time, as the festivities would become too impudent and rakish for the innocent at that point.

On Thursday, the fifth of January on the year of 2007, Felix climbed the dais and invoked another twelve-hour extravaganza. The throne sat between two long dinner tables at the back of the room, and he was about to sit on the throne. The upcoming Lord would soon take his place for the remainder of the night. Lydia had gotten the mumps, but her sister had taken her place, waiting patiently next to the bowl. When the chimes of the grandfather clock in the corner of the vast room resonated out, that was the signal. Everyone was seated, and Felix nodded to Cynthia, and she stuck her hand into the bowl, scrabbling around before ending up with her choice. All the men in the room were playing with their plastic chips expectantly. One of them was about to called up to the throne.

However, an extremely good-looking man over six feet tall had suddenly sauntered into the ballroom, and he looked like he owned the place and everyone in it...since the beginning of time. About thirty-five, he was wearing a grey three-piece silk suit. Already wearing a crown on his head, it seemed he had already been chosen. Holding an onyx scepter with a platinum top of coiled snakes in his right hand, he continued strolling into the center of the room until he stopped right in front Felix. He had a knock-out smile on his face, and the host instantly accepted his regal entrance with delight, whispering to the girl not to pick-out a number at all, telling Cynthia to get her empty hand out of the container. She did as she was told. Felix then bowed to the stranger standing before him, and he took off his crown and left it on the table.

Mr. Cleves had assumed one of his Hollywood buddies was behind this, assuming this splendid interloper was an actor about to blaze onto the silver-screen in an upcoming feature film. Whoever out of his cadre of producers and directors was behind it, was probably trawling for an investment in the project. And if that was true, so be it. It didn't faze him in the least. Felix loved gimmicks, especially if it magnified his own. He'd probably give them the financial boost they were angling for, at some point down the road.

"Good evening my Lord. My name is Felix Cleves, and this," he was gesturing towards his wife, "is my honorable wife, Katherine. We are here to accept the traditional responsibility of you over-lording us this evening. You may introduce yourself, my honorable sir."

In coming up with this off-the-cuff invitation, Felix was climbing down the three steps of the dais while grandly waving to his replacement to take the throne.

"I am the Lord of Misrule, Mr. Cleves, and you're right. I am here to rule you during these short Saturnalian hours."

He had a melodic voice, and an English accent. Felix could not pinpoint what part of England he was from in the strange lilt in his vowels. The elegant party-crasher gracefully lowered himself on the throne, still smiling. No longer looking up at Cleves, he now looked down on him.

To Felix, the guy was acting his role flawlessly; as if the expensive throne the seasoned artisans had built for him was more real with his 'royal' buttocks resting on the cushioned seat. The jewels and the swirls of gold in the mahogany really appeared to glitter more intensely as the Lord of Misrule turned his hypnotic gaze out to the entire room. Coming from a high window, a ray of light touched the fashionable shag of his brown hair, pleasingly supporting the simple platinum crown on his head. His clothing and his bearing may be up to date, but his expression was timeless…perhaps eternal, and the intensity of his natural charisma; inexplicable.

Picking up a pitcher filled with merlot, Felix went back up the stairs and filled the lord's goblet. He had instantly transformed into a servant.

Asking if the Lord of Misrule wanted anything else, he bowed and returned to his seat.

After the children had been escorted out, the celebration began in earnest. The entertainment became risqué, and later on, lewd and salacious. Jugglers cartwheeled into the middle of the room holding dangerous props including caricatures of well-known American and British political figures. Some of the performers were half-naked, plus fabric-free erotic dancers, male and female were also leaping between the jugglers. The tables were arranged in four long lines that bracketed the dance floor in the middle, and the guests enjoyed the sexually explicit humor and well-choreographed numbers up close and personal. After the flying heads of American presidents and the English kings, queens and prime ministers had landed, after the gymnastic dancers were done with their intense display, the more aristocratic guests brought dinner out to the rest of the party goers.

The room had quieted down some. The guests began to eat their jumbo shrimps, sea scallops and lobster tails on bone-white plates adorned with the family crest, and Cleves's own chef had made the cocktail sauce from scratch. The Lord of Misrule got to his feet, and clinked a fork against the side of a water glass to get everyone's attention. Somehow that distinct sound had risen above the clattering of cutlery, banter and the flute-driven back-ground music. His polite interruption had worked, and besides the ongoing muted music, silence reigned. His soft words were clearly heard by everyone in the ballroom.

"Forgive me, my dear subjects, but I must disturb your dinner with a short diversion. As you know, the world is disintegrating and my manifestation here on this day at this time can only be a harbinger of an apocalypse never anticipated. Now, I don't want you to get too upset," and at that point the Lord had raised his scepter, pointing it at the back of the room where a movie screen was slowly descending from the ceiling to face a projector already installed in the opposing wall, "but if you wish to keep worshipping yourselves and what you hold dear, you have to accept the painful facets of an evolving predicament. On your host's screen, I'm going to display twelve news articles that have been reported today…the day before Epiphany. Historically, the Christian faith celebrates a submission to the higher power right after midnight. Using this as a fable or a miracle, depending on your point of view, you're supposed to bind your soul to this invisible force. Aaah...well."

His extended sigh resonated throughout the room. Seconds later, he went on. However, now there was a hint of sadness in his voice.

"Alas, technological prowess and material knowledge seems to have confused your direction and undermined your spiritual foundations, and I can't help myself. It's my duty to bring these difficulties to your consideration. It's topsy-turvy out there, and in this upside-down predicament, some pretty strange miracles have taken place without any help at all from God. Not realizing the whole ball of wax was racing off the rails, you picked up speed until the end. My upcoming display shall be short, but not so sweet, and I'm sorry I can't dilute it. Don't worry. Afterwards, you can have an aperitif or a glass of wine or two to guide you back to forgetfulness, allow you to party without a single remembrance to haunt you."

As if his scepter was a magic wand, he waved it towards the ceiling. The main lights dimmed, and the ballroom became a theater for his slide-show.

Felix and Katherine were lapping up his latest antics with delight, and the rest of their guests enjoyed this surprise as well. Felix couldn't have made a distraction as exciting as this one if he'd tried, and he was even more likely to support whatever this Lord of Misrule was going to be starring in. Popping a lump of lobster in his mouth, he avidly read the first article displayed on the screen forty feet away from him.

TWELVE ITEMS FROM TODAY'S NEWS

The Traveler *January 5, 2007*

DUST STORM CHOKES BEIJING CHINA

By ***Fredrick Pender***

Air pollution zoomed off the charts in Beijing as well as the surrounding areas in northern China after a dust storm ravaged the region. When the high wind associated with the storm was over, a blocked stagnation in the atmosphere was responsible for storm's dust and the city smog to accumulate and hang there. Currently, the air in the city is unbreathable. Along the Gobi Desert on China's northern border, there has been a high number of dust storms so far this winter, pummeling the whole country with a higher level of pollution than the previous year. The World Health Organization considers the highest level per cubic meter of particulate matter in the air to be considered healthful should not exceed 25 mic. The reading in Beijing earlier today had registered at PM2.5, equaling 700 mic. per cubic meter.

The level of density of material suspended in the air was enough to make most residents stay inside. Almost all of the few individuals who had gone out on the streets had fallen on the sidewalks. Without a forecast for a front with wind to clear the smog out, the situation becomes dire. Emergency workers are inundated with casualties, unable to keep up with increasing numbers of people succumbing to the fumes. Attempting to avoid the side-effects of....

The Guardian *January 5, 2007*

MOUNT ONTAKE ERUPTS IN JAPAN: KILLING HUNDREDS

By ***George Monbiot***

Mount Ontake erupted without warning today. The volcano spewed out a huge plume of ash, rock and smoke, trapping hundreds of hikers on trails on the side of the mountain. A thousand soldiers, police and fire fighters began to comb through the ash that covered the slope to rescue the survivors. Seventy-one people are currently missing, and the volcano was still billowing out toxic steam. Certain sections of the mountain remain out of reach depending on the direction of the wind.

One of the largest rocks coming out of the eruption had plunged through the roof of a hut near the Delfta. Approximately seven backpackers seeking shelter there were killed. A volcanologist at the meteorological agency in Nagano, warned the eruption was ongoing. He foresaw a recurrence of the intense curtain of ash and rocks over the next two days....

The Fayetteville Sentinel *January 5, 2007*

FIREBALL LANDS IN MEXICO

By ***Craig Cohan***

A fire ball hurtled to the ground and exploded near the small village of Ichmul in the Yucatan valley. The phenomenon had started right after midnight, lighting up the entire sky. The resulting impact was followed by blue flashing lights and an electrical power outage for most of the Yucatan. Flames had been seen burning at the crash site until 2:00AM, however the authorities hadn't been able to get close enough to tell whether it was a meteor or space debris. There was a noxious effect of some kind surrounded the crash site, but what is responsible for the dangerous poison has remained a mystery.

Alan Lynne, a quantum physicist who works in an American funded group that delves into interstellar questions, had been sent to Ichmul right after the impact. In a telephone interview with this reporter, Professor Lynne conjectured that the intermittent blue flashes coming from the center of the crash could be radiation interacting with extreme temperatures generated at the center of the impact.......

The Boston Tribune *January 5, 2007*

ANGER IN KASHMIR RISES AFTER DISASTROUS FLOODING

By ***Crista Bahr***

After monsoon rain had flooded the city seven days ago, residents of Kashmir had turned their irritation to government administrators who failed to support them during the ongoing devastation. The first estimate of eight hundred and fifty people who had drowned had quickly grown to nine hundred and twenty-five over the past two days, and large parts of Srinager, the capital of Jammu, and Kashmir are still under water. Thousands are trapped on the roofs of their homes, while even more victims arrive at relief camps that are already overcrowded.

Many complained that the government had maintained a presence in the territory to keep a lid on any revolt, yet the administration and the troops vanished in the current disaster, leaving the local population to their fate. Stranded by high water that won't recede, the general degree of danger had increased with a forecast calling for ten more hours of heavy rains to begin within the next few hours…

The San Diego Patriot *January 5, 2007*

EARTHQUAKE KILLS IN THE ANDREANOF ISLANDS OF ALASKA

By ***Helen Thomas***

One hundred and thirty-five people were killed in an earthquake on the Adak Island in the Andreanof chain off the coast of Alaska. The earthquake had recorded 8.6 on the Richter scale, and it had created a long fifteen foot crack beginning at the north-east section of the island. On nearby Umnak Island, Mount Vsevidof, a volcano that had been dormant for two hundred years had been awakened by the quake, and many buildings were destroyed in the eruption.

The earthquake and the after-shocks were also responsible for a tsunami reportedly fifty feet in height. It had broken on the coastline of Scotch Cap, demolishing residential homes and businesses there. It had damaged the oil lines at Sand Bay as well. The small islands had not slowed the wave down, and when it reached Hawaii, it devastated the island's largest commercial dock, as well as demolishing two villages. The wave had inflicted fifty million dollars in property damages on Hawaii and the nearby islands, Oahu and Kauai.

So far, three hundred aftershocks have been felt along the Aleutian Islands, from Unimak to Amchitka Pass and…

The Telegraph *January 5, 2007*

FIRE TORNADO THREATENS MELBOURNE

By ***Thelma Nash***

A lightning storm was responsible for a bevy of ground fires, and the firefighters have only been able to control a small percentage of them. Rural southern Australia had been turned into a tinder box after weeks of drought and temperatures skyrocketing over one hundred and four degrees in an ongoing heat wave. The dangerous conditions worsened on Thursday morning with a forty-five mile-an-hour wind, and the ground strikes from the lightning started a barrage of wild fires.

There are four different fires currently out of control, besides a fire-whirl that became a Tornado. Witnesses described it as a fiery pillar over a hundred feet tall, and the fire was burning along its vortex. Tens of thousands of hectares on still on fire, racing through the outskirts of Melbourne. Hundreds of people are being evacuated from their homes.

Presently, officials believe the conditions are even worse than what was recorded in the 2002 inferno that had left 173 people dead in its wake…

The Daily Chronicle *January 5, 2007*

THOUSANDS LOST IN AVALANCHE IN PERU

By ***Bridget Johnson***

Buildings collapsed in an earthquake and thousands died in a major Peruvian fishing port called Chambile. Offshore, the tremor destabilized the glacier on Mount Huascaran in the Andes Mountains, and that touched off an avalanche burying the nearby town Yanque under a wall of mud and rocks. The avalanche had been moving at about one hundred and twenty miles an hour down the side of the mountain while many of the twenty-five thousand residents of the town had been at home watching the World Cup football match between Italy and Brazil. Only 350 people survived in the more densely populated part of Yanque. They'd raced to the highest elevation in the local cemetery as it was the only option they had in the very short amount of the time they'd had.

Mancora, a smaller village, was also buried. The Peruvian Government announced they will preserve Yanque's memory by forbidding excavation on the ruins, and they would build a new town with the same name, five kilometers away.

The exact number of deaths is not known, but it is estimated at eighty thousand. Another million people are currently homeless. To begin the monumental task of rehousing those who had…

The New York Journal *January 5, 2007*

LOST HIKERS IN SCOTLAND ARE FOUND: MYSTERY DEEPENS

By ***Donald Lawrence***

Twelve vacationers and eight residents were lost backpacking the trails in the Queen Elizabeth Forest Park within Loch Lomond. The long stretch of balmy days in the lee of the Grampion Mountains is believed to be a result of the rare Fohn Effect, and the good weather had enticed a lot more hikers out during that time of year. Law enforcement and park officials had begun a comprehensive search using blood hounds with no results, however they were all found in a macabre incident.

A sheep herder who lived on the outskirts of Thornhill, a town that bordered the Queen Elizabeth Forest Park, was riding through his forty-acre ranch when he saw a fifty foot wide sink-hole. Looking into it, he saw bodies lying on the uneven bottom of the hole, and he called the authorities. They quickly ascertained that they were the twenty missing hikers. So far, there has been no explanation on how they died or why they had all ended up on the bottom of a sinkhole miles away from park.

Doctor Charles Cavanagh, a local geologist, was questioned about the appearance of the sinkhole itself. He believed that an underground stream or cave could have slowly eroded the regular structure of the dirt that had been supporting the thin thatch of wild grass, and it may have simply disintegrated…

The Nebraska Gazette *January 5, 2007*

LIGHTNING STORM IN IOWA STARTS A DEADLY BLAZE

By ***Roger Riley***

Three homes on Applewood Street in Ankeny in Polk County, were struck by lightning at the same time in the most violent lightning storm ever recorded in the state of Iowa. Meanwhile, yet another strike hit the town's power station eighty feet away on Linden Street, triggering an explosion resulting in more fires in the populated area. The Abilene Free Church next door and the Growing and Learning Center across the street were set ablaze, and a southern wind drove flaming debris onwards into the city of Des Moines sparking even more fires.

Joel Hoffman, one of the witnesses, whose home was on an elevation in Cedarville, the nearest town to Ankeny to the west, called the storm apocalyptic. Having never seen lightning look like that before, he described it as awe-inspiring even if it had been deadly for some.

The resulting heat and smoke inhalation caused thirty-seven deaths in Des Moines and Ankeny. Every single fire department in the area responded, however the on-going lightning strikes continued to ignite more fires in different parts of the city....

The Alabama Eagle *January 5, 2007*

TWISTERS ERUPT IN A MASSIVE OUTBREAK

By ***John Ludlow***

Over one hundred and seventy-five tornadoes were confirmed in a fifteen state swath that included a Canadian province. Five hundred and thirty-four deaths and over a billion dollars of property damage has been left behind in the paths of these twisters. The sudden increase has dwarfed any previous outbreaks: The spate of tornadoes in 1974 had left three hundred and nineteen dead, while another group in 2011 slaughtered three hundred and twenty-four individuals.

Twenty tornadoes arriving at the same time with their severity, longevity, and scope had never been meteorically recorded before. The hellish outburst began right after midnight on Thursday in Indiana, Ohio and Kentucky. Eleven F5 and Eight F4 tornadoes were being reported at the same time, while forecasters in Indiana could not keep up with the activity. They called Governor Cooper and he put the state under a disaster watch. It was the only time in American history in which a bevy of tornadoes had been destructive enough to invoke the provision.

Thirty-one people were killed in Brandenburg, Kentucky, twenty-eight in Guin, Alabama, and another F5 tornado crossed the U.S. border into Windsor, Ontario in Canada, and thirty more individuals died at the Windsor Curling Club. Michigan was not attacked as violently as its neighbors. Only one twister touched down at Coldwater and Hillsdale, killing eight in a trailer park.

The thunderstorms surrounding the twisters had also caused flash floods along the entire weather front following the upper-peninsula towards the Appalachian Mountains...

The Chicago Chronicle *January 5, 2007*

DAM BURSTS ON RIVER ELBE THOUSANDS FLEE

By ***Angela Merkel***

The flood-swollen River Elbe broke through a dam above Magdeburg, the capitol of Saxon-Anhalt in Germany. Twenty-three thousand residents had to evacuate their homes. Many of the main highways are inundated as firefighters continue to rescue the stranded drivers. Twenty-two bodies have been found in the rising waters.

Victor Orban, the mayor of Magdeburg, said they have a catastrophic situation, and it is not normalizing. In a bid to sustain electricity in the city, hundreds of soldiers began to build a barrier of sandbags around the sub-station in Rothensee. And thousands of volunteers as well as conscripted convicts coming out of the nearby prisons were all reinforcing the banks of the Elbe and the Danube rivers with sand bags. This reinforcement must go on and support five hundred miles of river front land.

Parts of Saxony-Anhalt and the neighboring Brandenbury were under a flood alert as the rising crest moved north along the Elbe. Andreas Hamann, a spokesman of the Disaster Relief Project believes the other dykes will withstand the oncoming stress, however he was not one hundred percent positive. A dyke at Fishbeck, west of Berlin had breached the night before, leading to more evacuations.

In an anonymous letter to the Magdeburg Town Hall printed in the Magdeburg Advocate, the writer had indicated the town fathers had ignored the warnings of both a scientist and a botanist telling them about a lichen growing on the concrete of the dam over the summer. Believing this unusual plant life would weaken the concrete, they insisted that the powerful rain storms over the winter were not responsible for the dam's destruction. The letter went on to emphasize that the parasitic fungus\algae lichen was on many other dams, and the missive ended with a dismal pronouncement that the lichen will drag Germany into desolation from the ongoing...

The Florida Beacon *January 5, 2007*

CROP-CIRCLE OFF LIMITS BY AIR FORCE

By ***Ramon Yates***

In the corn fields of the Holbrook Farms within the confines of Tannersville town, a crop-circle appeared in the early morning hours of January 5th. A crop circle has never been seen below the thirty-four degree latitudinal line, and the United States Military's response to its presence was also unprecedented. The Air Force has built a barricade around the farm, plus a flight ban over the Holbrook land. Any questions surrounding the circle can only be posed to Major Jenny Harris, a liaison, and Major Harris explains they need more time to investigate the matter before she can give out any information.

Mr. and Mrs. Holbrook, the owners of the farm, were unavailable. In the hours before the air force locked the site down, a few locals had flown over the circle. Andy Paulsen, a crop-duster, and a friend of Mr. Holbrook, had seen the crop circle itself, and he had taken a picture of it. The large circle uses over thirteen acres to depict a generic warning symbol of radiation; three elongated triangles, points touching in the center interweaved with a portrait of a molecule of pelagic plastic. Flattened corn plants between the connected triangles indicated the lines and circles describing hexagonal form of the molecule, and when the structure moved into the triangles themselves, the corn plants remained upright connected perfectly to its opposite.

A copy of Mr. Paulsen's photo of the crop-circle was looked over by an expert in molecular-biology, and she told this reporter that the molecular form depicted in the corn is not exact. There is no natural particle like it on earth. Wishing to remain anonymous, she was concerned that if there really was a molecule of that form in our ecosystem, there would be global consequences of an extremely disturbing kind in our future...

The Lord of Misrule had been twiddling with his gold cufflinks embossed with the insignia of infinity and he'd been sipping the wine in his goblet. He had been patient. When his display rolled through the last article, he waited for a minute or two. Deciding the audience had had enough time to read all of it, he pressed two buttons on the remote in his pocket. The screen rose, disappearing into its dust free sleeve in the ceiling, and the lights went on. The crowd was quiet and subdued, and there was a hushed expectancy in the air. Hearing nothing but a faint giggle and whispering, the entire room went silent again. Looking over his court, the Lord saw real agitation in their faces. No, no. The soupçon he'd presented shouldn't dampen their holiday verve. He set his empty glass on the table had stood up. The Lord really didn't need anything else to get their attention, but he was ceremonial in temperament. He began to ring a small brass bell he'd found in the clutter near the glass bowl. When its final peal died away, everyone in the room stared up at him, agape. Of course, he had more than their attention, and the strange level of control over them had gotten deep enough to become enigmatic.

"Aaah," he murmured, looking out with a half-smile. "These articles were a bit distressing weren't they? Accepting this irrevocable chronicle is not a comfortable pill to swallow," yet he'd coated those words in honey and his smile broadened to a grin.

"Let us remember, it's twelfth night after all…and I am the Lord of *'Misrule'*." He'd placed emphasis on that declarative word in his title, accentuating his disingenuousness, and his duplicitousness. "Perhaps you've been giving too much credence to what you've been reading. Should we believe it? I'm not sure what's reported is actually there."

The elegant Lord bowed solemnly to Cleves and his guests, timing the gesture perfectly. He'd broken the ice. He had lightened the heaviness in the room, and a wave of chuckling ran through the crowd. He'd given them an escape; a way to really forget the whole thing. Clearly, the nasty crap on the screen had not been true. Just a practical joke orchestrated by their mischievous host. No one wanted to consider the complexity of what he'd said. If the Lord of Misrule hinted that he'd been lying, wouldn't that indicate he'd been telling the truth? But why would he do that? There's no reason for him to be tricky at that point, no reason at all…

"I know you're not done eating your dinner, and we have three and half hours during which you can let your hair down and forget the rules. Your carriage will arrive for you at twelve and your integrity will emerge on the platform to save you when the invisible becomes more intense, at least, that's the way it was in the old days. Anyway, we better have a hell of party until then. Come on and shimmy through these hours. I grant you power to blow the doors out and have a great time."

The Lord of Misrule sat back on the thrown. Holding a different remote, he nudged a button. The volume of the music rose and the lights lowered, and then he crossed his hands behind his head, and planted his booted heels on the edge of the dais.

Paul Harrison was forty-three years old and single. He lived in Lancaster on the coast of the Irish Sea. He'd flown to the United States for the party, and at that moment, he was one of the three individuals in the ballroom who were still sober as church mice. And he was sharp. Paul noticed the incongruity in the time variables in a lot of the articles. Whoever set this up had to have lined the stories up in a very tight interval, however there were problems. Unsurmountable ones. It was just too tight. Some of the actions couldn't have gotten there in time...if they were real. Nevertheless, the disjointedness of it pique his interest. He was also impressed by the lullaby coming out of this year's Lord of Misdirection, and this guy's control over his voice was a commanding gift.

Yes, curiosity drove Paul onwards. Using a photographic memory, he took his iPhone out of his pocket. He began with simple facts in the first article, and he was ignoring the merriment intensifying around him. Reading the information scrolling by on his small screen, none of it was reassuring in the least. He delved into more of the articles, with outside sources to support their veracity. He got even more nervous. Paul walked over to cousin Oliver, busy feeding a red-headed woman forkfuls of angel food cake.

"Olly...OLLY! Stop it, and listen to me. I think those articles were true. I haven't checked on all of them, but the first four were on the mark. Things are really going to the crapper *everywhere.* The whole world is crumpling, and there's no way to explain any of it. There's an end of the world feeling in those articles, and I feel like I'm living in an episode from the twilight zone."

Paul had been talking fairly loudly to be heard over the rock music, but it would not have mattered if he'd used a megaphone. The lady Oliver was flirting with had beckoned him to follow her to a back room. There were private rooms back there? It was obvious he wasn't going to get through to him.

"Sounds awful bad, governor," Oliver said it over his shoulder. He'd stopped feeding the woman and faced him. "But right now, we can't do anything about it. You've gotta relax, and go with the flow," and then he laughed. "Did you know we have a Lady for the Lord tonight? Seriously. Lady Gaga is going to perform in forty-five minutes, and I can't wait to see her costume...so listen, Wanda and I are going on an adventure, if you know what I mean. You should find a tasty tart for yourself, and eat her right up. Stop worrying, I'm serious. I'll be back in time to see the show. We'll talk about it if you still want to after that."

Oliver and Wanda strolled off, and they vanished into a corridor at the west wall of the ballroom.

Paul was left behind; warning ignored. Nevertheless, the blank expression on his face had not gotten there because of his cousin's avoidance. It had come from a revelation. He'd kept on linking his memories to what he could find on his iPhone, and the whole thing had suddenly become a monster. All of the news articles were true; even if some of the info could not logically be there. The Lord's insinuations that the show was a ruse had worked perfectly. Everyone fell for that! How the actor portraying the Lord of Misrule in collusion with Felix Cleves could have set any of that up was beyond his ken. But he was dumbstruck.

Multi-colored spot lights swept across the dance floor as couples boogied wildly around. Lady Gaga was about to appear on a stage against the back wall of the ballroom. Sitting motionless in his chair, Paul was pale, as if he'd already given up the ghost. And then logic kicked back into gear. The end may be perilously near, but Oliver had a very good point. There was nothing he could do about the end of the world. Might as well dance with the passengers of the Titanic while she began to sink beneath the waves. Blood returned to his cheeks, and he smiled. The Lord of Misrule had been right about one thing. There wasn't much time left, and he got out his chair with a goal. The young Duchess of Cornwall pranced by wearing the revealing clothes of a serving wench holding a tray of glasses filled with champagne. He waved her over and took a glass. He'd begin to douse those worries. Gazing out at the swirling crowd, he'd hunt down the sugary dessert Oliver had advised him to find.

After Lady Gaga's performance, carousing went on until the midnight hour arrived. The Lord of Misrule would abdicate the thrown to Felix Cleves, and the host had gotten got up and the music had stopped. Half of the tipsy partygoers turned their attention to the throne, wanting to watch the closing ceremony. The rest got the message, and the room quieted.

At midnight during this annual recreation, Felix Cleves would always re-climb the dais. It was time for the Lord of Misrule to relinquish the throne, take the crown off his head and bow and give it back to Felix; an echo of what had happened hundreds of years ago. The real king would metaphorically put things back in order. Felix had climbed the steps. He was standing on the platform, and the Lord had risen to the occasion. Since Cleves was five eleven, the Lord of Misrule looked gently down into his brown eyes as his hand traveled to his platinum crown. He was about to take it off and give it to Felix, and Felix felt funny about that. The regular one was still resting on the table. He'd feel better putting his own crown back on again; he would just give the more lustrous one back to whoever owned it after the ceremony. Of course, those thoughts were about to become irrelevant. The short trajectory of the Lord of Misrule's hand had stopped. The platinum crown was apparently staying on his head. He sat back down on the thrown, resting his onyx scepter across his legs, yet another psychological barrier symbolizing his abrupt departure from tradition.

"My dear man, I really hate to do this, but you need to realize that those twelve tidbits I presented for you on the screen clearly underline my ongoing responsibility. The rules organizing this world are gone. If the innate order can no longer support your foundation, and if the chemical basis to link it all together is gone, then…."

"But you can't…I mean, we should really…um…ah...we're supposed to change places now, and….and…" Mr. Cleves was mentally trapped like a deer frozen in some car's headlights.

"I'm sorry, my sir. No. We can't change places. You aren't going to be able to lead anyone. You have a logical mind, and you won't be able to accept the way the world is now. No one can govern this disorder, but myself. Up is remaining down, white is darker than black, and microscopic fluff has become a global freak. The scientists and military commanders can't grab a handle on anything, while the power and wisdom they used to have has shrunk to a wink and a promise. No, I must stay on this luxuriously throne of yours for a bit longer. There's a good chance I'll sit here forever, if forever can withstand the ongoing renovations."

The Lord of Misrule continued to calmly look at Felix, unconcerned about the fact he'd just thrown a wrench into the usual sequence of the annual ritual. The giggles and whispers from the guests was replaced with silence. The crowd was suddenly mesmerized by what was taking place on the dais as they waited breathlessly to see what the final result was going to be. Felix stayed stock-still like a deer frozen in the headlights. The unscripted actions of this man left him stymied, and he had no witty rejoinder to this impossible announcement. Staring up at the pretender's sleek finery and his miraculous physical charisma, he was then transported beyond his day to day presumptions. For a moment, the actor was no longer an actor on an elevator to stardom, and the transcendent quality of the Lord, like an otherworldly vision, beamed into him. Felix's certainty over what should be done wavered and fell, and the impasse over his Kingship evaporated. He decided to accede to him, and he relaxed and chuckled. It had become clear. The Lord must remain on the throne, it was the right thing to do.

"So be it, my Lord. I'm looking forwards to my own relaxation, since I'm giving you the ongoing responsibility to decide whose head rolls and how far," and then Mr. Cleves faced his audience.

"Outlandish things are running rampant out there this year," he said, "and I think we have no choice but to allow our new Lord of Misrule to go on with his rule until...until the broken egg shell is finally glued back together again. It's midnight, but this time we can keep on with our party as long as we can!"

A cheer erupted from the crowd, and Felix gracefully stepped back off the stairs to sit down with his wife again, while the Lord of Misrule himself stood up and spoke.

"Yes, my friends, topsy-turvy is the talk of the town. Put your left sneaker on your right foot and limp out to your car. You probably won't be able to open the driver's side door, as the keys in your hand will only fit the padlock on your neighbor's gardening shed. There'll be no solution for these shenanigans, and it's likely you'll go mad in the ongoing chaos."

He laughed, and raised his goblet in celebration. Almost everyone in the ballroom raised their own to honor what they thought was only a joke. It was all drivel after all, and he was probably being paid to act through this charade for their holiday pleasure.

Paul Harrison's glass was not raised. Instead, he swallowed the last drop of merlot on the bottom of his fourth cup of it with determination. The British royal he'd gotten his first glass of champagne from an hour ago wiggled in closer to him, and he put one of his hands on her ass and squeezed. He was trying very hard to divorce his mind and heart away from what he'd uncovered. As he dove head first into this bleak canard, he glued an off-kilter smile on his face, and no one, not even the countess, could make out the tears running down his cheeks.

PART TWO

8:35AM Friday January 5th, 2007 San Gabriel, California

Kitterman's was located in San Gabriel, a town in the suburbs of Los Angeles. It was fifteen miles from the coast. Johnny Monroe had been working in that factory for ten years. When the ownership of the company who owned the building changed twelve months ago, he'd gotten a letter in the mail telling him about new stock options offered by the Donnelly Foundation. A regular looking fellow with light brown hair and brown eyes, he was thirty-six. He didn't care what was going on in the drafty offices of the new owners in the city. It didn't mean a thing to him, and he tossed the letter in the garbage. All of it was a big fairytale; nothing to do with what he did every day.

It was his job to transport the tonnage of metal that had been imported from China or Taiwan or wherever, off the back parking lot outside Kitterman's warehouse doors, and inside the building. And line all of it up in logical piles on the concrete floor. Every day. His relationships with the other drivers and the floor manager were friendly. On Fridays they'd go out to Hushaby, a sports-bar three blocks away to play pool and watch sports games on the four strategically arranged large TV screens. Johnny was happy with his job and his rapport with Steve, the floor manager. Steve was the only boss he dealt with in a day to day give and take. Getting a raise of two-hundred dollars a month three weeks ago, he really thought it had come from his praise about his work. However, the pleasure the raise had given him was gone after a weird looking fly had bitten him on the arm a week ago. He'd felt an oddness floating around in his body, and instead of fading away, that strangeness got more intense. He was also dealing with interludes of lethargy, and it was the first time in his entire life in which he'd show up late for work. Almost twenty minutes late, lots of times. It was Friday, and he was looking forwards to going out to have some suds with the other guys at the end of the day, and he hit the gas and peeled out his driveway in his pick-up truck. He didn't want to be late *again*. Sitting in front of the wheel, the tightness in the waistband of his work jeans was pushing him forwards. It was irritating. For a second, he wondered if he was getting a beer belly, but he remembered the pressure hadn't been there yesterday. That couldn't be the reason. Nope. Besides lethargy, Johnny was having real problems remembering everything. He didn't remember the thirty-eight he'd secreted on the high shelf in the coat closet near the entrance of his house three days ago. Nor does he remember getting the same gun out of the closet that morning, squeezing it against the small of his back using the waistband of his jeans to hold it there right before he walked out the front door.

Arriving at Kitterman's, he parked and checked things out. There was a new shipment piled outside, and it looked like an acre of steel plate. Blowing at the coffee he'd just picked up at the deli across the street trying to cool it off a little bit, he watched a Mercedes skid to a stop right in front of the main office and Holly and Keith got out and walked inside. Of course, Johnny hadn't seen a Mercedes. In his mind, he'd replaced the luxury car with a white passenger van with *Emerald Point Missions* slapped on its side, and that the first of a torrent of necessary delusions to guide him into an unimaginable act. His visionary van had parked in the exact same place the Mercedes had, however in his now badly slanted world, eight kids got out and traipsed into the office, carefully supervised by two adults. Johnny thought it had to be a fieldtrip of some kind. The Donnelly Foundation must have opened their hearts so children could see what was involved in the complex building and manufacturing trades. A gratifying hallucination for him, their remarkable presence was poignant. Vigorously sipping at the coffee on his way to the forklift, he turned away. It was time to go to work. He would move the pallets of steel out of the parking lot into the warehouse…

Holly and Keith walked through the office and into the cavernous expanse of the warehouse itself. Holly had ordered the captain to dock Aspersion's Foil in a private marina next to one of the commercial docks in LA on Wednesday. Figuring out exactly what they needed to build twenty-two filters, Holly got on the computer to find a place to get it done speedily and precisely, as well as close by. Kitterman's popped right up. She remembered Keith's feeling about it, right off the top of his head. They both agreed: Kitterman's would be the answer. Using only a part of the building for the project, it would happen in a three-step process. Five by five feet square, the frames would be of high-grade steel. After they'd been poured, Keith and Wesley would line up everything needed inside the hollow frames before welding them shut. To let the different waves generated in the frames do their job, they'd decided to use Lexan as a window on the inner face. Glass could break or scratch, and it was harder to mold it into the complex corners of the frames. And they were in a hurry, a nerve-rackingly fast one. The idea of moving the newly built steel frames to another location for the final installation in which there can't be any floating dust or jarring coming up from the floor was scrubbed. Too many variables, and too much time to arrange. They'd stay where they were. Holly ordered yards of heavy plastic sheets to be stretched around a forty by forty foot section of the warehouse to close the entire area in. They would even create a lower ceiling from a larger piece of plastic, connecting the four plastic walls with airtight seams. This make-shift chamber would stop most airborne particles, and Keith's final delicate wiring wouldn't be contaminated. And Holly hadn't forgotten about the floor. An oversized mat would to cover every inch of concrete within, and a commercial mat was supposed to arrive on Saturday morning.

The frames should be done in two days. Keith and Holly would oversee the entire process without Wesley. They didn't need his help at that point. With schematics under their arms, they walked to a large work table in the middle of a wide aisle adjacent to the production line they were going to use. Unfolding the papers, they wanted to go over them *one more time.* If meticulousness was going to use up a little bit more time, so be it. They certainly couldn't afford any mistakes. The small window of time they still had to stop the catastrophe was shrinking, and so if anything goes wrong on the production line it would be too late to fix it.

Meanwhile outside, Johnny Monroe had been a very busy man moving pallets of steel for over forty-five minutes. When he saw a tendril of smoke slip under the corner of the outside wall of the warehouse and ascend in the air like a weaving snake, he was concerned. Making out more smoke rising from the far end of the building, he began upset. As those two hints both erupted into flames sixty seconds later to energetically blaze towards each other, Johnny's pulse rate soared. He was terrified for the children inside the building, and in his convoluted mind, he thought over what he could do to save them.

He shut off the forklift. He left the current load hanging in the air on lifted forks, as he sprinted to the backhoe that was parked sixty feet away. Swinging up onto the swivel seat in the cab, he turned the key and then he pushed the ignition knob. This backhoe was fairly large. At five tons, the highest part of the machine reached eleven feet off the ground not including the hydraulic digging arm. As the engine coughed into life, Johnny had come up with a radical idea to save the kids he believed were trapped in the warehouse.

He knew they must have been herded to the middle of the building, moving away from the two fires creeping towards them. He was going to save them by giving them the necessary exit between the encroaching conflagrations. He'd punch a hole in the metal wall with the backhoe. Of course, he was going to make this hole closer to one end on the building, not wanting to hurt them when he burst through. Speeding up, he piloted the neon-orange behemoth straight at the wall, and he didn't slow down; oblivious to the possibly devastating effects that may come from his crazy stunt. Johnny kept on going, bursting through the wall. And then he drove through a pile of equipment at the end of an aisle, flattening a lot of it beneath the treads of the backhoe while the rest scattered away like bowling pins. Johnny liked the breeze coming from the large hole he'd just made in the steel-plated wall behind him, and he stopped in the center of the aisle to see where the students were.

And he saw them! Two adults, with the kids cowered next to them farther along the wide aisle. (At least, that was what he thought was there). He wanted to cover the remaining four hundred feet left before he could get to them, and he tried to make the back-hoe trundle along faster. Johnny needed to save them. Maybe he could bring some in the cab with him, and lead the rest through the hole he'd made to escape the fire, but the reason he was really there was beginning to break through. Bubbling into his conscious mind, the concept of help was replaced with the word **'pulverize'**. He reached for the handgun pushed into his back, suddenly understanding why he'd bought it three days ago in a pawnshop. The necessity for it was clear. And there was no fire anywhere.

"Are you sure there's enough steel along the connection between the Lexan and the metal? It's got to be water proof, and solid as concrete," Keith said.

"Shush. I'm reading the specifications. It says '3.5 inches along the bead'. Sounds fine." Holly said.

"It doesn't sound bad."

"What about the thickness in the corners? Perhaps it needs to be a little bit more..."

But Holly stopped talking and spun around. Seconds later, the side wall bulged out with a screeching howl until the company's backhoe tore right through it. Holly and Keith watched Johnny power the machine through a pile of equipment before veering the orange beast straight at them. He was going twenty-five miles an hour. Johnny's eyes were glassy, and his expression was sickening. As this five ton backhoe bore down on them with speed, Holly seemed more irritated at the interruption than worried. Groaning, she picked up a tire-iron leaning against a trash barrel five feet away, but Keith had noticed the driver was also aiming a handgun at his partner.

"Holly, the guy has a thirty-eight, and he's pointing it at you."

"Thanks. Not going to be a problem."

Throwing the tire-iron like a boomerang, she'd used strength in its release. A precise spin, it left her hand in a blur, almost invisible. It pierced the backhoe's radiator, embedding itself into the middle of the working engine with deadly accuracy. The roaring advance of the mammoth stopped abruptly, however the following silence hadn't ended the ongoing danger. Another attacker was coming up behind Keith, and John Monroe was still wide awake at the wheel of the stationary backhoe with a loaded gun aimed at Holly's head.

Ervin, another driver working at Kitterman's, had been setting up space for Johnny to line up the new shipment of palettes. He had been bitten by one of the strange Borg-like flies, and he had a delusion in his head too. A ghastly one, urging him to use the forklift to knock over a certain section of the already stacked-up palettes he was traveling past at the moment.

'Go on boy...tumble them helter-skelter into the middle of the aisle on the other side. It'll crush that scallywag who's over there dead as a doornail....' This engaging voice kept on pushing him to action.

Keith had foreseen the lined-up aluminum falling on top of him in a clattering avalanche seconds before they fell, and he ran backwards as fast as he could. He didn't made it quite far enough. Two palettes bounced off the concrete floor like balls. One knocked him down, and the other landed on his left leg, breaking the femur bone in his thigh in two places and dislocating his knee. Sending endorphins into his bloodstream to block the pain receptors in his leg, Keith then used a jolt of adrenaline to magnify his abilities. He knew he was in a dangerous situation, and he needed to defend himself. That ability would be better served if he stopped the pain and shock from his injuries. Hearing the forklift running along the following aisle, the name of the man driving the machine, *Ervin,* popped into his head. It was going to be a lot harder for him to get out of the way of the next assault the guy was about to initiate; might be a deadly one...*or maybe not.*

Keith had some tricks up his sleeve. Not seeing the forklift didn't mean he couldn't 'feel' it. Using telekinesis, he flicked the fuel switch on the side of the Ervin's machine to **off,** and it instantly stalled out. The haunted man on the other side of the stacked palettes tried to start the engine, using the key and hitting the ignition button. It didn't work. He pounded his hands on the safety bar above the console with real frustration. Two weeks ago, he would have known to check the fuel switch, but after a metallic looking black fly's bite, he wasn't in control anymore. Ervin wasn't the same man. Going through a pointless endeavor with the key and button five more times, he finally gave up and got off of the fork-lift. The pallets he'd knocked over still represented an uncomfortable mound to climb over, and he decided to walk down the corridor to get to the other side. One way or another, Ervin wanted to defeat his quarry in a definitive way. If that meant he was going to have to fight him face to face, well, so be it.

Immobilizing Johnny's huge orange weapon, Holly turned her attention to the man himself. He was sat five feet off the floor in the cab of the now disabled backhoe. He was about to shoot her, yet she remained unflappable, staring straight back at Johnny. She even started to walk towards him, cold as ice, concentration riveted on him. She really thought she had the entire situation under control; hasty assumptions that would haunt her future.

Johnny was happy. He was about to pull the trigger of his 38 and blow her brains right out of her head…and then she disappeared into thin air. He stood up in the seat, and looked around. He even stared behind him. Nothing. No one anywhere, just towering piles of pallets on either side of the isle for hundreds of feet. He got out of the cage on the backhoe, and walked around waving the gun around; the best thing he could think of under the circumstances. She might reappear at any point, and he'd have her in his sights.

Holly had not really vanished. She'd just tinkered with his visual cortex. Getting out of the cab and standing on the concrete floor, had made her job a little bit easier. She strolled up to him with a smile, and Johnny Monroe felt a hard snap in his wrist, and the thirty-eight grew wings and flew out of his hand. It landed twenty feet away on the concrete floor. Then Holly reappeared, inches away from his face, and John was not happy as he looked deeply into her electric-blue eyes. Whatever he had in his mind to do next was quickly washed away as he fell into those swimming-pools. He forgot about everything he was supposed to be doing then and there, and any other future plans were washed away as well.

"Hello, John. Things are fine now. You need to go back to your seat in the backhoe and stay there for the next half-an-hour," Holly said, implanting this order into his mind.

"Yes…I will...ah…um, it's hard to know where I'm supposed to go these days. I'm not sure if that's a good idea, but maybe…"

Holly wasn't listening to Johnny's mumblings. He slowly climbed back into the broken loader. It didn't matter what he was saying. He was neutralized.

Resting her hands on her hips, she turned around. Beyond a pile of fallen pallets, Keith was badly injured on the floor, and a factory worker was lurching towards him with deadly intentions. Holly's blasé attitude to the attack thus far went through a sea-change. A streak of lightening, she blinked past her incapacitated friend, stopping right in front of Ervin. With only a faint flutter in the hem on her shirt sleeve and a tendril of her hair slipping back behind her ear, it appeared as if she had always there.

Ervin's travel was halted. It didn't seem he could walk around her or attack her, and Holly's mood would forestall those possibilities. And then she slapped him. It looked like a glancing blow across his cheek, but there had been hidden power in the strike. He was heavy-set and tall, yet he fell to the floor completely knocked out, and she left him there. Pivoting in a circle, she sent out all of her refined senses. Better late than never, Holly was making solid sure there was no one or anything else out there. Quickly enough she knew it was alright, and she dropped her guard. The echoing warehouse was safe for the moment, anyway.

The strange sounds coming from that part of the building had finally drawn most of the other workers in Kitterman's out to see what was going on. Seeing the hole in the outer wall, and the following path of destruction the orange machine had left in its wake, they congregated at the end of the aisle behind the disabled backhoe. One had found the wherewithal to step over to Johnny, and he was asking him how he was, when Ms. Donnelly noticed him. Ascertaining that Keith would be okay on his own for a few more minutes, Holly stood up and walked over to the increasingly nervous group. Raising her voice, she realized she needed to calm them and avoid panic.

"Everything is fine. Larry, please leave Johnny alone."

Holly had woven *influence* into her words, as she politely instructed the man who'd already climbed onto the backhoe to stop. While Larry climbed down, she went on smoothly painting a lie for everyone else, perhaps not as feasible as Holly would have liked. She hadn't had much time to come up with a zinger.

"Obviously, there was a terrible malfunction in the steering of the backhoe-loader John was using. Don't worry. He's alright…just badly rattled. Coincidentally, Ervin had also tripped over some of the fallen debris behind me, but he's going to be okay too. There's an ambulance on the way for both of them, just to make sure there aren't any hidden problems. The west wall has become a safety hazard. I'm shutting construction down until it gets repaired, or at least temporarily covered. It's time for you relax and to go home. I'll keep on paying you, regardless, and as soon as I can, I'll let you know when things get back to normal and work resumes. Shouldn't take more than a few days. Oh, and by the way, Kelly, Charlie, Jim and Mike, would you all please meet me in the office on your way out? Thanks."

Her explanation was accepted, even though it didn't really explain much or make a lot of sense, nevertheless the workers walked off to their lockers, talking calmly amongst themselves. The four Holly had invited to the office simply followed her there.

She needed their help on her side-project, and Holly told them she'd pay them over-time if they decided to do it. She'd spread out the blueprints on the filters on the desk, and they looked them over. She and Keith had been on the edge of agreeing the information was copasetic, before a backhoe tried to run them over, and since everyone in the office she'd invited to do the work had quickly nodded yes to her invitation, it appeared to be time to go. She asked Charlie to start up the line, as it was already set up in the east corner of the warehouse. This small group walked off to begin construction on the frames, encouraged by the upcoming bump in their paychecks.

Holly had sounded delighted as her employees left the office, but in reality she was miles away from pleased. Having taken care of necessary priorities, she wasn't happy that Keith was still immobile on the ground… for another half-an-hour. Done with the most pressing issues, she went back to him as fast as she could.

"How are you?" She had her hand on his shoulder.

"Broken, dislocated, and surprised, my dear. Which item on this painful menu would you like to order first? Right now, I'm stuck on a very hard and cold surface, and it doesn't feel very good."

Keith frowned up at her, but Holly was not looking back. She was staring at his left leg instead. Seconds later, she answered him, with a voice that sounded really weird; like she'd landed on mars.

"You're right. Your femur is cracked in two places and your knee in dislocated."

While she spoke, she had leaned over and tossed the sixty pound palette still resting on Keith's leg, fifteen feet away in an overdone heave, and that intensity was a reflection of her own irritation at herself. Then her voice when back to normal.

"Listen, I know you can heal yourself, but right now you look like utter crap. We have no time to heal normally right now, and I don't think we can handle your idea of speeding the process up fast enough. You should take my help. I think your injuries are my fault, and I'd feel better if you'd let me in. Relax and let it happen…okay?"

"I've never seen you rushing forwards with this kind of frantic energy before, and even if I don't agree with your guilt driven idea that you should have been everywhere and taken care of everything, you may have a good point about speeding things up. Alright, Holly…alright. I *can* heal myself, but I can't match the Donnelly miracle cure. Okay, I'll put my barriers down. Go ahead, girl, dive in, or plunge in, or whatever it is you do."

"Good, Keith. That's very good. *Relax and let go.*"

Her last words had gotten detached and robotic, similar to the way her voice had been when she'd been peering at his leg, but he opened himself up nonetheless. Keith needed to trust Holly utterly and completely, if she was going to be able to heal him. Her eyes electrified, while a psychic current seared out of her and into him so powerful Keith passed out. During the next fifteen minutes, Johnny helpfully stayed where he was in the backhoe, and Ervin remained unconscious on the concrete floor, and nothing else showed up to distract her. Holly was transforming a broken femur bone into one that wouldn't remember the trauma it had been in moments before, and that needed all of her concentration. After she was done, she reset the kneecap, rejuvenating the torn muscles and tendons throughout the joint.

Time to get their ducks in a row was truly running out, and getting him back to fighting order was something they both needed. If they slowed down, their complex efforts would be for naught. Soon the percentage of molecular aberration in the world's environment would reach a lethal limit and there would be no antidote. No way to come back.

A few minutes after Holly's cure was over, Keith's eyes opened, however what he saw was an ocean beach and some beautiful clouds on the horizon… and then a seagull flew by. She'd transported him to the same place she'd made for herself when she'd been in physical trauma last year. And then the beach dissolved, and he looked up into Holly's face.

"How are you feeling?"

"Fine…I think."

Keith stretched out, sat, and then stood up. He started to walk and he wobbled very badly, and Holly grabbed his arm.

"You did it!"

Knowing Holly would be able to heal him was not the same as *feeling* it, and he was deeply startled by its abruptness.

"I was injured, and now I'm not. It's a weird feeling. It's gonna take me a minute to adjust."

It didn't take him long. As soon as he was back to walking normally again, they turned their attention to the miscreants in the assault. These fly bitten assassins who had failed their evil tasks. Holly woke Ervin up with a single touch. He got back on his feet, way too confused to do anything to anyone, and she looked into his eyes. Holly overrode his previously innate directions, and inserted her own. They should hold for a while anyway.

"Go home, and stay home, and don't hang out. Don't go out unless you need food or beer or something. After buying that stuff, **go back home** and stay there."

She did the exact same thing to Johnny. Understanding that they'd been used as pawns in an increasingly cruel conflict, there was nothing intrinsically wrong with them and their innocence put Keith and Holly in a difficult position. All they could do was get them out of play, hobbling the power of what was behind the whole thing, temporarily. The culmination roared at them like a hurricane. There's a very good chance Johnny and Ervin and anyone else poisoned like that, won't come back to normal unless they stop the entire ball of wax. If they can't reverse what's happening, nothing would make any difference. Returning to the center table with the extra blueprints and paperwork the factory workers hadn't needed for starting up the construction, Holly dragged two stools out of the office. She wanted Keith to sit down.

"You didn't see it coming, did you? I mean, you hadn't had much time to react?" Holly said.

"No, but neither did you. That's odd. Very odd. Even stranger, the attack was done clumsily without any cunning, yet that ingenious unforeseen arrival remained in bed with these childlike tactics."

"Ah huh. And in this elegant review of yours, did you forget you were thrown to the wolves, badly injured by their so-called clumsiness?"

Keith chuckled, "Okay, okay. There was power in it, but you can also see my point, can't you?"

"I do. It wasn't complex, miles from outstanding, and there were only two of them. Yet, the mysterious force guiding those men has never targeted us personally before. The ineptitude of the assault may reflect a lack of information. Not knowing exactly what it was up against, our adversary certainly now realizes we are planning an attack of our own, and we are stronger than it may have thought we were. We should not be surprised if things don't get a lot rougher from now on. It's certainly unnerving we hadn't had much time to defend ourselves today. I'd only known about the damned backhoe breaking through the wall three or four minutes before it crashed in. That's terrible, Keith. And my reactions were sloppy. Sloppy... that's a very nice word to describe what I did...or didn't do. I was so blithe about what was going on. In retrospect, that cavalier attitude was more than reckless; it was irresponsible and dangerous. Johnny was all I needed to worry about, I thought, leaving you without any support."

"Get off your high-horse, Holly. Wailing 'oh woe is me' is not the correct melody of the day. You need to remember a few things too. This has never happened before. Yes, you may have abilities, but you were startled. If our enemy doesn't know a lot about you, we're in the same boat. What you did wasn't a mistake. We'll learn more from it, while our enemy will be doing the same thing. Belittling yourself chips away at our confidence, and we don't have time for head-games like this. Oh, and by the way, stomping right over my own talents like they aren't even here is a bit condescending. While you dealt with the backhoe charging at you, I managed to save myself twice. If you hadn't raced over there to punch Ervin's lights out, I could have handled him on my own just fine."

One of Holly's eyebrows rose. Then she pressed her lips into a grim line, not liking what he'd said. Keith had invited her to accept her faults and move on, and she quickly understood, regretfully, that he was hundred percent right. The stern expression on her face danced into a mischievous half-smile.

"Aaah," a long sigh leaking out of her like a release valve. "You're right. Of course, you're right. What happened, happened. Crying over spilled milk isn't the right reaction, figuring out why it spilled out, is. We need to decide what our next move is going to be, and the best way we can defend ourselves in the future," and Keith was smiling at her.

"I don't know whether this thing is coming from a centralized intelligence or a more web-like structure," he said. "But, right now, we only have a murky silhouette. It's like fighting a mirage shimmering out there in the desert. Since we can't predict when our next confrontation with it is gonna be, building the filters and placing them in the dredges will be more difficult."

With real frustration in his words, Holly's elbows had slid forwards on the table as she propped her chin on the palms of her hands. She smiled across the table at Keith, and his eyes narrowed in annoyance.

"Alright, okay…shit, I got it. Now *I'm* complaining. I'm stopping right now, okay. They're starting on the frames, and if nothing else goes wrong, they should be done in two days. You've set up the dust free environment so we can install what we need inside the frames before closing them up with Lexan. I don't know why I can't oversee the installations on the first frames coming off of the line tomorrow. That might speed up the process. Maybe you should see where the ships are, since there's a good chance the filters will be done by the tenth."

"I called up the captains up yesterday. They all believe they'd be out there by the eleventh. The Essayons and her sister ship, the Yaquina, who'd left Portland a month ago, will leave Los Angeles together. They can get to the center of the gyre in three days, so I'll tell them to start tomorrow.

We need all the dredges out there and in position at the same time. It won't take long to install the filters. It's very important not to leave them out there alone. One of us has to be there to defend them. It makes more sense if you stay here and oversee the construction in Kitterman's. Then you can manage the transportation to get them out there. I'll take the copter to the Cutaway in the morning. She's out there by herself right now, and I don't think we can leave the navy research ship alone out there anymore."

"That sounds fine."

Keith stood up and stretched…easily. He almost forgot what he'd just gone through.

Holly checked in on the crew molding the steel for the frames on her way out, telling them they could clock out whenever they wanted to. Later the better. She nodded goodnight, and told them she'd be back in the morning. They took the short drive back to the Foil. Drained from the battle, they needed to recharge. Five minutes into the car ride, Keith's phone rang. Holly looked nervous, and he glanced over at her while he answered the call; eyebrows raised in curiosity. He had no idea why a ringing phone would give her the heebie-jeebies.

"Hello."

"Hi, Keith, it's Wesley. Listen, I can't be alone right now. Please, can't you invite me over to the ship for a few of hours? We could have dinner or something. I gotta wind-down and talk this out. Nobody at the college understands any of it, and it is way too weird to bring up to anyone anyway."

"Hold on." Keith quietly asked Holly if he could invite Wes over to the ship. She nodded alright in response, and he went back on the line. "No prob. You can even spend the night if you want. We're not at the Foil right now, but we should be there in half-an-hour. Look forwards to seeing you there."

"Thanks a lot." Wesley was relieved. He said goodbye and hung up. Keith twisted towards Holly with a question on his lips, but Holly sailed in before he had enough time to form one word.

"I have a funny feeling Attison is going to call me. I don't know why. Right now, we're doing the best we can to win this war, but I'm afraid he's going to tell me some bad news."

"Yeah, okay. But I still don't know why it would make you nervous."

"He's a very busy man, and there's no reason for him to call unless there's a really good reason. I'm worried more stuff is unraveling."

"Listen Holly, it's really important you put your attention on what we have on our plates right now. Get your emotions out of here. Of course, there's a good chance more problems are going to arise, but your *'feeling'* is only a feeling. The pressure is getting to you. You're getting paranoid."

Holly took her eyes off the road for a second to glance over at Keith, and he was grinning. She shrugged, and went back to driving. Perhaps he was right. They were good at stabilizing each other; ironing out the glitch in the other's glide.

Parking the Mercedes in a small private lot next to the dock, they walked up the gangplank to shower and change their clothes. Wesley showed up an hour later, and they all sat down and had dinner. Having enjoyed praline pie to end the meal, they went out on the deck to watch the sun set. Keith and Wesley found that sipping a heavily dosed Irish coffee was calming their nerves. The group had reformed on the starboard side of the Foil, lying on lounge chairs. They were trying to relax and think about more soothing things, and silence reigned. It was supposed to be a moment of peace. A tranquil psychological island in the orange light bathed across them from an exquisite sunset as they appeared to be meditating in serene composure… of course, you can't read a book by its cover.

Keith was actually lining up in his mind what he was going to do in the morning at Kitterman's. Wesley was surreptitiously looking over at Holly and Keith. He wanted to talk things over with them, terrified a juggernaut was already descending on them, and a sunset and a double shot of heated up whiskey wasn't helping him in the least. Holly's anxiety over Attison's call had returned. She was tapping her fingers on the side of her cup in a frenetic beat, and that tempo kept speeding up. The idea of stepping away from the fight had been a good one, impossible to achieve. Five more minutes of this pointless endeavor finally ended with Holly's ringing phone. Her premonition had been spot on.

"Hello, Attison."

"Not interrupting anything, am I?"

"No, not in the slightest. We had a very tough day at the factory, and Keith and Wes and I were just lying on some lounge chairs trying to calm down. Your call was the escape we all needed to get away from the harmony done of us have within."

"Did something go wrong in Kitterman's? Were you attacked?"

"No....no, it was just chaotic. We're busy setting things up to make the frames. The workers were upset and I had to placate them. Things in general are getting more difficult."

Holly knew Attison always separates wheat from the chaff, but she'd lied to him anyway. She didn't want to hear what he'd say to her about her part in the altercation.

"Alright, Holly. I guess we'll talk about what took place at the warehouse today at a different juncture." She winced. Attison went on, "I called you because General Wyndham called me about what he considered a red flag. The man can't stand either one of us, so it must have been pretty bad for him to reach me on his own. He was almost out of breath while he was giving me the details, as if I could put the latest monster back under the bed as soon as he was done telling me about it."

In Attison's following pause, Holly heard a sigh of frustration come out of him, before his usually unbreakable aplomb returned.

"They'd found a crop-circle this morning in southern Florida with unfamiliar circumstances in its formation. The United States Air Force put a quarantine around the area, and a no-fly zone above it. It's also radioactive. Wyndham sent me a picture of it, and I'm sending it over to you."

Holly walked to her cabin, and opened her laptop and hit a key, and there it was. The circle. Hitting a different button, and a printed version of the picture slipped into the holding-bin on the table in the corner of her oversized cabin. She held it in her hands, and stared at the image and frowned. A molecule interwoven with the warning sign of radioactivity, and the molecule represented pelagic plastic, however there was an extra arm linked to another atom that shouldn't be there. The molecule was not quite exact. What was pressed in the corn was clearly a message directed straight at Holly and Keith. A malevolent one, done in a spiteful way.

"I see it, Attison. This isn't good. There's a terrible implication I don't like at all. I assume you can make that out too?"

"Of course. I'm irritated our opponent used its rudimentary intelligence to design a declaration like this, acting like a willful spoiled child reaching up and slapping us. Right now, you and Keith are the only adversaries it can sense, and it seems this Frankenstein has turned its sights on you. Probably fine-tuning its next attack."

Holly's belly knotted. What they'd gone through in Kitterman's had been their enemy's first fumbling attempt. Any uncertainty she'd had about what had been behind the attack was gone.

"I'm so sorry, Attison, but I didn't want to bother you with it. With this new information, it's important I get everything on the table. We *were* assaulted in the factory, but I took take of it. It hadn't seemed that important. Hearing about that crop-circle, and your angle on it, could be a sign that our level of risk could be growing. Yes, I'll tell you everything from now on."

Attison listened to her confession, and Holly didn't know he was smiling. None of his feathers were out of place. Or maybe she did know. After her lie had slipped out, she got a feeling he already knew what had happened.

"Maybe I should get closer to you and Keith as a precaution. I'll fly to LA, and blow some wind in your sails."

"I appreciate the offer, but I know you're really busy and things are working out okay for us. Every single one of the dredges are almost out here, and Keith is about to install the wiring on the first filters coming off line tomorrow morning. We should be able to stop the next attack as easily as we did the last one, and I don't think the influx of the monsters virtuosity is going to happen right away, if it's ever going to be a real issue."

Holly had started her conversation with Attison with a flat-out lie. Cornered, she had rescinded it, and told him the truth. Wanting him to believe in her independence, she went back to lying a few minutes later. Holly's pride had misled her into thinking that she and Keith were strong enough on their own, and the problems they'd encountered in the last battle had only been a hiccup. Next time, she'd include the entire battlefield and use every single ounce of power she has to get in front of anymore hidden surprises.

"Okay, Holly. Don't forget the scope of the struggle is titanic, and your concentration is more essential than your feelings. If things get dicey, *call me.* I do have powers of my own to support you."

"I know that, and I won't forget."

She was happy he was going to stay on his island, and leave the strategy to her. Early in the morning, she'd helicopter to the Cutaway, while Wesley and Keith would speed up the construction of the filters at the factory.

Attison gently placed the phone down on the desk in his office on Finalhaven. Owning an estate in Greece, and another in Belize, the residence he'd built on this small island off the coast of Maine was his favorite. From the inside balcony of his office on the second floor of the mansion, he watched moonlit waves roil over the surface of the Atlantic Ocean through the glass wall in the living room. Holly hadn't been the only one making things up during their very duplicitous exchange. His fleeting smile was gone, and with a more solemn countenance, he picked up his leather coat hanging off the back his chair. He walked quickly to the elevator in the corner of the room, and he could hear the helicopter coming in to the landing-pad on the highest part of his mansion's roof. The pilot had been told to arrive at nine thirty and transport him to Logan airport where his jet had been fueled and prepped; crew on board waiting for him. Waiting to fly him to Los Angeles. He would stay on the west coast for the foreseeable future to observe Holly and Keith's progress like a mouse hiding in the wainscoting. No. They didn't need to know about his closeness nor his increasing concern.

4:55PM Friday January 5th, 2007 The Caprice

Everything that had been painted white on the ship was transformed to a glowing pinkish-orange by the last rays of the lowering sun, yet the men standing on the landing-pad on the top of the Caprice were blind to this offhandedly beauty. They worried only about was the onset of darkness, and whether the cavalry will really arrive out there in the middle of nowhere. Captain Donald Walker, Officer Sidney Nugent, and the president of the Blackmore Coalition, Steve Boone continued fidgeting up there, and they'd lined up against a low steel wall, making sure they'd be out of the way of the upcoming landing. Hopes were hanging on his reputation. He had to save the day...he had too! Awful rumors were spreading through the ship, and their fragile instability was about to unravel. Captain Walker nudged Officer Nugent, pointing towards a tiny flicker of light above the western horizon. He was praying it was the helicopter, and he was right.

In a few minutes, they crouched beneath the backdraft of the swirling blades of an olive-green OH-6A Hughes 500 that was lowering onto the pad. The pilot wasn't going to shut his engines down, only staying on the Caprice long enough for the drop-off and pick-up; absolutely no longer than he needed to. He'd refuel at the battleship four hundred miles east of the cruise ship on his return trip. When the helicopter was still two inches away from a complete landing, the passenger door opened. The Captain and the security officer watched Porretta hop out and hunker over to them, while President Boone scuttled past him in the other direction. He grabbed the safety handle next to the door, and he got himself inside the copter and he sat down on cushions still warm from the previous passenger. Earlier, Boone had explained to the captain that he should oversee things with more accuracy 'outside the box'. He just wanted to get off the Caprice. Walker knew the real reason behind his departure, but he held his tongue.

"Hello, Inspector. I hope the trip was not too taxing?"

"It's great to be here, Captain Walker, and no, it wasn't too bad."

They were shouting over the engine noise while the helicopter lifted up and turned away. Ryan Porretta glanced over his shoulder to see Boone close and latch the door he'd just opened three minutes ago.

"Some captains don't have the nerve to hang around when the boat begins to sink, hmm?" Saying the jibe softly, Captain Walker had heard it nonetheless, and he glanced over and grinned at Porretta. "Let's go inside, Captain. Introductions will be easier if we get away from the noise, and I need to sit down on something more comfortable than a piece of foam rubber shaking under my ass like a jack-hammer."

Porretta nodded politely at the security officer as they made their way to a restaurant reserved to officers and their guests. It was near the bridge. Entering the fairly empty room, they sat down and ordered sandwiches and drinks. Ryan had a bass ale at his elbow first thing, a reward he was giving himself for enduring that uncomfortable ride. After hours inside the clattering helicopter, this sudden quiet was a wonderful relief for the Inspector.

He looked professional enough. He was wearing a dark blue three-piece suit, and the last of his blonde hair had turned grey. Thirty-five pounds overweight for most of his life, a case he went through over a year ago, the Donnelly mass murder reunion, had certainly peeled-off twenty of them, and they hadn't come back. Just under six feet tall, he looked almost svelte, but besides the physical changes, his grey-blue eyes had gotten a lot colder... and the lines on his face were deeper. He hadn't brought along much on this trip; a medium sized bag with essential clothes and toiletries, and an odd-looking valise that looked a bit like a paint box, and he'd left them on the carpeted floor near his seat. After going through introductions and anchoring themselves by talking over lighter fare while they ate, it was time. The real reason they were there had to be engaged, and it darkened the mood at the table.

"I've done some research on the Blackmore Coalition, Captain. More precisely, everyone from the firm who is also on this cruise. I have a theory on what the catalyst for this ongoing..."

"I've racked my brains trying to figure this out, Mr. Porretta. You have to tell me what you've come up with!" Too excited, Officer Nugent had interrupted the inspector. He'd even forgotten to use his title.

"I'm sorry, sir. There is no way I can rock the boat with any of my own theories unless they would be a stepping stone for resolution."

"Of course, of course...you're right, and I was out of line. If there's anything you need for your investigation, I'll get it for you. I can help you with anything else you want to do."

"Thank-you. Thank-you very much, Officer Nugent. However, right after this meeting, I need to sleep for a while and recharge my engines. After that, I'll avail myself to your offer."

Captain Donald Walker was swallowing the last of his turkey sandwich, and then stifling a burp. He was about to inform the Inspector about the unusual things breaking out in the general population on the Caprice, as well as the unpredictability now growing more intense with the actual direction of the cruise itself. It was important that Inspector Ryan Porretta know about any irregularities. After his explanation, these enigmatic problems would not confuse him in his hunt for the killer.

"I'm sorry, Inspector, but even if you're here to find the answer we can't, I think it's important you know about other problems that have nothing to do with the murders. About a quarter of our passengers have been afflicted with something our doctors do not understand. They would begin by standing in one position for hours. Our medical team has asked them questions when they are in that state, and they've all insisted they aren't doing anything wrong, even as the circumstances negate their claims. After a day or two of planting themselves in different places, they would slip into the next phase by going to their cabins and lying on their beds and staying there like the living dead. Right now, they look more dead than alive. None of them has moved a muscle. Since we have no idea how to fix what's wrong with them, we hope they will remain motionless for now. If another phase kicks in, it might make them aggressive. Currently, they don't respond to anything, and it's very unnerving. The number of our passengers out for the count with this thing, hasn't changed, so we assume it is not infectious. That said, I have more bad news for you.

The normal path of our commercial cruise has been dramatically altered by a tsunami. We were scheduled to dock and refuel in Hawaii, but the wave had devastated most of one of island's coasts a few days ago, and the commercial dock we were supposed to be at was destroyed. Obviously, we can't go there, and we can't refuel, but we're not telling the passengers. It's better to leave them innocent to the difficulties until it reaches a point where we have no choice. No reason to start a panic. The ongoing murders have not been announced either, since only the lawyers in the Blackmore Coalition have been pinpointed and no one else.

There's a chance the powers that be in Hawaii may repair the dock fast enough for us to get fuel there, but it's more likely we'll be meeting a Navy frigate in the Oliver Hazard Perry class out here instead. We might have had just enough fuel to make it back to LA, however our navigator as alerted me that we are in a stalemate right now between our engine power fighting against a mysterious current coming from the center of the northern pacific gyre. We happen to be in an inner ring of this whirlpool they call the trash vortex, and it's dragging on us harder every day. Currently, we can stay where we are, but what's left in our tanks won't hold us here forever, and if this abnormal pull gets any more powerful, it's not going to matter how much gas we have. This ship could be sucked straight into the center of the gyre, and we won't be able to get out. The odds for that are low, so I don't want you to worry about it. I just wanted you to know about these more intrusive items. I'm optimistic the intensity of this current will soon relax, and we'll either meet the frigate or dock in Hawaii in a couple of days."

Captain Walker looked over at Inspector Porretta, and he tilted his glass to let the ice slide into his mouth. Waiting for the man's reaction to his unusual report, he started crunching the ice into pieces.

"Wow. Sounds like you have some pressure on you. Oh, and by the way, call me Ryan. It'll speed up our communications. Having heard at least part of the list of abnormal stuff taking place on board, I will tell you, you're not alone. Things on land are getting pretty peculiar too. These stories don't upset me anymore than I already am, as disorder is always a variable in any murder I've been asked to solve, and I can handle disarray better more than most."

Ryan picked up his glass, and swallowed the rest of his ale in one gulp.

10:30AM Sunday January 7th, 2007 San Gabriel, California

The factory workers at Kitterman's had stayed on, only stopping for a couple of hours in the break room to sleep. They seemed to realize that something was going badly wrong, and what they were helping to construct would be instrumental in getting things back in order. Everything would be right again. They poured that steel as fast as they could. Keith had arrived that morning to begin installing the complex nest of wires and sustainable batteries into the first newly made filters; still warm when he began the process. Done with eight of them by the end of the day, they were ready for the watertight seal. He kept on working. At six that morning every single one was finished, and they were carefully stacked up on a wooden platform.

Four hours went by. Keith was busy setting up transportation to get the filters where they needed to go safely and speedily. Standing outside the warehouse loading dock, accomplishment swelled in his heart while the morning sun warmed his shoulders. He watched as a delivery truck backed in, and he helped load the filters. The truck drove off to the airport in Wallace holding these twenty-two newly formed weapons on the first stint of their trip to the vortex.

He'd had a heated debate with Wesley a half-an-hour ago, and it had been right on the edge of bubbling into a physical fight. It stopped when he sent Wes home. Keith was not going to allow him to follow them out to the center of the gyre. Unable to defend himself like they could, he couldn't allow his friend's genius to be snuffed out during a battle he had no reason to be in. Walking to the parking lot, he got in Holly's Mercedes, and started the engine. He'd supervise the transfer of the filters onto a rented cargo plane that he himself would fly to Hawaii. After that, they'd be loaded onto a coast guard cutter called the Washington. He would oversee that too. The Washington had been on the leeward side of the island, and the tsunami had not damaged it.

It was going to be a difficult voyage from Hawaii to the center of the gyre. They had to have a ship like the coast guard cutter to handle it, and Holly had been elected to persuade the captain of the Washington to help them with the trip. She started that enterprise by asking someone else to do it, by wheedling Captain Russell Gates of the Cutaway into calling Captain Dennis Quinn of the Washington. Holly hadn't needed to use any of her *persuasion* on to get Gates to ask the other captain for assistance, since he'd spent enough time on the Cutaway to understand the catastrophic extent of the problem. The strangeness of the environment surrounding the ship was certainly enough to make him understand the fight Holly and Keith were in, and he knew they were teetering on a ghastly tipping-point. It wasn't hard for him to insert a grave firmness in his request to the captain of the Washington. He made it sound a lot more like an order than an appeal, explaining that he needed him to carry some undisclosed items to an unknown location, and Quinn quickly acquiesced. He sent him the coordinates six hundred miles northeast of Hawaii, and he also told him that the cargo would be arriving where he was docked soon.

Holly had given the captains of the dredges the dimensions of the filters they'd soon have to install, and they in turn, told their engineers: five by five. They wanted to give them extra time to set up the necessary framework for them when they got on aboard, and it was a way to speed things along. It would make the entire process run much faster.

Five of the dredges on their way there were hopper dredges. When they were at work, they would normally suck up sand or mud and hold it in a hopper and transport the material they called 'slurry' to a different location and open the underwater doors of the hopper and let that tonnage evacuate to the bottom. Most of the dredges coming to the meeting were dissimilar, and their suction tubes hung at various depths. Of course, that wasn't going to matter on this particular adventure. The bottom would be over a mile down, so no dredge could touch it, unless equipment accidentally dropped off of one of the decks. Addressing the entire problem in an altered way, the only thing they'd be sucking up would be water.

In a working hopper-dredge transporting slurry, the load begins its journey on an open pipe or sluice that quickly splits into two channels. In their current plan, they would mount a filter in the center of both of these waterproof conduits before they re-join again. Sucking up a torrent of seawater, it would rush through the filters, and then this transformed water would continue into the hopper. The doors would be left wide open and this healed runoff would return back into the Pacific. The other six dredges transfer slurry by pumping it up, and dividing it in sluiceways in the same formation that exists on the hopper-dredgers. The main difference between them is in the final exit, as they would spray the slurry out by a nozzle at the stern of the ship and aim it at the desired location at a very high pressure. The filters would be installed in the same way on those ships too, however the transmuted water would be gushing out like liquid sparklers, and the purified H20 may possibly elicit jubilance on its more dynamic return to the ocean.

Holly, Keith, and Wesley had set up many diverse tests to see if their normalized water would have a cascading effect on the surrounding area. Their results were promising, yet those fast calculations weren't enough for a solid answer. They hoped the altered seawater would transform other molecules when it returned to the sea for the exponential and helpful effect.

Getting the dredges out there with the filters installed would be their last hurrah. A last stand against an enemy transforming like a chameleon using strategy from a Mobius strip in its surprising attacks. The weight of the world on their shoulders, their nerves were stretched to the limit. Filtering out the bad and reinstating the good would be their last breath, and they'd inhale and hold it as long as they could.

7:30AM Monday January 8th, 2007 The Cutaway

Holly Donnelly and Captain Gates were in the dining room in the Cutaway having an early breakfast, talking over their plans for the day. Holly was explaining how they were getting the filters out to the eleven dredges in the coast guard ship, and then she went on to describe the way they'd set the ships up with a mile between each one in a huge circle with a diameter of 3.4 miles. Quietly absorbing what she was telling him, the Captain gathered another forkful of scramble eggs and stuck it into his mouth. She didn't need the Cutaway during the upcoming delivery. The research vessel's job would act as a lookout. Not wanting to have the Cutaway too close during the handover, Holly needed them to remain afloat if things go haywire. Looking at the southern horizon through the window next to their table, Holly's gaze darkened and she stopped talking. Gates saw a tinge of electric blue flicker deep in her violet eyes, but it slipped by so fast he wasn't sure if it had really been there, however the change in her demeanor was unmistakable. It looked like she'd seen a ghost out there on the horizon. All he saw out there were clouds hanging out in the distance, and they didn't look dangerous in the least. Be that as it may, Holly got to her feet in alarm.

"I am very sorry Captain. Something has come up. I must retire to my cabin and check on something and I'll touch base with you later on. I advise you to batten down the hatches, or whatever you do when you know bad weather in coming in," and after that unsupported advice, she rushed off.

Two hours later, a thirty-five miles-an-hour southwest wind was sweeping over large waves, some reaching seventeen feet. A mottled blanket of stratocumulus clouds had covered the blue sky, and they were speeding over their heads at a fine clip. The clouds *had* to be stratocumulus. There weren't any other classifications in the book to explain the surreal configurations embedded at the altitude of fifteen hundred feet. The Washington had arrived, and she'd sidled up close to the Cristobal Colon; about to begin the first of her difficult deliveries. Captain Quinn stayed on the radio with the Captain of the dredge, Captain Hanson. They both had to be vigilant with their thrusters to control where they'd be in relation to each other. The wind and swells made it more difficult to hold their positions.

Quinn's radio connection to the dredge suddenly went dead, and the communication officer instantly tried to fix the problem, but dead air continued. Leaning against the back wall of the wheel house in the Washington, Keith didn't say anything. The dredge had been holding course, stable enough for the transfer, but just then, she turned her bow straight at the side of the Coast Guard cutter, as if Captain Hansen wanted to slam into the other ship...and...and sink her. If the Washington didn't pick her skirts and run, the unthinkable was actually going to happen. Captain Quinn barked an order out at the helmsman.

"Speed us up *right now,* and stay on course."

"Yes, Captain," and Officer Langhorn did as he was told.

The Washington shouldn't have a problem getting out of danger. She'd already increased the distance between the ships, and the cutter is a much faster ship. The slow advance of the torpedo-like dredge should not have bothered her. However, for some unknown reason her ability to move forwards with the necessary power wasn't there. Her engines were racing, but her simple escape wasn't taking place as fast as it should. She wasn't stalled, yet what she can do was not enough acceleration to save them. Keith had left the wheel house seconds before this preposterous holdup began. He jogged over to the port-side rail of the cutter, and he looked into the seawater lapping at the side of the ship, and the increased space between the two craft had begun to shrink again.

Virgil Burns was a crewmen of the Cristobal Colon, and his hands were in a death-defying grip on the wheel of the dredge. His eyes were glassy as if he wasn't really home. Of course, Virgil didn't want to guide the Cristobal into the side of the Coast Guard ship, yet something inside of him was controlling his actions for the past ten minutes. When the fire-extinguisher that had been clamped to the wall behind him crashed into the side of his head, Virgil blacked out and fell to the floor.

Seconds before human skull and extinguisher met, Holly stepped out of the shadows in the wheelhouse of the Cristobal in a black wetsuit with no symbols on it of any kind. She'd been almost invisible. A sinuous ink mark. Leaving tiny puddles of seawater in her footprints, she crept up silently on the crewman holding the helm. Holding the extinguisher in her left hand, she quickly put the meddler out of commission. Virgil hadn't even reached the floor before she started to use her other hand to expertly reverse the engines of the dredge in a last minute attempt to stop the collision. But the job wasn't over yet. The momentum built up by the forward motion of the dredge may be too much power to stop in the time and distance remaining. Holly roped the wheel to the steel post under the command chair leaving the dredge moving to the east, away from the Washington. Bolting out of the wheelhouse, she found Ian Hanson tied up twenty feet farther down the corridor. She released him, and advised him to go to the wheel house and take full control over his ship. The captain began to ask her about the rest of his crew, but she was gone, sprinting to the cabin where the rest of his men had been imprisoned. She unlocked the door, went inside and untied them, and then she took the same narrow metal stairs she'd taken to get there, back up again. Erupting out of the hatch and onto the deck, she was moving so fast there was steam rising from wet footprints she'd left ending at the starboard rail. She grabbed a rope, and jumped up on the rail and stood there with her bare feet balanced perfectly on the metal banister like a raptor searching for prey.

At that point, the Washington was a quarter of a mile away, and the Cristobal Colon had certainly slowed down. It should have been enough to avoid the collision. It should have worked, but now the cutter was moving closer to the dredge! Holly saw the latest difficulty, and it had tentacles twenty feet in width, disappearing into a mystery about the rest of it hidden under the water. Whatever it was had gripped the hull of the Washington in a powerful hug, and it was easy to make out the breadth of its fleshy arms as their mottled-white contrasted starkly against the dark blue marine paint on the steel of the ship. Obviously, their enemy didn't like the idea of the filters getting on the dredges. This malformed behemoth from the deep had to be the latest arrow in its quiver; a new weapon swimming up from its arsenal of contorted freaks.

Holly dove head first into the noxious water. She had to find a way to stop the monster one way or another, and a hands-on approach seemed like the best option.

Keith saw the speckled tentacles glued onto the side of the ship, and he ran to the bow of the ship where there was a stationary machine-gun twenty feet back from the edge of the deck. It might be a defensive tool, and he slid onto the seat of the fifty-caliber weapon. He'd even remembered to ask one of the crew to be there and help him by replacing the drum of ammunition, if he ran out. But he had a huge problem. Suction-cupping itself to the side of the Washington, it was too close in. There was no way he could hit it.

Holly was swimming straight towards the cutter. During the seconds before she got there, she raced over different ideas in which she could injure the creature. The idea of Jonah inside the whale popped into her head, but everything she was mulling over was violently pushed out as a tentacle circled around her, and tightened around her torso like a living girdle from hell. The sustaining breath she was holding in her lungs was also pushed out. It seemed that one of the countless tentacles on the Washington had been instructed to take care of a side-job. And it seemed its mission had been achieved. Thrown hither-and-yon in the water like a piece of yarn, the creature was playing with her as if she was a toy. It wasn't very comical to Holly. She was suffocating.

Plunging her dive knife into this alien flesh wasn't making any difference, and the stringy muscles just under the thick skin kept holding her tight. The girth of the tentacle was too wide to cut through it completely, and…and she was losing her strength. At that precise second, she wished she'd never told Attison to stay away, she wished he was there to save her. Her fleeting hope was swept away as the squid-like monster continued to play with her; exulting in the end of one of its most powerful opponents. It flung the end of its imprisoning tentacle fifty-five feet out of the water. A lot more fun. Let her breathe for half a minute or so, and then drag her under the surface of the waves forever. Holly broke through the crest of a wave, and she inhaled as deeply as she could. She rose higher and higher above the chop, finding herself hanging helpless in the wind.

Keith had been in the process of leaving the seat of the machinegun, when he saw one of the tentacles burst out of the Pacific Ocean, apparently holding Holly in its grasp. Dotted on one side with salmon-colored suction pads, it rose higher and higher above the surface, and Holly was not looking very well. His previous impulse to leave the weapon was erased, and he re-anchored himself in the center of the seat. Linking his telekinesis powers into his hands and fingers, he came up with a plan to save his friend. His window of opportunity to rescue her was small. He was going to have to do it *immediately*.

The thicker part of the tentacle was helpfully staying where it was, while the thinner end slapped her around like a flag in the wind. Keith had aimed his upcoming attack fifteen feet below where Holly was, and then he started an unending onslaught of bullets. His idea was to slice right through the thicker body of the limb. And he was using robotic precision in an uncanny speed. A terrible river of exploding metal kept on riddling through that flesh, back and forth over the exact same place on the tentacle. No one in the crew had ever seen that gun put out bullets that fast. It looked supernatural. Considering the mood of the man at the controls, unimaginable can easily become real.

The mottled tentacle began to lower beneath the waves, prize still tightly held in its deadly coil. Keith kept on firing bullets into it, not missing a single shot in his relentless strafe. This part of the boneless limb was now mangled and torn to shreds, currently hanging only a foot above the water. And then it finally dropped off! Nothing made out of flesh could withstand an ongoing salvo of bullets pounding in at seventeen hundred miles an hour.

Holly had been inhaling as much oxygen as she could, gaining most of her strength back. Shaken her around with gleeful abandon, the creature had assumed this savagery would addle her further, but it really had little effect. The tentacle around her middle was no longer attached to its source, and she was floating on the surface of the water actually free. The squeeze around her waist had lost most of its vigor, and it was easy for her to wriggle away. Keith was waving at her from the bow of the cutter, and she swam towards the ship as fast as she could. She'd stay on the surface this time. Making it to the Washington without interruption, she was guessing that after losing part of its body, the creature may be having second thoughts. Holly climbed the coincidental ladder of tentacles lined up on the side of the hull of the ship, and she swung over the rail to find Keith standing in front of her. He looked relieved.

"Hi, Keith." Dripping wet, she hugged him anyway, and he was happy to return it. "I have finally found a good reason for our relationship."

"Hello, Holly. Are you going to tell me about the..." But she interrupted.

"No time. We can't talk right now! The crash is about to happen and we have to stop it," and she looked over her shoulder and waved towards the Cristobal Colon. "I have the captain and the crew back in charge, but they can't control the momentum fast enough to stop the collision. Meanwhile, this slimy-slug is still pushing us right in the way and the props don't have the power to reverse it. There are only six minutes left. I assume you've come up with the perfect solution...Keith...hello...are you with us?"

Keith was running to the hatch that would get him into the wheel house. Holly was jogging along with him, and then he stopped in his tracks.

"Yeah, sort of, but you're right. We have no time. Go up there and tell them not to touch anything metal on the ship in the next few minutes, and that includes you. I'm going to the engine room and screw around with the main breakers. I'll reroute every watt of electrical power on this boat straight to the hull. Might not kill it, but it's gonna let go!"

Holly nodded, veering off to the wheel house. Keith had not seen the odd slant in her eyes, nor did he hear a whispering rejection about avoiding electrical shock. He was too intent on getting there, and he rushed down the steps and through the passage that would get him to the door of the engine room. Shouldering through, he saw the breaker panels on the far wall of the small room. He grabbed the safety rails of the wooden walkway hanging between the diesel engines. They were so loud they'd drown out the towering speakers in a death-metal concert. He picked up the earphones hanging on a nail near the door and he put them on. Walking the wooden planks between the engines, he got to the far wall, and he switched off the main breakers. He was making sure his pirating and rerouting of power wasn't going to damage the electrical system of the ship.

And then he pulled the disconnect lever, allowing him to open the lower panel where the wires from the generator itself were. He disconnected the ground wire and one of the hot wires, and then he reversed them. He closed the panel. Pulling the lever up again, he sent every watt of electricity on the Washington through the generator and onto anything metal on the ship. That included the hull. Keith looked at his watch. He was very careful not to lean into the metal rails. According to Holly's prediction, there were only three minutes left before the crash. He let the loose current run for another two minutes. The crew should be able to take control during that final minute, after he puts things back to normal. They wouldn't have the drag of the creature holding them back or pushing them forwards. They'd be able to get away. At least, that was what he was hoping for.

Holly told the officers what was about happen as Keith had asked her to do, even advising them to put it on the PA, or find the rest of the crew pronto and tell them not to touch anything metal anywhere on the ship in the next few minutes. Then she streaked out of the wheel house in an inhuman dash, flying down the stairs and onto the deck, already mentally insulating herself against the upcoming charge she'd withstand. Stepping over to the rail, she looked over at the side of the Coast Guard ship now ribbed by tentacles, and a cruel smile appeared on her face. It had really enjoyed torturing her, and she wanted to match that with something more, something that would give her a wonderful surge of delight in inflicting it. Besides, it would make a lot more sense to stop it completely instead of just shocking it. The monster could come back for more. Putting her own hands on the rail, she felt a potent current ride through her palms, and the tentacles were starting to shiver. It was obvious the creature was about to free itself. The hull was getting too painful to hold on to, but Holly was about to change her own physical form and that should take away the pain for herself. Her eyes burned into fiery sapphires while she amplified the charge. Intentionally. She'd turned into a human filament, vengefully quadrupling the current on the hull for another thirty seconds. Deciding that would be enough, she let go of the rail, eyes sliding back to their soothing grey/

violet. Seconds later, the current from the ship's generator stopped too. Holly looked over the rail. The behemoth had let go. More precisely, it had been scorched off, and it was floating in the swells like carrion. The tentacles had turned a yellowish beige, and they were disintegrated into pieces ranging from ten to fifteen feet in length.

At that point, the Cristobal Colon was only an hundred feet away and it seemed the crash was inevitable. The Washington's props were finally getting traction in the water, but it still didn't look like there was going to be an escape. The cutter was in full reverse. Did she had enough power to bounce away in time? Everyone on board both ships were praying for the impossible. Maybe that psychic appeal that had been the final straw, because she did slip out of the hopper-dredge's trajectory like a moonbeam.

Keith checked his watch again. The time to shock the monster off the ship was over. He returned the wiring to normal and left the engine room. Climbing the steps two at a kind, he wanted to know if it had worked. Jogging out of the hatch and onto the deck, he saw Holly against the starboard rail, arms crossed like a model on the cover of a diving magazine, neoprene suit helpfully reflecting the intermittent light peeking out between the bizarre clouds racing over their heads. But a high-fashion model would probably not be smiling at all, and Holly was grinning like a cat who'd eaten the canary. She was pointing down, and Keith quickly stepped over to her and looked over the rail. He saw the widening swath of bleached out pieces of the creature floating away and sinking, and there was a terrible smell of badly burned sushi hanging in the air.

"Redirecting the power in the generator was supposed to be a destructive force Holly, but I didn't think it could do that," waving his hand in the air. "I guess warning you about the charge had meant something completely different to you, and it had nothing to do with your own health. Mind telling me what the *hell* you did?"

"Does it really matter? We won't be dragging it around anymore in a more definitive way. Isn't that what you wanted? The current impediment is forever gone."

"If you had intended to fry it into a smelly slop, couldn't you have given me a hint?"

"Didn't have time to discuss it with you, as you may remember. We were counting seconds before the collision. Nobody should deal with that nasty brute again...and...and I was pissed, so I just magnified the current you sent out. Fool around with me that way does not bode well for anyone or anything if I survive the interlude. No, I don't play well with others if they're trying to kill me."

Keith shook his head, and smiled. He was impressed by her off-the-cuff action. She'd squashed the behemoth flat as if it was as inconsequential as a pesky fly.

And the project went back in gear. They secured the area around the dredges, trying to drop off the filters as quickly as they could. Keith and Captain Hanson and Captain Quinn realigned the two ships, and now they only had ocean waves and an occasional gust of wind to hamper their efforts. Side by side, the cutter and the dredge were stable enough, and they used the hydraulic crane on the dredge to lift the filters off the deck of the Washington and into the hands of the deck crew on the Cristobal.

Holly took the dinghy from the Washington to the Cutaway. No one would want to swim through that odorous crap. Wanting to peel off the wetsuit, as soon as she was showered and into some dry clothes, she went to the mess hall. She got a cup of coffee and sat down, and it looked like she had earned a short rest, but that was not what was happening. Holly was going through an invisible search through every crewmen on all the vessels. She had to make sure there would be no more possessions hiding out there, making sure what happened on the Cristobal Colon would not flare up again. And she found absolutely nothing. Implanting a solid barrier in everyone's mind to attempt to thwart any other insertions during the next few days, she was flummoxed on how the crewman in the Cristobal had been compromised so badly. Unhappy about not seeing the latest attack coming, she decided to go to every dredge and underline what she'd already done with a physical appearance. She'd support the barrier by actually touching the men themselves with a moment of hands-on experience. Captain Hanson had locked the poor man in a cabin until they found the time to heal him...if that can actually be done.

Putting her empty cup on the table, she went out to all the dredges, and after four hours of a more up front and personal scrutiny, Eagle 1 was the last in the circle. She got in the dinghy and sped back to the Cutaway, staring up at the helicopter she'd flown out in and landed on the Navy Research Ship. Tying the dingy at the stern, she climbed the ladder and raced across the deck and into the wheel house. She'd come up with an idea to use the copter to transport some of the filters out to dredges, and she wanted to talk to Captain Gates about it. He thought it was a fine idea, and she got on the radio to Keith who was still on the Washington, telling him she'd start on the ships farthest out. She would keep on going as long as the fuel in the tank held out.

It was after six, and the sunlight was waning. It didn't matter. All the ships had spotlights, and those who hadn't gotten the filters yet were frantic to get them in this last minute push, and of course the lights were on. Holly had taken care of the Essayons, the Geopotes 15, the Leiv Eriksson and the Vasco da Gama, and the fuel gauge had been on empty for quite a while. When she heard a fairly loud alarm coming out of the instrument panel, she decided it was time to land the helicopter...*right away,* since she didn't want to drop out of the sky and crash. Minutes later, she parked the copter on the landing pad on the Cutaway. There had been a very suspicious noise coming from one of the pistons right before she shut the engine off, and indication she'd been right on the edge. There was probably a low number of seconds left before those rotors would abruptly stop swirling.

And Keith had kept on going. He finished the last two boats by eleven, graciously thanking Captain Dennis Quinn and the crew of the Washington for the strenuous work they'd done. Holly and Keith wished them well on their trip back to Hawaii.

8:00PM Tuesday   January 9th, 2007   The Cutaway

The next day gave them good weather. The misshapen clouds kept on blooming over their heads, but there were less of them. More breaks of sunlight. The engineers on the dredges were installing the filters, and Keith or Holly would occasionally show up to help them. When the sun set that day, the final strap was pulled down, the last weld cooling, and the pesky watertight valve that wasn't doing its job, no longer leaked. Every filters was where it was supposed to be. They were ready for their last battle in a desperate war over the state of the world as they knew it.

The captains of the fleet of dredges had met at the Cutaway that evening, concerned over what they were about to do the next day. Talking things over, they cemented their plans. They'd start all the filters at high noon, and they would stay connected on the radio; touching base with each other throughout the day. The nervous group ended the meeting early, and by ten o'clock that night the Cutaway looked deserted. Besides the lone man on watch, the rest of the crew had retired to their cabins...besides Holly and Keith. Shoulder to shoulder at the bow of the ship, their elbows rested on the rail and they stared out at nothing. With the circle of dredges behind them, there wasn't supposed to be anything out there but darkness.

"Our enemy came up with an impressive display when the Washington showed up yesterday morning," Keith said.

"Impressive enough to almost kill me. Thank-god, you were there to give me a hand. Could that have been the last attack? I mean, Attison has a handle on the future cast, and he's not around. He hasn't even called. Isn't that a good sign? For a second or two, when I felt like I was in serious trouble, I'd sort of hoped he'd show up...but...but he probably already knew you'd take care of it. Probably kicking his heels up in Finalhaven, knowing we are just fine out here. Oh, I didn't tell you. I made sure the rest of the men out here can't be turned into drones. It's very unlikely it would happen again, and we've been worrying way too much, but it was a simple defense move and I took care of it. The filters will clear this whole mess out tomorrow. Simple and easy."

Keith pivoted around on the rail to face the brightly lighted deck. He wanted to support Holly's optimism with as much positivity he could find.

"I'm not sure about anything anymore, my dear. Attison's behavior or lack there-of might hint that nothing too dramatic is going to happen tomorrow, and I agree with you. It's a good sign. And we've gotten this far without getting killed. That simple fact should be enough to boost our spirits. It's easier to win the day if we have an innate belief we'll blow this monster to pieces tomorrow, just like we did to its oversized minion a few hours ago."

Holly stepped over to Keith, and they hugged. There was no sexuality in their sudden closeness as both considered the embrace as a mournful shot of spiritual sustenance. What they were about to do was going to put them in a very precarious place. Holding on to their bravado, they were talking a very good game, but in their heads they heard a susurrus of disconcerting whispers. The ghosts of devastation, desolation and despair softly muttered to them out of the limitless gloom surrounding the Cutaway, and those incessant faraway voices were getting very close, changing into a howl across the water of their souls.

8:30AM Sunday January 7th, 2007 The Caprice

The Captain and his officers knew they were stranded. The different problems would soon collide, and their delicate house of cards held in place by complex explanations was about to be scattered overboard with one more draft of the inexplicable. In the wheelhouse, the navigator and the ship's engineer, Lenny Rule, were looking up at Captain Walker, and they were frowning. Neither of them wanted to tell the Captain the latest news, and they glanced at each other. The navigator ended their silence.

"It's gotten too much, sir. It was okay when we could hold at seven knots, but now we must increase our speed to hold our place in the current. We'll run out of fuel in three days, and I'm not sure if that's an option you would want right now."

But even as he uttered these painful words, the situation had degraded farther, and his Captain wasn't listening to him anyway. The concern they'd had over the increased current no longer mattered. It was gone. The Caprice was floating in the center of the gyre; stuck slap-dab in the middle of the Trash Vortex. The cruise ship would certainly run out of gas if they tried to get out at that point. Wearing headphones, the communication officer was listening for anything...anything at all. And he did hear a message coming from one of the dredges, and he told the Captain about it. He was ignored as well. Captain Donald Walker was peering through binoculars, and he'd seen the Queen of the Netherlands, one of the hopper-dredges in the far-distance. Walker placed the binoculars back down on the counter. He assumed the other vessel had been sucked in too. Whatever his officer had heard on the radio must have come from that faraway smudge. Walker sighed. Their flimsy lies should be able to maintain an uneasy peace on his crowded boat for at least another four or five days.

6:35PM Monday January 8th, 2007 The Caprice

Almost the entire Blackmore Coalition had come on the cruise, and the group had been badly winnowed down. Only Michael Chandler, John Belton, and Eric Adler were left alive. The trio had agreed to have dinner at the Polynesian themed restaurant, The Sweet and Hot on the seventh deck. There would be guards in plain clothes at each of the exits to protect them, and at the moment they were both pestered by other passengers who thought they worked for the restaurant. People asked them ad nauseam about their seating arrangements, or what was the special on the menu that evening would be, and the young men were getting uncomfortable.

Captain Walker and Officer Nugent were the only ones who knew Ryan Porretta was the Caprice, and they hadn't seen him for two days. Ryan could have dove into the Pacific for all they knew. Earlier in the day, Officer Nugent had sent a security guard to check on him, and as the guard approached his cabin, Inspector Porretta had opened the door and walked past him in the corridor. Well, that was something. A speck of information to salve their worries. What he was doing was still a mystery, and so his reputation was all they had to bolster their worries over his ongoing invisibility.

The lawyers had ordered their dinners, and they were having a shrimp concoction as an appetizer before the main event. Avoiding subjects linked to untimely escapes off the mortal coil, the last of Blackmore's finest also tried to forget they were in the sights of a serial killer. Triviality and the unimportant, the flavor of the day, another description of a dance with Mr. Death would have turned their bellies.

"We're running very late on docking in Hawaii. Well, at least the Carnelian line is giving us more events. Tomorrow there's a new show in the main concourse about tropical snakes, plus a musical called 'Kinky Boots' on stage on Tuesday night. Probably something they were going to put out in the next cruise, but they are trying to make this extra time more fun with fluff like this," Eric Adler said.

"You know, I've heard a lot of the stories about snakes. I think I'm going to go to that show," Mike said, and he reached over and grabbed a roll out of the basket.

"Eric, you sounded like a cruise director. Shouldn't you think about getting a new job here on the ship? The only thing I want to do tomorrow is sleep late and lounge around near to the pool…and drink and eat." Sounding mischievous, John popped a jumbo shrimp dripping sauce into his mouth. And he chewed it up, and he kept on talking. It was hard to believe this guy was middle-aged, or that he gets paid top-line money to hold his own in court.

"I guess you guys don't know about the blow-out gambling fête happening tonight just two decks above us. They've even upped the limits, and initiated a more kindly percentage leaning closer to the gambling man…or woman. Of course, the house will always win, but during this Monday gala, it's going to take them a little bit longer to break us. Who knows? I might even win! The thing's been hyped out of its socks. It started about half-an-hour ago, and it's supposed to run all the way to sunrise. Anybody interested? Hmm?"

"You're nuts, John. You can't go into a crowded room like that without any security nearby. Strangers could get up close and personal, and you know exactly what that means!"

During his stern admonition, Mike was slathering a thick layer of butter on his roll. His eyebrows were squeezed together, brow furrowed, and he looked concerned. Eric chimed in.

"Why aren't you worried? I don't even know how you could get out of here. They don't want you to go out there on your own, and if you try, they'll stop you!"

"There's a lot I can do under the radar, my friends. Oh yes, if there's a chance for a pay-off in that gambling jamboree upstairs, I'm going to come-up with a distraction to get away. And that, my friends, won't be hard. I can use just about anything. I mean anything."

Vera Adler was one table away from her prey. There was security around them now, but she knew the end of her game was going to be harder. It certainly wasn't going to stop her. Changing her name to Janice this time, she had on a different wig; short, grey, and curly and a lot of makeup. She'd wiggled herself into a clutch of widowed women. In their communal attempt to rise above their sadness, they had decided to go on this cruise together. Vera had seen them in a bridge tournament two days ago. Telling them a heartbreaking story about her own husband lost somewhere in the wilds of Alaska piloting a small plane, she might have dipped her whole body in castor oil as she slid easily into this previously tight-knit group. The three women had fallen head-over-heels in love with her, and that was good. They were perfect camouflage. Vera had found the pawns she needed in the next phase of her deadly pursuit.

She'd heard John's *loud* pronouncements about his love of gambling and that he wanted to escape his safety net to go and play. Vera decided to aid him in his wanted getaway from the cheaply-suited men guarding the doors of the restaurant. Telling one of her gentle companions that she wanted to have her own birthday-dessert at 'Sweet and Hot', her dinner companion was surprised by Janice's idea. She'd never mentioned her birthday before. With a gimp in her gait, Vera suddenly got up and walked over to the man at the door, and it seemed she'd gotten arthritis in her hips and knees in only forty-eight hours.

"Today's my birthday, honey-pie, and I want to know if the chef has any cakes or special desserts for me. Could the waitress sing-a-long with me and my friends, and don't I get a free bottle of champagne? Which ice cream on a special today, because...um...I need to....."

Vera slowly melted onto the hibiscus adorned carpeting, suddenly dead to the world, and the security guard hadn't been able to get a word in sideways during her diatribe. His attention was completely directed at her, and he bent down to help her. The whole thing was taking place right next to one of the entrances. Her new buddies had been watching her antics at the door. When they watched her fall to the floor, all three rushed to her side. In reality, there was nothing wrong with Vera. Peeking from under her *almost* closed eyelids, her left leg got a convulsion of some kind and two of the worried girls were knocked over like bowling pins when they got close enough. The plan she had just concocted in her head was now in full gear. One of fallen women had twisted her ankle, and she began to scream. The guard moved away from Vera, and dropped to his knees next to the actually broken one, and he got on his radio and called for emergency medical help to be sent straight away to the entrance of the Sweet and Hot.

The lawyers had stopped eating, drawn to the commotion like everyone else around them. Mumbling something about going to the lavatory, John quietly excused himself. He walked towards the restroom until he stepped behind a column. Taking off his jacket and tie, he hid them under the fronds of a potted plant in the corner. In an ongoing attempt to change his appearance even farther, he brushed his hair up with his fingers as if he'd put his finger in an electric outlet, and then he sauntered through the main entrance. His dinner companions were still mesmerized by the older women lying on the carpeting and the guard hovering over her, and John Belton sailed through the door. No one at the table noticed him, and the guard was already so distracted he couldn't make out his own shadow. One of the two injured females suddenly got up. Quite smoothly, and the fluidity in her movements hinted at a younger physique. The two remaining lawyers at the table watched as the guard tried to put his hand out to restrain her, or perhaps support her somehow, but he ending up grabbing at thin air. Vera was gone. The medical team arrived, and no one could remember what had happened, and there was no explanation for her sudden disappearance in the growing confusion.

When he never came back from the bathroom, John's Blackmore associates knew he'd used the commotion to get out of there and go gambling. They really thought he would drink way too much while he was there, and of course, they were right. What they didn't know was that the killer had followed him, and Vera's attempt had been extremely successful. And John never looked back once. Weaving through the crowds washing in and out of the elevators, he still didn't glance over his shoulder as he made his way to the casino.

As soon as he got there, he sat down at one of the bars and ordered an imported beer and a shot of brandy on the side. These pick-me-uppers were going to trigger a winning streak, and he decided he was going to start with the roulette wheel. And he did quite well. After that, he tossed dice on the green felt-covered table, and that had been a godsend. He couldn't stop winning, and the money in his wallet waxed while his sobriety waned, but John kept on drinking. By eight-thirty he stopped gambling for a while. He needed to relax in a different way, and he sat down and ordered fish and chips; chasing the food down with another beer. A curvaceous female began to flirt with him, and he flirted back for a while, but his mission was not over yet. Leaving her at the bar disappointed, he returned to the tables. A little after eleven, he'd quadrupled his money, and he wasn't a stupid man. He knew he was way too sloshed. Time to cash out. John ordered the final drink for the road, and that had been a very stupid mistake. He was already real wobbly, and he quickly felt the effects of that last drink while he stumbled back to his cabin. Weaving between the two golden pillars at the entrance of the casino, paranoia slammed into him. In his muddled head, he needed to get away from everyone. His cabin was on the sixth deck, and he wanted to get there in a less traveled road. Ignoring the elevators, he opened a small door in the corner of the lobby leading to the service stairs, and he began to clatter down the metal steps. Ungainly in his stupor, he was moving fairly slowly. He didn't want to tumble head over heels down the damned things.

Vera had watched John Belton like a hungry hawk. She'd followed him when he'd left Sweet and Hot, and she'd perched like a vulture in a dark corner of the casino during the next few hours and she was in a great mood. Things had gotten more difficult, but John had unwittingly set himself up. He had become a very easy mark for her by peeling himself away from any security. With a wide smile plastered across her face, she quietly opened the service door. And she had been very careful not make any noise. Vera crept down the stairs behind him, taking the ten inch carving knife she'd stolen off a buffet table out of her purse. Getting close, she instinctively weighed the knife in her hand. The act would be fast and simple. A precise plunge just under his scapula, and there'd be a very good chance she'd knick his heart muscle.

John had slowed even more when he got to the first landing, with a deadly shadow almost on top of him. Holding the long knife above her head in both hands, she was half-a-second away from the ultimate coup-de-grace. She was about to thrust the blade into John's back, and she was using all the strength she had to put behind that downwards stroke. The drunken sot swayed right in front of her. It was a perfect, but things didn't really come out the way she'd foresaw. Her easy target suddenly pivoted around like a top, and his large hands instantly covered her own and she hadn't had enough time to even blink, forget about responding with enough wherewithal to continue with her attack. Or even get away. Stopping this wonderful downwards sweep of her weapon, he also kicked her legs right out from under her, and Vera fell flat on her back. He dropped his knee on her ribcage, using his weight to anchor her there, and then he wrenched the knife out of her hands. He tossed it, and it bounced off the metal stairs with an awful metal clang rebounding off the walls of the stairwell on its zigzagging trip to the bottom. Vera looked up into John Belton's eyes, and she knew. Grey-blue eyes were staring into her own, steadier than bedrock, and she knew. With a wig on his head, and concealing makeup and padding on his face that had, up to that point, reformed his identity, she now knew it was not John Belton. Whoever it was had done a bang-up job taking his place, however the truth was clearly revealed in a lot of ways.

"Hello, Vera…or would you rather have me call you Mrs. Adler? You probably aren't very happy that Mr. Belton is watching TV in his cabin right now."

"Who the hell are you?! And...and...get…off of me. I haven't done anything. Oh…and…" Vera was having problems getting a breath of air with Ryan's knee on her torso, "…and that was just a joke knife. The blade recedes back into the handle. John and I had already set up a cat and mouse game for tonight, and it's obvious he never told you about it. And I don't know who you think I am. My real name *is* Janice Topper. You can look it up in the guest registry. Get off of me. I can't breathe! *Get off! Get off of me!*"

There was absolutely no proof behind anything she'd just said. That didn't matter in the least. She was hoping her lies would give her a split-second of indecision in his mind, to loosen his tight hold on her by a millimeter. She didn't need much. Just enough to break free for a few more seconds. She could take this guy out of the picture just like she was going to do with Belton. *To all of them.* In this pivotal moment, a picture of Eric came into her head, the cherry on top of her poisonous cake. Vera had spent many hours imagining his warm blood throbbing over her hands, while she gleefully rode her own heart straight to hell.

"I am Inspector Ryan Porretta. The Blackmore Coalition wanted my help to find you. I know exactly who you are, and why you're here, my dear Vera. I advise you *not* to fight me. If you resist, the clinic will deal with incidental wounds I'll inflict on you to stop your indecision."

The furious expression on her face was replaced by that of a repentant child. Of course, real remorse had vanished out of her months ago, and the final dregs of her conscience dissolved soon after. Her free hand began to slowly creep inside Ryan's jacket. She'd seen his revolver snug in a shoulder holster under his left armpit. If she could get her hand on that gun, she'd have everything she needed. He hadn't seen her slow approach, and that was good. Porretta looked at her, and he started laughing. He could feel her tug at his sidearm, and in response, he slapped her hard enough to knock her out. Ryan tossed her limp body over his shoulder. He left the service stairs on his way to deck two, ignoring any questions he got from passengers on the elevator ride down.

Entering the brig, there was no one there. He found the necessary keys in a drawer in the desk, and he dropped her on cot in one of the two small cells. Closing the heavy steel door, he used those keys to lock her up tight. Ryan wasn't concerned about the bruise beginning to form on her temple, nor would he find a poultice of ice to put on the swelling.

Michael Chandler and Eric Adler, and of course, John Belton himself had known about the identity switch. Ryan had explained to them that they had to act as if Belton was really there at the table with them. Setting himself up as bait, it had to be realistic if his trap was going to work. It they got it right, there would be much higher chance they would not be murdered themselves. They'd done a bang-up job.

Inspector Porretta left Vera in her new home. He went off to tell the Captain, and Nugent the news. The remaining members of the Blackmore Coalition on land would also get a call, and relieve them from the pressure.

What was inside the odd looking bag Porretta had brought on board had remained a mystery for Captain Walker and Officer Nugent. Listening to what the Inspector had done to win the day, they quickly understood that it had to be a professional makeup-box. He wouldn't have been able to replace the lawyer that day without a lot of well applied paint.

8:30AM Wednesday January 10th, 2007 The Essayons

Holly and Keith were wound up over the upcoming confrontation the next day. When they got to their cabins, neither slept very well. Keith woke at eight. Stretching, he smiled, but reality wiped that dreamlike memory right off his face. He got dressed and he stepped out on the deck. It was time to eat powdered eggs and slurp up some coffee, but he stopped walking and looked around. Ultramarine blue, the sky was blazing bright; not a cloud in sight and the wind had dropped to a sigh. No nasty currents or swells bunching up on the surface around the ships. It was seventy-three degrees, too comfortable for words. Tranquility had replaced the gloom that had dogged them yesterday. Keith started moving again, and Holly appeared like a ghost at his heel, matching his stride. He looked over at her. She angled her head in a gesture that hinted about her own uneasiness about the weather. Then she rolled her eyes straight up.

"Nice day, isn't it, my friend. I don't see any disturbances in the foreseeable future," Holly said, and Keith opened the mess hall door for her.

"A dream come true. Ridiculously splendid. I don't know if I can get my breakfast to stay down, enjoying perfection like this."

"Oh come on, Keith. It's possible that last battle weakened it. It's possible. I mean, it had been a huge monster we killed. I couldn't get away, and I couldn't fight back either. It must have used everything it had to kill me and save itself. I've checked on the other ships by radio, and right now nothing is bothering them."

Keith did not say anything.

"*Hello?* Is there anybody out there?"

They sat at one of the tables, and Holly smiled over at him. Still nothing. Just more silence.

"Keith!"

"Alright, alright. It's certainly an option, but if we think about the entire thing, there are a lot of questions tugging at me with some pretty long claws. How was the guy on the dredge infected? And why didn't you know the tentacle was about to come out of nowhere to grab you? Just saying."

Holly frowned. Keith grinned back at her, and drank some coffee from his cup.

"Yeah. I know, but does it make sense to paint our future with a darker brush? I thought you were the one trying to put on rose-colored glasses last night? Can't change the past, so why shouldn't we imagine a more positive outlook? We did win that fight hands down, after all. Maybe our adversary is still mulling things over again, and it hasn't yet found the right combination for its next onslaught. There's a chance it's nice out because it's nice out."

And then her tone changed. It began almost harrowing.

"It seems you really want it down and dirty, Keith. Okay, how 'bout I'll give you a dose of what you crave. After we get the filters up and running later on, the whole show could easily go kaput. Over. Down for the count. Besides what is already bedeviling our internal predictions, let us now invite Senior Fiasco to have breakfast with us at the same time so he can describe what will go wrong with a flourish!!"

After another spate of silence, she finally got what she was hoping for.

"Of course, your right, Holly. It is beautiful out there, and it's clear as a bell. We shall overcome, we shall overcome it all," and with a nod and a smile as wide as the sky, Keith plunged his fork into his scrambled powder with sudden enthusiasm.

Done eating, they took the dinghy to the Essayons. It was the closest dredge to the Cutaway. They spent the first hours there in the wheelhouse as the plan was about to be put to the test. Captain Stewart Martin of the Essayons, had set things up as best he could. He helped Holly and Keith communicate to the rest of the dredges on the VHF channel, and everyone in the circle had responded with an A-Okay. Not a wrinkle during these silky-calm morning hours. The good-luck included the fleet of dredges. At eleven fifteen, Holly and Keith went out on the deck for a break.

The scene in front of them was an impressive one. The farthest dredge was almost four miles away, yet the fairytale climate allowed them to make her out pretty well. Closer in, they could read the home-ports of many of the ships by the insignia on their flags. Closer still, they could make out the letters of the dredge's name. Keith looked up. A flock of seagulls were swooping above his head, and he thought about that. They couldn't have found edible fish in this toxic dump, so they had to be surviving on scraps the cook was tossing out. The countdown was about to begin, and they went back inside the wheelhouse.

At 1:45, things were still fine. The engineers had all radioed in. The filters on the dredges were working perfectly. Holly had raced down the stairs to the lower deck on the Essayons to check on the filters, and they'd been humming along smooth as velvet. Then she took a sample of the water rushing out of the other side of the frame, and she took it to the lab in the Cutaway. One last test to make sure. She put drops of the filtered water under the electron microscope, and the molecules looked normal, floating there in what she considered molecular magnificence. She waited to make sure things would stay the way they were. And they did. Holly let go of the handle of the microscope, and she leaned back on the stool…and then she stood up and stretched and smiled. Time to return to the dredge.

Holly and Keith were catching their breath on the upper deck of the Essayons, after all, it was a beautiful day. Captain Martin opened the hatch behind them holding a pair of beat-up rust stained beach chairs in his hand.

"You guys have been racing around like maniacs, and it seems you have the tiger by the tail at the moment. Bobby found these crappy chairs somewhere in the bowels of this old scow, and I'm here to give you this cheap reward. I can't order you to do it, but I can strongly suggest you both take a load off. Use this needed recess as long as you can."

Holly smiled and thanked him, and she opened the chairs up and put them down in the sun. They sat down to absorb the soothing warmth of those rays more comfortably. For a little while anyway.

"Doesn't it look like a turn-around for us, and for everybody else in the circle too? If nothing goes wrong in the next few hours, we might get the idea we'd actually done it. The filters are working, and they should be changing the wrong direction into the right one. The whole environment is probably realigning as we speak."

"*Maybe.* At least I don't feel anything barreling at us anymore."

But Keith was lying threw his teeth. He couldn't lie any harder than he was able to at that point. The exact same prickly inkling that had burrowed into his head when he'd seen the headlines about the mass murder at Holly Donnelly's father's estate in their Thanksgiving reunion last year, had reappeared, only it was pulling on him even harder. Apparently not bothered by this unsettling shadow, Holly looked okay and he didn't want to pick up that gloomy brush of his again.

"Maybe I should call Attison? He'd love the good news and how things are going and stuff. What you do think?"

"Go ahead, Holly. He'd love to hear from you."

Taking her sat-phone from the back pocket of her jeans, she pressed a fast key, connecting her to Attison's land-line in Finalhaven. He did not pick up. She tried his mobile phone. Still nothing, and that was odd. He usually picks up her calls unless he was otherwise engaged. Holly assumed he was alright. *He's always alright.* He'd call her back in the next few minutes. There was nothing hiding behind the wonderful tableau she was gazing out at. There was nothing waiting out there. Nothing coiled up for a final strike to begin…begin what?

Her tangled thought was interrupted by a crewmen who'd bounded up the steep stairs holding two mugs of coffee for herself and Keith. The entire crew had been impressed by their diligence. As far they knew, they were sailing down the other side of the mountain, and this was a gesture of appreciation. They wanted them to know how they felt. Gratefully accepting the coffee, Holly and Keith thanked him, and the young man bowed and returned to the galley.

"Things are really stabilizing," Keith said, greedily sipping at his coffee.

"I must agree, my dear sir, and there is still not a cloud in the sky! I'm starting to really get the feeling this is going to work!"

After her happy declaration, one of the seagulls gracefully soaring above the dredge plummeted to the wooden deck right in front of them, transformed. A bird no longer, it was now a bloody lump of jumbled feathers, dead as dead could be. Fifteen feet away, the exact same thing took place. The beginning of a nightmarish flurry of falling birds quickly becoming a very short blizzard as the entire flock fell inexplicable to their deaths on the decks of the Essayons or the surface of the sea. The painful episode ended when there weren't any gulls left. Holly frowned. Her last statement really needed a new attachment.

"Or maybe not."

Tasting her coffee for the first time in a tasty sip, it was all she was going to get out of that pungent-smelling mug. Holly's uncertainty was replaced with a cast-iron truth, and a chill touched her skin, lifting away the gentle warmth of the sunlight. For only a second, their eyes locked. The premonition they hadn't wanted to accept was coming to life. There was no way they could make it go away. The only thing they could do was to fight, tooth and nail to the very last, and they raced down the steps the crewman had just climbed to bring them an offering of victory. Things were disintegrating very quickly. The Essayons had lost power. All power. Both generators on board were dead, and the diesel engines were quiet. The dredge was starting to drift. Obviously, the filters had stopped working as well, and it was time for Holly and Keith to rectify the situation anyway they could.

Keith saw a line of storm clouds moving swiftly towards them, and the breeze had picked up. With her long-distance vision, Holly knew the nearest dredges had lost their power too.

"Should I get into the dinghy and get over to Vasco Da Gama, or Eagle 1?" Keith said. The whole circle of dredges was collapsing.

"No. They're out of juice, just like us, and I have a feeling that the ships I can't see are down too."

"I think you're right, and they are all floating off their coordinates. Our first step has got to be getting the power back on the Essayons. If we combine our strengths we might get the job done faster...unless you have a better idea?"

"It's a good plan."

Keith looked calm, however the bleakness in his eyes was deep enough to drown in, and Holly didn't look any better. It seemed she was listening to a Pink Floyd song in which the lyrics advised her to crash on a rocky boulder someplace and die in a beautiful crescendo, but she appeared peaceful nonetheless. They knew it didn't matter how they felt. They were warriors, and they must stand and fight whatever the odds. No such thing as retreat. They cannot lose. The other option is incomprehensible.

The first wispy grey arms grasping out from the line of clouds had covered the sun, and somehow this little bit of shadow seemed to hold more darkness than a moonless night. Holly beamed out an ironical smile straight at Keith with so much force it slammed into him like a jolt, and it was enough to relight his hope. He smiled back at her and they pressed on.

They didn't see anyone from the crew. They might have been knocked out or worse, but they couldn't address that problem at the moment. There was not a second left to spare if they were going to get control of the dredge.

Jogging towards to the stairs that would get them to the engines, they both stopped on a dime when they heard gurgling coming from the stern. They couldn't see what was making the noises. It was climbing up the steel hull as if there was a ladder back there, and then they saw it clearly as it climbed over the rail and towered over them. A brutality from a thousand nightmares, it was over nine feet tall, and it mimicked the form of a roustabout; a crewmen who does heavy labor on any commercial ship. Of course, that was the extent of its familiarity. Their enemy had sculpted this form from tainted seawater out of the Pacific, and this new nemesis was an amorphous grey. Ripples banded across its surface by the ruffling wind as it lurched towards them on liquid legs, a thousand times more powerful than flesh and bone and muscle.

Holly's eyes seared into bright blue as she came up with an attack or even something to defend herself and Keith. Heating her skin hot enough to boil water, the monster weaved around her like a lightening stroke, and it slapped one of its turkey-sized hands across Keith's head. He was thrown five feet backwards, already unconscious when he landed and it wasn't a good place to be. His nose was tilted into a shallow puddle in a divot gouged into that section of the wooden deck, and it was difficult for him to inhale air. Getting a small amount of oxygen from the corner of his mouth, Keith was in dire-straits, yet Holly could not help him. The roustabout was not done attacking, now bearing its wrath on Holly with murderous intent. It knew that Holly was a more powerful opponent than Keith. Taking her out would be more difficult, and it had carefully thought over the best way to do. Strangling had come up as the most providential course of action.

Boiling the thing into steam wasn't working, and those crazy-large surreal hands with sausage fingers made from water had closed around her throat with clenching power. And that deadly grip tightened. Holly dove her own hands into its liquescent body to sever the hands of the ogre. Her desperate attempt was futile and gallows humor showed up on the face of her attacker in a lopsided sneer. It was about to win the entire enchilada. Just about over. Call it a done deal. Wiping out the crusaders would be devastating or delightful depending on your point of view.

Keith's skin had turned white. He was fading and he couldn't be woken up. Holly was flopping around in the playful hands of her enemy like a ragdoll as the Frankenstein's puppet held onto that strangle hold. Her eyes had wilted to normal grey-violet, and the only thing left blue was her face. Holly and Keith were slipping away, and the rest of the world was about to follow them down.

Attison had been leaning against the mess hall door, arms crossed and heel hung casually over the top of his other boot. He'd been watching the ongoing violence to his ward and her friend for almost a minute before he ultimately interjected with a whistle that sliced through the air like a scythe. Taking his fingers out of his mouth, he followed this piercing salute with a condescending taunt.

"Deal with someone your own size." Then Korybante smiled.

A sneer rippled across the lips of the caricature, and it dropped Holly like a bag of onions. She lay motionless on the deck, and she was hanging on by a thread.

Attison had put on his long black coat, a white dress-shirt and a pair of black leather pants. He'd even put on a heavy turquoise necklace, three silver and turquoise rings and a bracelet of the same type. Usually, he does not wear jewelry, but knowing what he was up against that day, he wanted to respect that gravity. Getting dressed hours ago, he'd shaken his head in regret. There was no way out. He had to challenge the usurper and he had to win.

When Holly had called him, he'd been on a speedboat gunning along at seventy knots. Hadn't heard the ring. The shaking of the engines had easily masked the small vibrations of the phone in his back pocket. He probably wouldn't have answered it, either way. There was no point in talking over anything anymore anyway. He was on the only path left to take.

Getting to the dredges swiftly, no one saw his approach, and no one saw the Merry Pace rumbling in the middle of the circle of ships with the unmistakable engine noise and the searing red hull of his speedboat reflecting glaringly off the gray-blue surface of the ocean. *Of course, he didn't want them too.* Tying up to a cleat on the stern of the Essayons, he'd made it just in time to save Holly and Keith. Probably. He'd turn his attention to the main event after this first problem gets taken care of.

Moments before Attison interrupted its murderous enterprises, the real millennium version of Shelley's Frankenstein had been happy. Assuming there was no one and nothing else out there to interfere with its project, ending those two lives and sinking all the dredges would solve its only problem, simply and permanently. Attison's whistle was an unsettling surprise. Having astonished Holly and Keith with the sudden appearance of that oversized roustabout dripping seawater on the deck next to the stern of the Essayons, it seems the same level of shock was now taking place in reverse. It seemed the shoe had somehow found a way to cover that watery version of the other foot. It was not in any way prepared for Attison Korybante. Didn't even know he existed. Instinctually, it understood he was going to be a formidable opponent. Perhaps more potent than anything it had faced before, and at that moment, it had no idea how to control him. Strangling him into submission was all it knew at that juncture, so…it would strangle the interloper to death. *If it could.*

The giant lurched towards him, and he stepped away from the wall and he confronted the monster. His eyes had gotten dangerous, shimmering into blue flames. He raised his right arm, palm out; stop. However, the gesture was exuding invisible force, and the nine-foot roustabout halted, and it hadn't wanted to. Attison had started his own assault.

The pearl grey fiend flickered, and the ripples rushed across its surface much faster. The monster was beginning to blow up like a balloon. Five feet wide at its shoulders, and nine feet tall, Attison's extremely intimate interference within its internal structure was pushing those limits outwards; three feet wider and four feet higher in the air. It was possible to make out the safety rail on the other side of the deck right through the expanded body of this watery thing. It was now a diaphanous mist. Attison had been able to insert space between each of the molecules within this mimicking creation. Of course, the usual physical connection between the particles was no longer there, and the only thing holding this disparate giant together was Attison's will. And he was leaving it like that for his own amusement. Be that as it may, the fiend had gumption. It kept on trying. The see-through hands were reaching at Attison's throat, and the jeweled antagonist broke into a laugh. Clenching his own hand into a tight fist, he swiftly pulled it close to his belly. He was letting go, and the monster disintegrated; countless gallons of water fell to the deck in an ongoing splatter and an oversized puddle replaced the roustabout.

Attison stepped through the wet patch of what remained of his opponent to get to Keith, and as soon as he got to him, he gently moved his head away from a smaller puddle he'd fallen into. The comatose man would need a lot more than that to come back. Lungs heavy with seawater, he was almost dead and in any other situation, they wouldn't have been able to save him. However, Attison was out of the ordinary, and so were his abilities. Putting his hand on Keith's forehead, his fingers glowed into a throbbing blue and that neon-light got even stronger, and he held his hand there for a solid minute until the supposedly fatally injured man's eyelids fluttered open. And then he started to cough up water and phlegm. Keith was coming returning to the land of the living. He won't wake up completely for hours, and he wasn't going to be hundred percent for days, but Attison had dragged him back from that eternal edge. It was time for him to take care of Holly. Or what was left of her.

A lump on the wet boards six feet away. He walked over and picked her up as if she was weightless. Attison saw the pallor of her skin and the touch of grey made it look like she was already dead. Moving a lock of her hair away from her closed eyes, he shook his head in painful regret. Until anger took hold of him in a very rare appearance, and the grievous force he'd been, became more intense.

Attison Korybante had never wanted to be where he was. He'd let himself believe Holly could take care of the entire thing on her own. His own cowardice had been behind this ludicrous optimism and his self-serving blindness had turned around and bit him on the ass. Oh, there'd been a chance. A chance she could have done it with Keith's help, but it was extremely unlikely. He should not have bet on it in the first place. Tying a gossamer rag over his eyes, he thought he could sidestep his responsibility to the planet, but the metaphorical chain around his ankle eventually tripped him up. He felt like an idiotic, like he was born yesterday, and even that was ridiculous. The human race was being eaten alive by a force created by their own ineptitude and selfishness. There was no choice in the matter. Now he must intervene.

Holding Holly in his arms, he opened the door into the mess hall with his shoulder. A crewmen lay against the starboard wall, and another was motionless on his belly under one of the tables. As he put her on the top of one of the tables, there was no time to see if they were unconscious or dead, and he lay next to her and held her in his arms. It wasn't a moment of tenderness. He wasn't grieving over Holly's possible passing. He was about to heal her as he'd healed Keith, however this time, he had to go farther out on that bridge to the thereafter to drag her back.

A swarm of tiny lights appeared and swirled around them on the mess-hall table, and the number of lights increased, and then radiance seemed to be coming straight out of their bodies. After that, they disappeared in a ball of blinding light. The pulsing cocoon held for fifteen minutes before it faded away. Attison was on his elbow staring at Holly while a snore purred out of her. For a moment he was at peace. He knew she was now climbing out of the bottom of that well. Soon she'd be healthy as a horse.

The second resuscitation over with, he left Holly behind on the table. Attison walked outside on the lower deck and then he stopped and stood there like a rock…thinking. After another quarter hour, he'd made a plan and he climbed the stairs to the wheelhouse. And he kept on going up the wall of the wheelhouse. It was slick, just a piece of painted metal, yet he climbed it as if there was a ladder soldered to the side of it. He needed to be at the highest point on the Essayons, and when he stood up on the roof of the wheelhouse, he'd gotten there. Gazing over his head, the cloud cover had thickened with a new hints of a curious green light emitting from within some of the twisted formations up there. Then he looked out at the horizon, and there was nothing to see. The other dredges had floated away, including the Cutaway. When he'd tied the Merry Pace to the dredge's stern, he'd used a form of telekinesis to anchor the Essayons where she was. He had to stay in the middle of the eye of the gyre in order to battle his nemesis. What he was about to do would certainly drain him; it may possibly suck-out way too much. Maybe more than he can muster. Attison shook his head as his black hair swept across the high collar of his coat. Hiding under his ferocity, something else had been born and for the first time in his life, fear had found purchase in his soul.

Korybante knew the radioactive cask had fallen off the transport ship many years ago, and it had gotten stuck between up-thrusting fingers of igneous rock two miles below. A gash in the side of the lead container was leaking out a plume of radiation riding an upward jet of scalding water shooting out of a volcanic fissure only feet below the pinned cask. Having tumbled into this absurd position in a devilish twist of fate, Attison was about to take away the gloating monster's favorite spice; take away most powerful ingredient in this ungodly mix.

Sitting on the salt-blasted paint-faded roof, he crossed his legs and closed his eyes. Remaining in a meditative position, he was ready and he unfettered himself from his body. He astral-projected out. One of the limited few who really can do so, he was the only one able to physically move things around in that ethereal form. He could even ramp that ability up to an astronomical level if he had to. Consciousness diving through the choppy surface of the ocean around the dredge, he plummeted down. Dark as pitch after twenty-five feet, Attison had his own radar and it didn't have anything to do with echolocation. Out-stretching and also extremely inclusive, he could make-out solid forms in the blackness as if he had on night goggles. Reaching the trapped cask, he stopped and fluttered there.

Fifty miles thick, the lithosphere was the outer crust of the earth. Composed of rock in smaller layers of differing density and composition, under the lithosphere was the mantle. There weren't many breaks in that outer crust to expose the lower stratum. But there were a few. A long crack on the floor of the Pacific Ocean followed a mid-ocean ridge; one of the rare places where volcanic bedrock is uncovered. The upper part of the mantle is made of nickel and iron, and it's usually in a solid form. Hanging above the radiated container, Attison was searching for something in the dense rock below it with a tentacle of mind. And he quickly found what he was looking for. A pocket of magma 2,400 meters away. Since just five percent of the upper mantle was molten, he was happy for the coincidence, and it was a mile and half down and slightly east of where the container was.

The easiest way to reach that hot pocket would be to follow the fissure that snaked off beneath the cask itself. Following its path with his mind, Attison made out that after three-quarters of a mile, the crevice divides. One side veering off to the left in an upside down Y, but he could still follow the main fracture almost to his ultimate destination.

With a thunderbolt of telekinesis strength sent into his astral hands, he plucked the barrel out of its rocky squeeze to begin this unbelievable trip, starting off by stuffing it straight into the crevice. The walls of the fissure were made of a bond of nickel and iron, and they were extremely hard. The main ingredient in the metal of the container holding the glassed-over rods was lead, a much softer material. Those natural walls would have crushed the buttery drum into a dented joke instantly, but Attison wanted it to remain undamaged so he'd used his telekinesis powers to change the tensile strength in the lead before starting this extraordinary voyage. And he'd sent it right off the charts.

The maximum width in the fissure was six feet, and the container was a smidgeon larger than that, but that disparity was not enough to stop him. Using a little bit more power, he squeezed it through the thinner fracture, pulverizing those extra inches into floating dust.

Soon enough, the barrel got close to the bubbling magma, and only a thin rock wall divides the two. Attison simply rammed the diamond hard drum through the wall, and it broke through into an irregular chamber holding the lava. Three thousand feet in width, some of the trenches were a mile deep. It was certainly big enough to absorb the poisonous invader without a burp. The lead cask floated graciously on its own for thirty feet in the molten liquid, but then it started to sink. Of course, nothing known to mankind would be able to withstand that location for long, so there would be no end to its final descent. At one thousand, eight hundred and seventy-five degrees Fahrenheit, the magma quickly melted the shipping container and the glass rods within, dissolving the entire thing and even the radiation had been dispersed into the vastness of the mantle. Unable to find the mythological inferno itself, sending the contaminated garbage to a real hell on earth instead would have made the devil smile.

Another job done, he raced to the surface like a shooting star. Thirty-seven seconds later, he was back on the roof of the wheelhouse blending into his physical body. Storm clouds were building, and he uncrossed his legs and stood up. He had just struck his inexperienced opponent with a very nasty surprise, and the roiling sky above his head was a symptom of this sudden displeasure. It was probably figuring out a definitive way to get rid of him. The puerile intelligence had to be livid, and Attison hoped his guess about its emotions was right. It'd be difficult to come up with a feasible attack in the time remaining if his enemy remains too upset to plan in a logical way. He'd be in much better shape if it *didn't* marshal its titanic strength together to attack him intelligently. Looking up again, he hoped the billowing thunderheads were there to unnerve him, to give him the heebie-jeebies. Attison certainly has misgivings coming from the deeper echo of real fear, but these atmospheric histrionics weren't bothering him in the least. The clouds had actually given him a unique idea. It wasn't going to be easy, but he thought it over. He might be able to pull it off, and it would take care of everything permanently, eternally and forevermore.

Attison wasn't going to give the millennium Frankenstein any more time to unleash what it might have up its sleeve, and any monster currently hiding somewhere inside the super-stellar looking storm up there wasn't going to be able to arrive. He could dissipate the thunderheads, but he knew it would just reformed the silly things. It would make more sense if he changed them into what he needed them to be before anything else happens. A first step towards a complete disintegration of his enemy.

There had been nothing wrong with the filters Holly and Keith had manufactured. If they hadn't been interrupted, they would have made a difference. However, it would have been a partial solution, and they hadn't had enough strength to defend themselves. Attison was about to create a filter of his own. He was following their idea into a larger and more inclusive cleaning system.

Facing the center of the gyre, he raised his arms. He was about to use all the energy he had in building this powerful creation, and his dark eyes flared up like the blue in a soldering gun. A thousand feet above the ocean, he imagined an invisible rotating wheel, a half-a-mile-wide. Then it came into being. This was going to be Attison's version of a filter, and it was aggressively active, vibrating in frequencies that were very magnetic. The invisible wheel thrummed out waves like a beacon. The twenty-two filters sucking in ocean water in the circle of dredges had been passive, and this one was not. Any distorted molecule in the atmosphere would be drawn in through this sphere by the hypnotic current to be repaired and sent back on the other side. It was interactive with the entire environment, and a mountain of ocean water had risen from the surface to dwindle up to an apex in the center of the Attison's unseen ring. Water molecules were going through the same cleansing process.

Singing the song of a siren, this new filter in the sky was bringing unnatural atoms on earth home, crooning a lullaby of lies made from a mix of complex waves. The melody was tricking the bad-bits into supposing it was the right place to go, and it drew them onwards, not fading out. No, the closer they got, the more intense it became. Finally, in the center of sphere what was interwoven in them was tugged out, and the influx of a powerful insertion of stable reality broke off the shifting additions in the jarring new evolution from the dark side. A small metallic looking ball had appeared in the middle of the filter, a physical reaction to the pulling apart. And it was slowly getting bigger. The warped particles that had been peeled off were sucked into a gravitational hollow so forceful they were stuck there like flies on flypaper wrapped around a minuscule marble.

A lot of passengers on the Caprice had gone to the starboard side of the ship to watch what was happening in the sky nearby. It was too spectacular not to watch, however their amazement was tempered by apprehension. It had a terrible quality of apocalyptic power.

Attison remained on the ceiling of the wheel house, arms raised, hands facing out to orchestrate the entire spectacle. Sending out influence of that magnitude, the radiance in his eyes was bright enough to blind.

He had decided to tame the bellicose thunderheads into long puffy bands of clouds, similar to chem-trails. They radiated out like a wheel from Attison's purifying circle where the summit of the wobbling sea-mountain was also connected. More delicate in their latest incarnation, these ribbons of white vapor were coming in from all points of the compass. And even more surprising, swarms of Borg flies were diving and swooping around those pale spokes. Occasionally, two of these swarms would mock-fight like World War II pilots in a deadly duel, aiming at each other in a fake battle. Then they'd get bored of it, and return to the hypnotic white road they were deeply linked too. Getting closer and closer to the filter, they were still utterly unaware of their upcoming dissolution. The metal-like looking ball hung in the distance, partially built by pieces of other Borg flies no longer buzz around anymore. It shone with the luster of hundreds of thousands of flies who'd been redistributed into it, and it was growing.

Attison's mission was reaching a triumphant close when a contingent of these flies veered away from their vapor trail on a new flight plan. They were zeroing in on the Essayons. Way too intent on what he was doing, Mr. Korybante hadn't noticed their deviation, nor how close they were getting.

The Frankenstein had had full control over the ecosphere minutes before Attison burst out of nowhere and knocked its apple-cart over. The millennial monster was besotted with rage, lifted to a higher plateau by the emotion, and its imminent downfall. It must save itself! Like an adrenalin boost in a human, this agitation allowed the creature to pull out all the stops. It has to continue to destroy what is correct in the world.

Attison was deeply distracted when the small horde of flies flew through the open window of the wheelhouse, and he hadn't seen their silent invasion. Captain Martin was unconscious in front of the wheel of the dredge, arms hanging down, head tilted back on the cushioned rest of the chair, and Engineer Reeves was slumped over the table in the corner of the room. Earlier, the monster had no interest in the unconscious men, besides knocking them out, but the situation had changed dramatically. In a last ditch attempt to get full control back again, every single inch of skin the flies could get to on those men was covered in a seething carpet of flies. And their writhed with demonic energy. Every single one of those insects was infected the captain and the engineer with even more venom with a fervor they'd never had before. Badly crowded, they crawled over each other to get to the flesh, and the skin that wasn't covered was swollen and red, and it was clear they were also getting under the clothes as well. The flies were injecting more of their poison on top of what was already too much, and if one bite makes a person into a drone, what would an overdose like this do? Five more minutes of this unrelenting spectacle, the swarm was finally satisfied. Rising en-masse from the bodies of the men, this rippling torrent of misery flew off to rejoin their kind in the clouds above. As if they hadn't done anything wrong, and what waited for them at the end of their journey still seemed to be heaven.

Captain Martin and Engineer Reeves's eyes opened, and they stood up and stared out into space as if they were blind. Skin mottled, red and pockmarked, it suddenly smoothed out and the discoloration went away. The officers looked fine; a nicety that was not going to hold for long.

Attison's nonstop assault had drained him to the limit. In consequence of that, his internal warning lights had flickered off. He did not see the captain and the engineer, or smell them, or hear the strange flickering of a bonfire burning bright as they climbed the side of the wheelhouse behind him. When Captain Martin's scorching tentacle slithered around Attison's waist, joined by another snaking out from the engineer to cover his neck and face in an attempt to suffocate him, he hadn't defended himself at all.

The eleventh-hour bid to rise out of Attison's blitzkrieg was truly an impressive one. The Captain and the engineer didn't look very human anymore. Their heads had dropped into their bodies, not much neck left to consider, and they'd each grown six tentacles on either side of their now extremely lengthened torsos. Just above the first and most powerful of the line-up of alien appendages, their normal arms and hands had atrophied into a much smaller form. Shriveled up tiny jokes, they were utterly ignored as they waved frantically around as a neurological hiccup from the intense transformation. The other tentacles weren't as long or powerful as the top pair, but the uneven ratio had no effect on the devastating strength coming from the nasty collection. Walker and Reeves were also on fire. Three inch flames rippled across their skin, and the heat radiated out of them made the scene behind them wobble and bend. Instead of suckers on the inside of their tentacles, dark mouths ringed with very sharp teeth were already trying to bite through Attison's extraordinarily tough skin. They wanted to break through and slurp-up as much of his blood as they could get. So far, their energetic grinding hadn't come up with any results.

The second he felt them on his body, Attison's response had been immediate and forceful. Leaving one arm up to keep doing what he was doing overhead, he wrenched the tentacle off his face and neck with the other with so much momentum, Reeves was thrown off the roof and into the Pacific. The other burning hot tentacle was putting a lot of pressure around his waist, but he didn't have good options to take care of it. The pillar of sea water had already fallen into the ocean. His strength weakening, it was getting very hard to support the filtering-sphere *and* the spoke-like clouds surrounding it. The tightening around his middle was increasing, but he wasn't going to be able to get this abysmal thing off his body with just one hand.

Meanwhile, throwing Reeves off the ship and into the sea, hadn't been enough. Whatever he had become, he'd had the wherewithal to not drown, instead climbing up the side of the dredge and out of the water. The burning tentacle waving engineer had suddenly appeared right next to his fiery companion. Flailing out one of his blazing tooth-ridden snakes, he lassoed Attison's ankles, and he yanked with everything he had. Mr. Attison Korybante fell to the deck hard. Very hard. The long clouds overhead quickly disintegrated and floated away from center of the sphere.

And then one of the inner mouths on the tentacle around his waist broke through. Slicing greedily into his skin, a pool of blood quickly puddling on the weathered roof of the wheel house as Captain Martin eagerly absorbed as much as he could from the wound he'd gnawed open. Reeves was busy nipping his way into Attison's body too, and his tentacle tightened on his prey's ankle. One of the circular mouths was snapping vigorously over a main artery. Breaking through at that particular point might send Attison over the top. He could succumb from blood loss.

He was on his back, apparently in dire-straights, yet he hadn't passed out and he certainly hadn't given up. *Far from it.* The bodies of his flickering attackers were swaying eight feet away from him, and he turned his invasive stare at their deformed faces, however the dangerous inference he'd put into that look apparently had no weight. In response, the captain sent out the secondary tentacles, swirling them around Attison's face, and then clamping them down. Why should he look at the man's eyes? It would be a lot more fun to suffocate him again. Deprive him from oxygen. Deprive him from life itself.

A strange calmness had fallen in the eye of the gyre. The linear clouds were gone, and the flies had been disbursed. The elevation of salt water had flattened-out ten minutes ago, and Attison's body was cocooned in tentacles. Waves of heat simmered in the air around this nightmarish husk intimated the end of many things. The flames erupting along the two deformed men had lowered; their concentration pinpointed towards their vampiric winnings leaking from the wounding of Attison Korybante. Things were finally reaching the ultimate end, and there was no reason why Frankenstein shouldn't win the day. Of course, there was a sticky-wicket in the optimistic forecast of ruin. The metallic ball was still rotating in the middle of the invisible filter. There was no good explanation for either of these things to still be there, and the sphere itself was an ongoing dilemma for the monster. Perhaps there may be something lurking under the surface like an iceberg. Harkening back to Hermes's quote, *as above so below* could have been a hidden a clue, clearly ignored.

Attison still had not given up. He was very groggy, and he couldn't see a thing, but he wouldn't let go of the sphere. Just enough strength to sustain it up there in the sky, he wasn't able to stop was being done to him. His life-force lapped up by his enemy, he became disconsolate.

But not for long. Unlike the reboot Frankenstein had gone through a half-hour ago, Attison was about to be infused by an atypical energy. Rising to meet an extraordinary circumstance, he was opening a conduit that was hard for him to accept. Rising up meant lowering down. Bowing to the undeniable fact that he had to call out to an outside force more powerful than he was…and then plead for salvation. He needed superiority to break this terrible hold.

In the painful darkness that Martin and Reeves had created, Attison's eyes were still bright blue. Normally, that blue would have remained in his eyes until the end, victorious or overwhelmed, however that truth was about to be undermined. He'd gotten an answer to his plea. The entire human race and every living thing on planet earth had gotten the same answer, and the sun itself seemed to burst in his head. White nuclear coals blasted the blue right out of his eyes, and whether this sudden alliance would be tapped for future endeavors or not, right now it was a death-knoll for the currently triumphant Frankenstein.

The captain and the engineer were attempting to rip out more of his skin in new locations, so far unsuccessfully, while the large mouth on Martin's tentacle was sucking in and swallowing Attison's blood as if it was nectar. However, that luscious liquid had suddenly picked up a taste toxic to the bloodsucker. Unable to stomach another drop of it, things in a general sense were unraveling. Their tentacles encompassing Attison were losing their hold. Like he'd been dipped in olive oil, and as these warped-looking creatures tried to reconnect, an invisible barrier had arrived to shield his body.

And Attison was free, lying in a puddle of bloody goo. He got to his feet again, and to his consternation, his long coat had been completely wrecked. The rest of his clothes hung on his well-built frame in tatters. Only his jewelry had made it through the battle unscathed. A thick layer of mucus was slathered on him, including his face and hair. The officers kept on trying to knock him over, but the buffer surrounding him was impregnable. Attison ignored the tentacle-wavers long enough to sweep his hands over his face and body to thin out the layer of drying drool. He slapped huge blobs of this slime onto the deck with awful plopping sounds. Having done the best he could under the circumstances, he looked over at his attackers and smiled.

Sometimes fate can be a cruel mistress. What had been wreaked on those innocent men could not be reversed, and Mr. Korybante had no other option. The wound on the side of his torso was still leaking blood, and he paused and heal it with an accidental glance. Then he raised his arms away from his body, palms up. Martin and Reeves slid four feet away from him. He'd pushed them both to the edge of the roof of the wheelhouse, and there they teetered. Gracefully flipping his hands over, he opened his fingers wide. Another well-known gesture; as if he was about to give them a wonderful gift. And he moved the two farther out. Off the Essayons. They floated over the Pacific Ocean, and their tiny human arms and hands were still frantically waving, tentacles reaching towards him...

As if they'd had dynamite in their bellies, Captain Walker and Engineer Reeves exploded. Hundreds of pieces of them rained into the sea. It was impressive that the pieces were still burning as they fell into the water. Not wanting to muck-up the Essayons, Attison had waiting to destroy them in a way that wouldn't leave any clutter.

Time to get back to business. Waving his hands over his head, he reinstating the mountain of water and the ribbon clouds and their respective magnetism. The Borg flies quickly resumed their misty path to dissolution, and any other twisted atom still mucking around out there was also being beckoned in to die. Working with more dispatch than he'd ever had before, he felt fine and looked like shit and the glistening grey ball in the center of the invisible sphere began to get bigger again.

During that defining moment, Mary Shelley's fictional Frankenstein would have been in pieces on the laboratory floor, or burning to a crisp on a funeral pyre under the devastation of Attison's magnified power. Of course, Shelley lived in a simpler world. The literary man\child she'd devised would have certainly rotted away to nothing on those flagstones, or in the other possible erasure, specks of burnt matter floating off in the smoke of that funeral pyre wouldn't matter either. But in reality, no portion, particle or percentage of this millennium Frankenstein could remain. Attison was adamant about that. The only thing he'd leave behind in the Trash Vortex would be flotsam, even if the modern version of it may be there forever.

The clouds were thinning out. There wasn't anything left to follow them in. The elevation of water from the Pacific had flattened out for the same reason, and the slowly rotating marble had grown into the size of a hot-air balloon. There was an hour of light left. Attison waited ten minutes until there wasn't a cloud in the sky, but in the meantime, he stared up at the grey ball. He was thinking. The mass of it had been created by pieces of the deposed monster, and he didn't want any of it to interfere with the environment. He came up with a solution in which it never ever would.

He closed his eyes, and visualized the Seven Sisters, also known as The Pleiades; a star cluster in a galaxy fairly near our own solar system in the sprawl of the Milky Way. Attison had picked out an unencumbered route the metallic orb would take to reach that cluster four hundred and forty light years away. The arrival there didn't matter, it was the long passage of time involved in getting there that did. Sending those compressed atoms into space and out of commission on an incomprehensibly long voyage was comparable to blinking them into nothingness. In a godlike way, he'd thrown the radioactive cask to hell, and the shining ball to heaven in a monumental way.

Attison began the interstellar trip for the weightless\black-hole heavy marble on a track to nowheresville with enough momentum to sustain it throughout. In three and half seconds, the compressed balloon bulleted through the earth's atmosphere leaving a blazing trail of incandescence in its wake. In five more, it wobbled only three miles above the pockmarked surface of the moon and then it was gone. Almost like an afterthought, he then erased his invisible filter out of existence. Everything he'd made was gone. What needed to be taken care was over with. Nothing needed to be sustained anymore. He remembered he'd send out a telekinetic net to bring the fleet of dredges back, right after he'd revived Holly and Keith, and one of the ships had appeared on the horizon.

4:15, and the sky remained a beautiful blue. The generators on the dredge had started up with Attison's help, and he climbed down the outside wall of the wheelhouse to the deck below. Stepping over to Keith, he checked on his pulse, and then he went inside the mess hall. Holly was still peacefully sleeping on the table, and he checked her pulse as well. They'd be up soon, and he left the mess hall.

Standing in the middle of the deck, he didn't have to do anything. The battle was finally over, and his exhaustion took hold. His insecurities began to haunt him again. The odd timing of his last-minute arrival could certainly be explained by the trickiness of the situation...even if things got more difficult to control. Illogical emotions linked to that disquieting choice were irrelevant now, and his eyebrows rose in a childlike 'who me' expression. An inch could be a mile, or in this case, a parsec. *The whole thing was taken care of, wasn't it?*

Since Attison was a physical wreck, he couldn't reign in his conscience nor override his confusing emotions. There was no way out of the moral conundrum in his head, ultimately accepting his own blunders. Shaking his head in regret, he replaced his guilt with the uncomfortable truth. Hoping that his adolescent truculence and trepidation wouldn't influence him in the future, he remained unsure about it. Emotions within are always unfettered. The only thing he may have learned in this stumble, is the disturbance itself. He may be able to see the instability within himself a little bit earlier.

Attison started to walk to the rail, yet his progress became more sluggish with every step. As soon as he got there, he leaned up against it for support. The white fire in his eyes had been banked a while ago, and even the last glow of his flickering blue had retreated. Pupils settling to a deep black-brown, the rest of his body was gearing down too. Some of the blood coming out of the now healed injury, had left a blotchy red pattern throughout his tattered clothes, but the only other indication of it, was the large circular scar on his belly and hip. He hadn't been able to get all of the slime off, and the thin layer had dried to the color of mustard with horrible shades of an orangey-rose along the creases of his skin.

Standing up at the rail wasn't going to go on for long. Out of the crossfire, and knowing his obligations had been met, whatever he was using for energy drained out of him. Somewhere deep inside, a voice was telling him it was okay to let go. Slowly sliding to the weathered deck-boards, Attison became dead to the world he'd saved.

And all the decks of the Essayons dredge were morgue-like quiet; apparently abandoned. The crew unconscious, Holly and Keith snored onwards, and any exhalations coming out of Attison were so weak they were inaudible. The shadow of the ship across the surface of the placid water seemed to hold more horrible surprises, but then Holly's eyes opened. The entire tableau changed in a heartbeat.

Sitting up like a snake bite with a question *'what happened to me'* pounding in her head, she leapt off the table, slammed through the door and ran onto the deck. Keith was unconscious a few feet away, but she instinctively knew he'd be okay. There was a pile of bloody laundry someone must have tossed next to the rail twenty-five feet away from her, but it really wasn't. Holly knew exactly what and who it was.

Belly clenching, she ignored the tear sliding down her cheek. Remembering his gracious offer to help her, she'd told him no. Stay away. The new reality slammed into her like a sledge hammer as she crouched over his body: Attison never listens to anyone. Not wanting him to know what had really happened in the factory the day he'd called, it had been easy as pie to accept his appeasement, easy to swallow his obvious lies like they were gummy bears.

A part of her still thought he might have been at Finalhaven when things got apocalyptic, but in reality, he'd gotten off the phone with her and did what he wanted. The opposite of what he'd said. Deep down, she'd known that…*or thought she had*. When Keith rescued her from the sea-monster, she'd gotten uneasy, afraid he'd fallen for her own bunk about being impervious. All of her doubts were washed away by the bloody garbage crumpled at her feet.

He'd saved her. No one else could have, but that hadn't been the only thing he'd done that day. He'd excised cancer out of the blood stream of the earth…yes, yes, he had…and that was peachy-keen, yet Holly wasn't getting any euphoria over the triumph. Her guardian was not looking very well, and that eclipsed everything else. She lifted his head with one hand and straightened his body out with the other. Over the past few minutes, Keith had woken up, and he'd come over to her.

"Hello, Holly. Do you know what's wrong with Attison?"

She looked up, and shook her head.

"Hi, Keith. I'm trying to figure out what went wrong…what happened after we were knocked out…and…and almost killed."

"The only thing I know right now is that our enemy is kaput, and his ruin didn't have much to do with you and me."

He crouched down on Attison's other side, moving what was left of his clothes out of the way. Keith was trying to find what could have been responsible for all the blood on his garments. All he found was a weird circular scar, nine inches wide on his torso and his hip, and it was the only blemish on his body.

"There aren't any wounds on him, Keith. I checked, and I can't figure out shit. Why can't I remember anything after I was knocked out? Usually, I can scour something up!"

"I'm having the same problem. Maybe we were way too far gone, and our memory-cards have no clearance for coma. Or wherever we were. I hate to say it, but if he hadn't shown up, we'd both be dead...hold on a second."

Keith trotted over to the rail. He leaned out to peer along the side of the ship, waiting for whatever was roped to a cleat back at the stern of the dredge to swing into view. A speed-boat. It had to be how Attison got on board. He must have foreseen their fiasco just in time. Helpful he had a boat like that at hand.

The crew was come around. A young roustabout trotted over to Holly, and he was unmindful of Attison's head resting in her lap.

"Have you seen the Captain, or Reeves? We've looked everywhere and we can't find them. Are they alright?" He was upset, and very tense. He was probably just as confused as they were.

"Sorry, mate. Can't answer your question right now. If I was you, I'd radio out to the other boats. Maybe they'd gone over to another ship for some unknown reason."

Three more dredges had come into view. Even the Cutaway was under three miles away. The worried crewman had nodded, disappearing into the wheelhouse to follow her advice. Keith had heard most of their short conversation, and when the young man was out of earshot, Holly gave Keith her gloomy prediction.

"Too early to be sure, but I don't think they survived. I can't find them, can you? I mean *anywhere.* Not on any of the dredges either."

"I've got the same feeling, but we can't do anything about it. We have our own problems on our hands," and he nodded towards Attison, who managed to look even worse. "There's a cruise ship nearby, and I think we should get him out of here and get him over there. I'll contact them on the radio. I have a feeling the captain is going to be very accommodating to the request. In the meantime, we should get him back to his own boat. Think about the situation we're in right now, Holly. We don't know what's wrong with Attison. There may be more resources we can use over there, and it will give us more options. Besides, we're not in great shape ourselves. The last round knocked us both out and the referee looked just like the angel of death. Attison isn't the only one battered and bruised." Of course, Holly didn't like his last inference, and she glared at him. Keith changed his tack for instant absolution… "I know there's a very good chance he's in danger, and we are not in the same shape. All I meant was we need to recharge too. All of us would be better off on that cruise ship than limping home in a hopper-dredge or even the Cutaway."

Holly nodded, accepting his idea.

"If we don't need the lab in the Cutaway for anything, I agree with you. Right now, I have no idea how to treat him, and the chance of finding anything on that research ship to heal him with doesn't seem promising. If you don't think we need a blood test or something for him, then it makes sense to get him over there. Get him to a comfortable place to recuperate, and I'm hoping that's all he needs. Anyway, they do have a more expansive clinic over there, and an MD…even if we end up avoiding it all."

As the unwanted slumber lifted off the crew on all the ships, Holly picked up Attison's shoulders, and Keith, his ankles. Transporting him to the Merry Pace may have been difficult for most people, however it was pretty easy for Keith and Holly. They climbed down the metal stairs at the stern, holding his body between them. The unstable journey was less so when Holly used a small smidgeon of telekinesis in the more challenging moments, and they got him on the speed boat without a scratch. They carefully laid him on a bunk in the small cabin in the rear of his boat. As soon as Keith reached the radio on the Merry Pace, he hailed the Caprice. He asked for harbor for the three of them, and the communication officer told him he had to okay it with the Captain. Keith did not wait long. The officer quickly came back on air and told him it was fine. Since it was almost dark, Keith didn't want to frighten anyone at the Caprice by arriving in the noisy speedboat, and he told the man about the design of the Merry Pace, telling him they should be there within the hour.

He was about to cut off when Captain Donald Walker got on the radio, wanting him to know he knew Mr. Attison Korybante...or maybe he'd heard of him. Keith hadn't been able to make it out perfectly, but it was clear that the Captain was swayed hard by his name. And he was an intuitive man, guessing that Attison was involved with the panorama he'd just watched unfold in the sky. Rolling out the red carpet for him, his connection with Korybante must be an impressive one. Happy about that uplifting link, Keith got off the radio. He was going to tell Holly about it, but she'd left the Merry Pace, and he saw her racing across the deck of the Essayons. She wanted to give everybody out there on the water an 'adieu'. It was important to let them have a general idea of what had transpired after they'd been knocked out. Walking into the wheelhouse, she picked up the microphone. The VHF working channel they'd agreed on at the outset of the project was already on, and she used it to get to the other ships. She asked all the Captains to broadcast her sayonara through their own PA systems so everyone on all the dredges and the Cutaway could hear it. After she got an inclusive thumbs-up from everybody, she knew it was time to say goodbye…

> ***"I honor your courage in getting here and remaining vigilant and unbroken in your efforts and I have very good news. We've won the war! The filters hadn't been the last brick in the wall, but they had certainly been a necessary step in getting us to the last conflict. If we weren't out here, fighting the ultimate fight, then the final blow wouldn't have landed. We were sending a bright flare so high in the atmosphere, someone or something had seen our planet-wide destruction and intervened. Many of us weren't positive there would be a happy ending to the whole thing. I was knocked out like everyone else, and so I don't know exactly what happened, but I do have the most comforting knowledge anyone out here would like to have. It's off our backs and the future of our planet.***
>
> ***Captain Stewart Martin and Engineer Robert Reeves, Officers of the Essayons, were killed, and their bodies were swept away in the deadly currents of war.***

Their role in this quest will never be forgotten, and they will live forever in our hearts. There will be a memorial for them when we get back to LA.

Well, that's about the extent of it. Possibility has been reinstated. There's a chance we can evolve into a sentient race with a conscience before our star implodes...oh, by the way, Keith and I are going over to the cruise ship out there in the distance. We'll see you at the memorial. If another wickedness slithers at us again, we'll reunite and take care of business! So with respect, Keith and I are bowing out for now."

She hung the mic on the wall near to the chair the captain used to sit in, blowing out of the wheelhouse like smoke in the wind. Keith was waiting for her, and Attison was still unconscious in the small cabin of his speedboat. Holly had to help him; get him to a better place. The only thing left was a very short talk with Cooper, Greg Cooper. He was set up to pick up the responsibilities of the Captain, at least temporarily. He'd lead the Essayons on her voyage home, and she wanted to make sure he was okay to handle the trip. Thankfully, her pep-talk with him was short and sweet. Almost instantly, she saw that Greg could do the job on his own without any *additional* support from her, and the remaining part of her trip to the Merry Pace was done in an Olympic sprint.

Tapping his fingers on the wheel. Keith had been wasting time in a mental doodle trying to figure out how fast the speedboat could get from the dredge to the cruise ship. It was a silly equation. Those few miles would evaporate so fast in the hungry pull of the oversized engines it was a dumb equation.

He wasn't feeling very well. Knocked out and half drowned, his weakness had set him on edge. He went back on the radio to the Caprice for more precise information on where and how to get on board...and where to leave the smaller boat. They explained they had a hatch in the stern, similar to the one in the Cutaway. The officer told him they would open it up as soon as the Merry Pace started her short hop over.

Holly came out of nowhere, and startled him. In an acrobatic bounce she'd taken the rope holding the speedboat to the dredge out of the cleat, setting them free, and then she ended her travels by sitting in the cushy chair next to him with her legs crossed. Looking over at him, she smiled with a nod. The engines were already purring along, so Keith slipped the Merry Pace into gear, and he also got on the radio to the Caprice to let them know about her upcoming arrival. The five engines clawed their props into the body of the sea and the bow lifted out of the water almost instantly. His estimate on travel time was wrong. He thought it would two minutes longer, but in reality, it seemed he'd gotten there in a 'blink-of-an-eye'. Well, he chalked his mistake off by the fact it was Attison's boat. The cruise ship rose around them and over their heads, as Keith carefully nudged the Pace into her belly. Shutting off the engines, three uniformed crewmen quickly aligned straps under the hull the boat, and a nurse was standing next to a gurney on the passageway next to the channel. (The captain had assembled a medical team waiting for Attison in the clinic). She was wearing traditional white, and she'd been ordered to transport the patient from the loading area to the largest center on deck four. Before Keith took his hands off the wheel of the Merry Pace, Holly leaped onto the metal walkway and sped up the ramp towards Maggie Rainer.

"No, no. He can't go to the infirmary, but thank-you. We can certainly use the gurney to get him to a cabin somewhere else on the ship, but he doesn't need medical attention at this point."

"Yes, ma'am, but Captain Walker insists Mr. Korybante needs to get the best care we have here on the Caprice. I've been ordered to transport him the main clinic. I could be in a lot of trouble if I don't get him there. He should be treated by one of our doctors…."

Holly took the stretcher away from Miss Rainer, wheeling it to the simplest egress for Attison to get off the Merry Pace. And she was an unstoppable force of nature, ignoring the nurse's ongoing objections as if she was deaf. Of course, that was not the case.

"Keith, get on phone, or the intercom, or whatever the communication system is on this ship, and make Captain…is it Wailer or Wilber? Oh yeah, *Walker,* understand. We can't accept medical help for Attison right now, but we do need accommodations to reflect his stature in the financial world. I'll go through any consultation with his doctor's to smooth out any confusion, if he'd like. Oh, and tell him the nurse he sent to meet us did her job the best she could under the circumstances."

Holly looked over her shoulder, and winked at Maggie, and then she disappeared into the Merry Pace to get Attison with Keith followed her into the small hatch. He was also punching in a sequence of numbers on his phone. The captain had given him his personal number, and he quickly gave him an update as Holly had asked him to do.

Minutes later, they emerged with the unconscious man, coordinating a perfect hop onto the causeway without a glitch or stumble. They put him on the stretcher, and Holly pushed him up the ramp onto the manmade stone that had been poured on a foundation of steel on the lowest deck of the ship. The main elevators were hidden around a stanchion, and she was rolling her way towards them with no idea where she was going. Stopping in front of the doors, they opened to reveal someone in an official-looking uniform. As soon as that individual saw Holly and Attison on the gurney, he stepped over with an expression of concern. Keith had been trailing behind her.

"Captain Walker sends his greetings, and his prayers. He has acquiesced to everything Mr. Fischer has told him you need. With that in mind, he offers Mr. Korybante the Champagne Suite on the top deck. It has heavenly views. Two other luxurious suites have also opened up during our cruise, and he hopes the other cabins will be up to your standards. I can escort you to deck fifteen as it would make sense for us to aid Mr. Korybante to his suite first."

The gurney squeezed into the elevator by a hair, allowing the whole group to sweep up through the lower decks. Stopping, the elevator doors opened on a carpeted landing, and across the short expanse were double doors inlaid with a brass sun. They'd arrived. In charge of domestic activities, the uniformed man gave Holly a plastic key card and a small slip of paper with a sequence of numbers. He told her she'd need the combination to get into the suite, and he gave her another key for a different elevator that allowed only certain passengers access to that section of the ship. Keith was going to stay with the guy to find his and Holly's cabins, and the doors of the elevator closed, leaving Holly behind with Attison. She'd opened the doors to the Champagne Suite, and while she rolled him in, she started to think even harder on what she could do to help or heal her mentor. Over the years, he had ultimately pulled an extremely profound attachment out of her, and that love could be a detriment to her abilities if she didn't hold the course.

The suite was quite expansive within the parameters of a ship. Carpeted in lavender and green, the geometric pattern ended at some sliding glass doors that led outside to a beckoning whirlpool. A California King overwhelmed the master bedroom, and the adjoining bathroom had a steam feature in the shower unit, plus a tub with power-jets along the inner surface. Holly was pleased. It was exactly what she was hoping the Captain was going to come up with. Of course, she hadn't foreseen standing on a cruise ship at the end of the battle, and considering the unusual circumstances, it was way beyond anything she and Keith could have imagined.

Thinking over what was wrong with Attison, she'd come up with the first step. It would be extremely intrusive, but Holly needed to distance herself. Using her augmented strength, she peeled Attison out of his ragged clothes. Now naked on the stretcher, she rolled him into the bathroom. There, she took off his turquoise jewelry, tossing it into a glass bowl holding multi-colored bubble-bath nodules. Filling the tub with warm soapy water, she lifted him from the gurney and lowered him in, making sure his head stayed above the waterline. Holly grabbed an oversized wash-cloth folded into a peacock perching on a shelf right over the sink, and she dipped it into the warm water. She used it to rub off the slime and blood and whatever else was on his skin, *off.* One of the very few things she could do for him, this single act was giving her a small amount of emotional release. When Attison's entire body was squeaky-clean, she drained the tub and took the flexible shower hose out of its bracket at the edge of the bath. Twisting the setting on the handle, she turned the water back on again. Now it was spraying out of the small hand-held shower she was holding, and she rinsed him off. Taking him out of the bath, she laid him back on the stretcher, and dried him with a towel, and then she moved him into the bedroom. She put him on the purple satin comforter that was covering the bed. Holly looked at his naked body, momentarily stumped. Attison didn't have any clothes. He certainly hadn't brought anything on the Merry Pace, and she didn't have any PJ's to put on him. At that point, someone in the corridor started knocking, and she walked out of the bedroom to answer the door. A housekeeper was holding a steel-cart, an inside the container was a variety of different garments. So there was the answer to her problem, solving her dilemma.

Blessed with sagacity, Captain Walker had discerned what was facing his new guests. He knew that Holly and Keith could find items in the ship's boutiques, but Attison wasn't up to that task. The housekeeper left the cart behind in the suite, and Holly thanked her and closed the door, rolling it into the middle of the main room. Searching through it, her hunt ended when she pulled out a small drawer right above the back wheels. Blue silk pajamas with silver piping in size medium. Perfect. Wriggling him into them, she re-arranged his body into what she thought was a comfortable position on the bed, and at least *she* felt better. Attison looked like he was sleeping…if you ignored the color of his skin and the utterly blank expression on his face. Hanging the extra clothes in the closet, she folded the rest of them into small bureaus on either side of the bed, and then Holly rolled the empty cart back into the corridor. She left it there and closed the door. The phone on the wall started ringing, and Holly picked up. It was Keith.

"Hello Holly. How are things going?"

"Okay, I guess. The Captain sent Attison some clothes, so after I cleaned him up, I got him into some PJs. He's lying in the master bedroom now, and he looks much better, but he's still out there, Keith, way out there. I'm not happy about it. What's up with you?"

"Well, our perky guide has sent me to my cabin on a lower deck, and farther down the corridor, he had me look in on yours. Lavish enough. We shall have a pleasant stay. Listen Holly, it's important to find more confidence for him. You know Attison is tough as nails, and there's a very good chance he's just healing. He'll come back to us, Holly. I know you're flipping out, and that's not a logic reaction. Remember, neither of us are up to par after that fight, and Attison is probably dealing with a pretty intense reaction. We don't know what he went through out there, but I assume it had been…well, let's just say turbulent.

I know you need to stay with Attison until things get a little better for him, but the captain wants to meet us. I think we should respect his wishes and meet him before we both lay down and rest for a while. Oh, by the way, it's got to be a small world out there. I'm still blown away by the news that he's on the ship. They were dealing with a serial killer on board, and a few days ago they called out for help, and Inspector Porretta helicoptered out. He caught the murderess in short order. She's in the brig right now."

"That's freaky. Reality can get stranger than fiction sometimes. It's weird to connect us all together again out in the middle of the nowhere. It'll be odd talking to him again, but maybe there's a reason behind the coincidence. Has it been a whole year since the reunion?"

The surprise in her voice was muted, and Holly sounded tired. The weight on the mattress in the next room wasn't very heavy, but it was bringing her down like lead.

"Where does Walker want to meet us? Maybe it'd be easier for me to meet you first, and then we'll go together."

"It's a private dining room reserved for officers. I'll wait for you on deck eleven where the private elevator from Attison's suite lets out. Can you handle this right now?"

"I'm on my way," and Holly abruptly cut the connection.

The expression on her face was almost as dead-pan as the one on Attison's, but inside she was churning. Opening the bedroom door for a last peek at him before she left, he was exactly the way she'd left him. She softly closed the door, and walked out of the Champagne Suite, and down the corridor to the elevators on her way to this short introduction with the Captain. And then what? She didn't want to think about that. She didn't want to think about anything anymore.

He was corpselike. Attison's breathing was shallow. And very weak. He could probably trick a practitioner of the healing-arts into thinking he was already dead. But in this dissolution, a reversal had become to swim to the top. He'd never giving up the ghost, and the fountain inside of him had not been bricked up. After she closed the door of the suite, Mr. Attison Korybante's eyes had suddenly opened wide. Then he wheezed, and after that he whispered very quietly, *"Holly? Are you out there?"*

His physical words of course, hadn't been heard, but he was also communicating in a different realm at the same time, and he had a lot more power there. Holly was impatiently waiting for the elevator to arrive when a thousand bulbs lit up inside her head like a silent fire-alarm. Sprinting back, she stumbled to a clumsy halt in front of the door, fingers a blur across the display as she raced through the numbers. And then the door opened, and she ran through the living room and into the bedroom, slowing down the second she saw him. Getting to the bed, Holly instantly sat down next to him and hugged him. Her shoulders became to jerk up and down, signifying that her uncertainty was gone, and she could weep without restraint.

10:45PM Saturday January 13th 2007 The Caprice

Day-to-day activities on board had returned to normal, as best as could be provided on the fly, and the recreation staff of the Caprice had been able to adapt to an extended schedule well enough. Captain Walker had already ordered the trip back to Los Angeles to begin, and he was discussing options for a refuel with the Navy on the radio. Just enough to get her to the coast.

Eric Adler, Michael Chandler and John Belton were the last surviving attorneys of the Blackmore Coalition on the Caprice, and they were enjoying a late dinner. It was a triumphant meal, and the men felt good. The murderer was caught, and their fears of being the next victim were gone. Of course, the entire thing had been traumatic for them. To avoid memories of their lost associates and friends, they imagined bank accounts swelling with the sudden influx of additional work when they got back to Massachusetts; the iconical dollar sign stamped on their souls.

After the meal, Eric Adler walked out onto the deck, and he looked up. Stars twinkled brightly in the sky and he smiled. It was late…almost eleven, and no one was around. Since it was a beautiful evening, he decided to climb those steep stairs to the overlook. They called it the 'Astro-Dais'. There was even a telescope up there. Walking to the starboard side of the ship, Eric followed signs directing him on his way there. Still hadn't seen anyone. It was going to be peaceful up there.

Using the telescope, he couldn't make anything out on the ocean, however the planets and stars popped out great. Like he was in the planetarium in New York. They were hundreds of miles from land, so manmade light no longer interfered with the more subtle radiance of the heavens. And the majestic sight over his head seemed to underline a grander future he saw for himself. Think what he could build out of the devastation within the Blackmore Coalition? His relationship with Tiffany bubbled up in his head, and his memory of her strident voice wanting him to marry her had become even more raucous in the recollection. Why should he lock himself down again? In the new situation at work, ending things with her was the best option. Besides, she'd been the mistress. The story has changed. The wife was out of the picture in a big way, and he could play the field without a care in the world. Better to disassociate himself from Vera who was cooling off in the brig. Tiffany was nothing but baggage from his old life when he was married. Married to a serial killer? He didn't want to think about that at all. It would be simple and fun to just invite a flirtation here and now. A one night-stand. When he was done with her, he'd throw the whole thing into the trash barrel like a used plastic fork from a picnic.

He was getting too sleepy. It was time to call it a day. He'd had a few drinks at dinner, and he was a little bit tipsy, so he'd put his right hand securely on the rail as he began climbing down those steep and endless stairs. Almost at the same time he started his trip, a good-looking blonde began climbing up towards him. It seems she wanted to see the stars as he had moments ago. Lustrous long hair, and a sexy looking short black velvet dress on her back, there were silver sequins scattered across the fabric. Like stars. Eric Adler instantly inserted the girl in a possible sexual exploit and a stupid grin appeared on his face. When they got closer on the stairs, the sweet maiden smiled right back at him.

"Good evening. It's a great night to see the stars, isn't it?"

He paused on the steps, oozing his words out like gobbets of honey. The young women had also stopped, one tread below him.

"Hello, sir. I certainly agree. The party at the Tropicana Room was way too fuddy-duddy for me, and when I stepped out on the deck, I came straight out here."

"What's your name?"

"Lyndsey. What's yours?" Of course, for Lyndsey the polite question had only a pretense.

"Eric Adler...hey, maybe during the next couple of days on our way back to the coast, we could meet up and have lunch or something?"

"Sure, sounds great," and she started to pass him on the stairs. Or appeared to.

"Wait a minute, Lyndsey. Wait."

She did.

"I'll give you my card. I'll write down my cabin number on the back. That way, you can buzz me anytime so we can have coffee or a sandwich or something."

"Okay...Eric." And then she winked at him.

Eric had taken his hand off the guardrail to get the card out of his wallet and the gold pen from the inside pocket of his jacket. Scribbling *Cabin # 1126* on the back of the card as fast as he could, he pressed the card into her hand. He watched her begin sliding it between her breasts, and he liked the idea of his card held in that warm sweaty well. But she'd past him, and he really hadn't seen her wiggle it perfectly into that nice place. Beginning the climb down the stairs again, he hadn't grabbed the rail quite yet, too busy putting his pen and wallet away and that had been a very careless thing to do.

Lyndsey had speedily twisted around to sweep her leg in front of his traveling ankle, and she kicked Eric's right foot straight out; never making it to the next tread. She was stable as a rock with a solid grip on the rail, while he was instantly off-kilter. Dangerously so. Her free arm shot out like a piston, and Lyndsey pushed him forwards in a wonderfully muscular invitation to fall.

And then Eric Adler did what she wanted him to do, and he did it head over heels. He clattered down nineteen of the remaining one-hundred and twenty-five steps still to go, until he bounced right over the rail. Tumbling through the air for a second and half, he landed next to a sign saying: Astro-Dias. Of course, Eric hadn't felt the impact when he hit the metal deck, since his neck had broken in his second cartwheel on the stairs killing him instantly.

Watching him summersault down the stairs, Lyndsey's flirtatious smile was long gone, and there was a kernel of ice in her gaze. But the deed was done, time to leave the scene of the crime as quickly as possible, and she reversed her course on the stairs. Racing down to the deck, she disappeared faster than the memory of a dream.

Eric's vision of Lyndsey putting his card between her breasts had been replaced with a more nasty reality. After tricking him with her graceful feint, she'd flipped it away like a piece of garbage. After the dead man's final landing a few feet away, the glossy thing had lazily seesawed to the deck, ending up squeezed between two support beams holding up the stairs.

4:15PM Sunday January 14th, 2007 The Caprice

Attison, Keith, Holly and Ryan Porretta stood as a group to watch the refueling. Seven hundred feet long, the Rappahannock, a Navy ship, was set up for the job. Meeting the cruise ship at coordinates 47 N 134 W, the Caprice needed more fuel to make it the rest of the way to Los Angeles. In landlubber's vernacular, she'd taken fifteen thousand gallons at eleven-thirty that morning. Five hundred tons of diesel had been sucked along a hose between the tank of the Rappahannock and into the Caprice's, supported along the way by safety-lines. Calm as silk out there, and the ungainly project ate up only three hours. Without a hitch. The Rappahannock motored off into the distance, leaving a wide trail of white water in her wake.

Turning to her companions, Holly suggested they have a late day snack on the ninth deck, and they reconvened at a large table on the veranda outside one of the restaurants. After a long separation, this unforeseen reunion seemed to be holding together peacefully enough, meanwhile, the entire staff on the Caprice had heard all about them. When the waitress saw them coming, she tried to give them a bigger table. They declined. Attison was already sitting a chair under an umbrella in the shade. The afternoon sun was painful for him at that point in his healing process. Ryan had sat down next to him. He knew Korybante more than anyone else there, however the restrained friendship he'd garnered with Attison, wasn't enough to allow him to understand the conversation they were having.

"I'm sorry Attison, but I need to know if you had been there right before the thing started to strangle me. I mean, right at the beginning of the fight," Holly said.

Attison stared at her. He sent her a question without uttering a single word out loud. *"Aren't you worried about Porretta hearing you?"*

"No. Anything he hears can be removed if it's necessary. Please, just answer my question."

The waitress arrived again to give out menus, and she beamed a smile and a hello to everyone. Badly tired, Keith just read the tag on her blouse instead of dredging it up out of her mind.

"Hello, Cathy. Bring me a *Magna*. Isn't that one of the seasonal beers from Denmark?"

Before she could answer him, he turned to Ryan, "If memory serves, it tastes like vanilla. If you like beer, you should really try it."

"Sounds like a great idea, Keith." He looked up from the menu, and then he directing his next words towards the waitress. "I'll have one too."

Cathy scribbled madly on her pad.

Holly ordered a gin and tonic; Attison, a double shot of absinthe, and their server went off to the bar to get their drinks. Attison was still dodging Holly's question, reading the menu as if it had information from heaven or something and Holly had her antennae up. Strange to see him sidestep *anything,* and a touch of aggressiveness was about to dribble into her curiosity driven questions. For a second, she forgot who he was. Forgot he could slice those inquisitive antennae right off her head in a single look.

"I'll order a Reuben sandwich since it comes with sweet potato fries," Attison said, and then he smiled at everybody at the table. The unusual grin coming out of him retreated when he rested his eyes on Holly, and she had returned his sudden chilliness with a snide smirk. After Cathy dropped off their drinks, he raised his shot glass in her direction in a gesture of conciliation.

"Alright. Alright, Miss Donnelly. I *was* on the dredge right before Keith was slapped into unconsciousness, and you were overcome. Now you know. I've answered your question."

"But that really isn't the point. Why didn't you intervene at that point? If you already knew what was about to happen, why did you hesitant?" And Holly waited impatiently for his answer.

During this extended and increasingly uncomfortable silence, Keith inserted himself into the middle of it. He brightly asked Ryan about the case he'd helicoptered out to the cruise ship to solve. The inspector responded, happy to veer away from the awkwardness as much as Keith did. He sailed into describing the murders as if they were as commonplace as a traffic violations.

Until Attison interrupted him. Holly's pinpointed secondary question had steered him into even darker waters, and it was hard to explain his actions under the circumstances. He'd simply dropped into redirection in the form of intimidation, a force almost impossible to withstand if he was behind the wind in those sails.

"Do you really have to know why I do what I do? You need my motivations behind everything, Holly? Perhaps we should travel back in time and hash over on the so-called win-win you claimed you had in Bakersfield. I'd love to know more about your own last minute decisions, since you did such an impeccable job taking care of that battle in the factory. At least, that's what you've told me."

The smirk on Holly's face became a frown. Attison's pinprick had triggered her paranoia, and her unease over the timing of his actions was washed away by her own, and then he went into a coughing fit. She got up and moved over to him, resting her hand on his shoulder. A faint glimmer of blue feathered out of her fingers and into his body, giving him a boost and he quickly got his wind back.

"I'm alright Holly, please. Thank-you for your concern, but you can go back to your chair and decide what you want to eat. You need to accept my injuries as a price I must pay. I won't stay like this forever. I'm healing. I should be completely back to normal within a year or so."

Attison was wearing a sleek three-piece suit in an odd shark-grey that Holly had found at one of the expensive shops on board. He still looked handsome and debonair, but the slump in his posture indicated he had a low-level of energy. He seemed a bit off-key. Before the confrontation with the Frankenstein, his skin had been a Mediterranean brown, however now he was a terrible beige. As if cream had been poured into his blood stream during the battle and then curdled. Of course, it was a temporary situation. What was dragging him down would be mended, and his final triumph fueled their celebratory mood. Attison had put his turquoise jewelry back on again, and no one but the inner-circle would be able to see any difference in his demeanor. One of the working actors on the ship sidled up to their table, and he was holding out a pen and a playlist of the show he was in.

"Please, Mr. Korybante, if you don't mind. I play Mr. Davis in the show, and I heard you had something to do with whatever went on out there. Your signature means a lot to me."

Attison smiled. He signed the playlist, and when the young man took it back, he politely bowed and walked away.

"How is it that everyone on board knows you were over there, and Holly and I don't seem to matter in the least?" Keith intentionally dripped a lot of envy in his voice, shaking his head and frowning. He put his bottle of Magna on the table with a thump.

"I'm guessing our captain's memory of me at a party in Washington five years ago must be a remarkable one, even though he certainly knows we were all there. I wouldn't be surprised if he didn't let the cat out of the bag about me, and if he did, then that gossip would expand and then distort. Since we're docking in LA tomorrow, I'm not worried about the extra attention. Actually Keith, I have a new commercial enterprise in my head right now, and extra recognition of my name may uplift my projects at some point in the future."

"Aaah, Attison, you keep on surprising me. It was you who got the dredges together for us, and in the beginning I thought it had been Holly. I still have no idea how you knew to do it. Figuring out which dredges, and getting them all there at the right time was a pretty impressive..."

Holly interrupted him, "I know how he did it, Keith, and when we have more time I can explain it to you. In the meantime, all that forethought and planning turned out to be for naught," and she sent a tiny smirk at Attison. "I don't know why you would go through that charade, if you already knew it was going to be a waste of time and energy..." and she faltered for an instant, before going on for another few seconds, "if you knew it was going to be impossible, then why would you...."

She stopped talking completely, and furrows crunched into her forehead and then, *"Never mind,"* slipped out in a soft whisper. His earlier comment about the factory came into her head again as a destructive missile. She knew he knew exactly what had happened that day, and it was possible she could have become too unreliable to him, weaker than he'd first believed she was. Her own bad lying about it may have helped Attison into a new track, and the reason the filters on the dredges hadn't worked was that she and Keith hadn't been strong enough to handle the attack. Perhaps, Attison had allowed the monster to overpower them as a traumatic remembrance. A way of telling them both to work on their abilities. Of course, Holly's invincible guardian would never ever own up to any misgivings or mistakes of his own. He didn't want to tarnish her image of him, and his perfectly sculpted misdirection had landed squarely into her uncertainty, and at least part of it had to be true. Then Holly dove herself verbally into dead air. She wanted to change the subject, and that was exactly what Attison was hoping for.

"Do any of you know which letter in our alphabet is the most prevalent one? Attison, you can keep on drinking absinthe until you pass out. Don't say a thing. You know the answer to just about everything."

Keith and Ryan stared at each other, and the technician bowed to the inspector, giving him first dibs.

"Well, how about E? Ryan said.

"Correct! You got the first one right. What about the second?"

"It's gotta be I. We hear it coming out of everyone endlessly."

"No."

Keith interjected, "What about A?"

"No."

"O?"

"No."

"Is it a vowel?" Porretta asked.

"No."

Keith tried S, and that didn't work. Then Ryan tried R, and then they both gave up. Holly told them it was T. Ryan guessed the third letter had to be A, and he was right again. He was swallowing down the last of his third vanilla-tasting beer, when Officer Nugent marched up to the table.

The Officer nodded curtly to everyone at the table, before he bent over to whisper into Ryan Porretta's ear.

"I'm sorry to bother you sir, but last night a porter found a body next to stairs leading up to the Astro-Dais. A member of the Blackmore group. We would really appreciate any input on this thing."

Inspector Porretta looked up at Nugent for a second, before he stood up and gave some parting regrets to his companions.

"I'm sorry, but I must go. I'll touch base with you later on, if I can. Who knows, maybe I can stop the latest outbreak much faster this time."

Holly, Keith and Attison looked up at him and nodded farewell, understanding his ongoing position on the ship. Ryan had just heard more extraordinary developments, and he followed Nugent to the service elevator at the end of the bar. Cathy came back to the table to pick up their plates, and Holly ordered another round of drinks. Silence remained supreme until the drinks arrived. She watched Attison sip at his liqueur. He seemed more peaceful, and that seemed to calm her as well.

"You're not worried about Porretta, are you? He's a very curious guy, and exceptional at his job, and as I remember, he'd gotten quite upset about my miraculous recovery last year. You let him go on worrying that impossible bone without end. He could easily become a problem, yet you allow him closer nonetheless. Not explaining the inexplicable to him becomes more and more unreasonable. What are you doing, Attison?"

"You're premise is correct, and you're right. I'm not concerned in the slightest. I don't want to erase his memories connected to our unusual activities, I'd rather build a relationship with him instead. He could be a solid link for us inside law enforcement. A more personalized interaction in that global network. We'd be able to accomplish our next goal faster with more diversity. We'd have new tools at hand."

The phone in Attison's pocket began to ring.

"Excuse me. I have a feeling this call is coming from a remarkable source."

Attison quickly walked over to the rail holding his sat-phone in his hand. (Keith had found the phone for him under a cushion on the Merry Pace while he was knocked out, and he gave it back to him when he woke up. Small as it may have seemed, he was trying to help the man who'd saved his life).

Attison leaned forwards on the rail, staring out at the horizon. And then he touched the screen, activating the call. A melodious voice softly caressed his ear.

"Hello Korybante. Do you know who this is…aah, of course you do. It's the Lord of Misrule jingling you up. I needed a moment to chit-chat."

"Hello, my Lord. I'm sorry about the unforeseen turn of events. I know our victory is undercutting your permanence, and I also know you are beginning to fade away."

The Lord of Misrule was sitting on the beautiful throne the Cleves had built for him in their castle in Martha's Vineyard, but Attison was a hundred percent correct. His bejeweled fingers weren't quite as solid as they'd been fifteen minutes ago, and he could see the armrest through his elegantly dressed forearm. Apparently, he had become a very thick fog.

"I was really enjoying myself with this court of ne'er-do-wells, and some of these noble maidens were *more* than accommodating…but it's turning out we can't keep on eating our cake and having it too. And if we wanted to be serious for a moment, there was no way I could have really gone on much longer without the necessary counterpoint. My gravity would have completely imploded. My fun would have ended in an ultimate finality, and so would have yours…forever."

"You really think you'll be reanimated again on Twelfth Night next year for another twelve hours of instability?"

"That's not a question, my friend. Of course I will."

And then the Lord of Misrule laughed with a touch of manic force and Attison frowned.

"I'm hedging my bets on that, sir, and I can never be sure what is behind your answers. Perhaps they will act more logically during this next cycle. You might not appear at all. They'll put the ducks in a row this year, and…." The Lord of Misrule interrupted Attison with another laugh that had risen to a screeching howl, and Attison couldn't hear any more of his own optimistic ideas in this loud onslaught of gleeful ridicule.

"Oh, I'll see you next year, Attison, and you're always invited to ring in these topsy-turvy changes with me. There'll be more surprises up my sleeve, and you can….."

But the burner phone the Lord was holding fell to the stone floor with a crack. What remained of his material form was almost gone, and conversational level of his voice had dwindling away to almost nothing. It seemed the Lord hadn't had much time left when he'd called Attison to say goodbye. Twenty seconds later, his final exodus from the material world was heralded when the last molecule upholding his temporary bastion there burst with a faint pop, and the throne was suddenly so desolate it looked haunted. The Ruler of Chaos was banished to his lair in dark space, and his physical return depends on what kind of race the race would be working on during those upcoming twelve months.

9:30PM Monday January 15th, 2007 The Caprice

The authorities had directed the Caprice to dock on the part of the wharf where ships of her impressive size had to go for repair. Normally, she would have invited another eager group of vacationers to sail straight out to sea in under twelve hours, but the police investigation had sidelined her normal schedule. Unable to replenish her supplies, nor debark the thousands of passengers still on board, the Caprice was stuck in the mire of a bureaucratic system handling the evidence in multiple murder cases. The situation had gotten more complex as another corpse was squeezed into the crowded ship's morgue, however this time, Vera Adler had nothing to do with its arrival. Getting into the act at the last minute, it doesn't matter whether an accomplice of hers had been responsible for the deed or not; a killer still roamed free on the ship.

The passengers were trapped, and they lined the rails to stare down at the parking area below crowded with police vehicles, news vans, and ambulances. They watched as more officials walked up the ramp and got on board. Having heard their captain on the PA a few minutes ago broadcasting an apologetic announcement informing them they couldn't leave the Caprice until they'd been vetted, his sweet patronization hadn't calmed anyone down. Why should it? Even if the presence of cops on the dock is a pretty good hint, their confinement on the Caprice hadn't been explained thus far.

Having gone through the evidence, and the placement of the Adler's body, Ryan Porretta spent all of Sunday night and into Monday morning on the computer, the radio and the phone. He needed to know what had happened on those stairs, and he'd questioned lots of people, most of them not on the ship. When the Captain invited him to the private dining room to talk things over, Ryan was going to try to alter the direction of the current enquiry if he could.

"I have no idea what to do, Inspector Porretta! The police captain of the local precinct is changing his bloody mind like the weather. He thinks there's another serial killer running around on the ship, and he tells me we have to increase our security, and after that we have to..." but Ryan stopped him.

"Wait a minute...wait! You haven't heard what I'm about to say, and it should take the wind right out of Carson's sails. There's a very good chance we've already apprehended the only murderer. I'm not positive, but I have a feeling the Caprice will probably cruise off by Wednesday. This week. I've talked over a few things with the lieutenant, and he's agreeable to my upcoming plans. If you're into it, we'll transfer the bodies and the suspect off the ship at midnight. More eyes will be closed; less irritation triggered by the move."

"Sounds fine, Inspector. You have my blessings. Please, include Officer Nugent in the arrangements of the relocation, alright."

"Of course. I'll talk to him about it as soon as we're done. He has the working knowledge of the entire ship, and he can direction us to avoid exposure in the most feasible way."

Captain Walker was shaking his head, "I have no idea how you're going to be able to straighten this whole thing out now with another maniac running loose."

"Well, I'm going to do it, and tell you how. Examining some evidence one more time to be sure, this last look will support my final answer. I expect to see his fingerprints on an empty wine glass found on the Astro-Dias right after they found his body, and if the blood test indicates a sizable amount of alcohol in his blood, then these facts support a contention that Mr. Adler was drunk. He may have simply tripped on those steep stairs without any help from anyone. Besides that, it was dark, and he was badly overtired, living on an emotional rollercoaster ride. I don't think he was stable when he went up there to commune with the stars."

"As awful as that prospect of yours may be, a fatal misstep of his own would certainly get us out of this quagmire a lot faster."

Ryan stared into Captain Walker's eyes across the dining room table, a shoulder rising in a silent implication that Eric's disingenuous timing in his lonely fall had been just that.

5:00PM Tuesday January 16th, 2007 The Caprice

Detective Porretta walked into the Star and Stripes, a bistro that overlooked the main concourse one deck below. Looking over the balcony, there was a sixty-foot long blue-chip marble counter where employees would meet passengers and help them with everything from shore excursions to reserving seats in a show; as well as alleviating a plethora of complaints. At the moment, the gleaming divide was deserted besides a security guard in the corner of the large hall.

Ryan wove through the predominantly empty chairs and tables of the Star and Stripes to get to a muscular-looking woman in exercise clothes printed in a burst of blue and purple abstract patterns. She was very appealing. Men would follow her into the gym for reasons unconnected to the services that business provides. Sitting by herself away from the counter in the middle of the lounge, she instantly looked up from the paper she was reading when he sat down on the other side of her small table.

"Hello, Lyndsey."

"I assume you're from law enforcement. Probably the expert they called in a few days ago, to stop Vera's wild ride."

She had a comfortable smooth voice, and Ryan looked into her eyes as she spoke. Lyndsey was staring back at him like a sphinx.

"I'm Inspector Ryan Porretta, and it's captivating to meet you," and he smiled and he stood up halfway and politely extended his hand. After the shake, he sat back on his cushioned seat.

"You killed Eric Adler, and I know why you did it," he said. Lyndsey was smiling too.

"That's an assumption, Inspector. I don't mind telling you I'm innocent to the charges."

Finding Eric's business card under the stairs, he hadn't put it in the bag with the rest of the items deemed evidentiary. He'd held on to it, and at that point in his conversation with Lyndsey, he slipped his fingers inside his jacket pocket and took the same glossy card out. He placed it on the tablecloth between them, and it just sat there like a guilty trap. She frowned, while their waiter arrived, and Ryan ordered an espresso with a shot of brandy on the side. Lyndsey asked for another cup of decaf with extra cream.

"You can keep on declaring you're innocent, as your personal history with the Adler's indicate something else. In your favor, I have no physical evidence to link you to the crime. It would be very difficult to convict you. Look, Lyndsey, I know he shafted you. Mr. Adler was not a very nice person. Be that as it may, he didn't have anything to do with your brother's disappearance, and there was no cover-up to hide whatever you think might have happened on that trip. The Carnelian Line has a lot of problems, and there is corruption in their ranks, but their dastardliness has nothing to do with Bryan's disappearance."

The waiter reappeared, leaving their beverages on the table, before fading away in the sea of furniture. Hearing any news about her brother's disappearance always jolted her into intense emotion, and Lyndsey wanted to throw her very hot cup of coffee into Ryan's face, but she controlled herself. She didn't want Sherlock there to think she was a nut. Who knows? He might actually have information about where he really was.

"Look, inspector, I have all the facts connected to his case in my head. There's no way out of the truths that surrounded Bryan's loss, but I still won't give up the search. He was on a cruise with his fiancé, and something happened to him out there."

"Maybe not."

"What do you mean, *maybe not?*" Lyndsey clutched the sides of the table and she squeezed it as hard as she could.

"I did research on all things Delft last night. I'm good at what I do, and my archeological efforts paid off. I know exactly what happened to him. I even know where he is right now."

The blood in her face drained away, leaving her pale and shaky, and in a very faint whisper, she said, "Is he ...um...ah...alive? Is he?"

"Of course. He's having a great time in his new career."

"Career? What career?"

"They call him Berenice, well, that's his name on stage anyway."

"What are you talking about? He disappeared on the cruise ship, and the ship had been out at sea. Somebody kidnapped him out and forced him into acting? It sounds ridiculous. Nobody would do that!"

"He's in LA. I'm fairly positive you'll be getting off the Caprice tomorrow afternoon, and since he'll be performing after the Chico's Angels at eight, I thought you'd like to see the Beatific Bee. It'd be a hell of a surprise for him to see you in the audience."

Inspector Porretta picked up his brandy with a serene smile as he swallowed it down, enjoying the warmth as it traveled to his belly.

"You're screwing around with my head, aren't you?" Lyndsey said, and she was far from smiling herself. "I think you're lying. I think you're recording our conversation. You are waiting for me to slip up and say something incriminating. Well, it's not going to happen! I'm not listening to anymore of this crap," and Lyndsey stood up, about to tramp away and sulk, but Ryan firmly grabbed her wrist in his hand before she could. Twenty years her senior, he'd been able to restrain her with an impressively quick reflex.

"Look at the flyer, Lyndsey," and he put it in her hand. "*Look at the picture.* It's an ad for his performance at the Cavern Club on Hyperion Avenue in Silver Lake. I think the photo should pluck a heart string for you."

Looking at the half crumbled paper, Lyndsey got even whiter.

"I am a busy man. I don't play games like the one you describe. It is what it is."

Lyndsey sat down again, and her eyes were glued on the ad.

"How on earth did he get there? None of this is making any sense!"

"I know you weren't happy about his upcoming marriage, but what you didn't realize was that Bryan was more upset about it than you were. Living a façade for as long as he could, he was terrified no one was going to accept who he really was. Dealing with his fiancé with an uncomfortable distaste was getting more painful every day. Going out to sea with her was the final straw. He considered diving off the ship and drowning, but it wasn't a very nice option. He had to overpower his paranoia over being ostracized, and he found a life-changing fortitude within himself to do that. He needed to get off the Caprice before she sailed, and he had to do it on the sly, not wanting anyone to see him. I'm guessing he used the luggage ramp. He probably thought about the fact they were busy loading and unloading luggage, and it may have been the only escape left. The drag-queen to be, likely hid on the conveyer belt like a seasoned commando, nestling in a wall of bags on their way to the dock. When he got here, he disappeared into the crowd to remake his life. His calling beckoned, and he melted into the belly of the city, carving a niche in the sequined world he'd entered. You're in the performing arts yourself, and I'm guessing he'd made a mistake about what your feelings would have been if he'd emerged from the cocoon he was hiding in. You would have accepted the butterfly years ago."

Lyndsey was crying, and Ryan reached across the table and held her hand.

"I...I don't care what Bryan is doing. I miss him and...and...I love him the same as I ever did. I just can't get my mind around this. I have to be by myself to...ah, process things." And then Lyndsey crunched over for a minute, before she stood up and walked away.

"Lyndsey...*Lyndsey!* Do you want to see his show tomorrow night at the Cavern Club?"

She stopped.

"Yeah...yeah. Of course. We'll talk about it later on, I have to..." Her voice broke, and she bent over again. Straightening up, she went on, "Just let me know where and when, okay?" And then she walked off.

Attison had been sitting on a tall stool at the counter of the Star and Stripes sipping an expensive blend of coffee beans from Italy throughout the entire encounter between Lyndsey and the Inspector. Neither had noticed this quite magnetic looking man on the other side of a fairly empty room. Of course, Attison could have easily invoked a bit of deflection, and Ryan Porretta, even after a lifetime of fine-tuning his five senses as a lawman, remained utterly surprised when he silently slid into the chair Lyndsey had vacated seconds ago.

"And a good afternoon to you, sir," Attison said, bowing his head in deference to the Inspector.

"Hello, Mr. Korybante. I pray you're feeling better," Ryan said, and he was shaking his head over Attison's bewitching appearance.

"Actually, in a gradual way, I am, and I thank-you. Do you mind if I talk with you for a moment?"

"No. I'm more than interested in what you might have to say." Ryan had been watching Lyndsey's progress towards the exit over Attison's shoulder, she'd gotten only fifteen feet away. The Inspector could not figure out where the man sitting across the table from him had come from, but he was getting used to his ways, and the heebie-jeebies he used to get from him weren't happening anymore.

"I don't think blind chance has drawn us all together again, and I'm giving the four sisters of fate an acknowledgment for this reunion. I believe it's going to be beneficial for us all, and I propose a different arrangement between us...oh, you should call me by my first name. Haven't I mentioned that to you before?"

"Alright, Attison. What proposal do you have in mind?"

"You were distressed by Holly's recovery after being poisoned at her family's Thanksgiving dinner last year, and some of the subjects we discussed at the table yesterday were probably just as troubling. I can't explain everything, but I can ease your mind over a lot of these particulars if you can meet me halfway? In this new relationship, I assume you won't incite the pitchfork-wielding villagers, and accept some impossibilities as valid, especially if these bugaboos will give you results you'd never be able reach before. On the flip side of our professional friendship, you'd support us with your own abilities, and we could also tap into your technological network; a global army of many more eyes on the ground. If problems become challenging, we can both extend our reach and punch up our strength in a way we hadn't been able to do before."

Attison paused, and sipped some of the mug of coffee he'd brought along, but Porretta stayed silent. He knew he wasn't done yet.

"Years ago, Keith helped law enforcement officials, and that included the FBI. With his helpful slant on things, they were able to lock up criminals they wouldn't have even known were there. However, things got painful for him, and he couldn't keep on. He kept psychically bouncing into a malevolence way beyond the simple lusts of a serial-killer or a state-jumping kidnapper, and those unwanted connections were draining his spirit."

Attison lowered his voice for a moment, "You should ask him about it someday. You yourself may have instinctively felt the same powerful force, and it could be a boon for him to talk about it with someone else in the field. Anyway, after many more years of experience under his belt, he's gotten a lot tougher. I believe that Keith could be an ongoing conduit between our dissimilar approaches, but if you reach a dead end in a case or the investigation gets dangerous and you lose control, you can call *any* of us. We will be at your disposal. On the other side of the coin, you could be *our* link to abilities we don't have, and I don't naysay your own deductive powers, Ryan. I wouldn't be here, if I didn't know we could scratch each other's backs, depending of the situation. We too can be deceived, bamboozled, and hypnotized, and our relationship with you could be yet another stopgap to avoid that mental quicksand...it'll also exorcise the bugbear haunting you over the enigmas linked to myself and Holly. I'm very optimistic you'll accept my offer."

At that moment, their waiter came up to the table in his red, white and blue smock, and Porretta ordered more brandy, (a double this time), and Mr. Korybante didn't need anything.

"It sounds like a fine idea...Attison. The like-minded banding together in an off-and-on association." And then he chuckled, "I'm assuming a hellish case is not about to snare me up. I'm optimistic this possibility is not really there, so it couldn't have sped up your wonderful revelation to make sure I'd know about these other options?"

Attison tilted his head slightly. He didn't say anything.

"And you're not saying *'of course not'*. You're not saying that because you're pulling my leg...*right?*"

The waiter dropped off his brandy, and Porretta picked up the glass and he swallowed the whole thing in one long pull. Meanwhile, Attison had taken one of his business cards out of his pocket, and he was writing Keith's and Holly's phone numbers on the back. Then he slid it across the table, and Ryan picked it up and put it in his wallet. Finally Attison spoke up, but he changed the subject before the Inspector could ask him anymore questions regarding his now possibly ominous future.

"Aren't you going to a burlesque show in Los Angeles tomorrow? Something to do with a brother and sister reuniting?"

"How on earth do you know about that?"

"Would it be okay if I came along with you? I haven't been up to par, and it might take my mind off some memories I'm trying to forget. Nice to relax in a completely unfamiliar environment, and I'll make sure Lyndsey won't be upset with me in the slightest. Dial my volume down a bit."

Korybante's sudden interest in shepherding the newly-minted murderess to the Cavern Club on Wednesday night was a real surprise to Ryan, but he thought over including him on the trip. Lyndsey must have heard about Attison's connection to the apocalyptic show they'd all seen in the sky, and she probably drawn to the mystery that swirled around him like everyone else. They were going to be part a large crowd anyway, and he decided his company shouldn't be a problem.

"It'd be fine, probably a great idea for me personally, since after the show, Lyndsey and Bryan will likely want to talk by themselves for a while. We could have a drink at the bar, and wait for them, and I might be able to ask you a question or two...why aren't Holly and Keith interested in coming along?"

"They wish to disappear on Holly's ship, the Aspersion's Foil. It's docked a few miles north of here. They are both exhausted, and they want to just hang out there for a week or so, before flying back to the family estate on Bass River. Thank-you for accepting my own invitation to your night out, Ryan. I'll meet you at the club tomorrow evening at seven...isn't that the right time? Doesn't the Beatific Bee's show start at eight?"

"That's sounds right. Look forwards to meeting you there sir."

Ryan Porretta was unsettled by Attison's knowledge about the entire evening. As if he'd overheard the entire conversation he'd just had with

Lyndsey, and then he'd read his mind for the rest of the information. Be that as it may, he was still excited about meeting him again, and they both stood up and shook hands. Watching Mr. Korybante walk off, he didn't want to think about what he thought had been a humorous question concerning his future wittily rolled off his tongue, since Attison's answer in the form of silence had been a very merciless reply.

6:24PM Wednesday January 17th, 2007 Aspersion Foil, Pacific

Eric Adler's death had been designated as accidental, and the investigation on the Caprice ended quickly. Vera Burrows-Adler was already in custody for the murders so it was time to let the passengers go. Having photographed, categorized and moved the evidence into storage from of all the crime scenes on the Caprice, the officials of the Carnelian Line and the police department also let the ship go too. By four in the afternoon on that Wednesday, she was slowly motoring towards the regular dock, and there was no one left on the ship but crew.

Earlier, Keith and Holly had raced out of her Rolls Royce and up the gangplank of the Foil just like kids getting out of the school on the last day before their summer vacation begins. Within an hour, they lay on lounge chairs on a high deck, watching the west coast of the United States recede away from them at a healthy clip. Lazily sipping at some fresh lemonade, Keith looked up at seagulls circling above. He glanced over at Holly, and she too stared up. Their thoughts were intertwined on the same memory, and she shook her head and they both smiled.

7:15PM Wednesday January 17th, 2007 Cavern Club, Los Angeles

Parking near the club was impossible, and there was a line of people that ran around the corner of the block. Ryan and Lyndsey had been fortunate in having Attison with them. Ryan Porretta's power as a detective from Massachusetts would not have made the slightness difference, but Mr. Korybante had been able to get them away from the line and through the front door like a movie star and his posse. And then he got them front-row in the center seats.

Bryan Delft preened in his dressing room, inspecting the entire package in a full length mirror. Slowly pirouetting, he needed to check his backside too; make sure the snaps and buttresses were where they needed to be. And then he crouched, staring into his own eyes in the glaring exposure of the searing lights of a makeup mirror. His extra-long fake eyelashes swept like fans across his bright blues, and then he pursed his scarlet lips in a momentary pucker. Erasing a smudge coming out of a glittering green coil of a wing painted right above his left eye, his makeup artist's idea of putting sparkle on his cheeks and the side of his neck had been a very good one. Sweeping out of his dressing room, he had a preternatural balance on his six inch heels. Almost as remarkable as Tina Turner, who, in her heyday, had danced across a line stages over the years on heels as high or higher than his without a single mishap.

No one at the club called him Bryan, and it was Berenice's back-stage fans made out of other performers and stage hands giving him thumbs-up and grins and an occasional hug as he flew passed them. He had to be in the right place in the next two minutes to do the correct breathing during the countdown; had to buzz on stage like a heavenly bee.

The curtain lowered on Chico's Angels review, and the audience clapped with appreciation as the theater lights dimmed. Soon the room was pitch black, and the only thing the patrons heard was the curtain rising up again, but still nothing happened. Another minute went by. Anticipation grew like hot air stretching out the elastic skin of a balloon. Thinner and thinner.

Until their momentary moonless night was suddenly replaced with intense lumen shock as spotlights zeroed in on The Beatific Bee. He was facing away from them, and when the band burst into Sammy Davis's old classic *I've Gotta Be Me!,* Berenice turned around in an exaggerated shimmy, belting out the song in the same key Sammy had recorded it in.

His sequined gown had horizontal gold and black stripes that began at the waistline, and they continued all the way to the floor, covering the svelte body of the Bee. He was wearing elbow length gloves, golden gloves, and the bodice of his dress was solid black. A sheer black and gold veil covered his face, and his hair was also hidden by a headpiece with long antennae. His singing was hypnotic, and it stayed that way.

Lyndsey, Ryan and Attison looked up from the front row with differing reactions. Lyndsey was stunned. She could almost touch her long-lost brother. Bryan was deep in his stage persona, and his day-to-day personality was barely there, but that didn't bother her. She was enthralled by his magnetism. As if he was a long term veteran of an operatic career, he sang the finale' like an angel.

I'll go it alone, that's how it must be,
I can't be right for somebody else
If I'm not right for me.
I gotta be free, I gotta be free
Daring to try, to do it or die.
I've gotta be me, I've gotta be me.

And then there was one more chorus left. The band went on a short instrumental, and the stage lights darkened and a strobe began to shimmer. Hard to see what was going on up there, but this odd lull was only forty-five seconds long.

During this short interlude, Bryan had taken off the veil and the head piece, and his blonde hair cascaded down his back. His lips, colored larger than life, would now smile out to the world, eyes revealed to hypnotize. The yellow and black sequins had all flipped to shimmering blue, with a touch of purple around the neckline, and four feet of the gown had dropped off to expose blue fishnet stockings and high heels. A stagehand had hooked large fake butterfly wings on heavy metal supports hidden under the back of the dress, and then her physical alteration was over. Only one more transformation of another kind was about to be revealed as one spotlight went on to illuminate the bee's change to butterfly, and the music got louder. As Bryon began to sing the last chorus, Sammy Davis had to have known there were people like him out there. People who broke barriers to live the dream.

The revelation vibrated out of the Beatific Butterfly's vocal chords as she sang an octave higher. It didn't sound as if he was in falsetto at all, and that indicated his range was massive. In one song, he'd sung three octaves without difficulty, and Bryan had held his higher altitude back until the end. Opening his wings completely, he'd flown into soprano as a final surprise for his fans. Flying over the rainbow, the butterfly could breaks wine glasses by the resonating power of his voice.

During the last notes of his astonishing performance, Bryan glanced down at the first rows of seats, and there she was. He instantly recognized his sister, and Lyndsey had blown him a kiss. Wobbling back on his heels, he was shocked and he almost started to cry. He rubbed at the corner of his eye to wipe any moisture away; he had to stop the tears. The show must go on. Berenice needed to put this miracle out of his mind until the act was over.

The next nine songs were all originals, composed by himself and his female manager. With a degree from Berkley, she had garnered three awards in composition so far, and she was a perfect match to his flame. Melodies elegant and exploratory, their complex phrasing was completely original, yet the songs were too pleasing to be anything else but right.

When the encore and thunderous applause faded away, and the curtain went down, a staff member of the Cavern Club sidled through the crush of the crowd leaving the theater to reach Lyndsey. She'd stayed seated with Ryan and Attison, and he'd told her that Berenice would love to see her. Nodding, Lyndsey got up and began to follow him, and she spoke to Ryan over her shoulder as he guided her backstage.

"Inspector Porretta, would it be alright if I went and talked to him by myself? I'm not going anywhere, and we'll both be back out here to talk you and Attison in a few minutes," but Lyndsey was already climbing the stairs at the edge of the stage. She vanished behind the curtain.

"Of course, dear. We'll be at the bar."

Ryan had been speaking to the back of her head and she had not heard a single word of what he'd said as she slipped behind the edge of the curtain.

Attison and Ryan picked out a table with a leather bench seat in the far corner of the bar, and a waiter came over and gave them bar menus.

Attison ordered a Long Island Ice-tea, and Ryan asked for an imported beer. After the waiter left, the Inspector read the menu, and Attison stared out into space. When their drinks arrived, Porretta ordered a hamburger, and Attison, a strip steak.

"Lyndsey and Bryan have a lot to iron out, and my guess is we won't see them for at least an hour," the Inspector said, and then Attison began to tease him.

"Not prosecuting her for murder and supporting her dreams, could be seen as unprincipled behavior on your part, accepting the act itself as the correct action under the circumstances. Pigeonholing her viciousness as a day to day accident was the best option you came up with? Dear Ryan, your nobility invites a shadowy dilemma even if the moral fiber of some of the fallen players may have me agreeing with you, and I do not think you'd give a seasoned butcher the same kind of leeway."

Ryan shook his head. Hanging around with this man is never going to be a picnic in the woods. How did he know about Eric Adler's murder? Well, maybe that could be the first question from the list he had.

"You do have a penchant for ribbing, don't you? Happy you don't have too much of a problem with it, Attison, but why don't you explain to me how you know what actually happened on those stairs?"

He sat back and drank some beer, and politely waited for an answer out of him. He'd been waiting for any answer to any question to explain the mysteries circling around him and Holly Donnelly for a very long time.

"I overheard the conversation you had with Lyndsey at the Star and Stripes, and that had given me more than enough information."

"You'd bugged the table or something?"

"No. I was at the counter, but I could hear you well enough."

Ryan stared at him and he looked unsure. Attison smiled.

"I have exceptionable hearing. My senses are, shall we say, tweaked, and I don't think you'd want to arm wrestle me."

Attison knew Ryan wasn't done with his questions. He wanted to include Ryan Porretta in his small cadre, so he was going to answer them the best he could. He had to pacify his curiosity, and make him understand the breadth of their relationship. There were a few things he wouldn't divulge, things he wouldn't talk to anyone about, not even Holly.

"You've heard the phrase, *'I think I can read your mind'*, haven't you?"

"Of course."

"Well, in my case, it's true. So can Holly and Keith, in varying degrees."

"Why can you do it, and I can't?"

"You probably can...if you put your mind to it. Everyone has this sixth sense. However, like all our senses, some can see a lot better than others. Whether its genetics, or the gravitational quotients lined up at the moment of their conception, some are born with a boost. They can use the sixth sense with the same dexterity we have over the other five. Keith has the ability too, yet he has a ..."

Ryan Porretta was glued to his words. The last thing he wanted to do was to interrupt Attison. He really truly didn't want to do that, nevertheless his duties began to summon him. Right then and there.

"Please excuse me, sir. I have to answer this call, whether I like it or not, and right now I'm not happy about my relationship with the Chief of Police in Massachusetts."

The phone in his pocket was ringing in an irritating cadence he himself had programmed into it. It was there to let him know that it was extremely important for him to pick it up. Only two other people out there knew about a numerical backdoor hidden in his regular phone number. Replacing the last two digits of it with a zero and a five, it was a quick way to alert him to a sudden emergency. They needed his help right away...

Weverton, Brownsville, Rosemont and Burkittsville were in Sheriff Hoyt's jurisdiction in Frederick County in Maryland. Strange behavior had crept into the local population of those neighboring towns months ago, and now it seemed Hoyt needed buckets of help since the problem had increased dramatically. A general uneasiness in the small communities had grown into flat-out paranoia after yet another arcane crime poured even more fuel on that nervous fire.

The whole thing started with personal possessions vanishing and reappearing in unlikely places. A lost table lamp had been found in the middle of Rosemont's town square, and a mother's baby-carriage (baby not onboard when it disappeared) was discovered in the woods where the Appalachian Trail passed Cedar Springs State Park; incidents out of an endless list of similar inexplicable events. The tension in the tiny towns had continued to rise, and three cars abandoned on the shoulder of Interstate 70 on a stretch of highway near Brownsville, certainly hadn't helped the situation. So far, the State Police had towed the cars away into impound, but they hadn't seen head nor tail of any of the people who'd left the cars there in the first place. Sherriff Hoyt's job had become untenable, and the latest episode pushed him over the brink.

He and his deputies' attempts at quelling an outburst of panic throughout the county hadn't been enough to calm anyone down when hunters stumbled onto remains strewn along on the muddy edge of Catoctin Creek. Bloody bits and pieces and a couple of internal organs had been hurled on the narrow shore of the creek like an afterthought. Painful to call it abstract art, it looked a lot more like an explosion of some kind. Something stuffed into an oversized grinder that burst leaving pink and red scattershot all over the dark mud. And the lab results were factual. All of it was human material.

The Sherriff had no choice but to answer the reporters and face their avalanche of questions; yes, the horrible gobbets had come from a man and a woman, and no, we have not arrested anyone yet, and on and on it went. At that point in the game, he no longer understood the rules, and he got on the horn to the Chief of Police in Baltimore, Charles Sawyer. He knew he couldn't handle it on his own anymore, and the state cops were giving him diddlysquat. Sherriff Hoyt pleaded to the Chief to send him a forensic expert, and get her to the creek while the evidence was still fresh. And… and he needed more men and a detective with a reputation to trap whatever was out there. Somebody to stop the nightmares sprouting up around him like mushrooms in the woods after a rainstorm.

Chief Sawyer listened to Sheriff Hoyt, and he quickly understood his terrible dilemma. Having told him he'd send help as fast as he could, Sawyer got off the line to get the ball rolling. He tried to dredge up a name he thought he knew, but he couldn't quite grab it. The guy had had a prodigious career snatching up bad boys and girls faster than a sidewinder, and the Chief was almost positive where he hung his hat, so he got on the phone again to tap John Lowery's mind, the Chief of Police of Massachusetts. He was pretty sure he'd know…and he did.

Inspector Ryan Porretta. And he said he was wrapping up a case in LA. If Sawyer can tell him that the state of affairs in Frederick County had gotten out of control, he could instruct Porretta to fly straight out of Los Angeles to Baltimore, and from there, he could drive out to him from the airport. To Chief Sawyer, it was imperative that Chief Lowery understood how bad things had gotten in one of his counties, and he quickly described what was going on in his neck the woods. And then he sent a list of news stories straight to his lap-top.

The first in the series had happened in 1940, and John began to scroll up to a more modern nugget about a drowned child found in Tappy East Creek five miles away from Burkittsville three weeks ago. Listening to Sawyer's ongoing lament on the speaker phone, Chief Lowery was absorbing the extra information coming over on his digital screen. The picture of a corpse of a child floating in the middle of a small stream had been the final straw. It was time to give the boys in Maryland a hand, *a big one.* He ended his conversation with Chief Sawyer by telling him he was about to do whatever he could to get the Inspector over there as fast as possible.

Using the last of his latest breath saying goodbye to the Chief, he yapped out at his secretary to set-up a flight for Porretta out of Los Angeles to Baltimore...and it didn't matter whether it was a redeye or not, or if Porretta needed to change planes in Chicago or not; just get him on a plane ASAP. His secretary has heard him come up with tyrannical orders before, and she went to work to secure the ticket, while Lowery called Ryan. Since the case was not in Massachusetts, Porretta could technically sidestep it if he wanted to. However, that was very unlikely as the request was about to couched in the voice of his superior in a mournful plea.

"Hello."

"Hello, Ryan, it's John. Guess you know what this is about. Normally, I would never bother you. Normally, I'd give you time to get your breath, but you're the best weapon we have against the worst of the worst, and we can't come up with anyone with your qualifications...oh, and congratulations. Captain Walker called. He complemented your decisiveness on the Caprice," and Chief John Lowery was grinning, impressed, yet again, by his officer's latest success.

"Anyway, something has come up in Maryland, and…"

"Please sir, hold on for a second."

The Inspector whispered over to Attison, "Sorry. This is going to take up too much time, so I'll go outside. I'll be right back."

Attison slanted his eyes and nodded alright, and Ryan walked out of the Cavern Club, already knowing he was about to hear about yet another chaotic murder mystery. He shrugged and smiled to himself, and it seemed his path as already been set.

"Go on, John. I had to get away from a public setting to have this talk with you."

"The extremity of what's going on had gotten the Sherriff on a hunt to find somebody like you. Look, it's out of state, and I know you haven't gotten home yet from the last one, but this is bad, Ryan. If I could, I'd order you to do it, but it's still up to your discretion. Either way, it's got to be stopped. Do you remember the tapes found in a hollowed out tree near Brownsville in 1999? Unedited video footage that was supposed to be part of a documentary about a local fairytale about the Blaire Witch. College kids were collaborating together on it, checking out sites described in some of the stories out there in the woods, and that was when they vanished. They'd parked next to the main trail going into the woods near Burkittsville and besides the car, they didn't find a thing until a jogger found the tapes weeks after their disappearance. Of course, looking at them hadn't helped at all, and helicopter passes to find the abandoned farmhouse in the last shots had found zilch. The only thing those tapes did do was make the whole thing more funereal. As time passed, the uneasiness in the nearby town relaxed. Until a couple of months ago. The entire county walked into a living nightmare. Whoever or whatever was behind the madness had gotten behind the wheel again, and it started with more disappearances and two murders. Sheriff Hoyt, the local guy, is tied to the cross out there. He really needs our help."

While he talked, the secretary had dropped off a printed flight confirmation from Los Angeles to Baltimore on the desk in front of him.

They both heard Ryan Porretta's sigh coming from the speakers above them, as if he'd actually seen her do it.

"Okay, okay. I guess I can get there, and see what I can do."

This querulous acceptance instantly hurled him into the thick of it. Any polite restraint Chief John Lowery had in his mind was gone. He enlightened him about what had already been set up with a joviality that was quite irritating to Porretta.

"Thank God, Ryan. There's a flight set up for you at LAX on Southwest Airlines. It's leaving at twelve-forty-five this morning, so you have just enough time to get there and grab your ticket at the customer service window. It'll be boarding at gate eleven, okay? Besides an frustrating transfer in Chicago, you'll make it to Baltimore by six. I'm going to set up a bank account for you in Weverton. You won't have any problems getting what you need when you get there. I'm also sending you whatever information I have about the disappearances off the interstate and the evidence on the murders to your PC. Check it out when you can, and get Hoyt on the phone anytime you want. He is looking forwards to giving you any help you might need. I have a gut feeling that what went wrong for those college kids eight years ago is linked to the latest flare-up."

Vexed, Inspector Porretta ignored John's 'feeling' and he wasn't very happy about everything else he'd said.

"My plane ticket is already paid for, hmm? I never really had a choice in the matter did I, John?"

"Well…ah, of course you do. You still have the final say. If you want to back out, you can back out right now!" Lowery was back-peddling hard. If he simply would have told Katy to get the ticket she'd already gotten, *after* Ryan agreed to go and then waiting another five minutes before saying what he said, he'd have been fine. Way too excited, he'd walked right into it. There was no way he could let the ongoing silence between them hold, "I mean, I was sure you'd be interested in the case since you love complex puzzles, and…and I just thought I could get you there a bit faster."

"I'll make it to the plane, Chief," and Porretta hung up on him with an impolite click.

Walking back inside the Cavern Club, he didn't want to think about Attison's answer to the question he'd asked him the day before, and he also disregarded the chill sweeping through his bones as he sat down at the table with Attison.

"Seems there's a disaster in Maryland. The Chief has me on a red-eye flight out of LAX this morning, early. Like right before one...hold on, Attison. Give me a sec."

Ryan got his phone out again. He called for a taxi, and the dispatcher told him the driver would be at the club in under five minutes. And then he turned to his companion.

"If you don't mind waiting, I'd appreciate it if you could give Lyndsey my regrets."

"Of course, Ryan. Remember, if things get dicey, you can call us anytime. Any of us can help you in a very significant way."

They both stood up, shook hands and made their final farewells, and Attison looked deeply into Ryan's eyes attempting to underline what he'd said about asking for help. And then the Inspector dashed out to the street. The cab was already rolling up to the curb in front of him. In his first act to get himself to Frederick County, he dove into the backseat of the taxi and slammed the passenger door behind him.

Fate designates. He'd have to solve the Blair Witch Puzzle whether he liked it or not. Bizarre violence, inexplicable disappearances, and a supernatural tinge chained to an outbreak of crimes in Maryland was dragging him in. Like a whirlpool. Ryan Porretta felt like a leaf in a powerful wind. He hadn't had any time to get his breath after closing the case on the Caprice. Being extremely good at what he does has a down-side, or more precisely, his job is getting exhausting.

Driving through the dark streets on his way to the airport, his uneasiness rode along with him, and for a second he thought he passed a signpost carefully camouflaged. For a second, he really thought he was in a current rushing him onwards to a place he didn't want to go.

****

The next book, 'A Happy New Year: The Blair Witch Puzzle Solved' should be out next fall. Holly and Attison will be busy elsewhere, however they will be back with everyone else in the fourth book celebrating Easter. Ryan Porretta knew about Keith Fischer's history working with police and the FBI, so he decided to call him when things got crazy. I'll be looking forwards to seeing you out there…unless of course, something comes out of the woods and drags you away.

Printed in the United States
By Bookmasters